EVE ARCHER

THIS IS NOT A STORY ABOUT JUDGMENT

A.P. COITEUX

TALONINK, INC.

Library of Congress number pending.

ISBN 979-8-9902102-0-2 (Hardcover) / 979-8-9902102-2-6 (Paperback) / 979-8-9902102-1-9 (epub)

First edition

for David, who still likes my brain.

and for anyone who hasn't been told lately that they matter
YOU MATTER.

PREFACE

The American justice system is bonkers.

The Judiciary Act of 1789 created the office of attorney general, then a part-time position for a fella who'd advise Congress and the president on Very Important Things Only Very Important Men Can Know. One hundred years later, the U.S. Justice Department was created. And almost 200 years after that, a nice girl from Oregon is wrongfully accused and awaits trial for something only a dragon from another dimension can corroborate her innocence in.

(The Justice Department has yet to recognize the field of dragonology as a science, let alone the existence of dragons. Hmph.)

Our story, dear Reader, picks up on the steps of the church during that memorial service for Jonah. You remember, the one where Libby is, like, *so rude*, and Eve loses her breakfast in the bathroom?

Qui Pro Domina Justitia Sequitur
~the motto of that pretty statue lady whose blindfolded and holding scales

1

AB OVO

I am not the murderer.

I am not a murderer.

I'm some random person who happens to be obsessed with dragons from a very young age, and that obsession may or may not have compelled a real-life, actual dragon to track them down and convince them that they're capable of saving the universe.

But honestly? I think being a murderer might be more believable than that dragon bit.

I leaned over the formica countertop and spit into the sink once more. The number of times I throw up from stress was getting problematic. I rinsed my mouth out with water from an old, tired faucet, wondering about the plumbing in a church. Was this water mixed up with the baptismal water? Was my drinking out of a church bathroom faucet the equivalent of communion? I spit into the sink again, and then a few more times after that. I didn't want any of that in me.

My footsteps were hollow on the linoleum floor that peeled up at the base of the heavy wooden door. Even the bathroom was like a tiny fortress. I hadn't been in many churches, but describing one as a sanctuary didn't feel appropriate. Fortress felt more like it. I could still hear the priest or father or whatever he was droning on down the hall. I pitied those funeral-goers held captive by his recitations. For a moment, I almost felt relief as I walked the opposite direction

3

of that sound, away from that awful site called a funeral for a classmate whose death I was accused of orchestrating.

I should be sad about Jonah; after all, I think he had been my friend.

I frowned, coming back to the same question that sat heavily in my mind: how long had he stopped being actual Jonah and started being one of those creepy clones reporting back to Obrenox? Had I been friends with an other-dimension lackey all along? What about his parents?

I pushed open yet another heavy set of double doors, inlaid with gaudy wood carvings and chintzy stained glass, only to be greeted by red and blue flashing lights.

"Shit," I muttered as I grabbed my phone to call my mom.

"She's armed! Drop your weapon!"

I dropped my phone on the ground and held my hands out in front of me. Overhead I caught the flapping of a familiar wing moving into the shadows of a spire rising from the far rooftop of the cruciform.

"She's not armed, good god! She's a child," my mom barked as she emerged from the back of a patrol car and jogged to me. "This is rather dramatic. Yes, thank you, I'll get her. Egg, I'm sorry about this – whatever this is. I think we just need to cooperate, and everything will be fine."

"What the hell is going on? I've, like, already been named as a freaking suspect," I hissed to my mom as she looped her arm in mine and walked me briskly to the car. "It's a funeral ... what did they think was going to happen?"

"They think they found more evidence connecting you to Jonah's ... um, to his ... his passing," my mom whispered, hesitating around the last word. She never had been comfortable using the word "death." For anything, ever.

I didn't recognize these officers, one a skinny and pale fellow who spoke too loudly, the other a quiet but gruff woman with narrow eyes and biceps that bulged through her uniform.

"They're the detectives on the case," my mom whispered. "Jesus, 'on the case.' What is this?" She closed her eyes and breathed deeply. Anytime my usually amenable, good-spirited mother had to engage in breathing exercises, the world tensed up.

I was glad I had already thrown up.

But something about riding in the back of a police car while detectives read you your Miranda rights stirs the stomach in a most upsetting way.

2

SEMPER PARATUS

Outside. What a grand place! I would never take it for granted again.

Those interrogation rooms, they're rough. They're smaller and better lit than they are in movies and television shows. But the stale air comingled with accusatory stares and the lingering distress of suspects gone before … it's suffocating.

Leaving Detectives Jasper and Serrano with their mouths agape had felt wonderful. I never figured Kip for that kind of rescue guy, but here I was, rescued by the fellow I had regarded as no more than Uncle Seb's lackey.

So much for rapid judgements about people. Er, clones. Er, whatever Kips are.

"Most sorry about the imposition, yep!" Kip said as he led us out of the station.

"Kip, don't apologize. You were there right when we needed you," my mom said gently. "Those detectives were getting out of hand, demanding and manipulating answers like that. We're relieved you showed up when you did to get us out of that ghastly room. And you could never be an imposition."

Kip stopped. His frame straightened as he adjusted his sunglasses. He stamped the ground twice with his right foot.

"Many thanks, yep. On to Father Sebastian, yep!"

I giggled. I still was not used to the reverence they used when referring to my uncle. From the look on my mom's face, neither was she. She sighed, but there was a smile in it.

"Kip, you know you can just call him Seb. I can count on one hand the number of times I remember my brother being called Sebastian."

Kip stopped again. His still-straightened frame turned tense and he swiped his glasses from his face.

"Madam, but he is father," he said with eyes so wide I wished he'd put his creepy glasses back on. "Yep. We have no life, no memories, prior to him, to his rescuing us from imminent destruction. Yep. He fed us, clothed us, bathed us," he paused to frown at me; that last bit made me choke on swallowed laughter. Bathed us? My mom elbowed me in the ribs, her lips tight from refrained giggling. "He raised us, yep, in the Ways of Flight. He is Savior, Nurturer, ergo, Father. Father Sebastian, yep!"

"Sure, sure, makes sense," my mom responded.

I snorted. She elbowed me once more; I elbowed her back. For a minute, I forgot where we were going and where we had come from and why. I was just holding in giggles with my mom, as we had done a bajillion times before. But in much more innocent settings.

Then I yawned. My body was a confusing mixture of adrenaline and exhaustion. Unfinished thoughts poured out of me, stilted and stuttered.

"Alright, so we head to Uncle Seb, I guess? Isn't that kinda far? We're not, like, walking to his hangar, are we? And even if we do, then what?" I asked.

"Then we strategize, yep."

"Yep," echoed my mom.

I followed my mom, who followed Kip, and we sojourned on, a tragic parade of backstories no one would ever believe.

I kept my head down, counting sidewalk lines. After about a billion, I finally looked up. We had left the police station on foot from its back lot and avoided the entrance that fed onto Main Street. From there we meandered through suburbia. Gradually, houses became farther and farther apart, and the sidewalks became less and less groomed before turning to gravel. Fields opened on either side of the road ahead.

"Where are we going, anyway? You guys, seriously, though. We can't walk to the hangar," I said as I looked behind me. The vista of houses paying tribute to the church spires was now a good distance behind us. "Can we?"

"You are keen," Kip clipped over his shoulder. "And correct! Yep, we rendezvous at 14:16, yep!"

I looked down at my wrist at a watch that wasn't there. My mom saw this and showed me her phone with a smile, mouthing two-sixteen. That was four minutes from now.

"Ah! Early, as usual, yep!" Kip quickened his pace toward a sleek, dark blue car that pulled over on to the curb opposite us. "Poor coordinates, however, yep," he muttered as he nodded to us to follow him across the street.

The driver's side door opened, and small figure emerged in a silky black dress that billowed up in the breeze. My palms turned sweaty and my face flushed. How had Ms. Neally gotten here so quickly? How did she know Kip? And why did she know Kip?

I watched the beautiful librarian delicately turn her cheek side-to-side in greeting Kip. Did people do that here? I had only seen French people do that in movies. Her head bowed as Kip whispered quickly to her. She nodded, put her hand on his shoulder with a reassuring smile, and gestured we get in her car.

Something told me now was not the time for questions. I silently slid onto the backseat, buckled my seatbelt, and slipped my phone from my pocket. I typed "car with triton insignia" into the search bar. My mom saw and giggled.

"I've gone weeks without seeing you use your phone," she whispered with a laugh, "and as soon as you see a beautiful car you just gotta know what it is." My face reddened and I shoved my phone back in my pocket. "I've never ridden in a Maserati, either," she added gently.

"Just trying to keep my mind off things," I grumbled. Good mood, bad mood, good mood, foul mood ... I was in constant flux lately with seemingly little control over it. My mom laid her hand atop mine. I wanted to pull it away, but I didn't. Who was she to offer a comforting touch? Her moods lately had been even more erratic than mine.

"Onward, yep!" Kip chimed from the passenger seat.

"You did not give me much time," Ms. Neally said as she glanced worriedly in her rearview mirror. "I left the church as the detectives did and felt quite conspicuous, as no other patrons had exited the grounds yet. I remained parked outside the police station until I saw you leave. I daresay you were there for quite some time; I may have nodded off. Please forgive me. I was roused when I heard your voices – yes, you walked right by dear little me sleeping in this very car! – and swiftly enacted Protocol 4275," she said. She stopped to smile at Kip, who stomped his right foot three times at the mention of Protocol 4275. "I am relieved the three of you made it out, and with seemingly good spirits."

"'Seemingly good spirits' is the name of my garage band," my mom said under her breath.

Any amiability I had carried was gone, just like that. I glared at my mom, who looked down with a shrug and an embarrassed smile. Why was I so hostile, so impatient with her? Designating silly phrases as "the name of our garage band" was one of our longest-running jokes. I ought to have appreciated her light-heartedness. It signaled hope.

"Old habit," she said, shrugging again, sensing my disapproval.

"So, Ms. Neally," I said, ignoring my mom. "We're not, like, fleeing, or, um, going on the lam or something, right?" I asked as I felt my cheeks redden.

I felt foolish, using movie lingo to describe the situation. But I didn't have any other words for "going on the lam." My stomach did a little flip as fear started to sink in.

Ms. Neally smiled at me in the rearview mirror. My pulse slowed a bit.

"Not at all," she said. "Those detectives were unable to hold you for myriad reasons, particularly when your crackerjack lawyer here appeared."

"I am not Jack nor of crackers, yep," Kip said with a frown.

"Indeed," Ms. Neally patted Kip's hand. "A silly colloquialism from a bygone era. You are everything you need to be, Kip."

He brightened. "Yep!"

The car's pleasantly growling engine quieted as we approached a familiar stretch of road with the outline of a small hangar on the horizon.

"Are you okay to walk a bit more? I'm afraid I'm short on time. But there is no one behind us, no one trailing us. I believe you are safe to proceed," Ms. Neally said as she drove to a pullout at the edge of the hangar's long gravelly drive.

"Would there be someone trailing us?" I asked as I scooted out of the back of the pristine car. I checked for crumbs or anything else I could have left on the backseat. I hadn't eaten anything in a day, but knowing me, I could still manage to dirty her Maserati with rogue crumbs.

Ms. Neally waved out the window as she pulled away. Kip took off toward his crowd of other Kips coming down the drive. They jumped and leapt in a reunion as though it had been an eternity since they were all together last. It was kind of sweet.

"I think maybe they're concerned about reporters or other nosy Nancies following you," my mom whispered. "I don't know why I'm whispering. Let's go."

Oh. Right. Reporters. Voyeurs. Gossips. No one at that funeral had been a friend of mine. I swallowed. Hard.

What it must have looked like to everyone! Eve Archer, plucky teen accused of a classmate's murder, driven away in a cop car from the deceased's funeral. My hands felt tingly. I had to catch my breath even though I had been barely walking.

Breathe in, out, in, out, I said to myself. I strolled in time to the rhythmic inhale and exhale.

Better.

The hangar was over there. Oof. Seeing it near made me catch my nerves and grab my breath all over again. What would it feel like to be there again? Would I find scorch marks still there? It had been almost two months since that … that … what do I call it? "Confrontation?" I could almost feel the heat of fireballs and smell the acrid stench of burnt metal. "Battle" felt more fitting. I swallowed hard again. My throat hurt.

"Eve? C'mon!"

"Yep! Yep! Yep! Yep, yep!" the group of Kips chorused as they sprinted back.

"Yep. Hate this," I muttered. "Breathe in, breathe out, whatever."

3

IL PRAESENTIA

The band of Kips running together had left dust wafting all around the gravel road. As the dust dissipated, the hangar came into view. I hadn't ever noticed how long the driveway was. The closer we got, the more my mom's pace quickened. Then she stopped so abruptly I almost my balance spinning around toward her.

"I don't know if I can go in."

We were aligned on that. But she hadn't seen the aftermath from that day. The black scorch marks, the dead clone, the bleeding Kips. Those things all live in my recent memory.

"Well," I started slowly. "We don't have to go in anywhere, you know. We're just gonna go over there, I guess," I said as I pointed to a table and chairs in the grass to the side.

"Sure, yes, I know. Only, I haven't really seen much of my brother since ... you know," she said. She pushed some hair behind her ear and whispered, "He hasn't even asked how she is, how you are, since ... since .... Ugh, I hate that I'm seeing him!"

I didn't know what to do as her voice trailed off in indignant tears. We would hug a lot, my mom and me, but we weren't especially demonstrative emotionally beyond that. Should I say something? Should I say how lonely that must feel, how it would suck to feel dismissed with the sweep of a clapped hand after the

12

world was saved, how frustrating it would be to feel like your family was restored and safe and then … not? Before I could muster some maturity to comment appropriately, we were stopped at the gate's opening in front of a line of Kips.

"Welcome back, yep!" they echoed as they each nodded to me and then my mom.

"Thanks, Kip, er, Kips," I said. "My uncle here?"

"You bet yer ass he is!"

A familiar voice boomed from the hangar. Uncle Seb sauntered toward us, outfitted in a new leather jacket (this one a chic, weathered, gray leather) that was not at all needed in this heat. I giggled as I ran up to him.

"Just really wanted to show off the new fashion, huh?" I said as I hugged him.

"Don't know what you're talking about. I'm cool as a cucumber."

"You're sweating."

"Am not. Hey, get on over here!" Uncle Seb called past me. He had spotted my mom, still standing near Kip and Kip at the edge of the hangar's shadow. In the background, a host of other Kips swiftly assembled a picnic spread, complete with a large, standing umbrella that only knocked one of them over during assembly.

"Charcuterie, yep! Napkins, yep!" they chorused as each fulfilled his choreographed duty.

"Thank you, Kips. Brilliant as always," Uncle Seb said as we walked to the charming setting. They beamed. "Be ready with some more beers, yeah?" he called over his shoulder.

"More beers, yep!" one called, followed by another, "How many, yep?" with yet another answering, "Many, yep!"

Uncle Seb turned around and motioned me over.

"Hey. Your mom not feeling hot today?" he whispered. "Is she doing that thing again where she doesn't eat during the day?"

I chuckled, appreciating how well he knew her.

"No, nothing like that," I said and glanced at her approaching, one giant frown. "I mean, maybe? But I think she's all," I gestured broadly at her, "like that because, um, like, you … you haven't really … you know …."

"Visited," Uncle Seb finished quietly.

"Yeah. Visited, asked about us, you kinda just ghosted," I added, glad I didn't have to explain more. I pulled out a chair as I eyed the charcuterie. "Not even a text?"

"It's not what you think, Egg," he said as he dropped into the chair opposite mine. "Honest. I've been there for you, I swear."

"Don't tell me, tell her," I said as I waved my mom over. I stacked a piece of sopresseta and a hunk of brie on a cracker and took a bite. Uncle Seb pushed another small metal chair out with his foot as a greeting to my mom.

"Glad you're joining us, Sis. Have a seat. Just taking in the view over there?" Uncle Seb rambled. "Sis, what can I get you? Please, anything you'd like, just say the word. Really, anything."

She stared at him with narrow eyes. He adjusted and readjusted his leather collar.

"Anything? Oh, wonderful! So, you can get Philippa all healed, then? You'll just snap your fingers, and your band of merry men will just do your bidding? And they'll even bring me a seltzer water while they're at it? Oh, that is so, so great."

"Pamplemousse or kiwi-lime, yep?"

My mom startled; Kip appeared at her side with two cans of seltzer water on a tray.

"Unpracticed in Western human medicine presently, yep. Apologies, yep. Perhaps … perhaps there are other requests I can fill, yep?"

My mom's face reddened. She snatched the pink can and opened it.

"I'm sorry; I, um, I didn't mean it like that, Kip. You're all doing a splendid job, I'm just…I don't know. Not myself," she said, her voice trailing off. She took a sip, then hiccupped.

Uncle Seb nodded encouragingly at Kip and grabbed my mom's hand across the table. She pulled it away.

"Look, you know how I feel about ... everything. You know I'm sorry. I'll never say it wasn't terrible. It was. But we really only have one option right now: to move forward. So, let's do that, yeah? We've gotta get a gameplan so Egg here doesn't—"

"Doesn't what? *<hiccup>* Doesn't also land in a hospital *<hiccup>* bed next to her sister? Or a tombstone *<hiccup>* next to Eamon?"

My heart dropped. I hadn't ever heard my mom speak that way before. I think that was literally the first time I even heard her say her deceased husband's name. Between seltzer- induced hiccups, but heartbreaking all the same. Dammit if those hiccups didn't dilute what ought to have been a very empowering moment for her.

"Look, I know you're upset, and I – crap, I *do* know you're upset. It's just that, well, you're hiccupping like a cartoon drunken mouse and I'm having a little trouble taking you seriously, Sis!"

My mom stood up so aggressively her chair fell back and rattled atop the gravel. She threw the half-drunk can of grapefruit seltzer water against the hangar and stomped off. It fizzled and foamed on the ground.

I watched my uncle watch my mom storm away. For a moment I thought his eyes were watering. I took a bite of my cheese and cracker. The wind fell silent. Uncle Seb was still. The only audible things besides rustling trees was my crunching. I was certain every bite echoed through the empty hangar to the hushed fields. I chewed slower. *Ccccrrrrruuuuuunnnnnccchhhhh.*

"Good cheese," I mumbled with a full mouth and a red face. I gulped down the mass of half-masticated gouda and saltine and cleared my throat. "Oh, that's right! Uncle Seb, how does Ms. Neally know Kip?"

He looked over at me. His eyes were wet. He hastily wiped his sleeve against his face with a cough.

"Right. Yaél was enlisted by Drahk to be a sort of ... babysitter? No, guardian, that sounds better ... to the Kips while they were recovering post-rescue."

"Yeah, about that," I said, my mouth now full of apricots. "You never really explained how or why you were in and out of, um – geez, it's still so weird to say – another dimension."

"I've been in and out of another dimension," Uncle Seb said gruffly. "Now you know."

"But why? And how?"

"What do you mean 'how'? You were there. You know how."

"Ok, but why?"

"Because I was able to."

I glared at him. For a minute I wanted to follow my mom's lead. But that would get us nowhere. The roller coaster I couldn't exit – Jonah's funeral, getting picked up by police at a church, being questioned by investigators – was bringing out some unsavory emotions in me. I sighed loudly, refolded my arms, and leaned back dramatically in my chair.

"So that's how it's going to be. Fine. Then let's make a freaking plan for whatever the hell is – aaaahhhhhh!"

I looked up. I was flat on my back. My legs stayed folded over the seat of my chair. I wheezed; I had fallen straight back and had the wind knocked out of me.

"Strange way to make a plan," Uncle Seb chuckled as he held out a hand above me.

"I can do it," I muttered as I turned on my side and wiggled away from the metal chair. "Ow," I said, finally pulling myself upright.

Several Kips sprinted toward me with a red first aid box, a bottle of water, and a fire hydrant.

"We've got to get you back in there, but you're on all the radars now. We'll probably need to go North, maybe Saskatchewan, but hopefully something just on the border. Those portals have been dormant for, Lord, maybe a century or so. Which is good news for you."

"All is well, yep? Blood, oxygen, water supply?"

"We're good, Kip. And, uh, next time just the fire extinguisher will do, if it does at all," my uncle responded with a nod at the last Kip. He promptly released the hydrant. It hit the ground with a deadening thud. In the background, a fantastic geyser shot into the air near the road.

Another Kip stepped forward and shoved a heel against the hydrant. It fell forward, slowly, heavily. We all stood, silently, watching.

"Best tend to the water line, yep."

The Kips turned on each other, arguing, jumping. Finally, one blew a whistle and the kerfuffle disbanded. Uncle Seb shook his head and turned back to me. I brushed gravel off my back and pulled the chair upright.

"I'm fine, thanks," I said dryly.

"I know you are."

"They're, uh, really something," I said, a little anxious, as I watched the Kips. "The Kip who's my attorney, he's—?"

"A different model, so to speak," Uncle Seb answered quickly. "Not all Kips have the same ... cognitive capacity.

"Like humans," I giggled and sat back down at the table with my uncle. "So, can we, uh, circle back to portals in Canada? And why they are good news for me?"

"Ah. Right. A dormant portal means a less potent guard."

"Guard? You mean, another peridiote?" I gulped.

"Should be smaller, less virile," Uncle Seb said as he spit out a cherry pit. "Nothing you can't handle. Especially now." He spit out two more cherry pits. They turned his lips an unsightly red. My stomach flipped; the image reminded me of a scene in the *Lord of the Rings* movie when Denethor grotesquely feasts with blood-stained lips. I shuddered and shook my head. There was no reason to paint my uncle like that. He was good.

Wasn't he?

"We'll have to dial in our route and schedule it with Drahk, through our thoughts. *<spit>* I don't dare speak any plans aloud. Not now. Can't risk it. *<spit>* In the meantime, let's get your new school dialed in."

I looked up, surprised. What did he care about my school? Like he was going to take me shopping for three-ring-binders and new shoes.

"What's it to you?" I said, completely ignoring the bit about going to a dimensional portal in Canada.

"Egg, be serious. With everything going on out there, you can't possibly be rolling into that high school, with all those same kids," he said and wiped his hands. "Hat's off to you if you decide to attend at all. But if you do, it's gotta be someplace new."

My blood froze. I hadn't thought of that. The public high school Philippa attended – the one I was meant to attend – would be the same school most of my matriculating class from Beecher would attend. The same class who made cruel memes of me on social media, who tried to get selfies with "the murderer," who stared at me at that funeral with accusation, suspicion, curiosity in their trespassing eyes.

"That's what Yaël is working on," Uncle Seb continued, still slurping down cherries. "Well, one of the things, anyway. She's very dialed into schools, you know. I think she's getting your application finalized, or had turned it in, I forget. But she's on it, so you know it'll be good."

"I'm going to a new school? Where? Wait, she's doing the applications? What school has an application? Do I have to write something? I … I'm going to a new school?"

I couldn't sort out the feelings that dripped off this information.

My mom finally showed herself again just then, holding a pile of binders in her arms as she emerged from the hangar.

"What's happening? Why didn't you tell me you had these?" she cried as she shuffled over to the table as if nothing had happened at all.

She dumped the colorful books on the table and knocked over the artistically arranged cracker piles and salami roses I hadn't devoured yet. I picked up a binder, flicked a smashed grape off it, and opened it. They were photo albums.

"Egg, this is when you were born!" my mom cried. She beamed as she opened a dusty cover to reveal baby pictures I'd never seen of myself. I stared at the wrinkly little person in a yellow onesie and frowned.

"All newborns are ugly," I said. "Wait, is my dad in here?!"

I lunged across the table as my mom swept the books up in her arms again.

"Let me see those! What the hell, mom?"

"So much to go through, let's table this walk down memory lane for another time. And don't swear, my lovely Eve. What's this about a new school, though?"

Frustration, only frustration, pounded through my body. It tried to sneak out through a few tears.

"You two, just, sort out my life, then," I snapped. I pushed my chair away from the table, swiped a pile of crackers and a hunk of brie, and stomped toward the hangar.

"Now it's Egg's turn to storm off," Uncle Seb called after me. "You and your ma taking turns or what?"

"I'm not storming off; I'm going to the bathroom!"

"With cheese?" he called behind me.

"It's a long walk!" I barked.

It wasn't a long walk. The bathroom was immediately inside the hangar; I knew that. I walked by it and to the back office. The last time I had been in there – the only time I had been in there, I think – I had taken cover from a vicious battle outside. I didn't want to see them, but memories from that day slid through my mind.

I slumped down onto the still-broken green vinyl chair and looked around, uncertain why I had come here. I opened my hands and dropped crumbled crackers and brie, warm from my sweaty palms, onto the ever-untidy desk.

Then I cried.

Yes, today had been a lot.

Even for me.

4

AMICI DIEM PERDIDI

Something occurred to me that stopped my tracks mid-way to the car.

Where was Dragon? Where was Baert? How long ago had they left?

"Eve, your uncle's waiting; let's go," my mom called over her shoulder. "I need to get this day off me. I need a bath or something. I need to see how Philippa's faring. Today was her first day of physical therapy! They sent a van to pick her up. Isn't that fun? Oh gosh, I bet she hated it, getting chauffeured in a medical van," she babbled up ahead.

He leaned coolly against his newly replaced MG and looked up at the sky.

"Going to be a beautiful night. Look at those colors! God, I love the Pacific Northwest," he said dreamily.

"Don't change the subject," I barked as if he had been privy to my inner dialogue. "Where are Dragon and Baert?"

His unruffled demeanor faded as he shifted from side to side. He put his hands in his pockets, took them out, and put them in again.

"You've not talked to Drahk?"

"No," I said squarely, unimpressed with my uncle's cavalier coolness.

"Or Baert?"

I shook my head.

He stared at me, then flung a small rock off in the distance. His evasive demeanor itched my nerves.

"Let's circle back to this some other time. It is late, and I don't want Philippa to come home to an empty house," my mom said, suddenly chipper. "I'm sure they're fine! Those guys have a different level of strength. So, shall we?"

She inserted her can-do attitude where we didn't need it. Her mood swung wildly these days. High then low then higher then even lower; it was exhausting. This new brand of optimism had to be some sort of coping mechanism. I'd seen her overcorrect her mental outlook during seasons of stress before; this time, though, it was getting problematic. I ignored her and inched closer to Uncle Seb, anxious.

"Where are they?" I asked again. My voice was quiet despite my heart beating like crazy.

"Look, Baert, well, he's old, you know, as far as Highland elves go. He, uh, he underwent a lot of stress in the last trip. It took a lot to set him right," Uncle Seb said, still avoiding eye contact.

"Just say it!" I cried. "Is he, is he –"

"Oh, he's alive, thank Christ," Uncle Seb interjected. "He just, he lost a lot of blood, and his punctured lung didn't quite make the comeback it needed to."

"So what does that mean?" I asked after a long sigh of relief.

"It means he's not going to be jumping between dimensions any time soon. It means he needs a lot of recovery time. It means, it means … shit, I don't know. That's all I got." He coughed and jerked his head toward the car. "Let's go. Get in," he said gruffly.

My mom and I piled into the tiny British car. No one spoke. She tried to sing. My uncle and I both barked at her to stop. I think he felt bad about it, same as me. But we said nothing and drove in silence the rest of the way.

That night, I'd eat as many peanut butter foods as I could find. Once home, I tore open a fresh bag of Nutter Butters and raised a cookie in the air.

"To Baert," I said solemnly and took a bite.

I lay in bed that night, I scoured medical websites for anything I could find on punctured lungs. The information was grisly.

"Ugh, why did I click on that image?" I groaned. I threw my phone across my room. It hit my door with an unsatisfying thud just as my mom was opening it.

"Geez! Were you meaning to hit me? What did I do?" she said with a nervous chuckle.

"Not you," I grumbled. "Bad phone."

"Oh! A fight with your phone? Very on-brand for you," she smiled.

I glowered and grabbed a book from my unending to-be-read pile next to my bed. The tower of books swayed precariously.

"Anyway, Philippa's not in the best of mindsets, if you wouldn't mind checking in on her tonight. Something positive, uplifting. We could all use some extra inspiration, yeah? Oh, and remember," she started to pull the door shut as she inched back into the hallway. "We'll need to go over the details of your new school tomorrow."

Before I could say anything, she blew me a kiss and shut the door.

It felt metaphorical.

5

NOVUM PRINCIPIUM

A new school.

Three of the most dramatic words in the English language.

I paused and let my thoughts wander to other common three-word phrases: I-love-you. I-am- sorry. You-have-cancer. Soup-or-salad.

Yes, *a new school* was more daunting than all of those.

As an incoming freshman, any school was going to be new to me. But I had just learned I was going to a fancy- schmancy private school that I hadn't even heard of before this debacle. It was so fancy it didn't even call itself a school but an *academy*.

I looked down at the letter in my hand and read it again. Willamette Preparatory Academy was thrilled ("thrilled"? really?) to offer me admission to its upcoming academic school year, and, as a first step of acceptance, would I kindly sign and remit the enclosed student honor code as well as indicate which after-school electives I shall be bolstering with my enthusiastic involvement.

I frowned and twirled a pen around as I looked over the other papers. "Enthusiastic involvement" seemed a bit of a big ask.

I don't know that I've ever been enthusiastically involved in anything. Maybe that one time I thought I was really good at playing chess and took to reading everything about Bobby Fisher and Garry Kasparov and anyone else associated with chess masters. I bragged nonstop throughout most of sixth grade, only to discover my one opponent – my mom – was remarkably poor at chess.

It took one match against Jonah the summer before seventh grade started for me to learn "palacing" was not a chess move (but did I perhaps mean "castling," he had asked gently) and I ought to choose another competitive outlet. I had cried and screamed at my mom for the embarrassment. She had pointed out how kind Jonah was in that situation, and how lucky I was to have a friend who didn't rub my nose in my ignorance.

My stomach flipped. That memory was a doozey.

What had happened to Jonah back then, and why?

I shook my head as if shaking it would release the questions from my brain. I shook it harder and harder – how I had so many memories I despised! Why wouldn't they shake loose?

My head hurt. I threw the letter on the counter. Willamette Preparatory Academy's fine vellum landed on a pile of mounting mail, get-well cards, evangelical brochures, to-do lists my mom kept making but never completing.

I rubbed my forehead and stretched. I flicked a thick envelope out of the way of the napkins. It was unlike her to allow piles of any type to take form in our house. She wasn't the most meticulously clean person, but she was tidy and abhorred visual clutter. "The brain can't function in piles," she'd say regularly, and then go out of her way to point out how productive and joyful Philippa and I seemed in any tidy space ever. I don't know if that's true, but piles were a red flag my mom wasn't quite alright.

The front door creaked open suddenly. I jumped.

"Phlee? Oh, no, Eve – sorry. How are you, Egg?"

My mom walked briskly into the kitchen, wearing her running clothes. I eyed her suspiciously. Her watch wasn't tracking anything, and there wasn't a drop of sweat on her.

"Are you just leaving for a run? I can help clean up while you're—"

"Oh, don't worry about that," she said quickly without any eye contact. "I'll get to it. It's just … whatever. Just getting back, actually. I kind of strolled, I guess. I was going to run, but, I don't know. Couldn't quite get it rolling."

My mom reached for a green juice in the refrigerator, put it back, and grabbed a piece of pie instead.

Red Flags. Numbers two, three, and four. She would never not run if given the opportunity. She was obnoxiously disciplined that way. She would never not drink a green juice if one were available. And she would never eat junk food in the middle of the day, if at all (even in the form of delicious homemade pie, which is bonkers). I watched her as she twirled out of the kitchen and headed upstairs.

"Gonna do some work for a bit, you need anything?" she called down. The question was just a pleasantry. I knew that. But just for my own sick entertainment, I challenged the ask.

"Yes, I need a calculator called a TI-84 and seven binders with colored dividers that have those little tab thingies!" I hollered. "And a large pepperoni pizza with cheesy bread, and a new thermos, and maybe a colonoscopy!"

"Ok, sounds good!"

Yeah. That's what I thought. I glanced at the clock. Philippa would be home from physical therapy soon. To what number of red flags should I let my mom get before I shared my concerns with Phlee? And would she even have the bandwidth (or awareness, as sometimes she gave in and took the super-strong pain killers even though I know she hated to do so) to deal with it?

I stared at the pantry, at the refrigerator. My stomach was in a constant state of upset these days. Maybe it was the stress of, you know, kind of everything; maybe it was my steady diet of crackers and cheese. But I'd give anything for a quiet tummy and regular bowel movement.

"Guess who has two thumbs and has graduated to level four of physical therapy? This guy!"

Philippa swung open the front the door and, balancing against one crutch, turned to wave the other at a car pulling away. She hobbled over to the sofa and plopped down, tossing her crutches to the side.

"Go on, celebrate me," she called over her shoulder toward the kitchen where I stood. I fished a string cheese out of the refrigerator and threw it to her. It hit her in the back of the head. I giggled. "You impale me rather than celebrate – oh, nice! Thanks, I've been craving cheese."

I giggled and walked over. She was squarely in the center of the sofa, one arm draped along the back, smacking happily on her cheese stick. She waved her hand across the cushion next to her. I took a seat.

"So, show me some level-four moves."

"Thought you'd never ask. Check this out. And a little bit of this, huh? I'm basically an athlete," Philippa smiled as she slowly raised one leg, wiggled her foot back and forth, lowered it, and repeated the same movements with the other leg. "Athletes get winded from leg raises, right?"

"Oh, absolutely," I said quickly and solemnly. "When you're at peak performance levels, your body is finely attuned to strenuous movements like that."

"I thought so."

I chuckled. She smiled. I envied her good-spirited approach to a shit outcome. She had nothing to do with all that business with Obrenox, yet here she was, damaged and still working toward recovery months later. I was directly involved, even had a dragon and some weird weapons, and I came away from it generally unscathed.

Except for that whole murder-trial-thing.

I frowned. Which was worse: possibly losing the ability to walk, or being on trial for a murder you didn't commit?

"Yo, what is going in your weird brain? Can you furrow your brow more? Like, is it even possible for your eyebrows to be down that low?"

I threw a pillow at her.

"Philippa, you're home? Oh, wonderful! How was it?" my mom called as she came downstairs. She hummed as she opened and closed different kitchen cabinets absent-mindedly.

"Dude, you can say anything to Mom right now," I whispered to Philippa. "Like, literally anything, and it won't register. Try it."

"I'm a level four ... Jedi now," Philippa called over her shoulder. "Next up is flying lessons!"

"I knew you'd progress quickly," my mom sang back.

"We're going catfishing later. I think the official term is noodling," I added, giggling. Philippa clapped her hand over her mouth.

"That's wonderful. I love it when you two spend time together." "You, uh, looking for something in there, ma?"

"Me? No, just checking on ... Oh, that's right. Laundry. I'll get to that now."

With that, she wandered out of the kitchen, still humming. Philippa and I giggled back and forth, and then my sister straightened a bit.

"How long has she been like that? I, um, haven't really been super engaged around here lately," she said and looked down, embarrassed. "I hate the painkillers, but god have I needed them. I know I shouldn't. I—"

"Phlee, it's okay. Don't even go down that road. There is no judgement here. And yeah, Mom's been a little ... dazed," I said, choosing my words carefully. "It's like, I don't know, she's here physically but definitely not mentally. She's not really sleeping; I'm sure that's it. It's nothing. And, oh my gosh, I almost forgot!" I brightened suddenly and faced her. "I'm going to a new school!"

"Yeah, you're a freshman," Philippa said. "Where's the remote? I need some dumb humor."

"No, like a *new*new school," I said, digging between the sofa cushions to find the remote and tossing it on her lap. "You remember Ms. Neally? She helped me with some applications, and she, well, she and Uncle Seb, if you can believe it, got me into Willamette-something. It's like some private school for dweebs."

"Willamette Prep?! Are you serious? I begged Mom to let me apply. That's only, like, one of the best schools around and it basically guarantees you acceptance to any college. Ugh, you're so lucky!"

"Crap. That means it's going to be hard," I muttered.

"Oh it is. Ugh, it's the stuff of dreams!"

"You can do my homework. Because I'm a giver like that."

"Deal. I'll be bored out of my mind with this online homeschooling curriculum they set up for me. Like, what a shit way to begin my senior year," Philippa said, her voice dropping. There it was – the chink in her resilience. "It better not get in the way of my being valedictorian."

I cozied up next to my sister as she selected a movie. But inside I felt hollow. She loved school. All she ever talked about was school. Going to school, being the best at school, graduating school so she could go to more school … And it was all thrown off.

Because of me.

A phone buzzed. My sister and I automatically patted our respective pockets.

"Ah! A reminder? For what? Oh –" Philippa's voice quieted, "a reminder for an arraignment just popped up."

"Shit. I almost forgot."

"Egg, don't swear!" my mom suddenly called from upstairs. "Hi Phlee, I'll be down in a minute! We have a conference call with Kip for the arraignment tomorrow!"

"What are you going to wear?" Philippa asked. I threw a pillow at her.

"Dude, I'm being serious. In one of my mock trial sessions, we watched this documentary about how much your presentation and demeanor and everything is super influential."

"So," I said, not wanting my skyrocketing pulse to stress out my sister, "you're saying don't wear my homemade Dragon Club jacket that I still have from the fourth grade?"

"Are you going for an insanity plea? Because then maybe."

Our laughter was interrupted by my mom's phone ringing. She sighed and answered it much too cheerfully. Philippa reached over and hit the speaker icon. Kip's chipper voice sang out on the other line.

"All set for the Ms. Archer arraignment, yep!"

Philippa reached again to hit the mute button on the screen.

"Are we absolutely certain this guy is a practiced legal professional?"

"Ssshhhh, it wasn't on mute!" my mom hissed as she hit the mute button again.

"I am just that, yep. A practiced legal professional, yep!"

Silence. Red faces.

"Oh. Um, I thought I had, uh, muted ... sorry," my mom mumbled.

Laughter. A lot of it.

It was nice to laugh when the world was kinda literally and figuratively crashing down on us.

6

DOLI INCAPAX

"**N**ext up on the docket, please."

A judge sat, square and disinterested, at the center of the enclosed wooden judge's bench. The hum of the courtroom droned on unaffected. He coughed and leaned closer to the skinny microphone.

"The court said, next up on the docket. Please."

The judge leaned to his right and conferred with a smartly dressed woman who was surely unaware there was a square of toilet paper stuck to the bottom of her loafer. She held her tablet up for him and took special care to point to something.

"Really?!" the judge gasped. The woman nodded. "Well, I'll be damned. Darned. I'll be darned."

He coughed, flustered, shrugged at the woman, who had taken her seat just below the bench on the left. I learned they called the giant wooden-podium-thing a bench from binge-watching every courtroom drama I could find that streamed for free. My mom didn't care for this and tightened the parental controls on my go-to platforms, leaving me to only access shows benign enough to warrant a PG-rating or less. I discovered an 80s gem called "Night Court" that featured a jeans- wearing judge and a laugh track.

Something about this austere judge with his shiny bald head and rectangular reading glasses perched at the tip of his nose told me there would be no courtroom antics with canned laughter today.

"Next up, Eve Gwendolyn Genevieve Archer, a minor," the judge trailed off as he scanned the courtroom. He raised his eyebrows and pulled his face back, producing several chins, as he strained to read the tablet the clerk had given him. "For the purposes of … that still can't be right. For the purposes of—"

"Criminal cause for arraignment," the clerk finished his sentence into a tiny microphone.

"Ah, yes. I see it there, it's just … a minor," he coughed uncomfortably again and shifted. "Now then, counsel, please state your appearances."

"Swan Rosencrantz, for the dear Nguyen family, your honor," a tall, lean woman stood ceremoniously and held her long arm out as if presenting herself to a much different court. "And standing aside the fine state of Oregon."

"I'll remind counsel not to editorialize, particularly at an arraignment," the judge droned into his microphone. The clerk typed dutifully along. "You know better, Mr. Rosencrantz."

"I'll remind His Honor that it's Ms. Rosencrantz. And I," Ms. Swan Rosencrantz flipped her hair and glanced around with a mischievous smirk, "will cross my fingers that this is the record that will finally show that."

Chuckles of support came from the pews behind her. The guard standing to the right of the bench nodded and raised a fist to his chest.

"Alright, alright, calm yourselves. Order in my courtroom," the judge reshuffled some papers and adjusted his glasses. "Some things are just different now. Back to the arraignment, if you please. State co-counsel. Oregon, state your appearances."

Swan remained elegantly, remarkably poised in her magenta suit and black necktie. The judge peered over his glasses expectantly.

"Also present for the Nguyen family is my co-counsel," said Swan Rosencrantz. "Whom you may also refer to as Ms."

A disheveled, round woman heaved herself upright. Her unpressed brown blazer might as well have been an extension of her choppy, frayed hair. Both were dotted with specs of lint and fuzz.

"Ms. York, Your Honor," she sputtered, clenching a bundle of papers against her as she stood. "I'm, uh, actually, um, here for the state. Swan, er, Ms. Rosencrantz, is a bit of a comic, heh. You know. Wishing we could join forces and whatnot, heh, heh … heh."

The judge had his head down again, flipping through papers. He looked up over his glasses at Ms. York, who was still standing, still clutching her papers, still smiling awkwardly. He waved his hand lightly toward her and shook his head.

"Oh, you're saying that I can sit; I can, now, can I? Yes, ok, I'll go ahead and sit," she stuttered and plopped down.

"And next, for the defendant," the judge said, drawing out the last word. "We have, we have … Ahem!" He stopped and looked directly down at us. Kip shot right up.

"Kip, yep! For the Ms. Archer, yep," Kip said with a stomp of his right foot.

The judged blinked and lowered his cheek to his hand propped up on his podium.

"Kip?"

"Kip, yep."

"Just … Kip …?"

Kip's lips stretched wider in what I assumed he thought must be a smile.

"He's asking after your surname," Ms. Neally gently whispered from behind us. Kip frowned, scratched his head, then smiled and looked up.

"Sebastian! Sebastian, yep!'

"Kip Sebastian," the judge echoed, his face heavy against the palm of his hand. "Typically these court documents would have been submitted with counsel's last name indicated. Uncertain how you managed to file them as such," he said and cast a disapproving look at the court stenographer. "Nonetheless, carry on,

Mr. Sebastain. Mr., yes? I feel I ought to check now, no matter how much time it wastes."

"Yep, yep," Kip said and glanced back at Ms. Neally, who gave him a thumbs up.

"What are you doing," I hissed, "that's a terrible, and I'm guessing inaccurate, last name!"

Ms. Neally just smiled and nodded toward the front of the courtroom.

"So you all understand, this is an arraignment, not a hearing; I'll not be hearing arguments or accepting witnesses, et cetera. We'll be mindful of the ongoing investigation and keep our opinions to ourselves. Clear?"

No arguments? Was there a chance I had no idea what an arraignment even was? My head shot up. I looked back and forth from Kip to Ms. Neally

"Clear, yep!"

"Noooo! Not clear! Don't you have, to like, consult with counsel before agreeing to things?" I hissed, pulling on Kip's sleeve.

"Then I shall continue," the judge said into a yawn.

"I object, yep!"

"I just informed you that this is not that type of hearing," the judge growled into the tiny microphone. "And what can you possibly be objecting?"

"Your continuation, yep. All is not clear, apologies."

Kip brought the tips of his fingers together, turned, and bent down to face me. His expectant stare grew with what felt like one hundred pairs of eyes behind him.

"Um, I just, um, didn't hear that first part. S—sorry," I mumbled slowly.

"The part where I said to take this seriously and pay attention because this is a court of law and serious matters are at stake?" the judge growled louder. "That first part?"

"Yeah," I breathed, "Er, yes. Yes. Thanks."

Kip gave the judge a thumbs up.

"As I was saying," the judge barked, looking up. "This is an opportunity to hear the charges against you only, after which I will ask you how you plea." He stopped and looked hard at me.

"Clear?"

I nodded, my face still burning.

A bunch of words fell out of his tired mouth then, words like "felony" and "crime" and "record" and "prison" and "judgement" and "due diligence." He was getting very impassioned, no doubt trying to either inspire or terrify, I'd never know. Words spun clapped around while my stomach did flips to the drumming of my heartbeat.

Was I guilty? Had I done it?

I tried to replay the ghastly chain of events. I thought I was defeating Obrenox, or at least keeping him at bay. I remembered the weight of the spear in my hand. The thrust of my shoulder as it careened through foreign air in a neighboring dimension. The grisly piles of Jonah clones that lay in the gray ooze that bled out. The Jonah I had known – eyelids open around flickering yellow pupils – spilling red blood.

That last memory froze my own blood.

"Ms. Archer, again, how do you plea? Mr., uh, Sebastian, is the defendant well?"

The judge's heavy voice pulled my focus back to the courtroom. I looked up at Kip, who had put his sunglasses on. Ms. Neally's hand fell gentle on my shoulder briefly. My heartrate slowed.

"Not guilty, sir. Your Honor. Um, yeah. Not ... not guilty. Thanks."

A tide of murmuring rippled through the courtroom.

"So stated. The court will convene for an adjudicatory hearing on ... shall we say, two weeks from Thursday. That work for you? You, Mr. I uh, Ms. Rosencrantz? Very good. The court adjourns until Thursday the twenty-third. I'm uncertain of the judge assignment that day. Counsel, you'll receive those details," the judge stated. He looked at the clerk for an affirming nod.

A beat of a gavel and a roar of people echoed in my mind for too long.

"Egg, my Eve, how are you feeling? Do you need food? What's around here, oooh! I think there's a great bahn mi food cart down tenth, or we can grab Thai?"

"Mom, it's okay. I'm not hungry. I think – I think I just need a nap," I said as I followed her toward the lobby.

My head stayed down intentionally; I wanted to see no one. Just get in and out, and back to bed. I smiled. I had almost done it. I had almost survived the day.

Funny how one forty-two-minute-long event can disrupt the entire balance of the other 1,398.

A stronger, more stubborn me would not have let them, based on the absurdity of the math alone.

But that Eve was on vacation somewhere. Where? No idea. I hope I was someplace grand.

This weaker, more bending me wholly accepted that some minutes are heavier than others, and the forty-two minutes I had just endured surely outweighed the other thousand-whatever.

The doors opened not to the relief of fresh air and freedom, but to the cacophony of greed and gossip parading as journalism.

"What do you have to say for yourself?"

My head shot up. Three phones were shoved in my face, each with the recoding icon flashing.

"Eve Archer, why'd you do it?

"Was it for love?"

"Why is your sister not here?"

A barrage of selfish voices calling themselves reporters barked and snorted one foul question after another.

"Keep your head down, you're okay," Ms. Neally whispered behind me. I spun around; she was gone. I scanned the growing crowds on the courtroom steps. Faces with wide mouths and loud eyes jutted out at me everywhere. I started to tumble off a step. Were they spinning around me now?

"Mom?" I called. "Mom?"

"I'm here, I'm here, stay close. Kip!" my mom cried through bodies. "She's a child! What is wrong with you all?!"

Kip bounded over and put his arm around my mom and me.

"Aced my first interview, yep!" he whispered excitedly to us.

I scowled. My mom reached across me and squeezed his arm. "That's wonderful!"

Uncle Seb's car honked and flashed its lights from across the street.

As we drove away, I looked back to see a familiar pair being interviewed on the steps. Detectives Jasper and Serrano had their hands on their hips, nodding and smiling at one while the other spoke and vice versa.

"Yes, that's great," my mom growled behind me. "Have your minute of fame, sensationalizing the death of a child. It's despicable."

"Yeah, the part about the other child getting accused of murder is, like, pretty messed up, too," I grumbled.

The car stayed silent after that. Until Kip spoke up.

"Hotdog, yep? Anyone?"

7

PRIMA FACIE

A new school.

Still the three worst words, I thought as I boarded the bus. I could have walked. But my mom insisted riding the bus was the "first step to a fresh start."

"Fresh" and school busses didn't really go together.

"That's her."

"Her? I didn't even know that girl existed."

"Yeah. She killed him."

"With her bare hands?"

"Dunno. Could've been wearing gloves, I guess."

"Don't be a smartass. She probably murdered him with that killer b.o."

"Sssshhhh! She'll hear you!"

"Don't make her angry – she'll bore you to death with facts about dragons."

I grabbed my books and moved to an empty seat at the front of the bus, swimming upstream through waves of whispers and snickers.

The first minute on my new bus on the way to my new school was off to a stellar start.

I could see the bus driver frowning at me in her overhead mirror. She was tall and lanky; every bone in her body creaked as she folded herself into the driver's seat. Her nametag said Jo. I historically am pals with my bus drivers. But looking at Jo, under the shadow of her glower, I think not.

The vinyl bus seat was warm. Unpleasantly warm. The early morning sun poured through the thick-paned bus windows. Oregon wasn't known for being warm. But this summer had been full of every eye-roll-inducing meteorologist quipping about the season's record-breaking highs. Get out your sunscreen, Becky. These rays are hot, and I'm not just talking about Ray our cameraman! Over-made smiles had beamed at the camera. It's so hot you don't even need a barbecue to cook your steak! Then a silly man would point to his backside and say, I'll bring the buns, they're hot too!

I hated summer. I hated maybe two things more than summer, though. Pun-spouting weather reporters, and this bus.

"You're in my seat, Dragongirl."

Without looking up, I held my hand out with a choice finger raised.

"Um, bus driver? I, like, don't feel safe! I'm being attacked!"

The bus driver scowled. She and the brakes heaved a sigh. Jo pulled her rectangular body from the driver's seat and lumbered back to us.

"Two things. You need to take a seat, Lizzy, and you – look at me when I'm speaking to ya – need to stop harassing my patrons."

"Um, it's Libby, and I couldn't sit because this murder girl is in my seat."

"There aren't assigned seats on my vessel. You, scoot. You, sit."

Libby plopped down next to me loudly with a louder sigh of disgust. Jo lumbered back to her command center and fired up the bus. I heard her speaking into her radio, "Yeah, I got an incident on bus 420, reporting an adjusted ETA of t-minus eight minutes to target ... every goddamn day I tell ya what."

"Every goddamn day," I said, mimicking Jo. Libby giggled, then cleared her throat. "Just, like, don't kill me, k?"

**

The excitement at being at a new school quickly faded.

"Murderer coming though, make way!" a boy I didn't know called as he waved his arms like a traffic cop. Some kids snickered; others pulled their phones out to record my walk of humiliation down a hall I wasn't entirely certain I should be in. I pushed past more students whose looks of confusion filled me with gratitude – they were unaware of my notoriety.

"Why's everyone filming that girl?" I heard behind me.

"Dunno. She's not even that cute."

"She, like, murdered some kid at her old school or something," another voice piped in.

"Wait, seriously? Then why is she at school with us?!"

Excellent question, I thought.

First, I survive the first day of school. Then, I survive a court room.

My pulse quickened as I thought about the court date getting moved up again. I had only just read the file last night: *In the event Ms. Archer poses a threat to future students, the prosecution requests an earlier hearing date, at the pleasure of the court, to avoid caustic fraternization and upset at the accused's new school.*

I hated that I had that letter memorized. I hadn't done so intentionally ... it's just that when you read something in disbelief, rage, and then despair about 300 times, it imprints on your brain.

The summer had been one legal document after another awaiting me in the mail. I hated seeing my name listed as "Defendant (minor)." I hadn't done anything wrong! Didn't they realize this dimension as we know it is safe for the time being because of me? My blood boiled again just thinking about it.

I had pleaded with my mom to move – China is rapidly becoming a world leader, I had argued, or Morocco with its vibrant francophone history would surely be a great home, or had she considered Democratic Republic of the Congo? Loads of philanthropic work to be done there, and didn't my mom love helping kids? – or at the very least enroll me in a home schooling program. She had cocked her head at each suggestion and finally accused me of just listing countries with no extradition laws.

I couldn't get anything past her. As for homeschool, she said she'd "think about it," which everyone knows is parent-talk for a big fat no. Ultimately, though, she'd put her arm around me every time and told me everything would be okay and to focus on being my "own, awesome self."

Whatever the hell that was.

A bell rang. I looked up and realized I had no idea where my first period was. Flustered, I pulled my phone out (that I had charged for a change!) to check my schedule.

"When the bell rings, we stow personal things," a whiny tenor voice behind me sounded. "Excuse me, miss, but being tardy and rule-breaking on your first day makes a foul impression."

I spun around to glare at whomever was speaking. But that glare quickly turned to an eyeroll.

"Oh, come on," I groaned. "You're here?"

"Oh, Ms. Archer, I, um, yes, er," Mr. Simmons stuttered, fidgeting with his brown tie that was awkwardly short on his lanky torso. He cleared his throat and straightened his shoulders. "That is, yes. Yes, I'm the new algebra instructor here, you may have heard."

"Congrats," I muttered.

I certainly had not heard, and one of the selling points for my coming to a private school instead of the public high school my sister attended was the assured absence of people from my immediate past. Now I'm stuck here with a math teacher whose wiry frame certainly had no room for a backbone to admit his clear disdain for me.

Neat.

I frowned, my mom's hopeful and encouraging smile from this morning popping into my head. "New chapter! You tell your own story. You got this, just be your awesome self!" she had said as she hugged me goodbye on the front step. Her running gear smelled of sweat, but it was mixed with her special scent blended of mint gum and dryer sheets. It was always oddly comforting.

"Ok, well, bye, have a good day," I stuttered, my head down as I searched my schedule on my tiny screen. There it was. Period 4, Algebra, Simmons, Room 208. Then my head shot up. "Hey, do you know where room 528 is?"

"Sorry, no," Mr. Simmons responded coolly. He tried to tuck his hands into his pockets, missed, and inelegantly ran his palms down his slight hips. "Well," he coughed, his hands against his thighs, "good day."

"I think I can help," a chipper Australian accent called. I spun around. The halls were empty, minus Mr. Simmons who swaggered down the opposite end of the hall, chastising a few tardy students running and giggling to class. "Down here! Right then. Ok, where are you off to, Sheila?"

I looked down to see a black, white, and tan spotted dog with its tongue out and tail wagging.

"My name's Eve," I mumbled, confused. "Are you – are you the one talking to me?"

"Sorry, let me start over. G'day. Name's Poppy. And you're Eve. And I'm here to help you."

I stared down. I should be disbelieving and incredulous, but something about hanging out with a dragon all spring made me unflappable if not am- bivalent these days.

Nonetheless, I eyed the dog suspiciously. She cocked her small, pointed head and wagged her tail slightly. A forest green vest was wrapped snugly about her torso, announcing her as a THERAPY ANIMAL

"You're the therapy dog? You're here to make me feel better, huh?"

"Nah. Just a convenient cover, but clever, in'it! Love how forward-thinking this school is. These posh kids, though. Just put 'therapy' on something and they don't give it a second look. Wanna get some brekkie? I know a spot with bonza avo toast. We could have a nosh, talk it over."

An Australian Shepherd. With an Australian accent. Masquerading as a service animal. Who wants to get breakfast with me. On my first day of high school.

"Sure," I sighed. "Why not. What could possibly go wrong here."

Her sweet brown eyes sparkled. Poppy lunged forward and took off down the hall, tongue akimbo and tail wagging. An excited yip escaped as she glanced back at me.

"C'mon, then! It'll be arvo at that rate, keep up!"

I grabbed ahold of the straps on either side of my new backpack – a sleek, black thing with minimal zippers – and jogged after her. Just once, I wondered, could the universe send me a creature whose regional slang I didn't have to decipher?

I stopped and considered a truancy on my first day might not set the best tone.

I watched the dog run off, curiously joyful. Curiously jaunty. I had to assume that an animal speaking to me knew of my checkered past year and would have a modicum of concern or sympathy or terror or something ... but jaunty and joyful? No one who knew about my recent goings-on would be chipper. Or even kind.

No one.

I turned back inside, grumbling to myself to recite my mom's self-affirmations. As I shoved the door open, a shrill voice slapped my ears.

"Oh my gosh, you are hilarious! I literally cannot stop laughing!"

I kept my head down, trying to just get past. No such luck. Libby quickly stepped in front of me.

"Dragongirl, Murderer ... I, like, don't even know what to call you these days," Libby chided. "We'll stay out of your way."

She knocked her shoulder hard into mine as she walked by even though there was (in my best Libby voice:) "literally" the entire hallway open on either side.

"Still so original, Libster," I mumbled.

Libby stopped, looked up, turned in a huff, and walked past me the other way in one, long continuous sigh. I guess she was back to being her old, reliable bully self. I hated the way this pricked my heart just a bit; I hated that I let myself think we might be getting on. I hated that I was disappointed in Libby just being Libby as I aways knew her.

"Glad you straightened it out, Big L!" I called after her. "My shoulder couldn't take a hit like that again!"

I shoved my hands in my pockets and chuckled smugly. "Big L," I laughed to myself. "I still got it." Then my head shot up. Oh no. Had I accidentally let out the therapy dog, and now the school's dog was running down the street?

"Um, Poppy?" I called out as a I glanced around. "Poppy?" I sighed and knelt. "Poppy! Er, uh, here, girl!"

Do I call her as a dog or as a person? Geez, this was awkward. I slid my backpack off and slowly crept down the halls, my voice somehow launching up two octaves.

"Poppeeeeeeee! Here, girl!" I made smooching noises, uncertain if that was a dog thing or a cat thing. My mom loved all animals, but we didn't have a pet because, in her own words, "if I have to keep another living thing alive, I may commit a crime, get a fake passport, and run away." Seemed dramatic, but if it's this hard to even get a pet to come to you, then maybe she was on to something.

"Whom are you calling?"

I met a tapping foot and looked up.

"Just whom are you calling?"

"Poppy, the therapy dog. For, some, um, you know, therapy," I grabbed my backpack and stood up clumsily. "And it's *who*, not *whom*, in that case."

Principal Fernhouser – yes, the very same one – put his hands on his hips and stared down his nose at me.

"Young lady, er, sir, er, person, er, student. Student!" he cried. "Young student, I strongly advise you to consider your churlish ways at Willamette Preparatory Academy. Your, ahem, record, among, ahem, other things, precedes you,"

"Wow, you're coming off as a little stalker-ish right now," I said. I was proud of my snark, but my face still turned eleven new shades of red.

"Ugh! Quite the opposite! I came to Willamette Preparatory Academy to escape any chance of encountering you, Evelynn Archer." He straightened his collar self-importantly. "And," he sniffed, "I was due a more prestigious position in academia. Not that you'd understand, Evelynn."

"My name is not Evelynn. And I came here," I gestured broadly, "to escape you! And judgmental assholes like you who assume a kid is a murderer."

He stared. I stared.

"Don't. Make. Me. Call. The. Authorities," Principal Fernhouser said through smugly clenched teeth. "You know, your friends." He split that last word into two syllables, dragging out the s. Fer-rendssssssss.

Buzzing took over my brain.

My heart beat loudly and my sweaty palms clenched.

That drawn-out Ssss mauled any rational thought.

I lunged forward.

I guess I snapped.

I guess I overreacted.

I guess I pushed my past and now-current principal in the chest with both hands.

He tumbled back and fell awkwardly against a recycling bin. Then he tumbled off of that.

My ears rang and my head hurt.

"Poppy?"

8

SINE QUA NON

Principal Fernhouser leaned against the wall across from me with the most scandalized look on his face. His glasses were askew above his open mouth. He clutched at his midsection with one hand, breathing heavily, while his other hand frantically reached into his pocket.

"I, um, it was a reflex! You sounded like, like … I'm so sorry," I said, flustered and awkward. "Please, let me help you up."

"Stay away from me," he stuttered. "Just – just stay – away."

"I really didn't mean to, it just happened," I said. My voice trailed off as I became aware of gathering eyes peering through the long classroom windows and doors that dotted the halls.

My head hurt. Doors opened and onlookers began to ooze out, phones in hand. The laughter that started mounting didn't help.

"Call security!" Principal Fernhouser cried. "You are out of here. Out!"

"That'll be enough," a soft voice I recognized came behind me. Hands reached below my armpits and yanked me up. When had a I sat down?

"Keep her out of here! Me, you, and you over there," Principal Fernhouser shot a shaky finger in various directions as his voice quaked. "And you! On my word, you all know – we came here to get away from her!"

"I said ENOUGH."

46

The soft voice turned dark. That last word thundered with an echo. My shoulders tensed. Sounds of shoes shuffling back to seats doors closing tightly petered out and the hall was silent. I stared nervously at the floor.

"Eve, let's go," the voice said, soft again, and someone had me by the elbow. I dared to glance up. Ms. Neally!

"You are here, too?!"

"I am here for you. I'm not due at Beecher's library until this afternoon, so I came to check in on you," Ms. Neally said tersely. "Thank Thoth I did. Best to keep your wits about you and be going now."

"But what happened back there? Is a principal allowed to outwardly hate a student like that?" I sputtered out questions as Ms. Neally yanked me down the hall faster and faster. Her delicate kitten heels tip-tapped rapidly in perfectly accelerating tempo. "Oh! And did you send Poppy? Where's Poppy?"

Behind us, as Ms. Neally's perfectly manicured hands heaved open the sets of orange metal doors, I heard Principal Fernhouser's annoyed wail: "There is no one here named Poppy! You've lost it, Evelynn Archer! You were so bright, and you've lost it!"

"That's not my name," I muttered. "And I think I have lost it."

The doors clattered shut abruptly, muting the principal's ornery cries. The sun was bright. Ms. Neally looked up, squinting, and held her hand over her eyes. I stared right into the sun. I had discovered as a kid that doing that makes funny black smudges appear when you blink. My mom would scold me, but it always entertained me. No mystery why I needed glasses (that I never wore).

"Such dramatics. Such a grizzly situation," she said and looked at me with a short sigh. "I hadn't scheduled in time for us just yet." Her face softened and she smiled faintly, maybe even empathetically. "Don't be concerned. I'll adjust my diary and make time for us to catch up, possibly this evening or next. You are available, yes?"

I blushed. Hard. Meeting Ms. Neally? At night? My throat tightened. Do I call her Ms. Neally or Yaél? I had heard high school kids sometimes got to call teachers by their first names. But how do you know when to start doing that?

"Yeah," I coughed, "when?"

"You'll know when it's time. Just," Ms. Neally paused to fasten her smart jacket and adjust her cuffs, "don't let your emotions overtake you. Trauma of the magnitude you carry can make you act out. With good reason. But I wouldn't want a repeat of today's … today's mania."

That last word punched me in the gut. Great, so now I'm some trauma victim with crazy impulses.

"And don't be so hard on yourself, Eve," Ms. Neally said, as if reading my thoughts. "You're not broken, you've simply been through enough that your brain is glitching in processing it a bit. A silly analogy, but an accurate one."

With that, Ms. Neally walked off. I stared at her for too long as she walked away from the school, away from the parking lot, over a large hill past the lacrosse fields. I assumed I shouldn't follow her. But I also shouldn't go back into the school. So, I was left to track down a dog whose presence I couldn't confirm and whose whereabouts I could only guess at.

"Poppeeeeee!" I began again. "Here, girl! Poppy! PAW-PEE!"

I wandered in no direction. I kicked at a pinecone. I missed and struck my toe hard on the ground instead.

"Ouch! Ugh! Dammit, where are you, you stupid mutt," I growled. As if it were the dog's fault I couldn't even kick a pinecone from the ground properly.

Ding! I swung my backpack around and fished out my phone (still charged!). I fumbled to hold it steady as I jostled my bag back over my shoulder and skipped awkwardly with my throbbing toe. The little rose gold-encased phone, its back covered in random stickers, toppled to the ground.

My jaw clenched. I breathed in heavily through my nose. Please don't be cracked please don't be cracked, I repeated over and over as I retrieved.

"Great. You're cracked. Freaking wonderful," I said to no one. "Anything else abhorrent waiting for me? What else you got for me today?" I held my arms out and swung around, daring the universe to double down on my day's misfortunes.

The little phone sounded again.

"Cute," I muttered as I brought my arms down to inspect my phone. One giant crack splayed out at the bottom of the screen and branched delicately. I swiped my forefinger across it as delicately as I could, but several miniscule shards caught in my skin. A small trail of blood filled in the cracks.

I wiped my finger on my jeans and popped it in my mouth. The message was from Philippa: *Sup nerd, hope you're having the best first day!! <insert inspirational cat poster here> Don't fart too much. You'll do great.*

A giant tear sprung to the corner of my eye. Then another, and another. I sobbed, blubbering, my bleeding finger still in my mouth.

"Crikey, what have I come back to?"

I spun around, sobbing and choking. I spat out some blood.

"Oh, Poppy! There you are!"

"Oh, Jesus, oh strewth!" Poppy rubbed her muzzle with her white paw. "Why's there – is that blood on your chin?!"

"What? Oh, yeah, it's um, you know how that happens," I said and flashed my wounded finger at her.

"Er, no, mate, I don't know. Anyhow, c'mon. We've got work to do," she shook her body, and then her ears went alert and her eyes flashed. "Oh crikey, really. We've got to go. Now. Now!"

Adrenaline pushed me after the dog, sprinting, speeding away from the school. What had she seen or sensed?

Up ahead a taco truck had parked and was playing some jolly music. Poppy stopped, barked, and took off running again.

"*Al pastor* tacos run out first, onya bike, then! Let's go!" I stopped in disbelief and bust out laughing.

"Oh my gosh, I was so panicked!" I wheezed between chortles. "I thought there was, like, an attack … and it was just – tacos…!" I fell forward, smacking my thigh.

"So it's funny to you, that? I'm tryna keep your nutrition sound, and you mock what little excitement I've got in the world." Poppy's head lowered and her hackles bristled slightly.

"Easy, girl, er, guy," I wiped my eyes and adjusted my backpack. "It's just, you really took off in full freakout mode. Over, over …." I trailed off, chuckling again. "So dramatic."

"Have your laugh. Rude, but understandable. Best street tacos around demand some haste. See if I show up to save you again," she sniffed and trotted ahead.

"Save me? Save me? I would just be hanging out in, in," I shoved my hand in my back pocket and produced a crumpled printout of my new high school schedule, "in ART – aw man, art? Dang, I was looking forward to that. Well, I'd be in art. Late, but in art. And, and instead I'm here," I gestured disgustedly, "probably expelled for something I don't remember doing to Principal Fernhouser and already the hot gossip for a bunch of rich kids who probably would've hated me anyway."

"Sorry 'bout that," she clipped. "Off we go, Sheila. Tacos or no, regardless. We've got things to get to. C'mon, then."

"What if I say no," I said slowly.

I clenched my backpack straps to my chest. I don't know who was controlling this voice of mine. Am I really holding my ground, indignantly, obdurately?

"Say no to tacos? Or no to gettin' onya bike. Time's ticking!"

"I – I am not, um, not going with you."

Earlier – had it been hours, or minutes? – I had rolled my eyes and began to ambivalently follow this adorable creature. Now I surprised myself with my stubborn incredulity. Poppy cocked her head and stared at me.

"That's your choice, in'it? But it likely won't end well. Especially when you're dressed like that. Though I see your bold choices and I do respect that."

Poppy turned once more and started toward the sidewalk. I looked at her, I looked at the school. I knew very little about either. If anyone should be here, surprising me, it should be Dragon. I walked in little circles, weighing some hypotheticals. Why wasn't Dragon here? It had been ages – weeks that fell into heavy months, anyway – since I saw him last, since I heard his voice.

You'll be under considerable investigative scrutiny, he had cautioned. *We cannot risk your being seen talking to a Dragon.*

Not everyone can see you, I had scowled at him. *Or was that bullshit too?*

I blinked hard. I hated that I had been so bad-tempered in that last conversation. I was – I am – so, so angry. Philippa in the hospital, my mom forcing this totally contrived optimism, stupid lawyer meetings and hearings and reporters trying to talk to me, and now I couldn't talk to Dragon?! It had been too much. I was cross. He was patient.

I'll still help, Evechild. I'll still be there for you. Let the trial pass, let the legal business settle.

I had wanted to punch him. Now I just wanted to hug him.

He had opened his arms, his wings perked upward. I had turned my back and stomped off. And that was the last time I had anything to do with Dragon.

I thought of those first few days with Dragon, of our initial encounters, of my thrill wound up in skepticism wound up in curiosity. And that turned out okay. Well, the friendship turned out okay, anyway. His presence heralding the potential demise of this dimension and dragging my mom and sister down with it was still a bit of a sore spot.

I stared after Poppy, bounding happily away. Man's best friend, right? Even if she weren't actually a dog in there, surely her assumed visage of something friendly smacked of trustworthiness, right?

I really was tired of arguing with myself all the time.

"Wait, Poppy ... I'm, ugh, I'm coming," I called half-heartedly as I jogged after her. At least, I jogged toward the spot I had seen her last. Man, Australian Shepherds were fast.

52

9

CAUSA SUI

New schools are a rough adjustment under normal circumstances.

But under my circumstances? I was proud of myself for even showing up.

My mom didn't share in this logic.

Yesterday I made it until third period.

Today I was determined to make it through lunch.

I checked my phone for the billionth time that day for any updates on Philippa.

Nothing.

I scanned the halls as I emerged from English class, looking for a rogue therapy dog.

Nothing.

I lingered briefly, bracing myself for something dumb or threatening or cruel to be said to me as schoolmates shuffled past between bells.

Nothing. No teacher, no mythical creature, no magical stone. Just the trappings of a yuppy school.

I sighed. Truthfully, I had been okay with the moments of upset that paved my way home. Who could fault me for leaving school early, given all I had been through. That's the phrase I heard most often: *given all I had been through.* Does that outfit suck? Well, yours would too, given all you'd been through. Was

I late to class? Good for you for showing up, given all you've been through. Crying in the bathroom? Makes sense, given all you've been through.

I had half a mind to take this enabling response on the road for some light larceny. I could hear the concerned shopkeepers now: *You can't be surprised she's shoplifting after all she's been through.*

You can't be surprised she broke into this bank vault after all she's been through.

I giggled. A girl checking her phone next to me looked over with a frown.

"No, not you – I was just laughing at … See, I had, like, this funny inner monologue … never mind," I muttered.

I followed the trail of teens down the left corridor. The energy and volume rose considerably. And there it was. The epicenter of the high school ecosystem: The Cafeteria.

Two sets of double doors were propped open, a disinterested student perched on a stool between them. I eyed suspiciously the lanky limbs and pointy shoulders jutting out from a green shirt that declared SECURITY in gold letters.

"Dude, don't mess with that guy. He will mess you up," said a voice behind me. I twirled around, about to speak.

"Yo, mind your business. I wasn't talking atchu," a boy snapped.

My face reddened.

"Bro, don't make her mad, either! Don't you know who that is?"

Hearing this, the student security guard turned and stared hard at me.

"Check it out, maybe they'll fight. Security Samurai versus Kid Killer."

"Kid Killer. Good one," another boy laughed.

I didn't linger to hear the rest of the conversation. Face burning, I kept my head down and charged down the hall. I heard laughter behind me.

Maybe I'll make it through lunch tomorrow.

For now, all I wanted was my bed. And a grilled cheese. And a mango smoothie. And my sister.

My phone dinged.

Somehow, she knew at that exact moment that I needed a little extra boost. A message from Philippa flashed on my screen. I swiped and read: *Hey loser, jk I actually miss you. Be cool. Love you.*

My chest hurt but I smiled. Then an idea brightened my day right up: another enabling excuse to leave! My homebound sister still recovering from a spine injury! And she missed me. Philippa missed me. And wasn't her health more important than anything at this dumb school?

"Just one minute, young student!"

I let the heavy doors at the school's entrance slam back shut in front of me. I turned and sighed.

"Yeah?"

Principal Fernhouser shifted side to side and folded his arms in front of his stomach.

"Oh, I, erm, it's you. Right," he said, not looking directly at me. "You'll be pleased to know that you are not yet expelled, nor am I pressing any charges on a personal level." He coughed and waved his hand. "Given all that you've been through, it doesn't seem appropriate. Or effective. Given all that you've been through."

I nodded. Entertained and relieved, I held my hand out to him.

"Thank you," I said. "And I, um, I truly am sorry."

"Yes, well, never mind," he said. Principal Fernhouser shook out his shoulders and took a step to the side as if shimmying away from something distasteful (oh, that's me). "You know, it behooves me to inquire if you've sought counseling. You know, given all you've been through. I'm sure I don't know the extent of your goings-on – nor do I care to! – but post-traumatic-stress-disorder diagnoses can be obtained with thorough evaluation. See? It says right there on that informational poster."

He pointed to one of the brightly colored posters adorning the hallway near the business office. Between dance announcements hung a yellow poster declaring that NO ONE IS ALONE with a paragraph below about how to obtain help for various disorders and issues.

"Well, if a poster says so, it must be true," I shot back.

"I've done my due diligence in informing you of as much."

With that, he spun around and walked off. Emptiness tugged at the hem of my shirt.

It was one thing to be fed up with stupid nicknames and storming away from a lunch line; it was quite another to have a school principal – and a poster – reduce you to your mental inadequacies in one breath.

An anger started to boil.

Who does he think he is, throwing around medical opinions like that? My pulse raced as I paced in little circles of rage. This guy goes from killing plants in a middle school front office to peacocking around the halls of a private school and now thinks he can dole out thoughts on my mental state? I was sweating. The straps of my backpack felt tight. My head hurt. I squeezed my eyes shut and rocked my head side to side. Something popped in my neck.

"She's still at it! Over there! Planning her next attack, take cover!" a voice from the cafeteria carried down the hall.

My mouth pursed. I reminded myself not to react, to be patient, to do those stupid counting exercises Malcolm had shown me in therapy that one time. I reached the door in time to see Poppy bounding down a hill outside toward me. Her happy face, tongue sideways out of her mouth, filled the window.

I pushed the front doors open fully this time, but not before I kicked over a large recycling bin. It made a satisfying clatter on the floors. I let the doors bang shut behind me.

"Poppy!" I cried. "There you are, girl! I'm in need of therapy, principal's orders. Yeah, what have you got for, like, PTSD? Principals and posters can diagnose you now, isn't that great? Isn[t that just terrific?"

I prattled nonstop to the little dog as we walked. She had stopped and was staring at me, head cocked. I was neither laughing nor crying, but my mouth made the sounds all the same and my eyes leaked all the same.

"Sheila, y'alright?"

"Yeah I'm alright. Lunch is still going and I'm just leaving, so I'm counting this day as a success. I successfully made it until lunch. Goal met, I am good," I said, shaking my hands in the air.

"When's the last time, y'know, you had a good talk with someone?"

"A good talk?" I asked, drawing out the two words as she had. "What the hell does that mean? Who do you think I'm talking to?"

Poppy's brown eyes looked down. Her ears slanted forward.

"Who, though? Oh, should I go get a random phone number off that yellow poster in there? Or you? Should I talk to you? My trusty therapy dog who talks for some reason?" I cried as I danced around her. "My sister? Was it during or after her surgery that I should talk to her? Or maybe my mom? Yeah, she's terrific for conversation these days. If I'm lucky, I can sometimes get three whole coherent sentences in before she drifts back to her special place of denial and red wine."

"Crikey, you don't have to be so—"

"Oh, but I can talk to Malcolm! My actual therapist who has no idea what has been happening! Because how do I tell a grown medical professional that I can't sleep because I'm worried scary guys will sneak through an interdimensional portal and kidnap my mom and sister again? But that he shouldn't be concerned because my uncle and his best friend, who happens to be a dragon, are on the case?"

"Sheila, I didn't mean to—"

"K, bye, thanks for the chat!" I yelled at the little dog as I took off running.

Ah, running. The thing that had always been the bane of my existence was now weirdly thrilling. I made a mental note to never divulge this to my mom, who loves running.

Barking grew faint. My lungs burned as my feet slammed the sidewalk inelegantly. These flat- bottomed platform sneakers looked cool as hell but were decidedly not designed for speed. It didn't matter. I just ran. I ran past my house, past the entrance to the park, past three more streets, until I arrived, panting and sweaty, at a white bungalow with a brick porch.

I walked up the steps, breathing hard. I ignored the smiling Buddha statue to the right of the colorful welcome mat and rang the doorbell.

I squeezed the straps of my backpack and clenched my jaw. What was I doing? I almost turned back; footsteps from within stopped me. I must do this. I breathed slower, deeper. I can do this. The door creaked. A small woman with black hair pulled back in a ponytail peeked around the open door and gasped.

"Get away! You are not welcome here!"

"Ms. Nguyen! Please! Please give me just a minute!" I said as I pushed lightly against the closing door. It was no use. The door shut; I heard the click of a lock. "I get it! I'd do that, too!" I called loudly. I leaned against the door and sank down onto the mat. "Ms. Nguyen, I just need you to know," I paused, listening. A faint shuffling came from the other side of the door. "I just need to know ... I, um, I'm just," my voice faltered and cracked, "I'm just really sorry."

My head dropped onto my knees and I sobbed.

"I'm sorry, I'm so sorry," I sputtered. Tears fell hard. I stayed there, in a ball, crying and spitting out inadequate apologies for felt like an eternity when the door opened behind me. I had been propped against it; I fell backwards with my backpack to catch me like a lame turtle.

Ms. Nguyen stared down at me. Her mouth was a perfectly straight line under her dark, steady eyes.

"Come in for tea."

I rolled upward and stood, suddenly very aware of my state. Sweat from my impromptu mid-day sprint mixed with snot stains and wet tearstained spots had no place in this tidy home. I instinctually removed my shoes and followed my host into the kitchen where a traditional green tea service was already waiting.

"Here, sit. You need sugar? I don't like to serve my tea with sugar."

I shook my head. I looked down and mumbled words toward the floor.

"What do you need? I'll get sugar."

"No, no sugar. I, um, could I, maybe use your bathroom?" "Third door down that hall to your left."

I nodded and walked slowly, trying not to disrupt the clean lines of the home with my heavy, dirty steps. "Hobbit feet," my mom and Philippa would jokingly call my feet, even though they honestly weren't that much bigger than theirs. A weak smile pushed itself out. I looked up.

The smile of Jonah met me, framed and young, on the wall. A dozen others came into focus then; smiling Jonahs highlighting moments of his 15 years stared at me. My stomach lurched. I dove into the bathroom just in time.

"Shit," I spit out between heaves, "not the bathroom."

But it was too late. I looked down at a small puddle of filmy vomit that had been spewn not into a toilet, but into a laundry basket next to a judging armoire. I wiped my mouth. My head spun too much to panic. I grabbed the laundry basket, and, checking outside the door first, tiptoed one more door down to the actual bathroom.

I locked the door and crept to the toilet, taking time to slowly and silently raise the toilet lid. I held the laundry basket up and started to reach into the clothing for the tainted garment. I paused. This is so gross, I thought, my stomach cramping in protest.

"Maybe I can just, like, pour it out ....," I said to myself as I carefully tilted the narrow hamper's opening toward the open toilet. "Easy, steady ... ah, dammit! Gah!"

The vomit did not pour out, as I hoped it would. A shirt came tumbling out instead. I looked inside the hamper. The putrid puddle remained. I fished the shirt out of the toilet and tossed it on the counter.

"I really don't want to put my hand in there," I muttered as I tilted the laundry basket once more. "Maybe if I shake it loose, yeah, ooze on down, that's right – No! Crap."

A pair of jeans toppled out with a small splash.

"Maybe I can just wipe it out," I murmured as I grabbed a wad of toilet tissue. "Oh, gross, oh, god, that made it worse!" The toilet tissue left little white fibers in the vomitous mess as I wiped. Little bits stuck to my hand. I tossed the disintegrating wad into the toilet. "Ugh. Back to shaking that puke puddle loose."

"You okay in there? It has been a while!" Ms. Nguyen called from the other side of the door. A soft knocking came, then louder. "What's going on there?"

"Um, sorry Ms. Nguyen," I called back, "I'll just be a minute for, um, changing, uh, changing my tampon!"

My face scrunched. That was better than saying I was cleaning up my own vomit? The hall was silent. Then came a tinkering sound from the doorknob. The door fell open. Ms. Nguyen's mouth hung open. She looked at the toilet, looked at me (frozen mid-tilt with the laundry basket), looked at the wet clothing strewn on the counter, looked back at me.

"It's, uh, it's not what it looks like."

"I do not even know what it looks like!"

"Eh, maybe like someone trying to shake vomit loose from your laundry?"

"Why is there vomit on my laundry?"

"Ugh, I know, right? I've, like, always had this stomach thing. I've gotten it checked out by, like, I don't know, a dozen doctors, and they're always like—"

"Did you vomit on my laundry?"

"Oh, um, yes, yes I did."

She just stared for a minute.

"I'm sorry, I was, uh, trying to clean it up. I'm really sorry. Again." "You are a strange girl."

My head dropped lower.

"I will get this; please, just grab that laundry and take it to the washing machine. It's two doors that way."

I nodded and collected the wet clothing into the hamper. The smell was acrid. I held my breath to lessen its power.

"Don't throw up in any more rooms, please."

I nodded in humiliated agreement and shuffled two doors down. I dumped the basket's contents into the washing drum. Something made a tinny plink and sparked. I peered inside. The bin flashed green.

"Ahh!" I jumped back. The machine had singed my fingers. I blinked; I saw green blobs from the bright flash. "What the … where did you go?" I felt around in the laundry pile for what I was so worried I had seen. "Ugh! Gross! Puke! Gah, why do I even – ah ha! AHH!"

I had no sooner recovered the source of the green flash – a tiny familiar gem, as I suspected – then it flared up and burnt me once more.

"Don't tell me you've done something wrong in there, too," Ms. Nguyen called from the kitchen.

"No, I, uh, just got shocked. Yeah, static electricity. The shock surprised me," I said lamely as I headed back to the kitchen, wondering why this woman was still allowing me in her house.

"Here, please sit. Your tea is cold. I'll heat more water."

"I'm really sorry about that back there," I said as I sat at the small table outfitted with tea service. She had added an assortment of small cookies. "I just, um, like I said, I have a wonky stomach."

"I understand. Emotions can cause intense physical reactions," Ms. Nguyen said quietly. Her back was to me as she tended to the kettle. "It's why I invite you to stay. That was an honest reaction to pain. I trust you now."

A small giggle came out.

"You trust me because I yakked all over your clothes? I swear I thought I was facing the toilet. I don't usually –"

"Nah, you did me a favor. I had been putting off doing the last of Jonah's laundry," she said as she sat down with a fresh pot of hot water and a small tray of tea sachets. She looked up at nothing in particular. Her eyes glistened. "Now I must do it. It's a good step forward for me."

Her positive spin was so earnest, so optimistic. I felt like the scum of the universe. This woman had a pile of her deceased son's laundry hanging about as a reminder of his smells, his style, him, and I blew chunks all over it.

I took a sip. I burnt my tongue.

Ms. Nguyen put down her teacup and leaned across the table.

"I've been wanting to talk with you. It's good you came."

Another sip. More burnt tongue.

"Okay," I said, wondering if I could burn my tongue badly enough to render me speechless.

10

AEQUAM SERVARE MENTEM

I cried into my pillow again that night.

Loud, heaving sobs accented by pitiful shrieks and screams. I slipped my hand under my pillow and pressed its sides against my ears to dampen my muffled agony. I nodded off at some point, only to awaken and repeat.

Yellow eyes flashed in my mind, Philippa's body under the hunks of broken glass hovered just beyond. I reached out toward her, and her body slid away, farther and farther away into blackness. Mrs. Nguyen was there, crying.

Birds chirped. The sun shone. I blinked.

It was morning, I had been dreaming. Nightmarish memories followed by screaming and crying. On repeat. My nightly ritual has left me exhausted almost every morning for two months now, but it had gotten really bad lately.

"Eve, lovely girl, are you ready?" my mom said as she poked her smiling face through the open door. "Oh! You'll be late! Do you have your things ready?"

I stared back at her. My mom lives in sweats, holding a water bottle in one hand and her phone in the other. Normally the sight would make me smile, for it was usually so endearing. She was so accomplished and had what I gathered to be a pretty important job. But working remotely had only fostered her love of activewear. At this moment I resented her upbeat if not blasé demeanor. What did she have to be so chipper about? I pulled my blankets over my head and burrowed under my safe layers of pillows and stuffed animals.

"No," I growled.

"No, you don't have your things ready, or…no, you won't be late?" she asked gently, walking over to my bed. She reached her hand toward me.

"Just no," I barked and turned away from her.

"Ok," she said softly as she bent down to retrieve Bartholomew, my stuffed dragon who had been my sidekick for going on a decade now. He had fallen off the bed in my ornery thrashing.

"Let me know when you're ready, no rush." She tenderly placed the stuffed dragon near my cheek. Her patience, her kindness, infuriated me.

"Go away," I muttered, swatting the stuffed dragon away. I secured my blankets even tighter around me and curled into an angry ball on my bed. "Please," I added.

"Oh, my Eve! Did you mean to – this must have just fallen in here," my mom said as she knelt at my small, always-overflowing waste bin by the door. "This is your favorite book! Here, where would you like it?"

"Where you found it," I grumbled as I thrashed about under my covers. I knew what book she was talking about. Dragonology had landed me in this mess. And that book, beloved though it had been, was more exculpatory evidence than childhood passion project at this point to me. Let it be dead and gone.

"I'll set it on your shelf in case you have a change of heart. I'm emptying all the trash bins, so … anyhow. It's there. Get some rest. Love you."

Through lidded eyes I watched her leave. The room was dimmed, and a cool breeze caught the top of my head and relaxed me all over. My mom had drawn the window shade and turned on the ceiling fan. I heard her humming down the hallway and my heart sank.

How could I be so nasty? She's trying to forge ahead and keep her good nature about her. I didn't have the monopoly on grief – surely, she felt pain as well. What must it have been like for her, I wondered, imprisoned in that tube? Did her thoughts continue? Was she aware of what was happening while she was hostage? I shuddered, reliving the discovery of her limp body, suspended in that tube. I blinked and shook the image out of my head for the hundredth time.

Which begged the question again, how is she okay now?

Anger rose inside me once more and I pushed it down with blankets. I burrowed deeper under covers, under sheets, under quilts, wishing I could continue burrowing into the bed itself. I would burrow into the floor even, through the floorboards, into the foundation, into the dirt, into the mud, into bedrock, into the mantle of earth, for surely there I would be safe. Safe from other dimensions, safe from intruders, safe from… Who am I kidding, I thought, shaking my head. I could drill through 1000 earths or jump through 1,000 dimensions and still never be safe from what was locked inside my own mind.

The parts of my brain had given up their scientific titles; only phantoms lived there. In the memory centers, the language centers, the bits that control responses and register emotion – all taken over by things beyond words. There are no lobes, no cortex, just phantoms, just ghosts, that haunt not the skull but the soul. They team up, they lie and wait, patiently waiting for my guard to be down. Wait until she sleeps, they whisper, and then they come out to play, to strike. My heart, my sanity, are their playthings. They commandeer my insides and make puppets of logic, they dance and laugh until their phantom revelry has distorted my reality.

But what is my reality even? The pile of bladed memories, scars I can't talk about, people in my house who are strangers to me now.

I sat up. Surely, I had been dreaming.

But no.

I replayed the evening with Ms. Nguyen in my mind, over and over, seeing her cry, seeing her flipping through photo albums of baby Jonah. She held my hand and made me tea. All I did was vomit in her laundry and use up a full box of tissue.

Shame greeted anger inside me and demanded I pull the covers back over my body. Maybe I could just stay here. On my bed, under these blankets, time stalled and the world waited, quiet. I needed that quiet. I needed to just exist, neutral and safe. Would I ever be able to do that again?

Too many heavy questions and heavier thoughts to greet a Wednesday with.

I had finally gotten out of bed.

That shouldn't have been such a victory, but alas, at 2:23 in the afternoon still in jammies, I took joining the day as a win.

The thing that got me up and into a shower, readying myself for joining society, was an invitation to join Ms. Neally for "evening tea" at a café I hadn't heard of. I couldn't say no.

As I rode the bus to the chosen destination – a kitschy coffeehouse in an old Portland Craftsman – a waterfall of guilt poured through me. I had promised Philippa I'd help her with her physical therapy "homework" that evening after I helped her proofread her college application essays.

Geez. I was the absolute worst.

Phlee I'm so sorry, I spaced our plans tonight. Back soon, don't give up on me! I texted her and hit send, the whooshing sound bouncing through the pit in my stomach. My phone chimed immediately. Ugh, that made it worse! She was sitting there, waiting, with her phone in her hand! Very uncharacteristic of the Philippa I had known.

Who dis was all it said. I smiled pitifully. Why did she have to be so goddamn pleasant and hilarious all the time?

I made my way off the bus down SE 12th Avenue. Seeing the place, weathered columns and shutters painted reddish-purple bedecked by a wide porch, compounded my guilt. Phlee would love this place.

I sighed and walked in. Ms. Neally sat, elegant and picturesque, at a small table shoved against an old fireplace. She looked up and smiled at me. I waved dumbly, dropping my head to hide my blushing cheeks.

"Oh, uh, hey. Cool spot," I said as I slid onto a rickety cane chair.

"One of my favorites. I, well, that is, people a little more like me, are always welcome here," she said as she leaned in.

I glanced around the place, dark and moody but with streams of lights and bright candles adorning its nooks and angles. A group of women in colorful crocheted garb chortled loudly at one table; at another, an Abraham Lincoln-looking chap sipped wine from a funky goblet. A couple at the counter giggled over which dessert to indulge in.

"You mean ... they're all, like, ancient or whatever? From other dimensions?" I whispered excitedly, my eyes wide with wonder.

"Not exactly. Not all. He certainly is," she said, nodding toward Honest Abe. "He's not great at understanding time's nuanced details, like fashion and progress. But nevermind. We can speak a bit more openly here, which is a nice change of pace from schoolyards and hangar grounds."

I sighed. Indeed, it was a nice change. A woman with loads of tattoos and orange hair asked me for my order. I really, really wanted to say hot chocolate, but, needing to appear mature, I coolly asked for a café Borgia and a piece of ginger cake. (I still don't know what a café Borgia is, only that it had enough orange flavor to mask the disgusting coffee taste and it kept me jittery and fidgeting for the next four hours.)

I sipped and snacked on delicious cake and let my eyes dart around the room. I wondered what was upstairs. I wondered why people ducked into the bathroom and came out laughing and comparing photos on their phones.

Philippa would really love this place.

What was I doing? Why was I here? What did I think I could even accomplish? A hard truth smacked me in the face: I wasn't here because I thought I could save the world. The last time that had been my goal, my sister got waylaid by an other-dimensional overlord whom I didn't even stop. I was here because I had a big, fat, stupid crush on my middle school librarian-turned galactic mentor or something.

And I hated myself for it. Nothing would change that. Not even that incredible ginger cake. I was frozen. Again. Locked in by walls and emotions that had no name.

"Eve? What do you think?"

Ms. Neely's voice startled me. Has she been speaking this entire time?

"I'm sorry," I said and coughed. "Can you, er, would you...." My voice trailed off as I felt my face burn and my throat crowd. Ms. Neely's face softened. She squeezed my hand and I jumped. I hadn't even registered human touch. How long had her hand been on mine? Was that allowed?

"Shall I walk through the plan again?"

"The plan, yes. The plan, yes," I said quietly.

"We will coordinate at Seb's hanger at 0700, promptly. Kip will be ready." I nodded dumbly. Just then she looked up.

"Ah! Here they are now! I believe someone is quite eager to see you."

Uncle Seb swaggered over, cool as ever. I stayed seated and \squeezed my arms tightly to my sides, suddenly very aware of the moist warmth growing in my underarms. (How was I supposed to know caffeine would make an already sweaty gal sweatier?)

Ms. Neely hopped up from her chair, slipped her smart loafers back on, smoothed her skirt, and went to greet Uncle Seb.

Baert stumbled in behind him, kicking a crumpled napkin. He missed the napkin, kicked the floor, hurt his toe, and punched the worn wooden planks.

"Baert!" I shrieked as I bolted up. My chair tumbled behind me. "You're here!"

We hugged. He smelled faintly of peanut butter. This made me hug him even more tightly. He laughed and pushed me away. I looked him up and down: His red hair, usually wild and matted, was smoothed and pulled back. And, wow, could it be?

"You're wearing shoes!" I squealed.

"Aye, lassie, I do be a brawn lad, when I choose," he said with a humph.

Beyond us, Uncle Seb and Ms. Neally were still whispering. He grabbed her into a bear hug. My eyes narrowed as his hands rested on either side of her tiny waist.

"I've seen that pure barry look before," Baert said, punching me in the arm. "*Aye, mairidh gaol is ceol.*"

"You don't know what you're talking about," I scowled.

"Boot I do!"

"Boot ye don't," I said, mocking him.

"Aye, so y'speak Gaelic now, is that it?" Baert said, bemused.

"I'm sure whatever it you said was dumb," I mumbled. I hated me just then. I adored Baert – just because I was irritated over the fact that visions of Ms. Neely's heart-shaped mouth wouldn't leave my mind didn't mean I should be cross with my favorite brownie. Everyone gets little school crushes on their teachers at some point, right?

"I'm glad you're okay," I said quietly to Baert. He smiled, a little sadly though. I could tell he didn't want to discuss his health.

Someone coughed behind me. I spun around. Dragon!

"Oh, hello, why, I only walked up," Dragon stammered, refusing to make eye contact. My thoughts had been loud. And he clearly had walked into their cacophony at the worst possible moment. My cheeks burned red.

"Shall we—"

"Yes," I cut him off brusquely and sat back at the small table.

I looked up, suddenly very aware that a dragon, a Highland elf, and three humans were casually meeting up for coffee. The same groups of people continued as they had been. The orange-haired barista walked across the room and turned the Open sign on the door to Closed.

"Huh," I said and took another sip from my coffee cup. Baert swiped my last bite of ginger cake.

11

CREDO UT INTELLIGAM

The coffee house had long since closed, and there we were, our motley five, deep in discussion about theoretical physics and quantum mechanics.

"Imagine a world where the concept of more dimensions inlaid with ours isn't a fascinating idea but a real thing, known and understood. Or if not understood, at least accepted," Dragon said.

"But there can't be," I shot back.

"Why?" Baert responded.

"Because string theory was disproven."

"Why?" he asked again.

"Because, because ... I don't know, they figured out the universe can't hold, like, multiple existences," I looked around, trying to be cool while having no idea what I was talking about after all, "And it was disproved."

"No. It just hasn't been proven," Uncle Seb added.

"Right. Disproved."

"No, not proved," he said. "Yet."

"Same thing!" I sighed, exasperated.

"Oh heavens, not at all! Proving something and disproving something are two entirely different prospects. Disproving something is not the same as not yet proving it," Dragon said as he threw his talons in the air indignantly. "String theory has not yet been disproven, so there's still a chance it may be proved."

"Yeah, well, by that logic can't I also say it hasn't been proven so there's still a chance it can be disproven?" I yelled back. "It's totally perspective. Doi."

"Doi?"

"Yeah. Duh."

"Duh?"

"Oh, for Christ's sake."

"Christ?"

"Oh, come on!" I wailed. Dragon's eyes twinkled.

"I am familiar with Christian lore and colloquialisms," Dragon said as his eyes twinkled. "I apologize, that was for my amusement."

Ms. Neally smiled from behind her teacup, bemused but not weighing in. She and Uncle Seb exchanged little smirks. I rolled my eyes.

"Ok," I started again. "Does being in a different dimension mean being in a different universe?

"Time is its own dimension, obviously. That is baby physics. Physics for babies," Dragon said impatiently. "In your plane of existence, you use the world 'time' incorrectly. You've created a construct for exacting the passage of carbon. But it's not time."

"Ok... but no? Because, because ..." I frowned and focused hard, "because we're in 3D, and those three dimensions are space, and gravity, and time. Boom."

Ms. Neally smiled and set her teacup daintily on its saucer. It made a satisfying clink. We all looked at her.

"You are right to hold convictions of science," she said gently. You are wrong in your tri- dimension definition. The Ds in 3D refer to length, width, and height. There is a fourth dimension of time, however."

"Whatever. I tried."

"Time behaves as its own dimension, isn't that fun? And thus, it opens up possibilities of different lines of time. However—"

"Ms. Neally, I love that you're an, what'd you call yourself?"

"Amateur physicist."

"Right, a physicist," I said with some snark; nothing about her ever seemed amateur. "But my brain is about to explode. I just need to know, do you, as someone who has apparently been in and out of dimensions for, like, a billion years, think defeating Obrenox is possible?"

Uncle Seb shifted uncomfortably, then got up, announcing he'd pull the car around. Baert slid out of his chair and made his way to the bathroom. Dragon suddenly took great interest in the millwork of the room, walking over to examine the stair banister.

The pretty librarian looked down at her hands, soft and manicured. She never wore jewelry, which I liked. She turned her hands over, so her palms were up, and rested them on the table.

"I had my palms read, once, by a fearsome wizard who claimed to have clairvoyancy," she traced the lines of one palm with the middle finger of her other hand, delicately, slowly. "He told me remarkable things, radical things, and very, very sad things."

"So? Did it come true? Was he right? Is that what I'm going to do?"

"No," she said, and clapped her hands lightly.

"No, it didn't come true? Or no, I'm not going to do that? What's the point, then?"

"Once I knew what my potential was – what could be mine, good or bad, I could project my steps backwards and determine my own path. If I wanted to arrive at the destination foretold, I could make a series of choices, decisions, and steps to arrive there. Similarly, if I didn't want to arrive that destination, I could intentionally select paths that I knew would veer so far off-course that the likelihood of it coming to pass was defunct."

I pondered this, puzzled. I felt I was being offered some profound key to life, but I couldn't make sense of it. Or maybe I just desperately wanted her to be offering me a key to life.

"Eve, humans don't operate under absolute fate. There are multiple possible outcomes for you, sure, myriad destinations. Examine which you feel most drawn to and act from there."

I just stared at her. My brain still hurt.

"What's the point of the human ability to learn and experience so much, if you don't get to use it to determine where you're going along the way?"

"Ohhhhh," I said slowly. "I think I'm getting it."

(I wasn't.) Ms. Neally smiled.

"You've learned all you have for a reason. Be confident in that."

I drank my tea, which had grown cold. No matter; I found tea equally disgusting warm or cold but very much enjoyed the aesthetic of it. So I drank it.

"Check, please," Ms. Neally called warmly.

She opened her small wallet and began to pull out several papers. They didn't look the money I was used to seeing; they were yellowish and looked more like small certificates. Ms. Neally blushed, folded them back in, and retrieved the green, wrinkled U.S. bills I was used to seeing.

"A 17th-century krona," she said sheepishly. "No one used Swedish banknotes anymore, but I hold onto them for sentimental reasons."

As we got up and walked out of the old building, I blurted out a question I had no intention of asking.

"Ms. Neally, how freaking old are you?"

She stopped, a bit taken aback. She paused, breathed deeply, and put on a pair of brown leather gloves.

"You understand enough about dimensions to know that time gets distorted just slightly or very significantly depending on where you've gone, yes?"

"Um, yes?"

"I have traveled a lot."

With that, she turned and walked away. Uncle Seb's little black MG rumbled up to the curb. He hung an arm out the window and waved awkwardly.

"Heyya, Yaél! It's me, you know that, though, alright, I'll catchya later."

"Smooth," I giggled as I got in the car. I would never get used to walking around to the left side of his British car.

"Shut it," he said good-naturedly. "We've got to make record-time getting you back. If I have a hundred missed calls and texts from your mom, you surely have a million."

I pulled out my phone. He was right. I scrolled through the messages from my mom, ranging from questions about dinner to thoughts on music lessons for me to inquiries about my timing ... that last question grew in impatience and panic the more recent it got. And then there were the messages I had missed from Philippa, in including a missed FaceTime call.

I felt awful.

That waterfall of guilt that had drenched me on the bus ride there soaked me all over again. But with more force.

"You good, Egg? Heh. 'Good egg.' Never gets old," Uncle Seb chuckled.

"No," I said. "I'm not good. And I don't know when I ever will be."

"Kinda dramatic, Egg. Even for you."

12

DOCENDO DISCIMUS

"**I**'m sorry, I swear I'm trying. I just do not get how this number and this letter are supposed to equal that," I cried as I pushed the calculus book away from me. "I know I'm supposed to be helping you study or whatever, but come on. We both know I'm, like, just in the way."

Philippa looked up from behind her neatly standing rows of colored highlighters.

"You just have to see the limits of the function. See, if you move *ab* here, and find that exponent, then – tah-dah! – you have solved for *y*," she said proudly and went back to her color-coded notes.

"If you're so perfect at this, then why am I helping you! I'm just in the way!" I wailed.

I pushed away from the table and stood. The rows of highlighters toppled over. Philippa frowned.

"By teaching you, I'm learning it better. Duh," she said as she balanced the yellow highlighters on their ends again. "If you can do it, then I know I've mastered the concept enough to show you thoroughly."

I started to protest, but that actually made good sense. My stomach grumbled. I looked down at her phone on the table and tapped the screen. The time illuminated against a background image of Barbra Streisand.

"Twenty-three-fourteen?" I cried as I slid the phone over to her. The high-lighters clattered to the table once more and spun around their sides. "Even your phone makes me do math to find out what time it is?!"

"It's 11:14! And really, you can't just subtract 12? If you're getting food, you wanna be a pal and make me a grilled cheese?" she called after me as I stomped off to the kitchen.

I wanted to protest, but a midnight grilled cheese would really hit the spot. It had been hours since I had devoured that ginger cake, after all. My mind began to wander back to the conversations in that delightful coffee house …

"Did you know time zones are calculated using the prime meridian?" Philippa yelled from the dining table. "Yeah! In increments of four degrees, starting with Greenwich Mean Time, which is obviously zero—"

"You want muenster or this weird gouda?" I called, intentionally cutting her off. She didn't respond. "It's goat-milk gouda! I didn't even know they could do that!" I yelled louder.

"So, each longitude is at a distance of ten, no, I think it's 15 degrees, from each other," Philippa yelled back.

"Is this calculus?" I called as I flipped the sandwiches in the cast-iron pan. Melty cheesy goodness oozed from the buttery, browned bread.

"Are you serious right now?" she returned. "Are you literally, actually serious?"

My mom appeared in the doorway of the kitchen, clad in pajamas. She rubbed her cheeks. Her hair, swept up in a messy bun, nodded as she did so.

"Oh, hey Ma. Grilled cheese?" I asked as I turned toward her with a perfectly cooked sandwich balanced on a spatula.

"Are … are you girls fighting about … math?" she said into a yawn. "Really, this is no time for fighting! I wish you'd just get along!"

"Yes, mom! I am shaken up at Eve's hateful speech about differential equations, as well as her disdain toward time zones!"

"Mom, ignore her. Everything's fine. For real. Have some sando," I offered her my sandwich on a plate.

She held up her hand and shook her head. She instead grabbed a bag of gummy bears I didn't know we had from the pantry and turned back upstairs.

"Back to bed. And you two," she paused on the stairs and tossed a handful of gummies into her mouth. "Be *nice*."

I rolled my eyes. Be nice, like stay up all night helping my sister with math I didn't understand and make her delicious food while I'm at it. My stomach grumbled again. I was secretly glad she didn't want the grilled cheese.

I slid a plate over to Philippa and joined her at the table.

"What, no apple juice? What is this, prison?"

"Is that how you imagine prison to be?" I giggled.

"No. Obviously not," she said and took a bite. "Prison would totally give you apple juice."

I threw a highlighter at her.

We chewed in silence. The night, light from laughter just moments ago, had turned heavy.

"Can I ask you something?"

"Phlee, you know you're going to ask me something regardless of how I answer that."

"Well, yeah. It's just the gentlemanly thing to do. Anyway. I think," she paused and wiped her hands thoughtfully, "I think I dreamed while I was ... you know ... in *there*."

I swallowed hard and looked down. I brushed some crumbs off the table. I knew exactly where *there* was. I wondered if we'd ever talk about her time captive in that tube, but I sure as hell wasn't going to bring it up first.

"Bad stuff?" I ventured finally.

"Bad stuff," she repeated quietly. "Voices I never want to hear again. High-pitched and sharp, you know? I dreamed they were trying to get something from me, cells? No, that sounds so dumb, saying it aloud. But yeah. Now it's this super familiar, creepy dream that comes back sometimes."

I was quiet. She started lining up her highlighters on their ends again, this time starting with the pink.

"Phlee," I said with a cough, "I'm really sorry. I – I didn't know any of that stuff would happen! You have to believe me. I'm, just, I'm just really, really sorry, that you –"

My voice broke. My sister's hands were on mine. I looked up.

"Walking over there to hug you is, like, a whole thing," she said and squeezed my hands. "Plus, I don't know what your deodorant situation is."

"You're such an asshole," I said, laughter breaking through my tears.

"Yeah, but I'm *your* asshole," she said, then paused. "That … didn't come out right."

"You didn't come out right."

We stayed at the table until the sun came up, talking, laughing, eating too much cheese. All the things sisters should do. And when we decided to tap out and get some sleep, I looped my arm under hers and aided her labored, pained limping up the stairs to her room.

It had been a good night.

13

SUMMUM BONUM

I slept through my alarms. All seven of them. But, I realized with a smile, I actually slept! I didn't wake because I was *sleeping*, not hiding from the world in a depressed ball!

I looked down the hall. Philippa was still asleep. My mom's room was empty. Perfect. No one there to ask me why I wasn't at school. I found my phone and clicked on my uncle's name.

Hey, no school today. (It wasn't technically a lie.) *Should we continue our convo?*

Just as I was about to give up on a response and start cleaning the kitchen, my phone chimed. *Owm.* I frowned, then giggled. My uncle must be thinking he was typing an abbreviation for "on my way."

"Old people," I chuckled as I readied to go. My phone chimed again. "Yeah, you're old! Did you hear me?" I yelled at the phone. "Oh, wait a minute."

I swiped on a message from my mom: *Running behind, will be to your conference in 10.* I read and reread the message from my mom, thoroughly confused. What conference? Where? So I did the only thing I could think of. I typed back: *No worries! Conference cancelled. They said they'll reschedule.*

I stared at the phone, more than a bit anxious. What conference?! Finally, a thumbs-up icon from my mom appeared on my message.

A honk from outside pulled me to the door and on my way to more pressing matters.

"Hey, cool that you had the day off. Perfect timing," Uncle Seb said as I climbed in. "Seatbelt. Oh, and I've got someone waiting for you back at the hangar."

I groaned.

"No more hangar. That place stresses me out."

He didn't respond.

We reached the hangar in record time, or maybe I was just so engrossed in my thoughts that the minutes didn't register. I was lost in our last conversations. Ms. Neally's words dripped over my brain, gooey and expanding.

"Oh, Evechild! Oh, what a delight!"

"Dragon!" I burst out of the car, leaving the door ajar.

"That's fine, I'll get it!" Uncle Seb yelled behind me, but I didn't care. I fell on my old friend with relief and gratitude, as if it had been years since our last encounter. His scales were warm.

Maybe it was the events in the Seventh, maybe it was just anxiety in general, but I sure was needy when it came to Dragon. How desperate I was for his validation and friendship!

I trotted after him, each of his mighty steps about seven of my own. We found our usual spot in the breezy shade across from the hangar; it was exceptionally warm for an Oregon September. A series of books and drafting papers were lain about.

"What's this?" I asked, sitting down next to it.

"Oh, I was sure your uncle would apprise you of our meeting today ... Eh, Sebastian, old chap?"

"I thought maybe you just wanted to, like, see me," I grumbled, only half sarcastic.

His face fell. Dragon crouched down across from me. His wings drew into his body. He looked smaller than I was used to seeing.

"Of course, I miss the days of constant interactions. You know it is not safe for me to be so ... present in your life right now, nor to be flying about this place at all. So, I couple business with pleasure. That is, presently. we need to chart out our course of action, and," he looked up and gave me a wink, "I wanted to see my old buddy."

I smiled and grabbed an apple from a tray near a pile of books. I took a bite and felt something rubbery. I pulled it away to see a tiny brown worm wriggling out of the core. I spit, screamed, spit some more, and threw the apple.

The Kips standing nearby bolted into action.

"Safety first, yep!"

"Tend to father, yep! Tend to the great wavy snake, yep! Tend to the egg, yep!"

"What's all the racket?" Uncle Seb cried as he jogged to us.

Dragon and I glared at him.

"After all our time, you present me as wavy snake to your gaggle of minions?"

"Minions, plus one lawyer," I corrected. "At least you're not 'the egg.' Wavy Snake isn't so bad."

"It most certainly is!" Dragon said and thumped his tail.

"What, that's your name," Uncle Seb said innocently. "It's good, Kip. We got it under control."

The crew abated. One Kip dropped a pile of gardening tools where he stood. A trowel hit the ground and spun. Two other Kips backtracked and gathered up the tools, apologizing.

"Speaking of one lawyer," Dragon continued, unamused. "Might we have Kip join us? It is pertinent."

Uncle Seb hopped up, and, a few minutes later, jogged back with Kip. Attorney Kip was now dressed in a suit. And wearing his signature sunglasses. And carrying a briefcase.

"Apologies for the delay, yep! Needed to change into my law uniform, yep."

"You look most becoming, most clearly a learnéd esquire," Dragon commented.

Kip beamed and sat down on the grass beside us. He sat with his legs straight out.

"So, we'd like to discuss strategy the upcoming trial."

Kip opened his briefcase and took out a sleeve of Ritz crackers. After very loudly opening the cellophane wrapping, he held up a single cracker.

"Cupcake, yep?"

"Oh, eh, no thank you, sir," Dragon said, nonplussed.

I shook my head and smiled. Uncle Seb waved him away. Kip shrugged and bit into the cracker.

"Mmmmmmm! Very tasty, yep!"

"Kip! Do you mind, bud? We need your attorney brain, my friend," Uncle Seb said with some impatience.

The three continued talking. About really big, really scary things that related directly to me. But my mind was already gone. My thoughts floated back to that conversation I couldn't shake, the one with Ms. Neally about the palm reader.

Could I really choose where I ended up? If I knew one outcome was A, and one outcome was B, could I simply reverse-engineer my path to or away from it? I frowned and thought of Philippa lying in that hospital bed after we had returned "victorious." She certainly hadn't engineered a path toward that. But some small choice must have shifted her trajectory in a different direction. Suppose she hadn't skipped her study group that night she and my mom got taken?

I shuddered. Peppering past choices with hypothetical questions was a dangerous game. That much I knew. Suddenly, I snapped back into the present conversation.

"Sorry, what? Did you just say 'when you were with Obrenox'?" I asked.

The three were quiet. Kip took another bite of Ritz cracker. Dragon coughed. Uncle Seb looked away.

"Go on ... you started to say something about meeting, um," I stopped and glanced around, "Obrenox!?" I finished in a whisper.

"It was nothing, Egg. Don't sweat it."

"You know I'm notoriously sweaty."

Dragon coughed to mask his laugh. I smiled, proud of my quick wit.

"What, I am. Just self-conscious about it, so I make jokes," I muttered. "Wait! Don't walk away!"

I jogged after Uncle Seb who had used my distraction as an escape.

"Gotta pack the wheel bearings and service the struts."

"Pack struts later," I panted.

"Gotta do it now or gunk builds up on 'em. Can't take maintenance lightly."

"The fact that you're working so hard on evading conversation just confirms you have something big you're hiding."

"I said it was nothing."

"Nothing doesn't get you all flustered and twitchy."

"Huh. I don't feel either of those things."

He turned to grab one more wrench to add to an already full bundle in his arms. A tin can of tiny bolts fell to the cement ground with a terrific clatter.

I looked back at Dragon and Kip, who were now in deep conversation themselves. I frowned. If whatever my uncle had said about knowing Obrenox didn't illicit a reaction from them, then it must be nothing. Or it must not be anything too worrisome. Or maybe I heard them wrong.

Or maybe they were all in on it together. And I was the idiot in the dark.

I stared at my uncle, his head buried in a toolbox. I gritted my teeth. This guy was getting on my nerves. The enigma had been understandable for a while, maybe even exciting. But what I was learning is that things only happened on his time frame. He'd tell you something when he was good and ready, regardless of what was going on.

"Alright, Kip. Back to my trial prep," I said half-heartedly as I jogged back.

Yes, I jogged back to a dragon and a rescued clone-something who was representing me while I was on trial for murder.

Every moment of my life, I realized, was stranger and more unbelievable than the last.

Better not stop and think about it too long, I decided, or I'll go mad.

That night, my body was as restless as my mind. I flipped and kicked as if trying to dodge every question that lambasted my brain. I had no means – no insight, no knowledge – to quash the questions. They lived, but buried themselves deep in my mind as their question marks floated away and skipped heavily in the air above me.

And that was life just then – question marks hovering above you, ready to attach themselves to anything at any moment.

14

CAVEAT EMPTOR

"**S**mart. Going for an insanity plea," a deep voice startled me. My hands jerked up and knocked my water bottle over. A stream of New Seasons-brand geyser water trickled down the computer desk and onto the plastic molded chair, where it pooled coolly under my backside.

"She doesn't need a therapist, she needs a parole officer," a girl added with a snort.

"You don't choose your own parole officers, dumbass," the boy shot back.

"Yeah, I know, it was still funny," the girl snapped.

I stared straight ahead at the screen, my finger holding down the delete key as "therapists for teens near me" unwound and cleared the search bar.

"I mean, are you though?" the boy pulled a matching blue chair over and slumped into it next to me. He propped a foot up on the desk, the other coolly directed the wheeled chair side to side.

"Am I what," I said dryly without looking away from the computer screen, nor really bothering to ask a question.

"Going for an insanity plea!" the girl tried to wedge a chair for herself between mine and the boy's. I moved slightly, he did not. "It's like, way smart. In my professional legal opinion."

"You don't have a professional opinion. Or a legal one. You just have a nice pair so people listen to you," the boy said.

Now I looked up, equal parts shocked, amused, and curious. The girl showed him a choice finger as she bumped the chair into place and sat down with a huff. She practically breathed designer brands. I had to catch my gaze as she leaned over to adjust a very lovely heel. Her shirt gaped open and seeing cleavage – young and new and so inviting – was not something I was used to. Nothing at Beecher Junior High had prepared me for this moment. I coughed.

"Too bad you knocked that water over. Because you should probably drink it," the boy said.

"That's not even helpful. Just, shush," the girl said. She unzipped a small Kate Spade waist pack and produced a business card. It was square and glittered like her manicured nails.

"Take it," she said with an encouraging smile.

I looked beyond her at the boy who was rolling his eyes, his fingers interlocked behind his head to recline his neck back. I grabbed the card and tossed it in my bag. I started to get up, then quickly sat back down. Christ, I muttered to myself. My butt was very, very wet. I swore internally some more, ruing the spilled water (that I had bought myself!), the wet jeans (that I had nothing on me to cover!), and just this whole situation in general.

"I'm Channing. Channing Reagan Barrenton. But you knew that already," she offered a hand covered with an intimidating number of baubles toward me.

"I did not know that already," I said as I shook the tips of her fingers.

"Yeah, you're new here," the boy leaned forward. "Channing's ridiculous. But she's right about the legal thing. You should totally take an insanity plea."

"Are you guys friends? You're not very nice to her," I said as I began collecting my things, plotting a stealth way to sidle backwards out of the study lounge to avoid my soggy Levi's being in their faces. "Nice to meet you, Channing."

"Relax, new girl," the boy said and shoved a chair toward me with the bottom of his shoe. It hit me squarely in the shin and buckled my knee. I dropped my bag and plopped down again.

"Fine. What? What shitty things do you want to tell me? You want a selfie? You realize I enrolled in this school to try to have the smallest amount of peace and quiet as I pretend like I can have a semi-normal freshman year, right? But lay it on. Let's hear your best," I said, surprised at my coolness. I leaned back, arms folded, and glared at the pair.

"Damn, maybe you did do it," the boy said. He had the air of confidence of one who's entirely too aware of how cool and good-looking they are. "You're way more intense that I thought."

"Um, wouldn't you be? Given ... all ... this," Channing said as she drew her hand in a circle in front of me.

A bell chimed. Thank goodness.

"I'm just trying to tell you that you seem like you could use a pal or two," he said unflappably.

"And also, we don't think you did it," Channing said quickly. "Like at all."

Holy cow, did I need to hear that! My heart warmed and tears pricked my eyes.

"Yeah, well, that doesn't do me a ton of good, does it," I said quickly with a cough to hide my vulnerability.

"Actually, it does. My mom is this big, huge scary attorney and we're kind of in a little tiff right now and she's, like, desperate to have me like her again," Channing said as she took a bag of fruit snacks out from another of her several posh bags. She opened it, ate three fruit snacks, and returned the pouch to its pocket. "So I think she should represent you. She'd totally do it if I asked."

I don't know what threw me more – the fact that this very beautiful upper-classman was advocating for better legal representation for me, or that she ATE THREE FRUITSNACKS AND SAVED THE REST FOR LATER.

"I don't know that I can afford another lawyer," I started.

"Attorney," Channing interjected.

"Oh my goSH, who cares," the boy blurted. "The point is, we're offering you a lifeline. Do you want it or not?" He put his arm casually around Channing's well postured shoulders and leaned in toward me. "What's it gonna be?"

"You make it sound like a blood oath is about to go down," I said.

"Ha. You're funny. She's funny, right? Yeah, let's do this," the boy said.

He stood, which apparently meant the tete-a-tete was over. Channing stood and smoothed her sleeves (something I had never thought to do). The boy shoved each of the chairs with his foot and stretched.

"We'll meet at your place, babe?"

I must have made a face because he frowned and challenged me. "What? What's that judgey look? Fix your face," he said.

"Um, nothing, you said ...," I trailed off, trying to come up with something besides the truth: teenagers calling each other "babe" was not something I had witnessed before, and I desperately wanted to mock it. "You said her name, but not your name," I brightened, pleased with my quick thinking. "Yeah, I like, can't meet you somewhere without knowing your name."

At this, Channing burst into laughter. She threw her head back and placed her hands on my shoulders.

"Ah, thank you for that! You made my day!" she chortled. "He thinks everyone knows his name! I can't even. Oh, this is too perfect!"

Still laughing, she turned to follow the pouting boy who was on his way out of the study lounge.

"He's Guy," she called over her shoulder, "Guy Cicero."

I waited a minute for them to leave. I grabbed my backpack and headed to the bathroom.

"That was weird," I muttered.

I felt myself smile a little, though. Someone believed me? Someone – two someones! – said aloud that they think I'm innocent. But my smile disappeared as I pushed through the bathroom door and faced the mirror. My own reflection startled me most unpleasantly. Matted hair, puffy eyes. And the piece de resistance: it looked like I peed myself.

"Maybe no one will notice," I grumbled as I tried to smooth my hair into a ponytail. It was lumpy. How was hair lumpy? I frowned and wiped paper towels against my damp jeans. I eyed the hand dryer and, checking that the restrooms were empty, shimmied my rear under it. I hit the button and a loud blast of air shot out.

I inadvertently let out a contented "aaaahhhhh" as the hot air dried my jeans and warmed my lower back.

"You need to be left alone, Dragongirl?" Libby snickered, suddenly in front of me.

"What? Oh my gosh. I mean, um, how long were you standing there?"

"Long enough to know you have the hots for the dryer. Get it? Hots? But anyway," Libby said as she leaned into the mirror and added a coat of mascara. She swung around and faced me, wide eyed. "I have to know, were you seriously talking to Channing and Guy?!"

"Why do you care? What, are you, like following me or something?"

"You wish," Libby snorted. She put her hand on my arm. "Like, are you guys friends? Tell me everything. I have to know. Does she smell as good as she looks? Is he still famous? Did you get a selfie with him?"

I shrugged off her hand.

"Geez, Libster. So you want to be pals or whatever now because you think that I am friends with some popular kids? That's just so heartwarming."

"Not just popular kids; juniors. The influencers. Not only of the school, but probably of the entire West Coast."

"Neat. I've gotta go," I said as I pushed past her out of the bathroom.

Libby was relentless. Somehow her hand had made it back on to my arm. She slid it around and linked her arm with mine. I quickened my pace. It didn't faze her a bit.

"They're probably in the top one hundred influencers in the world," she continued. "They have a podcast and everything."

"I don't know what they would possibly be influencing," I said. "They're beautiful people or whatever, and they were pretty nice to me, but I don't get the appeal. Or the concept, I guess. I don't even know why they were talking to me, really."

Libby stopped and pulled me to face her.

"The point is," she said with eyes wide and serious, "they were talking to you. You. A freshman. A nobody. Well, not a nobody," Libby squirmed and dropped her hand. "You're kinda famous, but not high school famous."

"They said they believe that I am innocent."

Libby laughed. I glared at her.

"Oh, I totally do, too," she said quickly. "Guilty until proven innocent, right?"

"You got that a little bit backwards, Libster. I've got to get to class. And I have a distinct memory of you singing a very different tune just a few months ago."

At this, Libby's head dropped and she shoved her hands into her jacket pockets. Was it possible she looked ashamed? I had never seen any hints of human emotion in her before. Well, not the good human emotions, that is. But honestly, I hadn't really looked before. She had checked the box of Childhood Tormentor since kindergarten, and I never thought to view her as anything beyond that. My beautiful tormentor. I swore under my breath.

"Look, I've really got to go. I've missed this class so often. If those two –"

"Channing and Guy, super-famous influencers," interjected Libby.

"Right, if those two very normal, but very pretty humans talk to me again, I'll try to introduce you or whatever. But I don't see what the big deal is."

Libby beamed.

"You are just the best, Dragongirl!" Libby twirled around; her skirt flared just high enough to make me blush.

"Calling me that probably isn't going to help you out here," I called after her.

"Can't hear you, too excited about my start to fame!"

So that was it. My notoriety here was just a quick rise to fame for these private-school peers. As if they didn't have enough going for them already, they had to use my drama to boost them higher in their petulant worlds. And Libby was just another one of them along for the well-publicized ride.

The bell rang. I picked up my pace again, half certain I was walking down the correct corridor to the correct classroom.

I did find the right classroom. But you know that sinking feeling of dread when you realize the world may be conspiring against you? Take that feeling, and then add a steaming heap of the grossest thing you can imagine on top of it. That was what sat in the pit of my soul as I shuffled into the classroom and made unwanted eye contact with none other than Mr. Simmons.

"Oh, Christ," he muttered.

"Good to see you too, old friend. I guess you can use more mature language in high school, huh?"

He glared at me.

"Take your seats!" The familiar, nasally tenor announced. I looked around, not a single soul had been standing. A snort escaped from me.

"Something amusing already Ms. Archer? Anyhow, I am Professor Simmons. I am covering for Ms. Batswell. She is on maternity leave."

I couldn't help it. I raised my hand, and without even being called on let the words fall unwittingly out of my face.

"Professor? I didn't realize you had achieved your Ph.D. since school let out three months ago. Very well done, sir. Er, I mean, professor."

The glare continued. His face slightly flushed, he turned around to face the whiteboard. He coolly erased "professor" from the front of his name and wrote "Mr." in its place.

"Now, then," he cleared his throat, trying to regain some dignity. But it was too late. I had unleashed the collective snarkiness of 18 freshmen. One kid next to me you raised his hand.

"So why did you say you were a professor? Seems like a weird way to start out the class," he said. Another girl chimed in, "Yes, isn't integrity in our school's motto?" Yet another added, "Honestly, your lying has me triggered. I don't think I'm able to continue calculus today."

Giggles and murmurs rose in volume around the class. I looked at Mr. Simmons, whom I believe was wearing a new brown tie. He dropped his head, a glob of hair gel showing near the bald patch ever growing on his head. I sighed.

"Goddammit," I mumbled. "Say," I said with extremely contrived enthusiasm, "how about that quadratic formula? I hear it's pretty exciting stuff," I stammered.

A voice behind me practically shouted at the class: "Nope! I am too shook up from having this authority figure a lying to us. Can't do math."

I heard some books close around me, I heard laptops shutting, I heard zippers zipping. A great shuffle commenced as most of the class filed out the door.

"Sorry," one kid said, holding the door open for his snickering peers on their way out, "I got to get to the counselor right away."

Mr. Simmons just nodded, totally defeated. I looked around and saw that the class was now just me and four other students: Twin girls who looked terrified and uncertain of what just transpired, a boy asleep in the back, and a foreign exchange student. She raised her hand.

"Yes?" Mr. Simmons asked feebly.

"We do not have class? The lecture is finished?"

Before Mr. Simmons could answer, I interjected.

"Nein!" I called out good-naturedly. "Let's get to that learning. Sorry, Professor. I mean that was your nickname in school, right? The professor? I should have put that together. You were just letting us know your nickname before I opened my big mouth or whatever."

I looked at him encouragingly. A weak smile spread on his face as he picked up his iPad and begin writing out several equations on the whiteboard.

"Yes," he stammered, "That's right. Kindly, scroll to section four. We'll be starting there."

Mr. Simmons turned nervously away from the board every few minutes, looking back with a sort of surprise that we few students were still seated, listening, watching. Well, the German exchange student, a very academic-looking girl, and the twins I now recognized from the mathletes club at Beecher, and I were paying attention. The very sleepy student, mouth wide open and eyes closed, snored in the corner. At last Mr. Simmons turned and faced us.

"Now then, um, that is, would you all assemble into work groups, please."

I glanced back at this crew of peers. I had been drifting in such solitude, angrily isolating myself to such an extent that the prospect of connecting with anyone on any level, even just academic, seemed altogether daunting if not pointless. I looked at the exchange student. She nodded and collected her things, moving toward me. I pulled another chair toward my desk with my foot, feeling very cool.

"Eh, what is up, I am called Elke," she said.

She had kind eyes, blonde hair cut neatly in a bob, and what looked to be a perfectly pressed t- shirt. As I marveled at the tidiness of this human, I was suddenly aware of the tea stain on my own white shirt from this morning, the grass stain on the knee of my jeans from who knows when, and the mud splattered on top of my (briefly) white sneakers. Elke's hand touched my arm, and I jumped straight up like a cat. She laughed.

"I said, and you are called?"

"Oh, geez, I'm so sorry," I stuttered, my face reddening to the same color of the Levi's logo on her flawless top. "My mind tends to wander, and ... never mind," I cleared my throat and tried to match her kind confidence. "I'm Eve."

Her eyebrows went up and she fell back in her seat.
"Are you!" she exclaimed. "What I mean to be asking is, you are the Eve Archer I read here?"

Elke took out her phone. I fidgeted nervously as her fingers deftly moved about her screen. She held it toward me.

"This is you?"

I peered down at a screenshot. A photo of me accompanied by my mom, Kip, and a gaggle of grotesque spectators leaving the courthouse was framed by German text. My entire body inside and out slumped in defeat. I wanted to die. Or at least hide.

"Oh, no, it is not like that," Elke said quickly. Her hand once again fell on my arm. "I do not mean to make you angry."

She looked flustered. I looked at her and shrugged. I coughed to keep that familiar lump from forming in my throat. That was an awfully familiar sensation anymore. I had no resilience left in me. I felt a tear form, loosen, and roll down my cheek.

"What I am meaning to say is," she said and put her phone away, "first, I am sorry to upset you," she paused and gently placed both hands on my arm as if to implore me to stay. (She seemed to know me too well too quickly.) I shrugged off her hands and pushed away from the desk. Elke continued, "What I am meaning to say is that, oh, *schiesse*, do not go, Eve."

I grabbed my bag, sniffling hard now.

"Shall we all convene and share our answers?" Mr. Simmons said suddenly, standing at the board. Had we been given an assignment? "Ms. Archer, I see you must be ready to present? Oh, I ... em, uh," he stuttered, having seen my tear-stained face. "That is, never mind. How about you, yes, you, young mathematician; I'm sorry I've not memorized all your names yet."

I was already headed to the door. I heard Mr. Simmons and Elke both calling after me as I fell into the hallway, breathing heavily. Would I ever make it through a full day of school? I had yet to even be present in fifth period. I don't even know what fifth period was.

I looked around. The hall was quiet, empty. The air conditioning hummed dutifully and sent a shudder through the posters lining the walls. One detached itself from a pillar and sailed toward me.

As I leaned down to retrieve it, my mouth open in a yawn, my gum fell out of my mouth and landed on my shoe, my bag slid off my back and pulled my shirt taut, and I'm pretty sure something came from my backside that I would have liked to blame on the squeaky floors.

"Crikey, is that how you exit?"

Poppy's Australian accent painted red on my face. I spun around, my back-pack unexpectedly heavy on the crook of my elbow, the errant poster in my other. Her tail was wagging, her tongue hanging to the side of her smiling mouth.

"G'day, then! C'mon, yeah?" she said, then frowned. "Er, if you're not otherwise occupied with..." she gestured her muzzle toward my hand, her wagging tail coming to rest. A giggle escaped from her as I looked down.

STD-ecide to be Protected, a neon-pink heart announced. The details of something called the Teens for Sexual Health Association were scrawled below. My already-red face deepened to a crimson.

"I just – it fell. Can't you feel that? The air conditioning makes, like, this insane breeze," I stammered as I dropped the poster back to the floor.

"Yeah, sure, alright," Poppy said, "if I'm not keeping you from your activities," she added with more giggling. "Onya bike, then."

I heaved my backpack up and followed the wagging tail of a talking Australian Shepherd down the halls of my new school for the second time this week.

15

PRIMUM NON NOCERE

"Egg! Eve! Thank goodness, hurry!"

My mom's small frame came onto view down the opposite sidewalk. She waved her arms wildly. She was wearing jeans. My breath caught in my throat. She never wore jeans. Suits or sweats, there was rarely anything in between. Donning casual, everyday wear was a sure sign something was wrong. I sprinted to her.

"Why weren't you at school? I wasn't sure it was you at first, I couldn't find my glasses, and I'm shit with my contacts," she rambled as she hugged me, breathless, and motioned toward her car. "Come on, hurry!"

Her black sedan was not so much parked as it was just stopped generally toward the side of the road. Other cars honked as they veered around it and us. Her hands shook as she pushed frantically on her key fob. The little car's alarm beeped as it locked and unlocked and locked again. I grabbed the fob from her.

"Here, I've got it," I said gently. I opened the passenger door and moved an unopened green juice from the front seat. I tossed it in the back, eying a backpack and one of Philippa's favorite blankets, the fluffy white one with hedgehogs dotting it. "Mom? What's going on?" I said, careful not to let any alarm into my voice as I buckled my seatbelt.

"It's Phlee," she panted. "She's back at the hospital. I couldn't get ahold of you, so I came to get you and, and… Oh, my Philippa!"

She collapsed forward, heaving, sobbing, against the back of her hands on the steering wheel. Her forehead hit the horn. It sounded brightly, macabre and untoward.

"Mom," my voice shook as I lightly rubbed her back, "what happened to Philippa?"

The familiar chirp of vitals monitors greeted me as I walked down the hall. I nodded as I shuffled past exhausted nurses and worried doctors and whistling janitors and scared visitors. Someone else had received tragic news; bowed heads congregated near the only entrance to Philippa's room.

"Here, she's here," my mom said and pushed through the group of prayerful mourners. "Just – excuse me – she's here. Yes, come on, Eve. Sir, kindly let my daughter through. Yes, ugh. Eve, maybe you can talk to her. Oh, good, they gave her warmer blankets! Phlee, Egg's here! Go on, I know talking with you will make her happy. She keeps mumbling the same strange things."

My mom pulled the door to my sister's room shut. It was dimly lit and quiet. Philippa lay hooked up to the same machines and tubes she had only recently escaped.

My heart dropped as she turned her face toward me and opened her sleepy eyes.

"Girrrrrl," she whispered with a faint smile, "it's just the fro-yo and pudding here. I can't get enough of it, you know?"

Tears sprang to my eyes. She had only been home three months, two of which were spent completing her rehab exercises with enough promise to graduate away from crutches.

A C6 spinal cord injury. That's what the doctors and radiologists had said. They made it sound so simple, so nonthreatening.

The surgeon, an athletic fellow whose white coat had Dr. Daas embroidered on it but insisted we call him by his first name, Maahir, had very gently explained that often surgery is necessary with "these types of injuries." With the cadence one might use to read an anxious child a bedtime story, he cited surgery as a means to remove fragments of bones, foreign objects, herniated disks, or fractured vertebrae that appear to be compressing the spine .... And that's where he had lost me. His voice had grown distant then, hollow, an echo haunting my ear canal.

I shook my head vigorously. No use dwelling on past fears, past horrifying announcements. Here my sister was again, and the same old surgeon, the one who had announced that surgery had been successful to stabilize the spine, was holding my mom's hand in his and droning on once more with feigned optimism.

"There appears to be a pressure ulcer where we removed the bone fragments from your daughter's spine. Surgery may be needed again to further stabilize the spine to prevent future pain or deformity."

"Wait, what?" I barked. "Another surgery? So, you did something wrong; my sister's back in this, this," I gestured disgustedly around me, "this place, and she's going to get cut open by you again? Because now deformity is in the cards? Pass. Hard pass. Mom, help me unhook her. This is bullshit. She needs better."

My hands shook, my vision blurred from tears I hadn't registered, as I traced the tubes from her nose and mouth, from her arms, up to the towers of god-knows-what liquids getting pumped into her.

"I – I don't know how to take this crap off of her," my voice quivered, and the ground was inconstant.

A hand landed on my shoulder. I shrugged aggressively, thinking it was Dr. Daas. I realized immediately it had been my mom's. Never mind. I grabbed Philippa's limp hand. It was warm and moist.

"So much fuss though," a drowsy voice sighed. I looked down. Philippa blinked slowly and looked up at me just for a moment. "It's good, Egg. Ha, 'good egg.' I've still got it." She swallowed hard, painfully. "Let them … let them do their thing."

Philippa's breathing was heavy, slow. The monitors adjusted their beeps to the cadence of her labored breath.

"I'm, um, I'm just going to speak with Maahir for a moment," my mom whispered brusquely. I could tell she was holding in her emotion.

"Mom, I'm – crap," I said as I spun around. But she was already out the door and deep in conversation with Dr. Daas. A nurse with a furrowed brow holding a chart joined them. "Gosh, can I suck any worse," I said under my breath.

"Unlikely. But that was … quite … the show. Unsarcastically … bold of you," Philippa's breathy voice sounded slowly behind me. I looked over. Her eyes were closed, but she was smiling on either side of the grotesque tube coming from her mouth. "Ow. I … hate … these …"

She trailed off again and was out. The concerned nurse with a still-furrowed brow popped his head in.

"Her pain medication is on a timer; she would have just received another dose and will likely be out for the next two hours or so."

I nodded dumbly at him; his forehead never released its furrow, but he gave me a thumbs up.

"Whatever," I muttered. "Phlee, this is so, so, so … shitty." I looked up, feeling immediate guilt and fear over swearing so haphazardly. But that was just a cover for what I really felt. Tears pricked my eyes again. "Oh Philippa. Phlee, I'm so sorry!"

I fell on top of my bedridden sister and sobbed. This was all my fault. The monitors seemed to chirp in agreement. Her fingers wiggled slightly under me. I lifted myself up and stood, wiping my eyes.

"You're … so … drah … matic …," Philippa breathed, a faint smile back on her face. "Night … girl … I … love … you …."

"I love you, Phlee," I sniffed as I pushed her hair from off her face. I tucked her hedgehog blanket up and around her shoulders.

"Oh, her blanket! Good, you brought it in!" My mom appeared in the doorway, her eyes red and her cheeks flushed. A pathetic smile was plastered on her face. "You're so wonderful to take care of her. Shall we let her sleep, get some food? Maybe some Pho?"

I hated my mom right now. Her sporadic positivity was wearing on me. Why couldn't she just tell it like it is? Had I never followed a stupid dragon, had I never told Philippa about the Peridiote stones, my sister wouldn't be here. She would be safe. She would be healthy. My mom knew this. And yet, she still swore her child could do no wrong, that her children were stronger than anyone ever, that no hospital bed could hold her child down, *blah blah blah.*

Her optimism bordered on delusion. And, frankly, it had me worried. Not just worried. Fully freaked out.

16

LUCTOR ET EMERGO

I t was the weekend.

    Phlee and I had planned to take advantage of the cold but sunny Saturday to hit up record shops and vintage stores on Alberta.

I couldn't bring myself to go alone. So I stared down an unscheduled day and finally gave in to responsibility: I would do homework.

My mom had forced me to check in with my teachers yesterday afternoon before school let out. I spent all of 12 minutes there to collect my homework and classroom assignments, half of which were spent dodging the salacious rumors that were whispered around me. A bright light named Elke, though, had smiled and waved. I had smiled and waved back, though a bit too late, as I was unaccustomed to the gesture anymore. She was walking the opposite direction by the time the reaction registered in my beaten down brain. I made a mental note to try more earnestly to be her friend. I could use one real, human friend.

"Dragongirl! You're, like, back! Oh my gosh, that book totally sucks," Libby had said, suddenly in front of me looking through the pile of schoolwork I held. She held up *Man's Search for Meaning* and grimaced. "*Très* depressing."

I hadn't the energy to dive into that comment and simply snatched it back from her and continued on my way. She had protested, but I had held my hand up in a peace sign and turned down the hall. My walk was haughty, but a smile had crept onto my face.

I smiled again, feeling proud of my response on this sunny Saturday morning as I spread my blanket out in the backyard. The pleasant weather would help me get through this drudgery of work, I hoped. I eyed the pile of books and binders. Even unopened, they challenged my discipline and motivation.

No matter. I couldn't visit Philippa, I couldn't think any more about Dragon, or Uncle Seb, or any of it, and I missed Baert. So a distraction was in order. And a distraction that would help me graduate (dimensional fortitude pending) seemed the best.

But my focus was … nonexistent. I sighed loudly and rearranged the blanket folds on the grass to make a pillow.

Birds flew overhead. A hummingbird landed briefly on a lowly rose still pushing a bloom. An ant crawled on my arm.

Eve! You idiot! I scolded myself. *Focus!* I buried my head in my book.

I had to look at the front cover to remind myself what I was reading – words, letters, were just nonsensical shapes at that moment. I chuckled as I slowly let the title on the cover sink in: *Man's Search for Meaning*. Meaning? I can't even discern shapes right in front of me. What has meaning got to do with anything when any moment it could all be destroyed?

Ah, Viktor Frankl. Should our paths ever cross, I think I should like to have a chat. You, Viktor, faced with outliving one of the most heinous events in human history, and me, on trial for a murder I didn't commit while the health of this dimension is compromised by a clone lord weirdo.

I shuddered. Best to not compare myself to an Auschwitz survivor. That could only bring bad juju.

Whatever the hell "juju" was. Something related to karma, I think. Was it bad luck to see some of myself in this famous writer's thoughts?

I lingered in that thought. What is survival, if not enduring something disproportionately difficult to your capability? If I were small, twee, weak, then perhaps surviving a car crash would be my magnum opus of life. (Does somersaulting out of a car count? If so, I can check that box.) If I were grand, powerful, with perspective and innate strength, perhaps I would have survived the horrors of an Auschwitz? I shuddered again. I couldn't contemplate such things; surely, I had no business ascribing those things to myself.

But the thought was humbling and deserved some introspection. Should the strongest among us be dealt the hardest hand? And are they?

What was I actually capable of?

"Why, nothing, at that rate!"

My head jerked up.

"Dragon!" I shrieked. I dropped my book and ran to him.

"Oh! Oh, Evechild! What a greeting!" he laughed as I leapt upon him and hugged him fiercely. His scales were strong and familiar and slowed my heartbeat.

"Where have you been?!"

Dragon shifted anxiously. I felt his pallor change. I pulled my arms away and stepped back to study him. My eyes narrowed.

"Where, Dragon?"

"That's neither here nor there," he sputtered. "Your mum, she is well? And Baert, why, he is quite well, and Sebastian, I daresay is thriving despite all the –"

"All the what?" I cut him off. "Uncle Seb was a ghost. Now he just shows up to make gooey eyes at Ms. Neally and drive me everywhere as...as... some act of contrition or something to make things better between my mom and him. He might as well have never been here."

My bitterness surprised me. Dragon raised an eyebrow.

"I, er, you know how it is. I, um, I just meant, maybe he'd be happier somewhere else," I mumbled lamely.

"I suspect you do not know the goings-on of your uncle."

"I suspect I don't."

Dragon cocked his head thoughtfully. I regarded him then as more of a peer, strange as that may sound. Geez, I had missed him.

But then I was immediately annoyed he had been gone so long. Here I was, casually catching up with a being I had idolized and studied my whole childhood, and I was feeling as impatient with him as I had with the kid in line at the cafeteria who took too long to pick out his pudding.

"So, Dragon," I said, "how the hell are you?"

"You swear a bit more openly?" he said, studying me. "You typically reserved your expletives for your inner thoughts, I may recall."

"Well, I guess, I mean, what's the point of censorship, or anything," I said, suddenly feeling very defensive, "when ... when ...." I trailed off as a lump rose in my throat.

"When your dear sister's life hangs in the balance?" he said. Leave it to Dragon to finish what I could not say. My head dropped.

"Yeah."

"How are you, though, my dear Evechild? Truly?"

I bristled. He noticed. I recoiled. He held out a talon.

I wanted to reach for it. Really, I did. But I was so tired of feeling ... what? I was tired of just *feeling*. One minute I was fine, cavalier, brave; the next, angry, cross, impatient. Or just plain sad. It was exhausting.

"I'm fine," I coughed. "Ms. Neally sent the dog, she's cool. Not totally certain what she's around for."

"Sent who?"

"Dog named Poppy? Australian Shepherd? Spots? Obsessed with avocado toast?"

Dragon just shrugged. I tossed my book back onto the pile of unfinished homework and stretched.

"My Yaél didn't want to leave anything to chance, I suspect," Dragon said with a small, sweet smile of adoration. "Just like her, just like her. Though it is curious you'd have a companion unacquainted with me. Curious, indeed."

"Is Baert with you?" I asked, wholly unfocused.

"Alas, tis just your dragon calling today."

"I didn't mean that," I said sheepishly. "It's always good to see you. I just wondered ..."

"About dear Cuithbaert. Quite understandable. He is making terrific strides. He even rode a unicorn the other day."

"Shut up, no he didn't!" I said, my head jerking up with a smile.

Before I could delve further, my phone pinged. I grabbed it, hungry to see if it was an update about Philippa.

It wasn't.

It was a new calendar event.

My mom had scheduled me a therapy appointment.

17

CURA PERSONALIS

"**D**o you think you're depressed?"

I stared at my feet. My new Converse, in a fetching blue color, already had a scuff on one toe and a drip of orange paint splatter from my attempt at oil painting in third period art discovery. They looked very out of place on the restored wooden floors of Malcolm's therapy office.

"Are you anxious, perhaps unusually irritable or quick to anger?"

"Well wouldn't you be?" I snapped, then retreated into the cushions on the giant armchair aware of what I just did.

"Are you still having nightmares?"

"Yeah," I muttered.

I was annoyed with myself that I had agreed to return to my old therapist. I really valued him as a therapist, true. But that was then – before I knew about different dimensions and string theory racket, before I knew a dragon and an elf, before Philippa was hooked up to a billion hospitals tubes because of an accident I caused. That list was on constant repeat in my mind. Every crappy thing that had befallen me played like some sick marquee in my brain, lights flashing the headline THINGS YOU CAN'T TALK ABOUT.

"Okay, you don't want to answer that one. We'll move on," Malcolm said congenially. I looked up. Paranoia that I had accidentally said something aloud shrouded my every move.

"Sorry, um, what did you ask?"

"Do you find the same excitement in your favorite activities?"

"I don't have favorite activities," I grumbled and looked back down.

"But you used to."

"I guess so," I said, looking up just long enough to see the very concerned, very furrowed brow on Malcolm's face. He crossed and uncrossed his legs, then flipped through his notebook.

"Why don't you tell me about some of things you used to love doing."

"Does it matter? Anything I used to do was when I was, like, a little kid, basically. Once you're, you know, in high school or whatever, you leave that sh—that stuff – behind for the noble pursuit of academia," I said, adding a snarky flourish of my hand at the end.

"You do not think you're depressed?"

I stared at him. He stared back. The small but very chic office was silent save for the ceiling fan, whose whirring spin was deafening just then. He leaned forward. I leaned forward. He adjusted his glasses. I adjusted my – drat, I had forgotten to wear my glasses again. I probably shouldn't be so fine with wandering through life just a teensy bit blind.

"Eve, I'm going to write you a prescription. I don't know what else to do to help you. But I want you to be able to function with some energy and optimism."

"Seems like you're giving in pretty easily, doctor," I shot back.

"Look, I thought we were making terrific progress. You were opening up more, your self- awareness was flourishing," he said as he closed his notebook. "And now, after you've gone through so much, I assume, when I feel I could help you the most, you're reverting to old habits. Old habits you worked very hard to free yourself from. The past three months you've grown more and more withdrawn, and, frankly, I'm very concerned about you, Eve."

"You have to say that because you're my doctor."

"I must provide thorough treatment options to the best of my ability. I can't force you to do anything, including talking to me or taking medicine," he said gently but evenly. He scribbled something on a small pad of paper, expertly tore it free, and handed it to me. "But Eve," his face softened more and his shoulders dropped, "Well, I must tell you, I do miss our camaraderie. I miss seeing you finding yourself and feeling good about who you are."

"Yeah, well, that makes one of us," I said as tears welled. I snatched the paper from his hand. I walked forward, face burning and eyes stinging, into a still-closed door. "So, uh, see you next time, or whatever," I said as I pushed into the door again. And again.

It stayed shut.

"It's a – yep, you got it. It's a pull not a push," I heard Malcom say as I let the door close loudly behind me.

One pointless therapy session and an obdurate door later, I had leveled up my self-loathing. I shoved my hands into my pockets and shuffled down the lobby stairs, almost walking right past my mom who was scrolling absentmindedly on her phone. I relaxed a bit: she was wearing gray sweats and a hoodie. Her usual daily attire. All must be well.

"How was it?"

I shrugged and pulled on the car door. Locked.

"What is with me and these damn doors today?" I snapped.

My mom just frowned and opened the door for me. I braced myself for another lecture on swearing. Which was hard to take, given how generous she was with expletives herself. *As long as you can balance it with supreme linguistic prowess, swearing is a bit fun*, she had said once. I had that phrase locked and ready to fire back at her should she scold me.

We drove in silence all the way home. It was becoming a new, unwelcome trend. Time in the car with my mom was unfiltered, to say the least, and we often covered many topics in a short amount of time. But lately ... I don't know.

I didn't have much to say. Or maybe I had too much to say, and that was the problem.

That night as I lay in bed, my stomach growled loudly and incessantly. I had been too stubborn to get dinner when I had the chance, and I didn't dare go down to the kitchen now. I thought about Malcolm.

What would happen if I just told him? What would he say if, when asked if I thought I was depressed, I responded differently. Depressed? No, I could answer. Traumatized from learning about and then flying through interdimensional portals to rescue my mom and sister from an evil overlord enslaving them while raising a weird clone gang of my middle school friend whose death I'm now blamed for? Maybe.

The nightmares would continue. I knew that by now. It didn't matter what I did, nightmares would be waiting for me. And that's the rub – the nightmare blends into reality and sometimes I can't tell which is which. I try to trick myself sometimes into thinking that all of that – the Seventh and Obrenox and Jonah and even Dragon – were just dreams I had once, bad ones, but just dreams, nonetheless. I had a remarkably creative imagination, or so every teacher had said (as an accusation more than a compliment) since kindergarten.

"Phlee," I said aloud, "I wish you were here to quote some dumb philosopher to me and tell me I'm overreacting and then challenge me to MarioKart."

I buried my head in my pillow and screamed. I remember a past version of myself desperately craving notoriety. For something academic, though, or brave. Not ... not the death of my classmate. Not when I can't tell anyone what happened, or why.

Was Obrenox really going to successfully keep enslaving humans, one death stone and weird clone guy at a time?

I fell asleep wondering how Jonah had fallen under his control in the first place. It wasn't a good sleep.

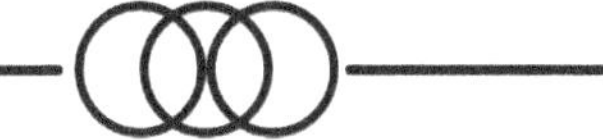

I awoke to my phone buzzing, buzzing, buzzing, enough to fall off my nightstand. I sifted through my blankets, groggy and trying to blink life into my brain. Too early for the sun, the streetlamps outside reached through my blinds illuminated my room just enough for me to catch the sheen of the little phone.

Eleven missed calls, eight text messages. All from the hospital. I sat straight up and hit the call- back number.

A tired man answered, no doubt very aware it was 4:03 a.m., and groaned into the phone. His voice became alert when I told him who I was.

"Thank you for getting back to us," he said quickly. "We've been unsuccessful in reaching your mother; although you are a minor, I see, you are listed as a contact for your sister."

"Yeah, fine. That's fine. What is it?" I said, my brain alert but my voice hoarse and groggy.

He said a lot of things. Medical things. I asked him to slow down and explain a bit more clearly.

He did.

My heart dropped. My phone dropped.

"Mom!" I screamed.

18

DAMNUM ABSQUE INJURIA

Fourteen hours. Technically, fourteen hours and six minutes as of the beginning of this sentence. That's how long it had been since Philippa last spoke.

"No, no, her vitals are otherwise strong," someone murmured outside my sister's hospital room. "Her coma? More common than you might think after general anesthesia. Yes, that's right, delayed emergence."

The voices melded into syrupy sound that stuck in my ears. I shook my head hard, then harder.

Philippa's eyes fluttered occasionally, long enough for me to scrutinize a sliver of brown iris exposed for something hopeful. But they hadn't fully opened. Not yet. Not *yet*. This disclaimer was important. Crucial, really. Her eyes hadn't opened *yet*, I had tersely corrected at least three different nurses as they gave updates to doctors. They floated in, these doctors, every three hours or so. Detached emotionally in their white coats, they were the sagely bookends to the flurry of nurses shuffling in and out in various stages of exhaustion.

I sympathized with their lot – so educated and generous with their time and skills – but I hated them right now, nonetheless. Their cheery effect and contrived concern weren't lost on me. They had seen too much, slept too little, and had gone too long without appropriate pay to be truly cheery. And I think that's part of the reason I hated them. Just stop trying so hard, you know? You're not the social worker, your job isn't to console the fearful and the mourners. Take the goddamn blood pressure and go steal a nap, for Christ's sake.

A younger nurse in pink scrubs gave me a smile and a wave as she passed the room. I glowered. Offer me a soda, fine. But don't tell me it'll be OK, that "she's strong" or "she's a fighter." You don't know Philippa. She's not strong. She doesn't fight. She trips going up the stairs and literally dressed up as the Statue of Liberty as a heated political debate raged on betwixt my mom and me. *Give me your tired, your hungry, your stubborn*, she had cried over our fighting.

I smiled, remembering how her ridiculous peace-keeping tactic had worked. No, she was not a fighter.

"Feeling better, I see! It's good to see you smile," Nurse No. Eight said as she pranced into check Philippa's vitals. She grabbed one of the small tubes dangling next to the hospital bed's rails. She swiftly detached one small bag while attaching another full of some unknown liquid. "Yep, she's a fighter!"

I got up and stormed out. I walked briskly toward an elevator bay, thinking that's where the café was. I pounded the call button about forty times. The elevator chimed, opened, then immediately began to shut its doors.

"Hey! Can't you see I'm standing right here?" I grumbled at it and shoved my arm between the closing doors. They bumped against my forearm and reopened. Something unintelligible, like swearing in another language, startled me.

"Aye! Lassie, let yer scan friend in!"

I jumped back and looked down to see saw a small, tattered boot pinched between the elevator doors. The doors hit against the little foot, almost in time to the cheerful ding of the elevator's arrow signal, over and over.

"Baert!" I pushed the doors open and nearly tripped over my old friend.

"Yer a real heel tah find," he said as he opened his arms wide exposing a still-bloodstained tunic. I gulped at the sight but bent down to hug him, nonetheless, thinking that's what he was after. "Aye, so yah did miss yer bonnie sidekick!" he laughed, surprised.

My face reddened. The gesture had not been for a hug. Before I could indulge in some self-pity I was recently accustomed to, Baert cleared his throat. He opened his arms once more and gave a little shimmy. A giant book dropped from beneath his shirt.

"I brought'ya a gift, besides a stolen hug because yah miss yer barry friend Baert so bad."

"Of course I missed you," I muttered, surprised by how quickly I became annoyed with my dear friend. I truly missed him. I wished I could regulate my emotions better though, geez.

"Drahk slipped it down thah neck of me tunic, and then I held thah front tightly to keep it right in place," he said proudly as he gathered the folds of his filthy clothing and cinched it atop his belly, pulling the back of the tunic taut enough to hold a giant tome in place.

"Because a bag wasn't an option," I sighed as I fetched the fallen book. Looking at it, I groaned. Fortis Librae.

"Bags be gettin' searched, picked at. Me hunchback doesn't," he grinned.

"Fair enough," I said, unimpressed and holding the book in front of me. "So you found me, and you brought this for some reason, now what?"

Baert frowned and hit every single floor button on the panel of the elevator. We began our ascent. Our slow, stilted ascent.

"Aye, lassie, it kills me tah see my bonnie friend thisaway. I am sorry, I truly, beseechingly, am sorry. I wanted tah come sooner, but thah timing and all," his voice trailed off as his doleful eyes shifted from mine to the ground. We stood in silence as the elevator dutifully rose, stopped, open its doors, closed them, seven times.

"You know, the 'close-doors' button doesn't actually do anything," I said as I watched Baert systematically hit it upon each stop. "Something about ADA compliance. But Americans are impatient, I guess, or something, so it's, like, what's that term? A placebo."

"Hmmm. Yah need tah cite yer sources fer me tah believe that. Ah, here we are, lassie! Off! Off!" Baert's voice brightened as the elevator ran its final ding. He stepped out onto the 18th floor. "Shall we?"

"Shall we what?"

"Get her better, of course! And work on striking a bonnie smile back on yer wee face."

"Two totally attainable goals," I mumbled, not attempting at all to hide my sarcasm.

Baert grabbed my hand and pulled me into a hallway I hadn't been in before. Its floors were dingey between the rows of vacant rooms. An exit sign flickered at the opposite end. His small hand grasped mine more tightly, more intentionally, his small fingers intertwined with mine. An unexpected jolt of warmth went through me.

I remembered reading about these horrid experiments in my Intro to Psychology class. Someone, or maybe a group of someones, wanted to determine if a child could grow normally in isolation, devoid of human touch. They can't. I shuddered as I recalled learning about the ghastly results from that "research." I squeezed Baert's little hand in mine, silently grateful for his surprise appearance; grateful to have a friendly hand in mine.

Had it really been that long since meaningful human contact? (Did Baert count as a human?) My heart lurched. Several days had passed since I had hugged even my mom. The only touch I could recall was my hand on Philippa's. A lump formed in my throat; in her prior hospital visit, I had done this, resting my hand upon hers until she woke up and made fun of me for it. Tears welled and anger returned.

Baert turned to me, grinning. But seeing me now, his eyes softened and his smile dropped.

"Here, lassie. Have a go. You'll like this."

He pushed the exit door open. I'm sure an alarm was meant to sound; a few stray wires, obviously clipped, swayed in the breeze of the open door. The sun hit my face aggressively. I hadn't dared to look outside in 14 hours and... 37 minutes? Funny, I had been counting the hours yet never acknowledged what time it was. It was 5:42 a.m., and we were on the roof of the hospital.

A group of pigeons chattered and flew upward, annoyed to be disturbed without the promise of food. Baert dropped my hand and stomped toward a more inquisitive flock. Their little gray bodies shuffled, heads cocked, toward us, closer and closer.

"Be gone, ye wee beasties! They'll be nary gossip fer yer foul-mouthed trysts today!" Baert cried as he flung his arms around and scattered the birds into the air.

They careened up, swooped down, and landed on the roof once more. A lot of Gaelic words strewed from Baert's mouth as he again kicked his legs and waved his arms. This happened three more times before the pigeons were alight and off the rooftop.

"Gossip, huh?" I said and smiled as he walked back. His shoulders squared but heaved a bit with his breathlessness. Clearly feeling very authoritative, he turned back a few more times to make menacing gestures toward the few pigeons who still swooped too close.

"Ye've no idea. Ruthless, they be. Yah think they hang out in urban centers fer the wee bits of rotten skan? Psh. All a rouse, and a damn fine one. Shameless," he said, shaking his head. "Fueled by salacious intrigue, those wee beasties."

"That's a vocab word," I said, amused at the idea of pigeons sleuthing and carrying gossip around.

"Beasties?"

"Salacious," I laughed.

Mrs. Moriarty, my new lit teacher (whom I liked if only for the sole reason she made no sign of knowing anything about me), was adamant (another vocab word) that we "expand our immediate lexicon." She'd get real sanctimonious (another vocab word) real quick if ever questioned about her mission to augment (vocab word) our conversational vocabulary, etymology and all. *It's your own language, ought not you know more of it?* she'd reply, which, honestly was a good point. Having the perfect word to describe the thing precisely as one wants – that's a feeling that's "divine!" "transformative!" "elucidative!" my classmates would chime. "Indeed!" she clapped, delighted, until me: "supercilious!" I had cried out in earnest. She had frowned. I had frowned.

"It so obviously means behaving or looking with an air of superiority, supercilious," a familiar voice said. I spun around, shaking my head out of my inner tangent.

"Dragon!" I squealed and lunged toward him. I wrapped my arms around his neck, his scales so wonderfully inviting, like your favorite meal after you've not had it for so long. Tears pricked my eyes again. But there was no anger. Just relief. Just comfort.

"Hmph," Baert sniffed. "Teeeee-ars. All I got was a half-wit hug, if yah could categorize it as such.

"Sorry, Baert," I said, at last smiling genuinely. I saw actual hurt on his face and it kicked me in the gut. It had been just as long since I'd seen him as it was since I'd see Dragon. "I was, um, not in the best headspace when you found me. You get it ... But, yeah, I'm an ass."

"Your outward expletive use is a new development, I've observed," said Dragon. "But never mind," he continued hastily as he saw me about to object. "You are quite in the morbs." He cocked his head, studying me. "And I daresay you've not slept, so consumed with worry. Oh, Evechild. I truly am sorry."

The tears returned a bit more forcefully. I hated how genuine kindness had that effect on me.

"Yeah, I haven't really felt myself," I choked pathetically. "I don't like it. I don't like me, I don't like this," I gestured ambiguously, meaning the hospital, of course. "I'm sorry, Baert. Really. I'm, like, so happy to see you, I just—"

"Saaaawry this, and saaaawry that," Baert mocked suddenly. "Ye'll a buncha nilly balloons. Let's get tah thah business, aye?"

Dragon's wing fell beside me. It still had a sort of renewing energy to it. My shoulders relaxed and I breathed a little more deeply.

"Anyway," I said with a cough to clear my throat, "I'm glad you're here. But why now, and, um, why the roof of a hospital?"

"Why, it's a lovely day, of course!" Dragon responded. I rolled my eyes. "Grab that tome, lassie."

"Right," I said, trying to match his seriousness. "But ... again, um, why?" I eyed Dragon and Baert suspiciously.

"So that we can do this!"

Baert struck the book from underneath; it fell open to two blank pages. Holding it balanced on his palm, his other hand grabbed mine and placed it on the parchment next to Dragon's talon.

"Evechild, think of dear Philippa's room. Her current hospital chambers," he added as Baert started to object.

I knew better than to ask why by now. I did as I was told – but too worn out to be hopeful – as my friends recited their Latin chant. I was starting to remember it, but I wasn't confident enough I had every word right. Silent, I squeezed my eyes shut and pictured every grotesquely sterile thing adorning my sister's too-sanitary space, the placement of the chairs, the bed, the screens, the tubes.... That crushing pressure and swift blast of air I had nearly forgotten about overcame me and then –

Beep. Beep. Beep. Beep.

I opened my eyes to the flashing lines of a monitor I knew so well already that I could draw it perfectly from memory if asked. Philippa's vitals chirped as steadily as ever. Dragon's talon rested gently on my shoulder as a dark rage rumbled inside me all over again. Baert reached a dirty hand onto the end of her bed, pulling her blanket over an exposed foot.

"Don't touch her!" I barked. Baert jumped, his face that of a scolded puppy. I froze. "I – I'm – I didn't mean it, Baert. I'm sorry. It, um, it just came out. I'm just on edge, or something, so … sorry again," I said as my voice trailed off into guilt.

"Anger is natural, dear Evechild," Dragon said gently. Baert grunted loudly behind him as he perched upon the windowsill. "Cuithbaert!" Dragon hissed back at him. Baert folded his arms and looked away.

"Drahk can do nary wrong, but this Leftenant, aye, storied and with a heart o'gold, his heid's o'full o'mince," he grumbled, not quietly.

"We are here," Dragon cleared his throat and spoke assertively, "to demonstrate that you can now appear here for your sister at any time. A tete-a-tete or popover, as you kids may say," Dragon chuckled, clearly pleased with himself.

"No one says any of that, and I can that anyways" I said, and was about to continue my protest when Baert hopped down.

"During viz-uh-teen hours only, lassie," Baert said, drawing out the word for emphasis. "Which, aye, have ended."

"It was Baert's idea, and a jolly good one," Dragon said. "You can be in and out with any unpleasant registration logistics."

I should have said thank you. I should have said, what a swell idea! But their cleverness elicited no enthusiasm in me.

"Why would I need to go in and out," I said sharply, "when she's going home any minute? She's not staying here. She's not."

Dragon and Baert said nothing. I nodded at the screens surrounding my sister.

"She's good. All of that says she's healthy. That's she's fine, that's what they say. That's what they tell me. These," I said with a shaky voice as I waved my arm at the monitors, "and them," I waved toward the hall full of white coats and blue scrubs. "She's fine, and she's coming home. She's a fighter, right? She's a freaking fighter. That's what they say, and they're the doctors, the experts, the gods, right? So, she's fine! She's just tired, see? She's just so … freaking tired!"

I choked out sobs, screaming at no one but this reality. Philippa's monitors chirped in response. I wiped my nose on my sleeve. My chest heaved and my head hurt.

Slowly, the door opened; its squeaking pulled my attention away from my tear-soaked fear.

"Everything okay in here?" a man's voice asked with a soft accent I couldn't quite place. A tall fellow with a gentle smile appeared. It was disarming.

"Um, yeah. I was just on the phone. Uh, sorry," I mumbled as I took another swipe at my nose. His brown eyes looked past me to my phone, which sat on the small tray table in the corner behind me, the screen black.

"Oh, that is okay. I'm the nurse assigned to your sister now. We are changing up how we do our scheduling a bit, so you might be seeing a lot of me," he said with slight upward inflection. He stepped all the way into the room, his muscles flexing under his scrubs as he pulled up on the doorknob and gently closed the door sans screech. "I hate that thing."

"Yeah, it's, whatever," I said, suddenly realizing a dragon and Highland elf had been beside me. Distracted and worried by their absence, I stumbled awkwardly to the window. It was open wide; I pulled it shut as I sighed in relief.

The nurse meanwhile deftly adjusted the tubes adorning my sister and quickly scrawled something on the clipboard at the end of Philippa's bed. And then he looked at me with a grade of authenticity I hadn't yet encountered in a hospital. His eyes widened with real concern and kindness.

"Now," he said gently, "how are you, actually?" Each word was enunciated with the same precision with which he carried out each of his tasks. He sat down – even that movement was gentle and controlled, his posture perfect. I glanced at his badge.

"Chur-gihn?" I asked as I sounded out an unfamiliar name next to a tiny sticker of a German flag.

"Close enough," he laughed as he got up and patted my shoulder. His muscled height intimidated me. "I'll be back with a coke for you," he said as he strode out of the room, gently, of course, belying his stature. "Then we talk more about your sister. And it's pronounced *yurr-gehn*."

19

DISCE AUT DESCEDE

I couldn't stop seeing it. Black robes slithered toward me as Obrenox thrust a bony finger in my face and repeated over and over in his tinny timbre: *The way isssss shut. You have lossssssssst.*

An alarm on my phone startled me back to the present. Chilling visions of Obrenox dissipated and white boards and posters of Shakespeare playbills came into focus. Literary arts, not Obrenox' lair.

"So, if you take the Latin root omni- and apply it to these – is that "By the Seashore" on someone's phone?" Mrs. Moriarty's steady academic tone turned bright as she spun around, mouth agape.

"God, turn it off!" someone barked behind me.

"Who even has that ringtone? How ancient are you?" another voice chided.

I swallowed pain and a tear as a memory of Philippa setting what she proclaimed "The World's Most Obnoxious Tune" as every alert sound on my phone, and then dancing awkwardly to it when it sounded.

"Sorry, that's, uh, I gotta go," I shoved my Lit Arts book and my blank page of "notes" into my bag and got up, tripping and knocking over a chair on my way out in true Eve Archer form.

"Don't be so affronted, Ms. Archer!" Mrs. Moriarty called behind me.

Affront this, I thought as I marched down the hall to my favorite bathroom. The one on the upper level near the language arts rooms was so far always empty

122

and, more importantly, it was away from most of the upper classmen rooms. So my risk of running into Guy and Ms. Perfect Rack was lower. My face reddened at my own thoughts. She has a name, I scolded myself. What that name was, I couldn't recall. Just recollections of her lovely pink blouse falling open just a little bit and .... The door opened and startled me out of my thoughts.

"Oh! You must be sorry," a familiar voice said. "I didn't know anyone was in here, I – hey, I totally know you!"

"No, you don't," I said, keeping my head down as I grumpily moved toward the bathroom door. A girl's chest blocked my path. It was *hers*. Snap out of it, I thought.

"What is wrong with you today?" she asked. I looked up, alarmed.

"Did you just say what – I mean, oh, hey! Cool to see you again," I said lamely. I tried to get my beat-red face under control, along with my sudden sweating.

"I swear I've seen you like seven times, and I've even waved. This is not something I do, and you have absolutely ignored me every time," she said, flipping her hair behind her ear. "That, my dear, doesn't really happen. If you have beef with me, just say it."

"Um, no, no beef," I grumbled, forcing myself to keep my eyes focused on her face. "Um, er, did you know the plural of beef is beeves? Yeah, ha ha ...it's true."

She said nothing but cocked her head and blinked. Perfectly expressionless. I was enraptured.

"I was, it's like, I was ....um," I fumbled for words, then brightened. "I was embarrassed. Yeah, embarrassed! I was, you know, all pumped to meet you, and you were, you know, totally great and everything, and, like, so pretty and nice," I rambled, aware yet again of my blushing cheeks, "and then I saw you, and I realized I had totally forgotten, er, I had not even paid attention to your name," I said with increasing speed. I sighed, finally taking a breath. "So yeah. Just embarrassed. Forgot your name. That's why I didn't say hi."

She surveyed me for a minute, one eyebrow raised. Then she smiled.

"I guess there's a first for everything," she said and offered a finely manicured hand to me once more. "Channing Reagan Barrenton."

I smiled and lightly shook the tips of her fingers. Once more.

"Go ahead, repeat it. Channing. Reagan. Barrenton."

I repeated each name after she announced it.

"Good. Anyhow, I was trying to find you," she said as she leaned over the sink and adjusted the green silk scarf around her head. "You're going to meet with my legal team, yes? Perhaps also fill an interview spot? I have this darling little podcast, but you knew that already."

"Oh, right. Yeah, sure, whatever. Sure."

"Perfect. You already have my pertinent info."

"I – I do?"

"Oh. My. God. Do you pay attention to anything?" she said. Her words were mean but her tone was nice. "The card," she smiled. "I gave you my card."

With that, she twirled out of the bathroom. Cool exit, I thought as I burrowed into my backpack for the glittery square business card she had offered me the other day. I moaned as I found the card. It was folded with a piece of gum squished inside.

"Guess I'm on her bad side now," I muttered as I left the bathroom.

"Whose bad side, Dragongirl?" Libby said as she rounded the corner. "Sorry, old habit. *Eve*," she said dramatically.

"Why is everyone coming to this bathroom? I've come here every day for a week, and suddenly it's, like, *the* place to be."

"The place to pee? Yeah, it's a bathroom. What are you even talking about? And why are you here every day? That seems executive," said Libby with a frown.

"Channing. And I think you mean excessive, Libster. 'That seems excessive.' Don't go to Moriarty's class, she'll eat you alive," I said as I tried to exit. Libby dropped her bag and pushed me against the wall. I blushed.

"Channing?! You were talking to her again?! Um, do you not remember how you literally swore to introduce us? But whatever. Tell me everything. Literally, everything. Holy shit, is that 'By the Seashore'? Why do you even still have that ringtone on your phone?" Libby's unending words ended in laughter as my phone sounded loudly again.

Flustered, I fumbled around in the front pocket of my bag and produced my phone, intending to turn off what I thought was a random alarm. But what lit up on my lock screen was an unknown number with "Maybe: Heritage Samaritan Hospital" written under it.

"Crap, it's the hospital. I've gotta answer," I stuttered as I swiped across the screen. My sweaty, shaky fingers failed at this simple task. "By the Seashore" droned on mechanically. It really was a horrid song.

"Here, I got it," Libby said gently as she took the phone from me. She lightly brushed her finger across and held the phone up. She pressed "Speaker" as the other line rang, clicked, and spoke.

"Heritage Samaritan, betterin' lives, intensive care unit, what can I do ya for?" a woman's voice answered. I rolled my eyes. I hated whomever this was.

"I, um, I missed a call? From you?"

"Well, glad you returned it! Can you tell me who this is, and then I can tell you why we were calling!"

"This is Egg, er, um, this is Eve Archer. My sister Philippa is there, and you —"

"Oh, oh yes," the woman's too-cheery voice flattened. "I believe that was our charge nurse calling you directly from this line. Let me," she paused and hummed a little, "let me just go on and find him for ya. Can you hold, dear?"

A thousand crushing weights filled my body.

"Yes," I said feebly. "I can hold."

There was no hold music. Just a woundingly silent line. And then a light click.

"Yes, yes, I know. But she needed to be told immediately."

"Yes? Yes, hello?" I said loudly into the phone.

"Ah, Ms. Archer, sorry about that," a familiar voice with a German lilt came more directly onto the line. "I was just conferring with my colleague, and ehm, anyway, I do think it is best that you come see your sister."

I was quiet. Libby squeezed my hand. How long had she been holding it?

"Um, ok, but," I searched for words to use. "Is she, like, is she ... good?" A lump formed with that last word. "Is my mom there? I, like, I haven't heard from her, so, yeah, I don't know. So, my sister?"

I pulled the phone away and opened my messages. Nothing from my mom.

"I have been unsuccessful in contacting your mother," Jürgen said carefully. "But, like I said, I think it is best you are here. Okay. I will let them know you are on your way."

"I have school, and you're like – oh, okay, bye, I guess," I said, starting to protest. But the phone clicked and the call ended. I dropped the phone and sunk to the floor. I pulled my legs into my chest and leaned my head on my knees.

"I'm fine, I just need a minute," I said as Libby's hand patted my shoulder. Through the crook in my elbow I could see her shift side to side. Unscuffed Doc Marten boots met insanely smooth shins. I don't think I had ever shaved my shins that perfectly ever in my life; although, admittedly, I had tried very few times. I shook my head and sat up.

"You good? You're, like, whiter than usual," Libby peered down at me, again with surprising amiability. No bad puns, no nasty remarks ... just kindness, and, and really cool boots.

"Yeah, thanks. I've got to go," I said as I ignored her hand up and stood inelegantly. A very real wedgie was distracting me from both my anxiety over that phone call and Libby's suddenly very beautiful, very kind face.

"Alright, well, let me know if I can do anything for you," Libby said, then smiled sweetly and winked, "Dragongirl."

I walked away, confused. Was that a term of endearment now? Or was she being cruel again and I missed it because I unwittingly realized how cute she is?

Just as thoughts of Channing started to float back into my head, my stomach flipped and brought me back to reality. I had to get back to Philippa. Fast.

20

IN SOMNIS VERITAS

"**G**osh, just answer already!" I yelled.

I held the phone close to my ear, my breath anxious and heavy, as I walked through the school tennis courts and cut across the field towards home. Doing the math in my head, it was faster and cheaper to run home where my mom hopefully was, and then drive to the hospital with her. The phone continued to ring on in my ear, redial after redial.

"Mom? Hello? Did the hospital call you? Mom?" I yelled as I unlocked the door, out of breath.

I barreled down the hall. Unopened mail, neatly folded laundry, empty green juice bottle on the kitchen counter – all the usual things were in place to signify my mom had indeed been here. But where was she now?

My heart pounded as loudly as my feet as I charged up the stairs. I checked each room: mine, still looking like the aftermath of a tornado; Philippa's, tidy and coordinated with each odd tchotchke, book, and obscure musical instrument in place; my mom's, bed made with a slew of papers and books spread out upon it, but otherwise empty.

I grabbed one of the books that was open face-down: *A Scientific Approach to Trauma*. I rolled my eyes. My mom swore she was above health trends and fads, but apply the word "scientific" or "medical" or anything hinting at evidentiary research and she was the most gullible sponge in the world.

"Mom?" I called again as I peered into the bathroom, then her closet. I grabbed my phone and hit her number for the hundredth time. I paced anxiously around her room, picking up this, looking at that. A book vibrated slightly on the opposite end of her bed. It stopped, then vibrated again. "What the ... oh my gosh," I screamed as a I grabbed the book to reveal her phone buzzing away under it.

She was gone. Flashes of finding her missing last time crashed in my mind: images of the sinister little fellow, of seeing her suspended in that awful tube ... I made a beeline for the bathroom, lunged for the toilet, and threw up every piece of the hastily chewed croissant I had grabbed on my way to school this morning. I kept heaving, the taste of acidic bile turning my stomach over and over.

"Eve? Egg, oh my gosh, Egg! Are you alright?"

I coughed, spit into the toilet, and spun around on my knees. I looked up and, as the toilet flushed noisily behind me, watched my mother wet a small towel and hand it to me.

"Are you kidding me?"

"Eve! I'm so sorry you're sick – do I need to call the school? What can I get you?"

"You're fine?! You're here? You were ... you were what," I said as I stood, panting in anger, and looked my mom up and down. My eyes narrowed. "You were running?! Running?!"

My mom, bewildered, and shuffled backward.

"Of course I was! I do every day. I – Eve, what has you so upset?"

"Your phone," I said as I gestured dramatically to her bed, "is *here*. You didn't tell me where you were going, you didn't know the hospital was calling, you, you, you could have been taken again and I, I just can't!"

Every word out of my mouth crashed into the next. One, long run-on sentence accented by snotty coughs shot at my mother. Hot, indignant tears rolled down my cheeks. I stomped past her and to the bathroom Philippa and I shared.

I grabbed my toothbrush with a shaky hand. I think I jabbed my gums more than I successfully brushed vomit off my teeth and tongue.

"You need to answer your phone," I slurred indignantly while spitting toothpaste in the sink.

"Egg, my sweet Egg, I'm so sorry," my mom said gently, putting a hand on my shoulder. I shrugged it off. "I didn't consider what it would look like to you. I just needed to get out of my own head for a minute, get a break from just the onslaught of information, so I left to run – no music, no mile tracker! It really was grand. I swear I was faster. But I didn't think about – hold on," she said, frowning. "You were at school when I left; it shoulnd't have mattered. How long have you been home?"

"Ugh!" I screamed as I wiped my foamy mouth, threw the towel on the floor, and darted downstairs. "I'm here because the hospital called, and we have to get to Philippa! Which you would know if you had your f—your freaking phone on you," I yelled, catching myself before I swore.

She fell silent. From downstairs, I heard sounds of her quickly changing from sweaty running clothes, then padding down the stairs, into the kitchen to grab a bottle of water, and to the front door, where I was waiting. Cross as ever.

"You good?" I snapped and headed to the car.

She stayed silent. Silent as we got in the car, silent as she backed out, silent as she wove through Happy Valley backroads, silent as we merged onto the freeway, silent as we drove along the Willamette River. That was when her silence was the most deafening. I have never once been near a body of water – that body of water, especially – without her commenting on the boats or the water level or the reflection of the buildings on the water or the freaking geese or some dumb crap. My heart softened a bit, knowing this brand of silence wasn't borne of anger, but of something far more damaging.

"Look, I know I should have had my phone on me," she said quietly just as I was about to open my mouth with a bad joke or some other lame attempt to mend the air. "I realize some moments can be – and excuse my use of a now very overused word – triggering for you. But I don't deserve the way you reacted."

I stared at my hands on my lap. I felt low. Selfish, erratic, imbalanced … but really, just low. My mom's voice stayed quiet, and I caught a glimpse of her watery eyes when I sheepishly looked up.

"I'm sorry," she said. "Anyhow, what did the hospital tell you? When did they call last?"

I checked my phone, ignoring the seven unopened messages. I never had messages, unopened or opened. but I was too distracted by worry over what awaited us inside the walls of Heritage Samaritan Hospital to give the mystery messages more thought.

"They called about an hour ago now," I said. "Can't we just use the valet? It's here for a reason!" I pleaded as I sensed my mom about to find the cheapest parking possible, which always ended up being several blocks away.

To my surprise and delight, she obliged. We pulled up the hospital valet where a kind woman with sad eyes nodded and gave us a tag. In another life, having valet service for anything would have been the stuff of fantasy, a next level of luxury that would prompt me to say things like, "and treat yourself to a joyride, my good man." And then I'd wink and do that handshake where you covertly tip someone with money folded in your palm.

Today was not that day, and I was no longer that kid who had such a dumb fantasy.

My mom and I zigzagged our way through regrettably familiar elevator bays and reception desks until we reached the fourth floor. I didn't have to follow the signs anymore. As far I was concerned, everything in that building existed solely for one department: the ICU. And that department existed solely for one person: my sister.

"Oh, good, you are here. Thank you," a warm voice greeted us with a smile.

"Yeah, sorry it took so long," I said coolly, doing my best to hide any emotions. "Mom, this is Jürgen."

They exchanged pleasantries, my mom suddenly very charming. I rolled my eyes and started toward Philippa's room. Jürgen's large frame swiftly blocked me.

"Eh, can we talk for a minute?"

"Me? Why?" I stammered.

"Your mother, too. Yes, it's fine. I need, eh, maybe a little more background on your sister's mental state."

"Her mental state?" my mom cried. "So, she's awake! She's awake, right? Let's go see her!"

"Mom, hang on," I grabbed ahold of her bag as it swung behind her. "If she were awake, he would have, like, you know, led with that information," I said and then shot Jürgen a look. "Right?"

"Right, of course. And no, regrettably she is not quite awake, not how you mean. I'm very sorry about that," he said. His voice drifted. He shook his head and blinked rapidly several times. "Sorry, very tired. All good. What I mean is," he paused and glanced side to side. "Is there any reason your sister would begin, eh, saying things – mumbling them, really – about, eh, about dragons?"

The way he said that last word, his voice hushed and cautious, his eyes checking his periphery for anyone who might be in earshot, it crushed me. Every atom in me went alert, desperate to protect my sister.

"Why, um, why do you ask that?" I said as my mom clutched my forearm.

"Well, really, it's the strangest thing," Jürgen said, his voice softening away from caution. "There is great debate among medical communities regarding whether someone in a coma has dreams. But there is zero debate – because everyone agrees – on the fact that someone in a coma does *not* 'talk in their sleep,' dreaming or not."

We were quiet.

"But talking must mean consciousness, which means she must be awake," my mom said slowly, starting to inch forward.

"That is what I'm telling you. Her vitals, her charts, all the monitors, everything we're seeing and learning in there ... it all says she is, I'm sorry, still comatose," he paused, his hand at his chest as he so earnestly continued. "But she is, somehow, magically, I truly do not know, repeating the same word ... sometimes as a mumble or like a ... a whisper, sometimes a little more clearly," he said, still whispering, his eyes wild now. "But it is always the same word: *dragon*. So, does this mean something, or is it something like a subconscious tick? Like Tourette's, but from a comatose mind?"

My mind was spinning. What did this mean?

"Well, she doesn't seem to be swearing, so must be nothing," my mom said with a smile and a weak laugh.

"No, no I don't, uh, know what that is," I answered honestly. "Must be that tick thing you said. Super weird. But she's okay, right? Can I – can I just go see her?"

I didn't wait for confirmation. I heard my mom's quick footsteps behind me, and then the heavier gait of the nurse's. I pushed the door open and stood in the dark quiet.

There on the bed, eyes shut and body limp, lay Philippa chanting over and over, "dragon, dragon, dragon, dragon ..."

"You see? It has only been off and on for the past few hours. But what does that mean?" Jürgen asked, his large brown eyes wide and wild. "This is truly unprecedented."

I stared at my mom. She looked away and walked to Philippa's bed. I joined her, thinking hard.

What would Dragon do? What would he tell me to do?

"Um, Jürgen? I know this is bizarre, what's happening," I began, slow and uncertain.

"Uh, yeah. Bizarre. To say the least," he responded, still wide-eyed.

"But, um, it's just, well, if it's not medically necessary, or detrimental, or whatever," I continued, searching for something smart to say, "maybe we don't have to tell anybody that this is happening?"

Jürgen frowned. My mom cocked her head. Her hand was on Philippa's forehead, stroking her hair back. The kind nurse started to protest, but I carried on, growing more confident.

"I think if her talking is, like, truly groundbreaking, then it'll draw all this unwanted attention, and put her in medical books and stuff," I said, pleased with my burgeoning argument. "We don't want that. We don't want more, you know, spotlights on her. Or to have her, um, be some test subject or something when she comes to."

My mom nodded and smiled at me, satisfied with my reasoning. Jürgen frowned still. He put his hands on his hips and looked off in the distance. He cocked his head slightly, raised his eyebrows, and then nodded in agreement, clearly having some great debate within his own mind.

"Okay. I understand this and respect your wishes. So long as there is no medical threat present, or potential for medical threat, I shall document this as occasional sounds and nothing more."

My shoulders relaxed. Holy cow had I been stressed. My mom rocked her neck side to side and smiled in relief. She grabbed my hand and squeezed it.

"Ew, weird," I said as I pulled my hand away. She shrugged and leaned down to hug Philippa. "Don't smother her!"

"That's what moms do. It's my innate right," she said, winking at me as she sat up.

"Ew, don't wink either."

"You have any questions for me?" Jürgen coughed behind us.

"No, thank you, Jürgen. Truly. We appreciate your protecting her and will not forget this kindness," my mom said solemnly.

Anyone but a German may have deemed her formal gratitude over the top. But Jürgen simply nodded and exited.

"Crap, what the hell is happening in her brain?" I hissed as soon as he closed the door. My mom's face fell.

"I don't know, my Eve. You'd know better than me," she murmured.

"What's going on in there," I whispered more softly, ignoring my mom and looking down at my sister.

"Something wonderful, I hope," she said.

"Something wonderful," I repeated.

We sat with Philippa for hours into the evening. The shadows drew out my nerves. The darker it got, the more anxious I became. What if she awoke and divulged the whole vivid nightmare? She'd surely be swarmed with every medical researcher questioning the workings of her comatose brain and every mental health professional questioning her sanity ... I shuddered. One thing at a time, I reminded myself. One horrid, terrifying thing at a time.

21

GRAVIORA MANENT

"**I** have saved this seat for you," Elke said as she patted the desk next. It was the first time I smiled walking into Mr. Simmons' class. Or I thought I smiled, but I guess that was becoming a forgotten skill. Elke shrugged and said then, "But you don't have to if you are not wanting to."

"No, no, I want to. I, um, thanks, or whatever," I said as I put my bag down. "Crap! Was this open the whole time?"

I looked at my bag, it' zipper fully undone and the contents of my bag on display. Nothing too damning – a few binders and a phone charger ... but those were hidden by *An Illustrated Brief History of Time* in its enlarged hardcover version stowed dominantly in front.

Elke giggled as she looked down at the black book that I shoved deeper into my backpack. I yanked hard on the zipper.

"Why ... won't ... you ... ugh ... I zipped you this morning ... before I ... left ... THERE!" I said and sat back, victorious, and possibly panting a bit too much.

"I did not know Stephen Hawking had his books illustrated," Elke said with a grin.

"What? Oh. He, uh, he didn't, I don't think. It's the, um, the illustrated version," I mumbled.

"Oh! With pictures to understand better!" Elke smiled bigger. "I was thinking it was a picture book, like, a book for children!"

"It might as well be, hmph, so big and illustrated!"

My head turned. Now Mr. Simmons was teasing me for my book?

"At least I'm reading Stephen Hawking!" I exclaimed. Should I laugh along? I had no comeback. I remained indignant.

"More like you're *looking* at Stephen Hawking. Oh, Ms. Archer, I do apologize. I suppose I'm feeling a little sassy this morning," Mr. Simmons said and shook his hips.

"Um, ew. Never do that again. And," I said as I sat back in my chair and put my hands behind my head. "Don't, like, apologize or whatever. We're cool. Totally cool."

"Holy crap, how are you so sweaty?" a male voice blurted from a few desks away.

I dropped my arms. Quickly. That was my cue to exit. A little sooner than I expected. But I was painfully aware of my inability to live anything down these days. I began to collect my things and wondered if I'd ever make it through a full class period.

"He is just saying that to, you know, distract people from looking at the toilet tissue on his shoe," Elke whispered. I looked over and, sure enough, the several squares of white tissue were stuck to his left foot.

I smiled. The universe was showing me just a bit of mercy.

"Fine," I mumbled and sat back down. I dropped my backpack; one of the zippers popped off as the bag slumped against my chair.

"Hey," Elke whispered, "This came off your bag. Also, you should know that I know about you."

"Yeah, so does everybody," I grumbled. "Not really an announcement I need."

"No, no, no," she said. Her eyes were locked intensely on mine. "I am knowing about ... about *de Junge den du getötet hast*." She looked up and raised her hand for the attendance check, then leaned back on my desk. "I do not believe it, though."

"Elke, you went Deutsch there for a minute," I whispered, disinterested. "Maybe we just, you know, stick to doing math?"

It's not that I was so keen on this class, but I really didn't want to discuss any of *that*. Compared to *that*, algebra was a party. Elke looked at me, though, as if she had a desperate secret, it made my insides stand upright.

"Ms., or should I say Fraulein, Mischler?" Mr. Simmons called with a cough. "Oh, I love German so much. Kindly write out the third problem please, and show your work on the board for the class. You know, math is the universal language," Mr. Simmons' voice faded as he busied himself in papers at his desk.

"I would like to talk more with you about this," Elke whispered in my ear as she stood. Looking at Mr. Simmons, she added, "Also, it would be Frau. *Fraulein* is, eh, a little ancient and perhaps offensive. I am *Frau* Mischler."

I liked how soft her *r* was at the ends of words. And I liked how she was confident enough to correct a teacher, just like that. Was that part of her culture? I made a mental note to learn German.

But what had she said? The "yoong-ih" what? The "geh-too-tet" or "gih-tuh-tet" ... that second bit was probably a lost cause. But whatever it was, she had gone white saying it.

The day finally went on, uneventful and quiet after that. I thanked heaven I made it to – and stayed the whole time in! – sixth period. Which was a not a bad class, as it turns out. Whatever science class I was meant to be in was in breach of the "Willamette Preparatory Academy honored student-teacher ratio," or so the note mailed to me said. Thus, I was moved into Intro to Film Studies, after which I'd close out the day with Literary Arts. Maybe this yuppy private school wasn't so bad.

As I sat in the back row squinting at "Citizen Kane," I repeated the phrase from Elke earlier that morning over and over in my mind. "Dee yoong-ih-some-thing-geh-tuh-tit." I'm pretty sure that was it.

22

PROPRIA MANU

I'm not one of those people who is glued to their phone screen. Malcolm had told me once that was a good thing, a healthy thing. He had adult clients who really struggled with that, he had said. Tech addiction, he had called it. Of all the addictions in the world, that one sounded the lamest.

My addiction, he had informed me, was self pity. I had wanted to march out of his beautiful office. Moi? Indulging in self pity?

I didn't see it.

"You get validation from the voice you care about the most – yourself," Malcolm had said evenly from his smart leather chair.

"I don't ever validate myself!" I had started to object.

"You do, in the form of pity. You tell yourself you've *earned* this feeling of woundedness. You tell yourself you are unique in your pain. You shower yourself with pity and it feels. So. Good. You indulge in it," he had said in his cool, melodic voice. "It is common. And it is retractable."

I shook my head hard to toss the memory from the front of my mind.

I wasn't pitying myself. I had been through some real shit. I was dealing with things literally no one in the word understood, Malcolm included.

Because I never told him. I couldn't tell him.

Right?

So, what did he know? He didn't have the whole story. He couldn't just accuse me of indulgent self pity.

The more I argued against it, the more I feared he was right.

My phone buzzed. I shook my head and looked down. A message from the hospital illuminated my screen: *This message is from Heritage Samaritan Hospital. Patient [Philippa Archer] update available. Visit Station 6 on floor 4, login to your Heritage Portal, or call your outreach number. Respond STOP to end messaging service. Data rates may apply.*

My heart jumped.

I threw some snacks in my backpack and headed toward the bus stop. I was getting quite adept at navigating public transit, something my mom adored in Europe but was comically frightened of in the Portland metro area.

Settled on the bus, I texted my mom that I was headed to the hospital. My phone buzzed immediately. *Perfect, already en route. I'll meet you there!*

I frowned and typed back: *Why didn't you pick me up first? I'm on the smelly bus.* I waited for a minute, started to take out my headphones, and then smiled. The phone buzzed.

"There it is," I murmured with a chuckle.

You're on the bus? Alone? Didn't you read about the guy who got his ear bitten off by a transient bus rider?!?!

I knew better than to engage. Portland was home to more than a few peculiar transient groups. And my mom, bleeding heart though she was, kept tabs on the goings-on of Portland metro streets a little too closely. Even though we lived in the safe, lovely burbs of Happy Valley. Happy is in the name! And no one's happy while they're unsafe. Ergo, Happy Valley equals safety. I tucked this argument into the back of my mind to use on my mom later and popped on my headphones.

I cued up my current go-to playlist for my melancholy moments. The Cure, Joy Division, and, of course, no playlist is complete without a smattering of Beatles. But, like, the 1966-era Beatles: a little more psychedelic and angsty.

I leaned my head back, grateful for rad music to pull me away from my own thoughts. Just as I was nodding off, the buzzing of a phone call interrupted my tunes and my relaxation. (I had learned to silence all notifications, lest I have a "By the Seashore" moment again.)

"Yes, um, hello? Is this, is this Eve? Eve...Archer?"

"Yeppers, I mean, um, yes," I said, wondering why "yeppers" came out of my face. I had never said this in my life.

"Oh, good, so, um, you're Eve?" a man's voice stuttered on the other line.

"Yes, why," I said slowly, not feeling great about answering.

"I, eh, I was wondering if we could meet. You see—"

"No way, perv!" I yelled into the phone. I pulled the phone away, ready to hit the red end-call button, when I heard the man shouting over and over.

"Don't hang up! It's me! It's me! Don't hang up! It's me!"

"It's ... who?" I said as I raised the phone back up.

"It's Chad."

"I don't know a Chad," I barked and started to pull the phone back again.

"No no no no no! I'm your dad! Eve! I'm your father!"

The buzzing took over.

The world spun.

My body shook.

My dad?

Was calling me?

I have a dad ... and ...and his name is *Chad?*

Ew.

And also, WHAT?

I walked through the hospital halls in a trance. I had taken a screenshot of the number; saving it in my contacts just didn't sit right.

"Sweetie, she's not there," an elderly woman at the registration desk said as I walked by.

"What? What?" I said, a tremble arising in my voice.

"They moved her!" she continued quickly. "Didn't you receive a message? Yes, to the sixth floor. Private room, too. Fancy!"

I didn't respond. Too antsy to wait for the elevator, I heaved open the door to the stairwell and trotted up one flight, then two. By the third one, I was gassed enough that the name Chad had stopped pinging around my cranium.

I tumbled into a sixth-floor hallway, sweaty and panting. My mom appeared in the doorway of a suite a few doors down.

"Eve? Goodness! Getting your workout in, good for you!" she rattled. "No change in your sister. But that means nothing is worse, right? So, that's good. And this room! Not much bigger, but definitely nicer. And isn't this floor nice and quiet? I brought her book for us to read aloud, but it's almost done. Have you eaten? You can have the other half of my tuna. Was Dr. Daas downstairs when you came in?"

I stared at her, this woman I felt I no longer knew. She prattled on. With each word, her voice became more foreign.

Who was Chad?

Was he really my dad?

How did *he* know if he was my dad or not?

Did she know he was … around?

Why tell me some elaborate story about my father being an unknown sperm donor?

Was Chad the sperm donor?

Why lie?

"Eve? Are you listening?"

I blinked and looked at my mom.

"What? Yeah, whatever," I said about nothing in particular.

"Great. You finish this Tolstoy and I'll be back with a new book for her."

I looked down at the tattered paperback my mom had thrust into my arms as she trotted down the hall, humming. I snorted.

"Of course you'd be reading Tolstoy's *Childhood* for fun," I said as I sank into a chair near Philippa's bed. "Where's the part in here where the kid learns his mom is a lying hoebag?"

A jab hit the inside of my stomach. Overwhelmed with confusion and anger though I was, I felt guilty thinking so little of my mom.

But I did. I did think so little of her in that moment.

23

VERBA VOLANT, SCRIPTA MANENT

Ms. Neally had given me her school email address a while back.

With communication from Dragon and Baert so limited, I appreciated the gesture now more than ever. Like everything else in my life, I had scoffed when I received it. I think I even made a joke about going back in time to 1996 to send an email. She had looked puzzled but had graciously smiled and carried on.

I couldn't remember the last time I sent an email. If a teacher needed emailing, my mom usually did that. I sighed and fired up my laptop. After nine failed password attempts and several minutes before I could try again, I stared at an inbox cluttered with OFFERS I HAD TO SEE from merchants I had never heard of, a slew of messages from "girls" with subject headings that made me blush, and dozens of school announcements from Beecher I never knew had tried to reach me.

Scrolling through was pointless. I highlighted the whole of it and hit delete. As I watched the folder clear itself, I swear I saw a message from a Chad ... I shook my head free of the impulse to go into the deleted folder and check. I had no time for that guy. Not right now.

I needed a snack. I started to get up, then scolded myself.

"Just do this one easy thing, you self-pitying waste of space," I muttered as I clicked to compose a new message, "Send one freaking email to get some freaking help. You can do it."

I began to type. And as I typed, I realized I wasn't typing so much as deleting.

Dear Ms. Neally,

This letter is in regards to

<delete delete delete>

Hey Ms. Neally, it's Eve

<delete> Of course it's me. My name is the goddamn sender line.

Yo, Yael. It's been a minute.

<delete delete delete>

Greetings,

<delete>

Salutations,

<delete>

Bonjour!

<delete>

What was wrong with me? Had I even sent written correspondence in my life?

I pondered the question and concluded that, no, apart from the occasional text or the handwritten thank you card to my nana on holidays, I really hadn't sent written correspondence.

I typed "how to start an email" in the search bar on my phone. And immediately hated myself for it.

Deep breaths. And another string cheese. You can do this, I told myself.

Hi Ms. Neally

Okay, that's normal.

I'm having a hard time with my sister's health. I feel like it's my fault. I learned something upsetting about my mom. With everything else going on, I think I ought to take your offer for a therapist more seriously. Would you be willing to still help with this?

I paused and frowned. Started strong, but how does one end such a message?

Cheers

<delete>

Sincerely

I stared at that one for a minute. Then shook my head. What, am I applying for a job? <delete>

Best wishes

<delete>

And many fine returns

<delete> Where had I even learned that phrase?! I scowled and hunched over my laptop.

Thanks, Eve

Fine. That would do. I hit send and sat back, proud of myself for taking action. I felt a little warmth inside. But I shook it off, unwilling to give my mom's "tiny victories" lecture any credence. My hand was on my laptop to shut it when a little chime came from within.

She had already responded!

Wow. I figured someone has cool and beautiful I mean just cool as Ms. Neally would be busy on a Friday night. I didn't know with what – what did grownups do on a Friday? But definitely not chilling with email at the ready. I clicked her message and read eagerly.

Dear Eve,

Yes.

Kindly,

Yaël

Alright. So, the message was a bit of a letdown, but the sentiment crucial: she was still willing to help.

Maybe there was hope for this self-pitying dragonlord after all.

I closed my laptop, satisfied with The Very Responsible Thing I had just done by asking for help.

"Suck it, Malcolm. I can do self-care," I mumbled as I swapped out my uniform of jeans and a sweater (I had upgraded my wardrobe from the daily hoodie to the more mature sweater) for sweats and an oversized alien tee-shirt Philippa had gifted me last Christmas.

A rustle outside my window made the hairs on my neck stand on edge. I felt around for something – anything – weapon-like and grasped at a pair of scissors on my desk. They weren't closed; I grabbed them in the middle of the two blades and felt a swift cut stinging my palm.

"Crap!" I cried, sucking on my bleeding hand and forgetting my defensive stance. I peered out my window. My mom was in the yard, humming. I shook my head, disinterested in seeing what asinine thing she was doing now. From finding her green juices in the bathroom cupboard to retrieving a stack of folded laundry from the stove (thankfully not on), I was clocking a few too many concerning moments in my mom's behaviors of late. I didn't have the bandwidth for another.

I shut my window with a sigh and made my way downstairs for an evening snack. Just as I was adding another sleeve of Ritz crackers to my armful of treats, more rusting from outside caught my attention. I didn't have time to arm myself – bushes in the backyard were moving and two loud thuds sounded from the patio.

I swung open the door and thrust my sleeve of Ritz at whatever was lurking in the backyard. A jar of peanut butter and my bounty of string cheese fell to the ground.

"Aye, and she has skan for us a'ready! Lassie, how'd y'know?"

Baert shook some leaves from his hair and beard. Dragon emerged from behind him.

"So sorry for the unannounced visit, Evechild," he said as he stretched. "We bring news!" I scooped up my snacks and joined them in the backyard.

"You guys suck with your arrivals. Couldn't you, like, tell me in my head or something first?" I said, trying to be gruff but secretly pleased with the unexpected visit. I hadn't seen them since that night at the coffeehouse.

"Quite right. I ought to be better with my telepathic communications, quite right. Excellent note. Consider it taken under advisement," Dragon said. "But this news couldn't wait!"

"It couldn't? Boot what news?" Baert hopped up and grabbed a string cheese. He bit into it, plastic and all. "Aye, what the bowfin boggin is this?" he cried, yet still took another bite.

"Baert, it's, uh, yeah, you've gotta, nope, stop taking bites, that's a wrapper. There you go, you got it," I said as I coached him through the intricacies of string-cheese eating. He threw the wrapper with a grunt. It barely floated and fell into his lap.

"Well kin me th'dobber," he grumbled and took another bite.

"So you have news?" I said to Dragon.

"Aye, news?" Baert repeated, his cheeks now full of all seven string cheeses.

Dragons eyes widened.

"Indeed! Someone of a celebrity will be coming for you, Evechild."

"A celebrity?" I asked, unimpressed. Celebrities had never really been my thing.

"Well, someone whose panache and cache of exquisite collectibles is unmatched."

Dragon smiled and folded his arms. Baert furrowed his brow, then looked up at his coy friend.

"What. It can't be. Who? You mean—?" Baert said.

Dragon nodded excitedly.

"What about him? What? Tell me already," I said, trying to stay cool even though their excitement was a bit contagious.

Dragon cleared his throat, closed his eyes, and brought his palms together in front of his chest. Baert danced side to side, his arms over his head as he did a little hop-step.

"This person is," Dragon started.

"Yeah? What? He's what?"

"The only human," Dragon said, pausing for emphasis.

"Go on."

"To own," Dragon paused dramatically again.

"All — EVERY SINGLE ONE — yes, you heard that right, all Beatles' first releases in original vinyl in mint condition," Dragon declared and then bowed at the information, his arms and wings ceremoniously outstretched.

Baert hollered and stamped his feet. He and dragon erupted into a shrill celebration of fandom and disbelief. They held each other's hands and hopped up and down, laughing, speaking insanely fast and unintelligibly, and, where those tears?

"Are you serious? I mean, that's pretty rad and all, but," I started. The two stopped their revelry and stared at me.

"Are you not a fan?" Dragon said.

"Oh, god, I'm the biggest fan! For, like, so many reasons. So many songs have been there for me, but, it's just …" I trailed off, uncertain how to fix their aghast and now disappointed faces. I coughed and smiled. "You guys, I think I was just, like, in shock. The Beatles?! Originals?! I can't even handle it!"

They stared at me a second longer. I launched into some shrieks and jumps, trying to match their enthusiasm. They joined in. And there we were, a dragon, an elf, and a teen freaking out over the Beatles. I really wanted to watch A Hard Day's Night again just to see if I could superimpose our crew over the gaggles of screaming girls in the concert scenes.

"Ok, so who is this, uh, cool collector," I asked, panting from the jumping and shrieking and hand clapping.

"Only one of the finest psychological minds alive, my dear protégé," Dragon said, wiping his eyes (yes, actually) and giving a few more fist bumps and hi-fives to Baert.

"Does not e'en come close t'thah pure barry bliss o'my mate," Baert said wistfully. "Quite right. Prepare to be amazed, Evechild."

"I heard George himself was a mate," Baert added.

"Always my favorite Beatle. Should have been knighted. Taken before his time, indeed," Dragon said. Baert straightened up and did his funny salute; he and Dragon stood in reverence for, like, a really long time in what I assumed was a moment of silence for George Harrison.

"I, uh, saw Paul McCartney in concert," I said finally, unsure if I'd upset whatever sacredness they had going on at the moment. "And Ringo."

They looked up, delighted.

"Oh, Sir Paul! Such a chap," Dragon said and thumped his tail.

Before the two could launch into more chittering fandom, I spoke up a little louder.

"Um, who am I supposed to be preparing for?" I asked. "And, uh, when? Where? Any of those little details ready?"

"Yes, yes, of course," Dragon said hastily. "Yaél is handling all of that, naturally."

With that, the two turned back to their Beatles trivia.

"You guys just gonna leave me hanging? Someone super cool is apparently coming? Guys? Alright, whatever."

I took their lack of follow up as my cue to head back inside. It was fully dark. I was tired. And hungry (and now without snacks; don't you just hate it when an elf steels your cheese and crackers?).

But I should check on my mom first. I could hear strange noises from the front yard. I gave Dragon and Baert a wave that went unnoticed and left them to prattle on.

"Seems about right," I muttered under my breath. Then I found myself unwittingly softly singing as I made my way through the side yard and into the front, "It's been a haaaaard day's night, and I've been workin' like a daaawwwwg. It's been a haaard day's night; I should be sleepiiiin' like a laaawwwwg."

"Great song choice!"

My mom's chipper voice greeted me. She was, in fact, still in the front yard, kneeling in the garden bed along the edge of the grass. A pile of small onions, garlic bulbs, and a single potato lay next to her.

"Oh, hey girl," I said. My mom smiled and dug another gloved hand into the dirt and produced a small, white onion. She held it up for me to admire. "Very nice. Isn't it, you know, a bit late to be gardening?"

She held up the one lowly potato in response.

"We shall feast like kings! But maybe you don't need to be harvesting in the dark?" I offered.

"Eh. It was too hot during the day, and I didn't find the time. It's kinda pleasant, though. Maybe I'll work this into my nightly routine."

She shrugged off the question, but I knew better than to believe her response. She was avoiding the same thing I was avoiding: sleep.

"'Harvesting in the Dark' is a great album name," she called as I walked past her into the house.

Normally our years-long joke of announcing a choice turn of phrase as a garage band name or an album title brought a laugh or at least a smile from me. No smile came. For two reasons. Philippa was the master at turning everyday lingo into hilarious names. And I was worried about my mom.

Really worried. Again.

24

SANGUIS POLLICETUR GLORIAM

I spent most of the afternoon at Philippa's side, babbling on about my new school, my classes, the books I was reading, basically anything but how I was actually feeling.

Which was scared, alone, stressed, and generally hungry. My stomach grumbled loudly to confirm this last bit.

"That's as good a spot as ever to stop," I said to my sister's unmoving face. "I gotta get some food in me. Maybe I'll eat a vanilla pudding right in front of you. This one nurse showed me where they're stored in the cafeteria, and, bro, these puddings here are sooo good."

Her monitors chirped and beeped. I thought I saw an eyelid flicker. But probably not. My heart dropped. What did I care about teasing my sis with food now?

"Please just say something," I murmured.

"Oh, sorry to interrupt! I am just here to change out her fluids."

Jürgen's friendly voice startled me. I nodded and kept my head down, tired of others witnessing my constant state of tears.

"It is alright, I can do it later. I'll be back in, say, twenty minutes," he said warmly as he pulled the door shut.

"Wait! Jürgen," I hissed and started for the door.

It fell shut just as I reached it and smacked me in the nose.

"Ugh! Ow! Hey Jürgen," I called as I pulled the door open with one hand and held my nose with the other. Something warm streamed along the top my lie. "You're, like, German, or whatever?"

"Uh, yes," he said with a chuckle. "You finally cracked the code. Oh! You are bleeding!"

"I am? Oh, it's fine. Noses just, like, do that," I said as I held my nose more tightly and winced in pain.

"Blood should never leave the body," Jürgen said with a frown. "There are very few instances in which it is okay that blood leaves the body. And nasally is not one of them. Please, sit."

I did as I was told and waited silently as he swabbed and dabbed at my face.

"I am going to insert this to absorb any more blood. It may make you have the sensation that you need to—"

"AHHH-CHOOO!"

Blood splatters with a heaping side of snot shot out of my face.

"Sneeze," Jürgen finished. He dabbed his own face with some of the gauze now. "I will be right back. Hold this, yes, firm but not tight, like that."

I marveled at his patience. I had just sneezed multiple body fluids all over him, while he was helping me, and he kept helping me as though nothing happened. It was my own blood and snot, and I was so disgusted I wanted to puke.

"Good day to bring extra scrubs," he said as he jogged back to where I still sat. "Now, you have something to ask me?"

"I wanted to ask you something, about, um, a word, er, words," I said, then paused. I racked my brain for those German words Elke had said in class a few days ago. "Oh yeah! Ok. What does ... young, no, yarn, no, 'yoong-ih'? Is that a word? What does that mean? And, also, damn, what was it, oh! 'Guh-toe-tet' or something? Are either of those words?"

"The first word I think you're saying is *junge*, is that it? *Junge*? That is a boy. Or a young man," he said. He shifted his weight and looked at me, puzzled. "Say that second word again?"

"Yeah, um, uh, something like 'guh-too-tut,' but I can't totally remember it," I said, feeling my face redden.

"Well, *getötet* is 'kill.' So, I'm sure you are misremembering," he said with a chuckle and opened the door to Philippa's room. "Is that everything? Keep holding that compress on your nose. Back to work I go!"

"Yeah. Probably misheard," I mumbled, unable to move.

What did Elke know?

25

REDUCTIO AD ABSURDUM

I remained unfamiliar with the school's grounds. Not because they were so grand; I just never hung around enough to clock its layouts and details. At Beecher, I knew every nook and cranny, every squeak of every door, every corner that remained quiet and undisturbed by the riffraff known as a student body.

Something rumbled in my heart, something akin to homesickness, as I entered Willamette Prep that day.

Annoying. It must be Ms. Neally. Being around her all the time. She was really one of the only highlights on my time at my junior high. I thought of its familiar corridors, its welcoming fields, every nook and cranny that I knew so well. I knew where to hide.

"Forget this," I muttered as I headed out the side doors of Willamette Prep to the side yard.

It was lined with beautiful gardens proudly kept up by the school's horticulture department. Placards describing each herb, vegetable, and flower lined the cedar fence.

"Psh. Yuppies," I said under my breath as I walked briskly past it. I shook my head at myself. I loved gardens; that putdown didn't even make sense.

But these gardens were new. This school was new. And lovely though it was, it was different from what I was familiar with, and therefore unwelcome to me right now.

Was I really feeling sentimental toward Beecher? A thousand memories – each more embarrassing than the last – flashed through my head. Then a memory of Dragon. Of Baert. Of Libby ... what?! Of Jonah. Double what?! Jonah, then Obrenox, then Jonah, around and around they went.

I shuddered and shook my head.

"You alright? You're whiter than a kipper!" Poppy chirped. I jumped, not realizing the little dog had joined me.

"Yeah. I, uh, it's nothing. Just a weird moment."

"You've a lot of those," Poppy said, her body alert and her gaze sharp.

"How are you liking life as a therapy dog?" I asked the question as a redirect, but I was wholly disinterested. I rubbed my temples, squinting my eyes shut. Jonah-Obrenox-Jonah-Obrenox ...then the herd of Jonahs, then the herds of small gray men mutilated and sliced and dripping with their own innards, then Jonah's lifeless eyes ... Each image spun with immaculate detail on a depraved carousel. My stomach lurched and a buzzing grew loud in my brain.

"Hey, I've got to sit for a minute..." I stammered as I dropped onto the grass.

"Oy, Sheila, we've no time for rest," Poppy said, her bright eyes falling dark as she looked back at me in alarm. "Hang on, love. You're not quite looking like the full quid." I felt her muzzle me and whimper a bit. Instinctively I pet her, then recoiled.

"Crap, I'm sorry. Is that, like, invading your personal space? I should have asked. I mean, you're human in there, right?" I said, grateful this distraction pulled me away from whatever bog my brain was sitting in. "Or something? I feel like you're not actually an Australian Shepherd ... if that makes sense."

"Don't worry about me," she said and licked the back of my hand reassuringly. "But thanks, you're a real bonzer. And while you're at it, maybe you hit just behind my ears, then?"

I giggled and obliged. As I scratched her soft, piebald ears, they tilted forward suddenly and she lunged forward, her tail erect.

A figure appeared on the hill before us. The silhouette of wild hair and a billowing coat moved shakily toward us. Poppy's hackles announced her distrust, and just as I was beginning to get the hell away from there, she yipped and ran forward.

"It's you! Blimey, but I was expecting a real dag," Poppy said as she jumped about the shadowed person, whom I could see now was a very tall, very curiously dressed, very unkempt woman. She clutched a Victorian-era medical bag in one hand while she adjusted a headscarf with the other.

"Hmmmm, yes! I didn't want to ruin the surprise, hmmmm, you must be the dragonlord!" The woman dropped her bag to the ground and was now prancing in circles near Poppy, hopping as the dog hopped, laughing delicately as the dog barked. "Oh, but enough of this silliness, hmmmm? Tell me, how is the subject?"

The woman straightened, her mishmash of fabrics falling still under her dark purple overcoat. She removed her brown wool hat and leaned down in what looked like a curtsy. I quickly copied the gesture, not wanting to offend whatever – whomever – this was.

"Terrible bunion I've got," she murmured in a whisper as she produced one sandaled foot from beneath her long, wrinkled garb. Her toes wiggled grotesquely, making the world's largest and most disgusting bunion dance atop her foot. She looked up at me.

"Oh! Your greeting is so very formal, hmmm! I was not expecting such formalities, hmmmm, but yes, as you are."

She adjusted her glasses and withdrew her foot back under her skirts (thank god), and gave an obvious curtsey toward me.

"It's fine, I thought you were, like, doing that first, so I ...yeah," I stammered lamely. "I'm Eve," I said and thrust my arm forward, trying to reclaim some of my dignity. "And you are?"

"So you are, hmmmm."

She leaned in close to me. So close I could smell hints of peppermint and ... was that curry? ... on her. Her pupils widened and focused through thick, bulbous glasses. The lens curved and magnified her eyes to an unnatural size. She licked her lips and pushed a curly purple strand from her forehead.

"How kind of you to meet me," a breathy alto voice twittered. She finally extended a gauze- covered arm with a limp, bejeweled hand at the end. "Gil Baudelaire. M.D., THC, RD.f, WZP.d.7, Esq." She produced (from nowhere?) a small card with exactly that inscribed upon it.

I meant to smile but I think I only awkwardly showed my teeth and sort of bowed again. "Your name is ... it's Gil?"

"Gil, yes, hmmmmm. Dr. Baudelaire is fine. Quaint, but fine."
I stifled a laugh. Her eyes narrowed, looking like slits in her coke-bottle glasses.

"You object, hmmmmm?"

"Eh, um, it's just that, here," I said, gesturing broadly around us, "like, in this dimension or whatever, Gil is, eh, generally a name for, erm ..." I trailed off, surveying Dr. Baudelaire again, who certainly looked very female, for several reasons. "It's just, um, a typically masculine name. That's all."

"Yet it's what I am called," Dr. Baudelaire said nonchalantly. "Hmmmm, I am here as a human female woman. And a doctor, hmmmm, a therapist, where your own species has failed you, hmmmm."

"Is Gil short for something?" I asked.

"Yes. Gilbert."

"Gilbert," I repeated.

"Ah, don't you love spring?" she said as she picked up and fingered a yellowed, crunchy maple leaf.

"Uh, it's autumn," I said as I inelegantly accepted the crisp gift.

"Hmmm. So it is," Dr. Baudelaire shrugged. "Drahk and Yaël foretold of my coming?"

I looked at her with a cocked head. *This* is who had Dragon and Baert all in a tizzy? *This* is who Ms. Neally sent in response to my email?

"Wow," I said under my breath.

"Hmmmm, you're angry, with … everything and everybody? Hmmmm. Have you tried, let me look at you, hmmm, yes, have you tried nipplewort?"

"What?" I gasped and choked on the bottled water I anxiously sipped. "Have I tried what?"

"Hmmmm, *lapsana communis*. It's so lovely sauteed in butter when it's young. And excellent for your constitution," she winked at me, looking more like a spider than a woman with those fun-mirror glasses.

"Polite pass," I said quietly. "And I'm not angry. Ok, well, sometimes, yeah, I'm pretty angry. Fine."

Dr. Baudelaire rested a bauble-covered hand on my shoulder.

Her palm no sooner touched me than she shrieked and jumped back. In the distance, Poppy barked.

"By the eye of Thoth, demons let me be! Aaaaaah!" she cried and recoiled.

Dr. Baudelaire fell backwards with such force that the ground sunk and cracked around her.

"What – what did I do?"

"You, you –hmmmm!" she shook as she looked at me. "You carry so much. Too much. You carry you too much."

She looked up at me from the ground. One final crack stretched out along the grass and came to a stop as the soil groaned. I stepped forward slowly; I'd never been suspicious of the ground before. The doctor smoothed her gossamer layers and retied her scarves.

I lamely offered a hand for the second time this morning to someone on the ground because of me. In the background, I saw Poppy shake her head and run off.

"We must get to work forthwith," she said as I heaved her upright. "I need my spells; no, Gil, you mustn't use spells here. Tokens, yes, tokens! Hmmmm. Brilliant, Gil. Yes, hmmmm, let's fetch the tokens. Eve! Eve Gwendolyn Genevieve Archer, ah, yes, there you are, hmmmm! Lovely, er, a bit rough, but no mind. Just as Yaél said, strong and powerful and, well, hmmmm, there's that, but that can fixed, and this part is, well, alright, hmmmmm, so we just adjust that bit, and yes, maybe, well, perhaps it'll be okay. Hmmmmm?"

She danced about, witchlike, as she devised what I guess was a plan. She pulled things from the folds of her skirts – small vials and books – examined them, and tucked them back away.

"So, um, I'll leave you to it …. This was, uh, super useful. So, tell Ms. Neally thanks and all, but I'll take my chances with the crazies," I said as I backed away, ready to turn and run.

"Sorry?" Dr. Baudelaire stopped, her arms fully outstretched with little castanets affixed to her fingers. She cocked her head. "We've only begun. You need help, hmmmm. And I, alas, am the one, hmmmm. Let us put aside the conceptual for the concrete, hmmmm. The trial."

She sat upon a wooden bench that appeared out of nowhere and gestured for me to join her. I obliged, but patted the wooden slats a few times before sitting on them.

"Thanks for, like, coming all this way, or whatever," I said and looked down. "But we all know how the trial's gonna go. They'll say I'm crazy and that'll be the end of it. I'll be in some institution somewhere with people who eat crayons on purpose."

"First, hmmmm, that's a rather unfortunate if not ignorant reduction of those with mental health disorders, and second, hmmmm."

"Okay, mentally ill," I said, making air quotes with my fingers. My own bitterness surprised me. "What's the point," I grumbled.

A lump formed in my throat. I could picture my mom's disappointment stare over my dismissing mental health. A frustrated tear formed, and I turned my back to the peculiar woman.

"Oy, if you throw in the towel already, maybe that'll be your lot," Poppy called from down the hill. "C'mon. Give her a try. G'on."

"We've much to discuss, hmmmm. Tell me of your sister, Philippa Jacqueline Archer."

Rage inflated inside of me like a circus balloon.

I stood abruptly and took an assertive step away from the bench, but something jerked me back. I rubbed my neck and took another step. Some sort of force held my skull in a vice. I winced and whimpered as I tried to step forward once more. A strange voice rushed into my mind.

"You are not ill. You are battered, traumatized. You have seen too much, you know too much, and no believes you," a voice, dark and layered, echoed into my brain. "The humans cannot and will not. You are imbalanced. You are unhealthy, but you are not ill. And your sister ....," the voice trailed off, its echo sprawling after it. "Your sister ... is ... hmmmm .... that can't be right."

My blood froze. My eyes shot open; I hadn't realized I had closed them.

"What? My sister is what?" I snapped and spun around. "She's what, you crazy old bat? Why are you here? Why? Why do you all keep popping up? To get me out of here? And leave Philippa? You all show up, but all the shit's still here! It wasn't here before you all arrived! You weren't here, neither were my problems. Just ... go ... away!"

My voice rose louder and louder, but not loud enough to overpower the ringing in my brain. I cautiously inched forward. No resistance. I rocked my neck back and forth and exhaled, relieved.

Dr. Baudelaire fell to the ground. She slumped down, backward, back, farther, farther, until she was supine on the ground, curled up in a little ball. She didn't cry, she just ... withdrew. Into herself. She became smaller, and smaller, a tiny snail shell.

"Your sister will not agree!" a tiny voice shrieked from the ground.

I stepped back. Had she said that? My head spun and my vision turned fuzzy. Dark splotches danced around me. I gulped in air. My fingers seized into strange shapes. Was I standing?

"Eve, Eve, hmmmmm," Dr. Baudelaire's hushed coo washed over me. "You're having a panic attack. Hmmmm. Think about Sleipnir, with the noble brow and silky hair."

"I don't know what that is," I wheezed and gasped. My fingers stiffened into immovable claws. I sputtered and gulped. "This is a panic attack?"

"Hmmmm, yes. Surely you know Sleipnir. Odin's preferred mount? Eight-legged horse-like fellow? Quite fast? Hmmmm? Sleipnir?"

I shook my head and felt my blood returning to its normal pulse and my feet feeling the ground again. I breathed in and out until the tingles drained from my fingertips.

"Yes, think of Sleipnir. Hmmmm, yes, breathe more slowly, hmmm, good," she purred. "Let Sleipnir pull you from the panic, hmmmm."

I leaned against her, uncertain how close we had been for how long. I breathed deeply from my stomach and felt my shoulders relax.

"Um, thanks," I whispered finally. "Panic attack? That's what that was? I think ... I think then that I have panic attacks a lot. Is that ... I mean, are they, normal?"

I felt pathetic; how suddenly and earnestly I wanted help from this weird, intriguing woman in gauze and scarves and beads. But who else could give it?

"Hmmmmm. For you, it is absolutely expected and must be so normal," Dr. Baudelaire's tone softened. She cleared her throat and fidgeted with her bracelets. "I might offer here, I don't believe Yaël would have called upon me unless you really, truly needed me in some way."

"You're the first person to diagnose my panic attacks, so that's something," I mumbled.

Although, I really hadn't admitted those moments to anyone. Not to Malcolm, my mom, no one. Minus a few thousand internet searches, I didn't even know if they were true panic attacks.

"Really? Hmmmm. Oh, that's sad. I shall keep to myself my thoughts on some Western medicine practices. Medicate this, and overdose that! Hmmmm, that's the healthy way, is it?"

"Hold on. What were you saying about my sister?"

"Hmmmm. I sense perhaps now is not the time to be discussing … and, it really was just an errant thought. Yes, hmmmmm. Fleeting, at best."

"What did you see?" I asked slowly, feeling my pulse quicken.

"I'd like you to tell me," I said, inching closer. I had no endgame; I just knew this gauzy grandma with purple hair knew something about Philippa.

"Uncoil your bristled suspicions. Hmmmm, come. Have a seat," Dr. Baudelaire walked a few paces and sat down in a patch of sunshine, gesturing for me to join her. "Your shifting emotions, so erratic, hmmmm? Must be rather exhausting. Please, hmmmm, sit?"

I folded my arms and stared at her.

"Not until you tell me what I need to know. What about Philippa?"

"Hmmmm, this child is tormented, so true, so true. Incredulity, but more than that, hmmmm." Dr. Baudelaire cocked her head as she stared back. The breeze passed through her purple curls and drew her hair across her face. She remained unmoved. Overhead, a single seagull soared, then another, then a whole, frantic flock cawed past.

"Mind those hawks, hmmmm," she said and finally adjusted the hair from her face (which was driving me mad). "Caaaaawwwww!" A startling sound erupted from her previously whispering lips. "Anger. It's more than incredulity, it is anger and distrust and …hmmmmm," she looked even harder at me, "fear."

"I don't know what you're, um, rambling about," I said, trying to keep girded in stoicism. But I felt so uncertain under her steady gaze and even, breathy tone.

I shivered and found myself taking a step forward, then another. "Hey, what the – you're doing that! Stop doing that! I don't want to walk … I –"

Fighting against her was useless. I walked beside her, unwillingly, and then found myself next to her on the ground. I scowled. Gil fetched a thick grass from a nearby plant and pressed it to her lips, blowing hard. A terrific whistling sound came out. She smiled, pleased.

"Hmmmm. Such lovely little things I miss about this place."

"Yeah, like controlling people's minds?"

"I didn't control your mind, hmmmm."

"Um, I'm sitting here now. I was standing," I gestured behind me. "I didn't do that."

"Hmmmm. Of course you did. I connected with a thought, small but still powerful, and greeted it. Hmmmm, the thought of sitting down next to me was all yours; I simply spoke to that thought."

My skin felt prickly; my heart pounded. My own thoughts betraying me, exploited!

"Whatever. You got me here. Now tell me whatever you saw or sensed or know about Philippa. And who – or why – you are here, for that matter," I snapped. "Please," I added quickly.

"Hmmmm. You know who I am. You know why I am. Hmmm …. You simply do not know what I am." She uncrossed her legs and turned to face me, blinking heavily. She offered her hand. "Here, hmmm."

I looked down at her shriveled palm. The undersides of her fingers were stained from years – centuries? – of wearing rings and secrets. I swallowed hard and laid by hand on hers.

A billion images flashed before me. My brain seemed good at that lately. Scenes swept by one after the other at a dizzying speed: Ms. Neally shelving books high up, Principal Fernhouser watering his dying plants with a hand on his hip, Libby guzzling Pellegrino, my mom pulling open desk drawers and thumbing, frowning, through pages of strange books, Philippa back in her hospital room – I gasped. Philippa!

I looked up at Dr. Baudelaire. Her eyes opened. She pulled her hand back from mine. Her mouth opened with her lips over her teeth in some garish smile.

"I'm seeing … I'm seeing the future? But –"

"No, hmmm," she cut me off. "Not the unique future. Hmmm. But your thoughts, your experiences, as you expect. This is what you see."

"Why? What good is that?"

"To understand the power of your thoughts, hmmm. This is what I do, yes. Hmmm. Your most powerful thoughts – your most fearful, your most hated, your most desired, your most joyful, hmmm. These impact, shape, create, hmmm, your reality."

"Bullshit," I spit, then reddened and looked at her. "Sorry, I, uh, that's just … a bit hard to swallow. You sound like some influencer talking about manifesting." I looked down. "No offense."

She frowned and tilted her head.

"You have no reason to carry this skepticism. Indeed, yours is a life that ought to have made you more open to the fantastic, to possibilities."

"Look, Gil. You're just talking about everybody's favorite buzzword. Manifesting. Anyone wants something, they just manifest it. And you're saying that's magic or something," I said, my voice somehow emboldened. I looked at her, level and unapologetic. "So, like, if I think hard enough about a million bucks, I can just, like, yeah, make that happen?"

"Hmmmm. Have you seen one million dollars?"

"Well, no, but –"

"So, no, hmmm. Your recall – your own experienced reality as you perceived it – shapes and creates your future. For those things we hold onto, we find comfort in their familiarity and seek to recreate them. Hmmm. Yes, as you do."

I blinked, dumbfounded, definitely no longer feeling emboldened.

"Yeah, just don't, like, don't really buy that. But I have heard my sister talking about something similar, maybe. For one of her dumb philosophy papers; this one guy, Jester or something, was big on that. So, it's a nice idea, but, whatever."

"*Gestalt*. Not a person but a German word meaning shape, hmmmmm. Also, a fascinating concept applied to your human psychology, hmmm, regarding the need to see shapes, patterns, that are not there. Hmmm, I believe this is what you are referencing?"

"Yeah, maybe. Whatever. You're just telling me things I already know but in a weird, useless way. No offense to Ms. Neally," I said as I got up. "but I don't know that this is going anywhere. So, I'll, um, just be going."

"Hmmm, you are wise, and I believe you do understand what I'm saying. You're not seeing anything absolute, only hints of what you fear to be true, hmmmm. Lean too far into that fear, hmmm, and it does manifest that way in your own reality."

I spun around and opened my mouth to respond. But nothing came out. I was irritated with myself over my lack of words. But I was more irritated over the fact that Dr. Gil Baudelaire in all her gauzy weirdness had captivated me, shook me. I shook my head hard and picked up my pace toward the street now.

"Oh, finished, hmmmm? I shall, hmmmm, count this as our first session!" Dr. Baudelaire called behind me. "A real success! Hmmm, well done! And Eve Gwendolyn Genevieve!" Her voice, though raised, remained eerily breathy and low somehow. "Mind your thoughts!"

I threw a hand up behind me in a half wave, not looking back. A dark voice boomed into my brain repeating the warning: MIND YOUR THOUGHTS.

I ran all the way home. In my school clothes, my backpack thumping against me in time. Like a nerd. I chuckled, amused that now I yearn for days when getting laughed at for running away from school was my main concern. Now, I'm trying to make sense of strange "helpers" popping up and spewing nonsense about the great, daunting power of thoughts. I snorted.

"So dumb," I muttered.

My brain hurt. I wanted tea and a blanket. In my bed.

My pace stayed quick. I think I was trying to outrun my thoughts.

26

ANIMUS NOCENDI

*T*hank you for joining me in another true-crime adventure. As always, a
*reminder that these episodes follow the real-life chapters of grisly stories
from our own backyards. Please like, share, and follow for all the latest updates
as this grim yarn unravels....*

"If you're going to listen to crap like that, could you at least take it off
speaker?" I said loudly.

"Hmm? Too much for you? I figured a murder podcast was totally your jam
these days," Libby giggled as she popped on headphones and tapped her phone
screen. "I guess I don't want to give you any tips for how to get away with it,"
she chuckled.

"Aaaaand that's enough for me," I said. "I'm going to pack up; see you in
Keller's class to get our project assignments."

"What?" Libby yelled.

"We're assigned that group project, remember?"

"Shhhh! You're making me miss the best part. They do, like, this *super* dramatic introduction of the new plot twists. Oh my god. You *have* to listen. You'd
love it."

I rolled my eyes and grabbed my bag. I had entered some sort of new territory
with my age-old nemesis. Something bordering a friendship, I think. But, ugh,

she was so pretty. I rotated between a quickened heartrate when she was kind or a quickened heartrate when she was horrid. The heart's distinction between excitement and fear was really up for the brain to decide. And my brain was perpetually tired, so I toed the line between love and hate with her, and hoped to balance on a line of amicable acquaintanceship.

"See ya, dragongirl! Sorry, I mean murdergirl; sorry, I mean Eve," she yelled too loudly behind me, giggling to herself.

I exited the library with nowhere to go. I just knew the combination of Libby and true-crime podcasts were not what I needed, let alone what I could tolerate. I started toward my favorite restrooms upstairs, hoping they'd be empty for a few minutes of quiet before the bell rang again.

"Hey! Oh my gosh, it's you! Guy and I were just talking about you!"

I spun around. Channing appeared at the top of the stairs just as I alighted. I turned back, ignoring her. "Hey, hey, don't be like that, girlfriend. But I get it," she said coolly as she caught up to me. Coolly enough to distract me from the ick of being referred to as "girlfriend."

"Sorry, I, er, uh, was going the wrong way."

"Well, now you're going the right way! Speaking of rights, what was it like to have your rights read to you? Was it wild? Just wondering. Just curious," she said as she shrugged and smiled sweetly.

"My rights? Um, geez, I don't even know. Wild, I guess. Upsetting. Surreal," I paused; I'd never given it much thought. That bit had just been one of many bits that comprised the whole unbelievable, awful situation. I half-smiled, considering it for the first time. "Honestly, they said they were telling me my rights, but I have no idea what any of those rights are. Still. Something about a fair trial and an attorney, I guess, but I think I already knew that part from, like, movies and stuff."

"Uh-huh. Interesting," Channing said as she tilted her head and looked up. "Would you say, maybe, your rights weren't explained to you?"

"Explained?" I asked, chuckling as I recalled Detectives Jasper and Serrano bumbling around their squad car and the investigation room. "Hardly. But, uh, again, I really wasn't in a super-focused state, you know? Like I said, surreal. It was all just … surreal."

Channing held her phone up, nodding at me with the scrunched-up face you'd see an interviewer on a news show using to feign concern and sympathy.

"Um, yeah. Anyway, why do you ask?" I asked as overwhelming suspicion set in. It made me sweat.

The bell chimed. Halls above and below the staircase where we stood filled with students hustling from one room to the next.

"Great talk, so good to catch up!" Channing said as she quickly tucked her phone into the pocket of her pink blazer (who wears a blazer? Let a long a pink one?) and floated down the stairs. She turned and flashed a smile, "Ciao!"

"Oh, you're done? Uh, okay, bye," I said as I marched up the stairs, not toward my bathroom but to my next class. "Popular people are weird."

"I absolutely agree!" Elke said as she came up behind me. She pulled hunks off a giant croissant. "Would you like a bite?"

I shook my head, even though my stomach growled to the contrary. My weakness for all-things- bread was still very much intact, despite my constant nausea from what an internet search suggested were stress-induced ulcers.

"You left before we could talk further last time," Elke said, lengthening her stride to keep up with my speed-walking short legs. "I still want to show you something, something that I think you need to know about. I do not know if it is helpful to you."

"Look," I said as I stopped abruptly and faced her, "I think you're cool, and I've never had a German friend, and I think we'll do great in math. But whatever you need to show me, trust me; I've seen it, or heard it, or, whatever. I just thought you'd be different, not so into all that stuff. Although, I mean, I get it."

"Wait! Do you know about the other boy, then? The German one?" she called after me as I hurried off.

I stopped cold.

What other boy?

I spun around. Elke jogged toward me, panting a bit.

"You walk very quick. Or is it quickly? Quickly, yes. So then, yes, the boy. The German one, from Freiburg. You know of him?"

The bell chimed.

"Why would I know of him?"

"Because he, eh, he looks like ... here, see for yourself."

Elke scrolled through her phone for a moment, then held it up to me. It was a news article, I gathered, with a photo of someone who looked exactly like ... I pinched my thumb and forefinger together on the screen to enlarge the image under the German text.

"Holy shit," I whispered.

"I thought you would like to see it," Elke said. "Shall I translate it for you? The headline, anyway, it says 'Boy Collapses Unexpectedly, Medical Officials' – what would that word be in English? *Verwirrt*, hmm. Ah! Stumped! – 'Medical Officials Stumped.' And that photo looks like the boy in the memorial posters I have seen around. This is the same boy, yes? The one they say you, eh, eh ... you know."

I stared at the photo. My heart pounded so intensely I was certain you could see it beat through my sweater.

Pictured in grainy color was a kid with black hair wearing a red pullover lying on a stretcher in what looked to be a school classroom.

I was quiet for a long time, awaiting some – any – coherent thought. None came. Only a question.

"Is that Jonah?"

27

ANIMA MUNDI

Uncle Seb was silent. Ms. Neally was silent. Dragon opened his mouth then closed it several times. Kip took out a yo-yo. We sat at a table outside the hangar, my phone sitting face-up in the middle of us. The article Elke had shown me, the one in German, illuminated the screen.

"It's him, right?" I said.

"Well, not exactly," Ms. Neally started.

"It's a rather complex issues, Evechild, one we were perhaps naïve to imagine hadn't reached this depth," Dragon added.

"I've mastered walking the dog with my yo-yo, yep!" Kip said.

"This the only one?" Uncle Seb asked.

"The only article? Or the only boy? How should I know? My freaking classmate showed me this," I said.

A mid-September breeze made the weathervane atop the hanger creak. We all jumped.

"Prepare, yep, for around the world, yep!" Kip said and stood proudly with his yo-yo.

It whipped around his head and landed expertly between the string he held taut with his other hand. Uncle Seb coughed. Dragon yawned. Ms. Neally stretched. I just stared at the phone.

"Tough crowd, yep," Kip said dejectedly and sat back down.

"What does this mean? Who the hell is this? It can't be him, can it? Right? Soooo … what does this mean?" I asked again.

"It means your clone lord pal was a little busier in the Seventh than we thought," Uncle Seb said finally.

"Really, Sebastian, that sounds so crass," Ms. Neally spoke finally. "But your uncle is correct; I assume the same. Jonah, whenever he was captured and enlisted to do Obrenox' bidding, had more replicas of himself released than we previously believed."

"I should have guessed. I am disappointed in myself, indeed," Dragon murmured.

"None of that, Drahk. That woulda-shoulda-coulda bullshit won't get us anywhere. Kip," Uncle Seb said.

"Yep! Another trick? I know just the one!"

"Nah, buddy. We need you to gather some intel. You fellas still comfortable with the phone and laptops I gave you?"

"The technological devices, yep!" Kip said, his yo-yo falling as he jumped up. He whimpered in surprise when it hit the ground.

"We'll get the Kips scouring all media outlets, all social platforms, for any similar phenomena," Uncle Seb said. "In the meantime, Egg, you've gotta keep that story under wraps."

"But … but it's a news article on the internet," I said slowly. "How exactly am I supposed to do that?"

"Have the investigators brought this to your attention, Evechild?"

I shook my head.

"Has your legal team uncovered it?" Ms. Neally asked.

I shrugged and looked at Kip, who was vigorously rubbing at a scuff on his yo-yo.

"I'll take that as a no," Uncle Seb said. "Drahk and I will work on destroying any other stories like this one."

"How –" I started.

"Don't worry about it, Egg."

They got up from the table and began walking together toward the hangar. Kip stashed his yo-yo in his pocket and sprinted after them.

"Um, guys? Really not feeling great about this … Could you, like, give me a little more info on, I don't know, what to freaking say to Elke when I see her at school again tomorrow?"

"Don't say anything," Uncle Seb called.

"We're in the same math class! And we're partners!" I yelled back.

The three of them leaned in and spoke quietly. Wild gestures ensued, and then Dragon looked up, smiled, and walked over to me.

"What can I help you better understand, Evechild?" he said with a gentleness that erred toward condescension.

I stared at him. I was uncertain which emotion to yield to. Rage, fear, overwhelm, hunger … Indignation won.

"Are you kidding me? I mean, are you seriously freaking kidding me? You must be kidding me."

"I assure you I rarely kid."

"This girl, a German exchange student, from out of nowhere, shows me on her phone a picture of someone who looks exactly like Jonah," I said, the words racing out of my mouth, "and I'm supposed to, what, just hope she's the only one who has seen it? Just, like, hope she's the only one who has realized *that* dead kid and *this* dead kid look exactly the same?"

I shuddered at my own words. I hated that I just spoke so callously of the deceased. Clone lord or not, the Jonah I knew had a family who loved him. I thought of Mrs. Nguyen, or her sad smile, of the photos of young Jonah that lined the walls of her home.

My head shot up.

"Hold on, how are these clone Jonahs getting around? The one here who I knew, the original, right? Well, that one had parents and stuff and could, like, just assume that life …. But what does a clone do?" I grabbed my phone again and pointed to the photo. "This kid clearly had a life, see? That's a classroom."

Dragon stared at the photo, hard. His eyes widened with panic.

"Evechild, your schoolmate whom you received this information from, what did you refer to her as?"

"Uh, my math partner?"

"No, no; you used a specific title for someone schooling with you from another country."

"Oh! A foreign exchange student?"

"That's the one. Precisely. Now, listen to me, carefully: you must inquire of her parents, her family. You must see concrete proof she is who she says she is."

"But why? What does that have to do with – ohhhhh."

"Yes. It is the perfect guise, the ideal ruse. This Jonah, this clone, could insert himself into culture as a foreign exchange student in Freiburg."

Dragon was speaking quickly now, piecing together theories and fears at an alarming rate.

I was filled with dread. I couldn't go through another Jonah incident. I couldn't … A lump formed in my throat before I could finish that thought. Elke was so kind, so lovely. Maybe a little straightforward, but that was the German way, right?

"Where did you say this occurred? Freiburg, yes, this makes sense. The *Schwarzwald* would be a perfect portal location. I cannot believe I didn't think of this, didn't anticipate this," Dragon spoke in one long run-on sentence; each thought quickly cascaded into the next.

"The shvarts-what? Why does that make sense?"

Dragon stopped his monologuing and looked at me, surprised.

"The *Schwarzwald*, the Black Forest. In Baden-Württemberg. Why, because of the trees, of course. It's a prime spot."

"Yeah, I, uh, don't follow," I said, now only able to think of the black forest cake my mom made regularly for my sister's birthday.

Dragon sat back with a sigh and motioned for me to join him. Great, I thought, this is a whole thing now. And all I could think of was chocolately sponge drizzled with kirsch … I sighed.

"As I was saying," Dragon said impatiently. He must have sensed my daydreaming. I couldn't help it. I hoped he knew that. Dragon coughed and continued, "Humans regard science most peculiarly, and since the dawn of man – no, that's too much prologue. Shall we consider outer space, then? You look up, yes? Imagining that the stars and the planets – these ancient things twinkling in the sky – must hold your answers. And indeed, they do in many ways. But you overlook the ancient things within this very planet."

I stared at him blankly. He nodded expectantly at me, as if I were going to make whatever asinine connection he was getting at.

"What is ancient on this planet?" he said finally with a little nod, as though this hint would get me to wherever he was going.

"Uh, ancient things … Stonehenge? Lascaux?" I stammered.

"No, no. That is, why, yes, but what is *natural*and ancient?"

"Dragon, I, uh, love a good riddle and all, and normally I'd eat up these little nuggets from you," I said and fidgeted with my sleeve, "but I've got homework, and I want to see Phlee, and, it's just …."

"Trees and rocks," Dragon interjected. "Trees and rocks have always existed in some form on this planet. Well, almost always."

"Yeah, I want to follow you, I'm just not," I said apologetically.

Dragon picked up a rock. The parks, the grass, the trails, everything in the Northwest was invariably peppered by varying sizes of gray rocks – the same kind people pay gobs of money for at home improvement stores to fill their riverbeds or landscaping tableaus. I kicked another with my foot. They were so commonplace you don't even notice them.

"How old do you believe this to be?" Dragon asked as he held up a smooth, grayish, bean-shaped rock on his palm. I stared at it for a moment and shrugged.

"Rocks many miles under our feet can range in age from 50 million to perhaps 400 million years old! They are more commonly known as ..." he paused as though I could finish his sentence, "cratons!"

I looked at my dear friend and tutor, smiling expectantly with his arms and wings stretched out in a grand "tah-dah" pose. I yawned. My stomach growled.

"You're saying that rock in your hand is a billion years old?" I said flatly.

"I never said billion," he muttered. But he brightened and continued, undeterred by my waning interest. "This little fellow isn't that old, of course, but most of Oregon's rocks and minerals are basalt. Which, as you know, is incredibly hardy thanks to its largely magnetite composition—"

"Dragon. Please. You're losing me. What has this got to do with me and Jonah and Obrenox and all of that?"

Dragon frowned again and tossed the rock to the ground.

"The older you are, Evechild, the more you know, the more you've seen, yes?"
"Yeah, I guess so."

"Rocks are old. They've seen a lot, they know a lot," he said gently as he motioned to follow him back toward the hangar. "The ancient things growing here hold energy, hold strength through evolution and change that we have barely begun to understand. Something as powerful as an interdimensional portal would naturally be tethered by ancient strength, by atoms whose essence was created and evolved through the very properties of the universe that created wormholes and space-time wrinkles and supernovas and the whole lot of it."

"The trees hold the portals in place?"

"In a manner of speaking. Doesn't that make sense? And the great rocks ... Why, try asking someone in Sedona their age. They will invariably evade the question, for most are dimension jumpers. That whole town is one galactic enterprise."

"Sedona? I've been there!" I said, my attention now rapt in this new idea. I turned it over in my mind; new ideas tumbled about like rocks. "I ... I think I get it ... There were some pretty trippy things in Sedona. I went to this one store, and the owner, she was so cool. She taught me about all of these healing properties of—"

"Rocks and minerals?" Dragon finished with a wink.

"Rocks and minerals!" I echoed. "Yes! Oh my god. Now it seems so obvious. But why –"

"—are rocks not more commonly accepted for and known by their powers?" Dragon finished again.

"Something like that, but yeah," I responded.

"Because humans suck!" Uncle Seb called as he strode toward us.

"Ah, Sebastian. Yes, kindly weigh in ever so eloquently. Where has Yaél disappeared to?"

"She had to jet. And sorry, but that's an accurate summary. Anything that promotes the strength of the Earth is discarded as all hippy-dippy and Gayaist bullshit. It sucks. People suck," Uncle Seb said, spitting at the ground. "How we strayed so far from the basic elements and their energies, I'll never know."

I studied my uncle; I was unused to his being anything but obnoxiously calm and understated. But this, this topic, certainly struck a nerve.

"Probably enough for the day, Egg? Let's get you home. Your mom asked me to get you home and get you fed."

"Yeah, well, she asks for a lot of things," I said, suddenly bitter at the mention of my mom.

"What's that, Egg?"

"Nothing," I grumbled. "Wait, do you know—"

"Know what?" my uncle said as he sped up and held a middle finger out his window.

"Nothing," I muttered again and sighed.

A conversation about Chad would have to wait. I didn't know if my uncle would have any insight, anyway. He and my mom had drifted apart for some years, as I understood it.

I hadn't heard from this Chad fellow again. Just the one phone call. Who calls, drops a bomb like that, then freaks out and hangs up?

My brain, sluggish from processing all of this on top of everything else, turned back to rocks and trees. Slowly, little tidbits and factoids tumbled around and around in my brain like stones in the rock tumblers I watched at shops in Sedona.

28

COMMOTIO CORDIS

D ays tumbled into each other. Responsibilities and tasks clinked against themselves like those damn rocks I couldn't stop thinking about. I sat in the living room after school, spinning an old wooden globe that stood near the piano.

"How many portals are hiding on you," I murmured quietly as my finger glided along the equator. I held the tip of my forefinger just over the spinning surface, then dropped it hard. I peered down to see where it had stopped. Burma.

"Ma, how old is this globe?" I called with a chuckle. I wandered into the kitchen where I could hear her hard at work at … something.

"It's just so easy to not go outside," my mom murmured as she dried an already-dry pan over the sink. "Out there, in here, what's the difference. Would you like a sandwich? I have ham."

Her unblinking gaze remained fixed on the horizon as she turned the pan slowly in her hands, moving the orange dishtowel around and around its rim. I walked over and put my hand on the pan.

"Think this one's good, Ma," I said and gently removed pan and towel from her. "Would *you* like a ham sandwich?"

"*Jambon.* That's what it's called in French. It's so good with camembert. That's a difficult cheese to find in the states. I don't know why. It's just a variety of brie. But a little firmer because of the lower fat content."

"That's, um, that's great," I said.

She drifted away from the sink. I walked behind her and laid my hands lightly on her shoulders. I carefully directed her out of the kitchen and to her desk. She had moved it to the living room "for better light and vibes," although I rarely saw her working there. I moved aside some papers and books and opened her laptop.

"Here, you sit, get those work emails read, yeah? I'll get you that sando."

I headed back to the kitchen, shaking my head. Why did I have to be the rational, functioning one? I'm still the kid! I opened the refrigerator and stared at its odd mélange of offerings. Capers, chevre, poppyseed bagels, a bottle of Portland ketchup, an empty apple juice jug, some lettuce that had gone beyond wilting ... and the ham. None of these things go together.

I looked around the kitchen and spotted a mostly fresh baguette amongst the uncharacteristic mounds of dishes, papers, and laundry items forming little towns along the countertops. I frowned. My mom hated cluttered countertops almost as much as she hated piles. And yet, here we were.

"Maybe we go on a trip!" my mom called from the other room. "We've not been to the coast in forever!"

"Yeah, sure, sounds great," I called back halfheartedly. I sliced the baguette and placed a piece of ham on it. I grimaced. It was slimy. "Mom, I've got your —"

The bread and slimy meat dropped to the floor.

My mom lay slumped, face-down on her keyboard, row after row of b's tiling the screen. A limp hand hung at her side.

I think I tried to scream. A buzzing filled my head, a prolonged beep that drove into my skull. I heard nothing else beyond that.

I didn't hear Dragon crashing in.

I didn't hear Uncle Seb yelling through the phone (had I called him?).

I didn't hear the chair falling over as I pulled her out of it.

I didn't hear her labored breath as she lay on the floor.

I didn't hear her wheezing and gasping as blood splattered from her mouth. I only heard buzzing.

Buzzing. Buzz. buzz.

A commotion arose outside. Paramedics rushed in. One knocked over the vase of hydrangeas on the hall table. My mom will hate that. Those are her favorite flower.

"How long has she been like this?"

Buzz.

"What has she eaten or had to drink?"

Buzz.

Blue fingers snapped in front of my face. I blinked. A young woman in a navy jumpsuit was waving her blue latex-gloved hand in front of me.

"Yo, what has your mom been in contact with? Anything you can tell us is helpful."

Behind her, three similarly dressed saints kneeled over my mom, holding her wrist, shining a light in an eye held open, gently pressing two fingers along her stomach.

I blinked hard. The buzzing quieted. It was replaced by a roar of activity.

"What? Nothing. She hadn't eaten anything. I – I was making her a sandwich, and then ...." I trailed off as I spotted Uncle Seb frantically looking over her desk, checking its drawers, feeling underneath it. "I had just come home from school, and, um, she was just, like, staring."

"Staring?" the paramedic repeated.

"On three!" another shouted behind her. The band of blue jumpsuits kneeled in concert. "One- two-three-and up!" They lifted her expertly onto a stretcher. Two carried it out while a third held a breathing apparatus over her mouth and nose.

"Yeah, staring," was all I could say.

"Egg, you're with me. We'll follow you," Uncle Seb said to the paramedic still in front of me. She nodded and stood. I liked her thick boots. Was I still sitting?

Uncle Seb's arms were around me. "And here we go!" He heaved me upward, keeping his hands on my arms as I steadied myself.

"Did … did they get my mom?"

"Who, Egg? The paramedics? Yeah, they got her, she's breathing."

"No, no … the … whatever they're called … Obrenox's guys … did … did they get her?"

"Fortunately – not fortunately, that's weird thing to say – it does not look that way."

Dragon emerged from somewhere – I don't know where – and extended a talon. I didn't react.

"On our way then, Egg. Hop in," Uncle Seb said as he headed out the door.

I guess I hopped in. I guess we drove to the hospital, the lights of the ambulance up ahead a blur in the late afternoon sun. The siren's pitch matched the buzz still pinging around the walls of my skull.

I needed to visit Phlee anyway. A two-for-one. Howdya like that?

My head fell back against the leather bucket seat of the tiny MG. He had managed to replace his beloved right-hand drive automobile.

I smiled weakly. Then I vomited.

29

NOSCE TE IPSUM

I was really tired of being in hospitals.

A pit formed in my stomach. What an awful thing to say, as the only healthy one *not* currently admitted to a hospital.

"You ready to come in?"

I looked up. A nice man in a blazer smiled and waved me over.

"She's okay? I can see her now?"

"Oh," the man said and shifted uncomfortably, "I'm not sure. Here, have a seat and fill these out to the best of your ability."

He gestured toward a chair and table in a small, drab room. I looked down.

"Insurance forms? I don't know any of this stuff," I protested and waved it away. "I'm a kid. Where's my mom? When I can I see her?"

"Hmm. That is a pickle. Is your father here, by chance?"

"I don't have a father," I glowered. Chad's voice pinged around my mind. "Any more questions for me? Where's a doctor?"

The man folded and unfolded his arms.

"Well, I'll just leave these with you, then," he said and practically shoved the paperwork into my arms. "A doctor should be along shortly."

I tossed the insurance forms in a trash bin and sat back down. The waiting room was crowded. The first one we had entered, the one for the emergency

184

room, was even more packed. I looked at the people around me; were all of them also waiting for someone in surgery?

"What's the scoop, Egg? Here, some sugar. Take anything you want," Uncle Seb said suddenly and dropped a handful of candy bars on the seat next to me.

"Where have you been? Have you seen her? I hate this place," I said. I pulled my knees into my chest and rested my chin on them. I felt more overwhelmed than I had in a long time.

And that was saying something.

"Look, it's not … what you feared it was," Uncle Seb said in a low whisper. He crouched down next to me. "It was something with her heart, but she's good now. They're patching her up."

"Her heart?!"

"Of all the organs, it's the one with the highest rate of success in surgery. Just read that somewhere," he said as he moved over to a chair, opened a package of M&Ms, and poured it into his mouth.

"What the hell is wrong with you," I growled and swatted away his offering of more candy.

"Ms. Archer?"

My head jerked up. A lean man with tattoos peeking out from his navy scrubs held a clipboard in one hand. He held the other hand up to his mouth as he yawned.

"Yeah, here," I said as I scurried over to him.

"Sorry about that, long day. Anyhow, I'm Dr. Alkowitz. You are …?"

"Her daughter," I said quickly.

"And her brother, hi, Sebastian Barras," Uncle Seb said over me as he stuck his palm out to the doctor.

Dr. Alkowitz nodded at us both, ignoring Uncle Seb's handshake.

"The percutaneous coronary intervention was successful," he said as he scribbled more on his clipboard. He looked up at our confused faces. "That is, the stenting was successful." He looked up at us again. "Her heart is pumping and healthy again," he said at last with an air of annoyance.

"Her heart?" I choked, still dazed to even be there.

"Yes. Very curious for someone as relatively young and healthy as she to sustain a heart attack of this magnitude. But she performed beautifully. Some nitrates and aspirin should be all she needs, going forward."

"Her heart?" I repeated.

"She's in recovery now."

"Her heart?"

"Yes," he said impatiently. "This is Glenn. He'll take you back. I'll be by to check on her again in, let's see, approximately 42 minutes."

With that, Dr. Alkowitz handed his clipboard off to a nice-looking nurse named Glenn and was gone.

"Come here often?" Glenn chuckled as he led us down a maze of hallways.

I hated Glenn.

We entered a dimly lit room, my uncle and me. Glenn waited respectfully behind us. Maybe he was alright. I had gone in and out of hospital rooms who knows how many times, but there's something about walking over that threshold that changes you a little bit each time. Maybe you age, maybe you weaken. Hard things are meant to make you stronger; whatever strength might be mine was elusive.

"Christ, sis," Uncle Seb murmured under his breath.

"You're here," my mom said with a feeble smile and a labored attempt to sit more upright. The action made her monitors hasten their beep.

"Of course we're here," I said as I forced a smile. "How are you feeling?"

"Like a giant loser," my mom chuckled. "My own body let me down. After I've been so nice to it, trying to take care of it and whatnot."

She said it with a little light-hearted laugh, but I knew her heart failing her was deeply upsetting to her. For all her odd habits and peccadillos, her need for control always manifested in one area: physical fitness. The more out of control life got, the more toned my mom got.

The silver lining was that she cared. There was a time not that long ago when she had shrugged off running, shrugged off nourishment. That had really worried me. Now I had a new thing to worry about: her heart.

I leaned down and hugged her lightly. She smelled different. Not bad, just not like *her*. I didn't like it.

"So, your ticker's busted, eh?" Uncle Seb said, looking over the monitors and tubes and wires standing guard over her.

"Ssshhh! You're not the only sick old bag in here!" a voice from the other side of the curtained partition barked suddenly.

We three were silent for a moment, then burst into giggles.

That felt nice.

Uncle Seb started in on tales of replacing his beloved MG, how he had dealt with crazy car collectors until he found just the right one, how he had worked on this new model to get in what he deemed perfect shape.

I sat at the foot of my mom's bed, smiling throughout but paying attention to nothing. There was only thing I wanted to ask: how bad is it? My uncle's special brand of denial-soaked rambling and my mom's perpetually bewildered face made me keep that question to myself.

Dr. Alkowitz sauntered in. He elbowed past Glenn who still lingered in the doorway.

"Excuse me, Glenn, if you would. Great news, Mrs. Archer. There is absolutely zero reason to believe you will undergo such an event like this again any time soon."

"Its Ms. And, uh, I was a wee bit groggy when you were explaining things earlier ... why was I here, exactly?"

"You suffered a myocardial infarction," he said. "Glenn, what's the coffee like on this floor?"

"Which is--?" my mom said quietly and looked down guiltily.

"The coffee maker at the nurse's station is broken," Glenn replied quickly.

"Not now, Glenn. A heart attack. A mild one, anyway. An episode, really. Owing to your abnormal blood apolipoprotein levels and hypertension."

"Sure, *that*," I said with a scowl.

"Her lipid profiles were off and her blood pressure too high," Dr. Alkowitz said as he looked at me, a bit annoyed. He then turned to my mom, "Are you stressed?"

Uncle Seb let out a snort. I sneered. My mom's eyes watered.

"But how would I have known my pol… polipo… whatever levels were off? My chest didn't hurt! I don't smoke, I'm not obese," my mom whimpered.

"Only about half of women with an MI present with chest pain," Glenn chimed in suddenly, all too happy to have something to offer. "Fun fact, women are more likely to present with atypical symptoms. Your classics, like shortness of breath, fatigue, inability to stay asleep, back pain, chest pain, nausea, vomiting."

"Classic you," I said dryly and looked at my mom. She attempted a smile, but still looked down. "Ma, I don't think you could have prevented this, is what I'm gathering."

She still looked deeply ashamed. I stared at Glenn, at Dr. Alkowitz for some sort of validation. The doctor continued to flip through his clipboard. The light from the hall made his bald head gleam. Glenn hummed as he checked tubes around my mom.

"I've written you several prescriptions for nitrates and beta-blockers," Dr. Alkowitz said. He finally looked up. "Try to control that stress. Save that, there's really no reason I should ever see you again. Glenn here will give you some discharge instructions."

"Discharge?" I blurted. "Weren't you just operating on her heart?!"

Dr. Alkowitz stared at me blankly. Glenn stood just behind him and shook his head nervously at me.

"Why, no. I performed a semi-invasive non-surgical procedure, in which, I – damn. I must be going; duty calls. Glenn, would you, just – yes, you got it. So long, Archers. I wish you good health."

As Glenn puttered about and finally strode out of the room, I found I missed Jürgen. I wondered if he was working that night. I wondered if my mom would be upset if I went to the other building to visit Philippa.

As if reading my mind, my mom suddenly burst into tears.

"Oh, Eve!" she sobbed. "Here you are, your mother in one hospital room and your sister in another! It's just awful. It's just awful! I'm so sorry!"

She wailed inconsolably. I understood, I think. She so rarely expressed emotions to me anymore; everything she must have already been feeling combined with the exhaustion of a … a … I couldn't even say the words to myself. That old familiar lump rose in my throat.

"Ma, Mom, don't put anything on yourself. Just, um, focus on, like, getting better. I'm good. Promise," I said.

While I was talking to her, I noticed Uncle Seb slyly hitting the button on the side of the bed. Another dose of something swam swiftly through her IV. Her eyes blinked heavily.

"Mmmm, that feels wavy all over me," she murmured with a smile.

Uncle Seb nodded his head toward the door and pulled up a chair next to her bed.

"You go check on your sis, and I'll hang out here with my sis."

I felt I should I hug him.

But I didn't.

I wound my way through the maze of hospital departments and, a few wrong elevators later, found myself in my sister's hospital room.

Its familiarity and solitude were comforting.

"Hey, Phlee," I started as I paced around, "soooo, crazy life update. Mom's actually here, too! But not like, *here*, in this room. She's here, getting worked on, just like you. Well," I glanced at my sister's sleeping face, "not like *you*. Our mom, well, can you believe it? She's, like, so freaking healthy or whatever, and her heart, it just like … it, um, you know … ugh, why can't I say it? I think you get it." I stopped to wipe my eyes. "She's fine. She'll be fine. This is fine."

I collapsed into the blue vinyl armchair across from the bed, shifted uncomfortably, and got up. I moved to the recliner by the window. I pulled the lever on the side – not falling this time – and stretched out. The horizon was dark between the twinkling stars appearing above and the city lights scattered below.

"Phlee, you're really not missing anything out there," I murmured and yawned. "It's just bullshit. Chaos and bullshit. There are some good bits, I guess, but …you're not missing out."

I dozed off in that recliner against the large, metal-rimmed window. My sister's breathing apparatus was soothing white noise to me these days. But something tinny and high roused me momentarily, a small clinking. I turned my head lazily toward my sister. All was still. I wondered briefly if our dreams could merge. My eyes dropped and I feel deeply, deeply asleep.

30

PIA MATER

A chewing sound, no, a chattering, high-pitched and convoluted, wound its way into my consciousness. A tick, a chirp, something foreign that seemed far away. No, it was close. It was – my eyes shot open. In this room?!

I jerked awake, surprising the tiny recliner into its upright position. I toppled forward. From my hands and knees on the ground, groggy but panicked, I looked up and gasped.

"Get off her! What are you doing?!"

I lunged to Philippa's bed where a dwarfish form with dark purple hair and a snarling smile crouched over her. A sickening grin accented by yellow eyes glanced my way, as a gnarled finger pressed a purple stone against my sister's forehead. I watched the grotesque nail, long and pointed, slowly pull away. A thin trail of red followed it. Blood dripped along Philippa's brow line.

I grabbed something metal from the table closest to me and launched it at the creature. An aluminum tray struck it in the back of the head. It tumbled backward off the bed and hissed, then darted out of the room before I could get much closer.

"Phlee! Are you – aaaah! Ouch!" I cried as I pulled the tiny stone from her head. It was white hot. I yelped in pain and sent the stone flying. The singe on my finger was familiar. Fully alert, heart racing, I took stock of the place. Nothing disturbed, save a dented tray on the floor. Nothing abnormal, save a glittering gem by the door jam.

Oh. And my sister. A tiny stream of red ran along her still face.

Thinking fast, I grabbed a mound of gauze from the cabinet above the small sink near the door. I carefully dabbed her forehead and pressed the gauze lightly on her wound. I used another mound to swipe up the purple stone, and, still feeling its burn through the gauze, dropped it in a biowaste bag. I rolled the bag several times on itself and dropped that in another bag. I stashed it in the opposite corner by the curtain I use as my secret *Fortis Librae* entrance.

I moved quickly back to my sister. The chirping of her vitals, going crazy just minutes ago, had slowed and leveled.

"What has happened? Did you notice anything?" Jürgen said, suddenly at the door, breathless. He removed his stethoscope and pressed it along Philippa's breastbone. He frowned and examined the monitors.

"I, uh, was just giving her face a little wash," I said as my shaky hand pressed a wet washcloth to her forehead. Had he seen the blood?

"You see this? Here. Just minutes ago there was a flutter of cardiac and cognitive activity," he said as he pointed to the various screens. "You did not hear the change in beeping? I heard these monitors freaking out from halfway down the hall."

"Oh, I, um, probably didn't hear it because," I stammered as I glanced around the room. My eyes landed on the recliner, "because ... Ah! I had fallen asleep. That's right. Yeah, it must have been the beeping that woke me up. But by the time I, um, came over, it had, like, stopped. So, I grabbed this washcloth, and yeah." I trailed off as I studied Jürgen's concerned face.

"Hmm. This is odd, though. I will call the doctor."

Before I could protest, he was out the door. I peered down the hall after him. I surveyed the floor, the elevator bay, the nurses' station. All hummed on as monotonously as ever. No sign of a rogue evil elf.

Was that a relief?

I perched atop the bed next to Philippa. A small welt grew dark where the stone had been. A few more drops of blood pricked the surface. I pressed the washcloth gently to her forehead once more. I closed my eyes tight and yelled into my brain with the hope Dragon would somehow hear me and make everything better.

Back at the recliner, my phone buzzed. I had dropped it in the all the commotion, I guess. Each buzz sent it spinning, vibrating on the tile floor. Buzz, stop, buzz, stop; it made its way under the recliner and out of reach.

"Goddammit," I sighed as I slid off the bed and over to the recliner. I shouldered into the chair. It did not budge. The phone started buzzing again. "I *know*! I'm trying!" I cried as I heaved my body against the cold vinyl again.

"You need help?"

I looked up. Jürgen had returned with a doctor, who was already studying the monitors and printouts.

"I, um, dropped my phone under it," I mumbled.

"What's this on her forehead? What has happened here?" the doctor demanded.

I left Jürgen and bolted over to Philippa. The doctor held the washcloth in one hand as she peered closely at the small, circular welt. The bleeding had stopped.

"Thank goodness," I murmured.

"What was that? Did you say something?" the doctor looked up at me. "This hasn't been here. Where did this come from? Odd for our coma patients to get surface injuries. It's not like she's picking up a quick rugby match."

I scowled at her, uncertain how to take her humor.

"Yes, that is strange," Jürgen said, suddenly next to me. He held my phone and wiped it with a sanitizing cloth. "Here you are."

"It was me," I said hastily. "Curling iron. It burned her forehead. Yeah, uh, curling iron burn. Clumsy me."

The doctor frowned.

"Her hair's not curly."

"I was straightening it."

"It's not very straight, either."

"I'll apply some arnica cream while you review the vitals I was telling you about," Jürgen said.

As they fussed over charts, I snuck into the corner to grab my book and the bag, then quietly turned out of the room and checked my phone. A few missed calls from Uncle Seb, accompanied by a bunch of messages from him inquiring of my whereabouts, hunger level, breakfast requests ... I smiled. That must mean everything is fine with my mom. I needed that good news. I scrolled down. A message from an unknown number caught my eye.

Hey, dragongirl! Jkjk. I think you need to see something. Don't let me forget to show you. Also I totes don't remember what I'm supposed to do for Kellers class pls help! Kthx

I frowned. How had Libby gotten my number? I turned back to Philippa's room, only to be shooed out by a growing number of medical folk milling about her bed. I didn't like that. I stashed my phone in my hoodie pocket and charged across the hospital campus toward my mom, toward Uncle Seb. Any other day, a random text from Libby would have totally piqued my interest.

But I had more pressing things occupying the space of unanswered questions in my brain: How had an Amythystic gotten into my sister's room? That's what that had to be, right? The purple stone, the yellow eyes. That little elf-like creature had to be one of those nasty buggers. I shuddered. Why was he there? What the hell was it trying to do with that stone?

"Whoa, hey! Hold up! You barreled right past me!" Uncle Seb cried and grabbed my arm.

I must have really looked frazzled. My uncle's whole countenance changed as I turned toward him. He put his hands on my shoulders and looked hard into my eyes.

"Egg. What's happened?"

**

Uncle Seb didn't say much. I followed him to his car, which he parked across two spots in the hospital parking garage. I was so shaken I didn't even give him crap for that.

"You're sure it was—"

"Uh-huh," I whispered.

"And it was on top of –"

"Uh-huh."

"And it was holding—"

"Yep."

"You're *sure*?"

I held the orange bag up for my uncle.

"Egg, what the hell is that? I don't want your biowaste."

"No, ugh. Here," I said as I unwrapped the bag within the bag and produced the tiny purple stone. It immediately singed my palm. I yelped, and the gem fell onto my uncle's leg.

"Jesus, put that away!" he cried as he swatted at the little stone as it singed his jeans. "Shit! The road!"

I stowed it back in its wrapping and tossed it behind me. Uncle Seb clenched his jaw as he muscled the vintage car back to the center of the lane.

We stayed silent again until we pulled up to a familiar coffee house, its inviting red porch illuminated with a CLOSED sign. Inside, I could see outlines of patrons. One, though, stuck out. A mighty set of wings and a long tail swished near the window.

I sighed with relief. Dragon will know what to do.

31

ACTA NON VERBA

There are different moments of bravery, different categories of control.

Usually, to be brave and in control, it's you who takes charge of the action. You've calculated the risks, you've presumed a series of steps, you've surmised an outcome, and you move ahead accordingly. You are initiator.

That's easy. Anyone can *do* something. Action doesn't mean bravery. And planning doesn't mean control.

The harder part of bravery, the bit about control no one glorifies, sits in the moments between the action. The waiting. The waiting! The control it takes to wait, the bravery you must contrive to trust in the waiting, it's enough to make someone go mad.

Be brave enough to wait. Be in control enough to trust patience.

That's what Dragon had left me with at the coffee house. Then he did the most infuriating thing.

He sent me home to go to sleep.

Armed with a little bag of dried herb sachets from Ms. Neally, I stomped into the kitchen late that night certain I would never sleep.

As the kettle warmed, I assembled my favorite mug on a plate with some stale animal crackers I found in the pantry from who knows when and selected a sachet from the paper bag. I took a whiff and immediately pulled away. *Whew!* A blast of orange, cardamom, anise, and a host of very strong, peppery smells

I couldn't place shot through my nose and hit me in the back of the throat. Coughing, I went for a glass of water and noticed a small paper rolled up in the bag.

"Probably just steeping instructions. Or maybe it tells me what weird herbs are in this tea," I mumbled to myself as I took sips of water between little coughs. On the paper, though, was a short message in Ms. Neally's handwriting.

Sweet, young Eve: Consider energy a finite thing. Where you expend it will hold it indefinitely, with no chance of returning it for greater tasks.

p.s. sip slowly

I frowned and tossed the paper back in the bag and grabbed the kettle before it could whistle. As the stream of hot water hit the sachet, aromatic steam swirled up to my face. I inhaled slowly, deeply.

I yawned and headed upstairs, hitting the lights on the way. I wasn't sure at what age a mom doesn't have to wait up for her kid or tuck them into bed anymore, but some nights I felt like I wasn't at that age yet.

I took a sip of tea and wished my mom cared enough to wait up for me that night.

Cinnamon accented with citrusy pepper lingered in my throat. I yawned and downed the whole cup before I got in bed.

"Gonna be a long night waiting," I said with a sigh as I adjusted my pillows and blankets around me. "Better get some books ready to pass the time – *yawn* – until Dragon gets back to me – *yawn* – oh man ... I'm so ... sleepy... after all."\
**

My eyes were suddenly open. No alarm, no gradual coming-to as I bargained with Time to let me stay in bed just a bit longer. I was awake. Just like that.

I sat upright and stretched, befuddled by my rested alertness, then reached for my phone. I stared at it, blinking.

"That can't be right," I murmured.

It was 7:12 a.m. One full day later.

I had slept an entire day. Yesterday and come and gone, and tomorrow arrived too soon.

"Ma?" I called as I wandered down the hall, slowly, like a guest in my own house. "You home?"

I reached the kitchen and found a note from her taped to a bag of black and white cookies from a deli downtown.

Quick getaway to the hotsprings. See you tomorrow after school. I love you!

I grunted and crumpled up the note. It lay next to a smaller bag, the one I had brought the tea leaves home in. I must have not even noticed it the other night.

I took out a cookie and chewed it thoughtfully. I could be mad at my mother. Or, I swallowed and grabbed another cookie, I could acknowledge that she needed to briefly escape to a healthy and healing spot and be proud of her for being brave enough to step away from everything here.

Nah.

I was mad at her.

But still in a fine mood. Strange.

I left for school early, made it there on time, and didn't feel like I might start crying once.

I guess sleeping well really is as useful as they say.

I smiled as I collected my notes and books and colored pens at the end of class. I had enjoyed it. The conversation around Kafka was focused and titillating, I hadn't done anything dumb, no one had looked askance at me or muttered something about me being a killer, and Mrs. Moriarty only smiled and gave me a faint nod as she dropped my graded essay on my desk. It had an A stamped on it.

I heaved on my backpack and headed out the door. I hated having lit arts at the end of the day. I realized now that I had really short-changed myself with all those absences early in the school term. I chuckled to myself; would I be feeling that way if I had algebra at the end and missed it a bunch?

My mind drifted to Elke. The one good thing about algebra. I mean, I guess algebra as a concept has provided loads of problem-solving over the years or whatever. But for me, it meant only one equation: me plus Elke.

I laughed out loud at my own dumb inner monologue. Where had *that* come from?

"Plotting for your next victim?" a kid bumped into my shoulder as I descended the staircase. I turned to look up – I don't know why; would it have mattered if I knew him? – and lost my footing. Down, down I went, surfing along the wide, stone steps before finally coming to a rest against a pillar at the landing.

A chorus of giggles and "oh-my-gods" pulled my attention up to my left where a group of super compassionate peers recorded this choice moment. They all stood in the same attitude: elbows slightly bent, phones upright in their paws, eyes down on their screens, smiles plastered on their faces. It was creepy.

I stared at them, then made like I was going to get up, all quick and threatening-like. They spooked and disbursed. I leaned against the pillar and sighed. Somewhere, a clip of me falling down the stairs was getting posted, liked, shared.

Do I laugh or cry?

So much for my pleasant mood. I wished I had Philippa with me. She'd make fun, sure, but her humor had this great slant that always lessened my humiliation somehow.

A lump rose in my throat. I coughed it away and swiped a rogue tear from the corner of my eye.

I reached for my backpack, about to pull out *Fortis Librae* to go visit my dear old sis, when a hand fell on my shoulder.

"Do you need help?" Elke said gently, looking down at me.

"No, no," I said and blushed. "Just, uh, having a quick stretch." I shot my leg out to the side to demonstrate and kicked Elke in the shin. "Oh! Damn! Sorry!"

"It is nothing, do not worry," she said and knelt next to me. "Here, I picked these up on the steps behind you."

"Oh. Crap. Geez, I mean, sorry, er, thank you," I stammered and swiped the notebooks from her. I shoved them into my bag next to *Fortis Librae*. They barely fit with that book's heft, but I just felt better knowing I had the option to get to Phlee anytime.

And I needed that.

"Here, I have an extra," Elke said as she offered me a crueler in a plastic bag.

I looked at her, confused. She smiled and shrugged.

"I have an uncle who always says, 'food fixes life.' I find this to be true. Good or bad, something can always be made better with food."

"I like that, and, uh, thanks," I said as I took the offering. I was trying to be cool, but this beautiful girl with her beautiful accent was not only being kind to me, she was offering me one of my all-time favorite foods ever.

I took a bite of the morsel, the brilliant achievement of light, airy dough fried to perfection with just a hint of glaze kissing its signature ridges … My eyes closed as I slowly chewed.

"You are really having a moment over there, yes?" Elke said with a little giggle. "I can leave you alone with your doughnut."

"This is no simple doughnut!" I cried.

I surprised her.

I surprised myself.

"Tell me more," Elke said and shifted her bag behind her to scoot closer to me.

"I thought you foreigners were supposed to be all refined or whatever. And you don't even know what a crueler is," I said with a tsk-tsk.

When she smiled, her whole face smiled. Her blue eyes and her round cheeks and her hard jawline, it all smiled.

Philippa would totally mock me for using a conversation about a doughnut as my big in, but so be it. I was warm all over.

And this girl was nice.

So nice.

32

CASTIGAT RIDENDO
MORES

We kept talking. The bell had rung, who knows how long ago. And she and I were just there, on the stairs, shoulder to shoulder, laughing and talking about nothing.

It was grand.

"You're going to think this hilarious. I mean, I hope you do," I said, trailing off, suddenly very aware how close her face was to mine.

"What is hilarious?"

"I, uh, would kind of, like, try to scribble down the German words you'd say so I could take them to this German guy to translate."

It sounded even dumber aloud than it did in my head. Elke didn't help. She burst out laughing.

"But you have translators on every device! Show me! I must see these phrases you scribbled."

My face fully red, I dug into my bag and retrieved a small notebook. I flipped past the pages of dragon doodles (old habit), past the unmarked to-do lists, to a page of "German" phrases. She peered at the paper, still smiling.

"Ah. I think what you were trying to write, here, is *vielen dank*. That means 'thank you very much.' And this, this must be *gern geshehen*, which is the same as 'you are welcome," Elke said and paused. "Wow, I am so polite."

We giggled, looking over my scrawled phonetics of her beautiful language.

"But ... what is this one? I cannot make out what this is supposed to be," she said with a frown.

I grabbed the notebook and snapped it shut.

"Nothing. That was nothing, just jibberish," I said quickly.

But the phrase that gave her pause was not nothing. I had written it the same day she had shown me the German news article on her phone. I shuddered, hating my increased knowledge of dimensions, of clones, of danger.

"Can we, uh, sit for a minute?" I said, sinking involuntarily toward the floor. "I'm not ... I'm not feeling so hot."

I leaned my head back. The books lining the shelves were uneven and had that old-book smell that I always wanted to love but never could. It made me queasier.

"Can I do something to help?" Elke had sat down next to me. Her hand was on my shoulder.

"No, sorry. Just ... no. But thanks," I said, closing my eyes and smiling. "It's fine. This is fine."

Elke chuckled and stretched her legs out. I hugged my knees closer to my chest.

"You were saying, there was someone you know to translate?"

"I was? Oh, right. Yeah," I said, coughing. "This nurse. At the hospital where my sister is."

"Jurgen?!" Elke squealed.

"Yes? You know him?"

"This is my uncle!"

"He is? What are the odds?" I said, my disbelief releasing me from nausea.

"I would say, pretty good," Elke laughed. "How many Germans do you know around here?"

I frowned. Our little hamlet on the West Coast was not especially diverse, but it was fairly international. There was even a German American school on the other side of the river. Was it so crazy that I didn't assume the only two Germans I knew were related?

"I am sorry," Elke said, still chuckling. "*Es tut mir leid*. It is wild to me that you know my uncle. He has never been to school functions. The encounter was not likely."

"Does your uncle go to your stuff usually? That's cool. Mine just kinda waltzes in and out of my life."

"You live with your uncle?" Elke said, brightening.

"No. He's just – I don't know – around a lot. It's complicated. Families are weird. Wait, do you? Live with your uncle, I mean. I thought you were a foreign exchange student. You live here?"

Elke's smile fell. She looked down, playing with a thread on the hem of her sweater.

"I live here for school terms with my uncle. On holiday I go back to Berlin with my father. It is," she paused and looked up, "complicated. Like you said."

"I, um, I'm sorry I never asked. I just assumed ...." I trailed off lamely.

"It's cool. *Alles klar*," she said, then giggled. "You know my uncle! As a nurse? That is wild. Even I have never seen him in his profession."

"Maybe you could come with me some time," I said, my face reddening as the words came unexpectedly tumbling out of my mouth.

"When you visit your sister? I do not want to be in the way," Elke said, clearly taken aback. She softened. Her hand gently brushed atop my knee. "But if it would be a comfort or a help, I will happily go. I will see Onkel Jurgen at work!"

She clapped her hands and stood up. She offered me a hand, which I sheepishly grabbed. Her grip was strong and warm. I liked it.

"You, um, like, you know, want to, um, get a coffee or something?" I sputtered finally.

Elke squeezed my hand in hers. Do I take that as a yes?

My face burning, I walked in sweaty silence with her through the school grounds, down the sidewalk, past the crosswalk where the obnoxious volunteer crossing guard always yells at me to pay attention, to the street that turns on to the main drag.

"I hear that place is good," she said, gesturing down the road where a familiar café sign blinked on the horizon.

I hadn't been there since that one night with Uncle Seb. The one where he had stormed off after trying to explain worm holes or some shit to me. I shivered, remembering meeting Jonah that night as I walked along the darkened streets, contemplating my place in the universe. I swallowed hard.

"Yeah, good pie there."

We continued in silence, my gait awkward and halted for fear of upsetting her hand in mine. This was a new sensation – in every way – and I didn't dare disrupt whatever thread of energy in the universe that had made this transpire. I liked it, my hand with hers. I liked it a lot.

"Two? For dinner?"

A chipper voice startled me. I jerked my head up. Elke laughed.

"I think we are only having coffee," she said quickly to the server who stood impatiently holding menus. "Can we sit over there?"

The server smiled curtly and nodded.

"I will never be used to restaurant servers here," Elke whispered as we slid into a booth against the window.

I shrugged. I didn't know how servers behaved in other parts of the world.

"Please excuse me," Elke said, getting up and nodding toward the restroom. "I will be right back."

I pulled my phone out and did a quick search for the differences in servers between here and Germany.

"Right," I said as Elke slid back onto the cracked red vinyl bench across from me. "In many parts of Europe, restaurant wait staff are salaried, so their response time is generally quite different from that of their counterparts in US eateries."

"What? Oh, right. Yes. Are you – wait," Elke said and leaned across the booth, "I see you! You are reading that off your phone?!"

My face turned red for the millionth time that day. Humiliated, I shoved my phone back into my coat pocket. Elke giggled and patted my hand.

"What'll ya'll have?"

A server in a red polo with a black apron appeared suddenly at our side. Grateful for the change in focus, I buried my head in one of the menus stacked on the table and gestured toward Elke.

"I'll take a cappuccino, please," Elke said.

I smiled behind the menu. I liked how she ordered.

"I'll need to see some I.D. if that's what you're ordering from," the server said.

I looked up, confused. The server glared at me. His nametag, which had Jeremy scrawled on it, was upside down.

"I, uh, just want some tea," I said. "I can't find it on here."

"That's the bar menu. All alcohol," Jeremy said flatly. "So, tea. Iced or hot?"

"Sure," I said.

Elke smiled. Jeremy rolled his eyes, swiped our menus, and exited in a huff.

I looked out the window, uncertain what to do now. Did this count as a date? Was I on a date? I wished I could text Philippa right now. But she wouldn't know any better than I – her dating record was as nonexistent as mine.

"Alright, one cappuccino, and one," Jeremy said and paused as he set down a small tea pot and a cup in front of me, "tea."

Before I could ask for anything else, he was gone. I poured some tea into the small cup and took a sip. It burned my tongue. I should have just stuck with pie.

"So, you live here," I said finally. "But not in the summers?"

"Yes, that is correct. My papa, back in München, he is not so good since my *mutch* died. So, I live much of the time with Onkel Jërgen. It is better this way," Elke said. She swirled her spoon in her cappuccino, not looking up. "It is a lot of responsibility for just a father," she added quietly. I got the feeling she was reciting that last part, trying to believe it herself.

"Geez, I'm so sorry. I – I had no idea," I said.

"Why would you know? Why do you apologize?" she said quickly, her eyes narrowing.

"I just meant, shit, I don't know. That must be hard, is all I'm saying. And I am sorry, that, like, you have to go through that. Or ... yeah."

Elke looked at me. Her face was expressionless. It was remarkable.

"So, I do holiday in München," she said coolly.

"Mewn-chin?" I repeated.

"Oh, sorry," she laughed. "I should pronounce it 'Munich' like you do here," she said, enunciating the name dramatically. "This is how I know about the other boy. The one who is like the one in ... in ... I am uncertain what to call it, exactly."

I stood up quickly. My tea spilled.

"Shit. Sorry," I said as I shakily wiped up my spill.

"It is no problem; let me help. Sit, this is not a big deal," Elke said gently.

"Yeah, I, uh, just remembered I have to go," I stammered as I zipped up my hoodie. "I, um, shit! I don't have any cash. I'll get you next time. My treat, I swear. Try the pie though! Um, bye. And thanks."

Elke frowned. How I wanted to stay! But her mention of the other boy, well, that sent alarms going off in my head. They blared and demanded attention. But I stopped, paused, and turned around.

"Look, that thing ... that boy you're talking about ... it was, like, discredited, or whatever. Nothing to it. So, um," I paused, hating myself for what I was about to say. "Don't, like, talk about it here because, uh, you'll come across as real ignorant. And offensive. So ... yeah. Ok. Bye."

I did all but sprint out of there.

Once I was around the corner, I paused just long enough to check my phone. My pulse raced. How much did she know? What, exactly, had that German news article revealed?

I opened my messages and scrolled until I found Uncle Seb.

Pick me up? I typed.

Now? Where? he typed back. I frowned. His responses were never immediate.

I shared my location with him and checked to make sure Elke wasn't in sight. My head spun. My heart pounded. For so many reasons.

A shiny black MG pulled up to the curb within minutes.

"That was so fast!" I exclaimed as I slid in, but not before I walked to the wrong side of the car. The right-hand drive got me every time. "Where were you?"

"Waiting for you, believe it or not," Uncle Seb as he hit the gas and peeled out away from the sidewalk. "We've gotta talk."

That should have been a warning, too, that phrase. But I was still stuck between the light airy cloud of spending all day with Elke and the dark, thundering raincloud of suspecting Elke to be in cahoots with the Obrenox posse. At the very least, she was aware of multiple Jonahs and a weird yellow stone.

There was some intense weather happening in my brain.

Uncle Seb pulled the car over and turned the engine off. I didn't recognize the street, a one-way road lined with creepy, empty buildings made creepier by growing evening shadows.

"We've been talking, the guys and me," Uncle Seb started. I smiled, thinking about how "the guys" in this machismo scenario were an injured elf and an ancient dragon. "And we think we have a working idea of why that bugger was in your sister's room. And, I know what you're thinking, it was to get *Fortis Librae*. Well, no, it wasn't. Not this time anyway. Something more –"

"The book!" I gasped.

I forgot my backpack at the café with Elke! I looked back. We hadn't gone far; I could see the café sign still illuminated in the distance.

"Sorry, Uncle Seb, I've gotta go. Can you, like, turn around?"

"No, in fact, I cannot turn around. Are you even listening to me? This shit's important!"

I groaned, fiddling with the weird foreign lock and handle, and pushed against the door.

"Hey! Stop that! Good lord, you're stubborn," Uncle Seb said as he hit the brakes. "Let me turnabout, wouldya?"

But I had already burst out of the car and was running back.

I didn't have to go far. Elke came up the street toward me. She held a very large, very distinct book in her arms.

"Oh! Hey! Yeah, thanks, I, um, left all my stuff," I said as I pulled the book from her arms. "I'll just take that guy, thanks again. Sorry I left in such a hurry. Um, yeah. Really. Sorry."

"I could not close your bag entirely with this large book inside of it," Elke said as she handed my backpack to me. "I hope you do not mind that I took it out."

I gave her a thumbs-up (really? a thumbs-up?) and turned to go back to Uncle Seb's car, which was already approaching.

"It's a beautiful book!" she called after me. "I can't wait to see what sketches you put in it!"

I closed my eyes and exhaled. That meant all she saw were blank pages.

I opened the car door to be greeted by Uncle Seb's yelling, and another man's voice yelling back. I giggled as I buckled my seatbelt. Two grown men arguing –haggling – over the phone about some plane part was a nice distraction.

Plus it kept my uncle occupied the entire ride home and unable to talk to me about serious things anymore.

I was so tired of serious things.

33

VOX POPULI

I woke up that morning still dazed from the events of the week but strangely rested, thanks to another, albeit much smaller, cup of Ms. Neally's tea.

I kind of felt like I could even handle the day.

Other days, my eyes would open in the morning and before I could even register the day or time, my brain would flood my roused consciousness with fear, pain, panic, and ultimately hopelessness.

It made for a rough start.

But there had been a handful of mornings now – tea or no tea – where my eyes opened to a quieter mind and a gentler psyche. All the scary stuff was still very much there – often shaken up with a dash of self-loathing – but something had shifted. The pointy parts of fear had dulled a bit; the panic became less sticky; the hopelessness eased its white-knuckled grasp.

Maybe I was just getting used to all of it. Novelty has a way of exaggerating things, after all. And these anxiety-promoting feelings of mine, these companions, grew commonplace and less harrowing.

School was less scary. So there was that.

I stretched out on the floor outside my lit arts class, closed my eyes, and sat in my thoughts for a minute. Could the brain work that way, conditioning itself to bad things? If you were constantly consumed by stress, is there a tipping point at which your spindle neurons just shrug and go back to sleep rather than freaking out in fight-or-flight arguments? Something akin to the brain saying, "same crap, different day."

I suppose I wondered because the alternative that could be happening – apathy and ambivalence – seemed far more problematic.

There's a fine line between getting used to something and just not caring about it anymore. It was a line I walked so regularly I couldn't always tell which side was pulling me and which was balancing me.

I hugged my knees into my chest and stared at the posters lining the walls announcing dances and spirit assemblies and clubs. I wasn't getting used to all those debilitating feelings; I was becoming ambivalent toward them. I sighed.

"Whatever gets me through the day, I guess," I muttered to myself. "Better here than in bed, right?"

I pulled my lit textbook out to finally attempt the assigned reading when a screechy voice from down the hall startled me.

"There you are! Ugh, I have been, like, looking everywhere, literally everywhere, for you," Libby yelled, panting.

"I am in the most visible place possible," I snorted, waving my arm around the empty landing that opened to the floor below. "You can see me from both floors."

"Never *mind*," Libby said, making 'mind' into two syllables with an impertinent hard "duh" sound coming off the end. "I totally texted you, like, two days ago. You, like, must hear this. Oh my god, you don't even know. Just, shut up, I'm finding it, k, listen."

I had said nothing, but I smiled a bit at Libby's focus and enthusiasm. She kneeled next to me; her brow furrowed as she concentrated on something on her phone.

"K. Ready. Here, just listen," she said.

"Ugh, Libby," I said, looking down at what was playing on the phone. "You know I hate true crime stuff. These podcasts are, um, not really my thing."

"Just. Listen," she said, enunciating the words forcefully as she shoved the phone back in front of me.

Our story today comes to you unlike any other we've previously delved into, for a lot of reasons.

I looked at Libby. The voice was familiar. I looked down at the phone. "OreGone: Murder in Oregon" scrolled across the screen. I had never heard of it.

But the main reason this unfolding tale is so frightfully compelling is because we're talking about a minor. Yes, that's right, a teenage perpetrator this time, walking free, maybe even roaming the halls of a school you or your kid goes to ....

I looked up at Libby. My heart pounded.

"Is that—" I started.

"Channing," Libby finished. "It's so utterly messed up. Like, parading as your friend like that."

"That's not the part I care about," I whispered, feeling clammy and flushed.

...Because this is an ongoing investigation, and there are teens involved – whoops, I mean, minors involved, don't want to give too much away – we're super-not at liberty to disclose any names. So, we'll refer to our victim as Noah, found in a pool of his own blood on his home's front porch one fateful night last Spring ...

"Just turn it off," I barked. "Turn it off!"

"There are two parts. The first one came out the other day, which, is why I totally texted you, even though you *super* ignored me, and the second part—"

"Came out today?" I finished. Libby nodded and flipped her hair.

"What should we do?"

"We? *We* don't do anything. It's just some dumbass podcast made by dumbasses listened to by dumbasses," I said as I got up and gathered my books. "The bell's gonna ring. I've gotta go."

Libby's head dropped. She stayed seated on the ground, her phone still in her hand with the screen brightly showing "OreGone." The cleverness of the name irritated me even more.

"Yeah, well, I might be a dumbass, but, but," Libby trailed off.

"But what? You wanted to taunt me some more with this garbage? This is too much, even for you."

"I, like, wanted to help you," she said quietly.

"Right," I snapped. "Because you're such the helpful type. Always have been."

I let the door shut loudly behind me. Mrs. Moriarty looked up from her desk, startled.

"Ah, Ms. Archer! From total absence to now arriving early. What a splendid metamorphosis for you."

I ignored her and slumped into a seat in the back. I took out my phone and quickly searched for "OreGone podcast." It was the first hit in the search results. The podcast, its description, and a cringe-worthy photo of Channing and Guy, "co-producers and co-hosts," populated on my screen. In the photo, Guy sat in a leather armchair, white collared shirt unbuttoned way too low, elbows on his knees, looking coyly at the camera. Channing stood aside him, a hand lightly on his shoulder, her face tilted the other way to produce a perfect silhouette of blonde and pink. What was she even looking at? What teenager has a pink suit? Who takes photos like that?

I rolled my eyes. But my stomach still churned with anger and anxiety.

I scrolled furiously through their podcast archives, each with a higher listen rate than the last. There were two episodes about me so far. Well, about "Elle" and "Noah." I wanted to scream.

"This was quite good," Mrs. Moriarty said as she dropped a paper on my desk. I jumped straight up.

"Um, sorry. Yeah, thanks," I said as I looked down at my essay on Kafka's *The Metamorphosis* and snorted. Leave it up to me to be insightful about feeling like an alienated monster. "Damn straight I got an A," I grumbled.

"Pardon?" Mrs. Moriarty said, looking over her shoulder.

"Nothing. Good book. I liked it," I said quickly, grateful for the distraction of other students now filing in.

I sunk into the plastic molded chair and zipped my hoodie up to my chin. I leaned down to retrieve my tablet from my bag and yelped. I had caught my hair in my zipper.

"Owwwwww!" I hissed as I rubbed the side of my head.

"You have something to add, Ms. Archer?" Mrs. Moriarty bayed.

My face reddened. I jerked upright, still pulling hair with my zipper.

"I was, um, just thinking about what it would to wake up like an insect," I said lamely, trying to save myself. "I, you know, bet it would hurt."

Mrs. Moriarty stared at me and sighed.

"Yes, I suppose it would hurt," she said, then turned to the class. "Which opens up our conversation on Kafka's intent with pain: is it physical, emotional, psychological, existential...."

She continued addressing the class as I uncoiled, a bit dumbfounded and relieved. I looked around the classroom: students were nodding, talking, writing, a few were sleeping, one was making little effort to hide their flurry of texting. No pointing at me, no snickering, no bad puns or dumb jokes. Was it just because Libby wasn't there to spur them on?

Before I knew it, the bell rang. I had successfully made it through the entire school day. I could count on one hand the number of times that had happened.

Tiny victories.

I shuffled out of the classroom behind everyone else. I took my phone out to check the bus schedule for routes to the hospital. I'd have to fill in Phlee on all of this. She couldn't respond, sure, but talking to her had become my new therapy.

I chuckled. I had two therapists – Malcolm and Gil Baudelaire – but it was the sessions with my comatose sister that felt the most productive.

"Before you go," Mrs. Moriarty called after me, "I wonder if you might consider some additional reading."

I spun around.

"Me? Oh, right. I guess I need to get my grade up?" I asked dejectedly.

"On the contrary; you've the highest grade in the class currently. I offer you additional sources to pique your critical thought, should you desire," she said coolly and handed me a paper with several titles and authors written in perfect cursive.

I stared at it, then straightened. Wait a minute. Is she ... could this teacher be, one of *them*?

"Is this, like, um, a code for something?" I whispered.

"A code?"

"You know, you hang out at that one coffee place? You know, like how Ms. Neally had me look at the antiquities section in the library to find ... *the book*?" I drifted off and my face reddened again as I saw Mrs. Moriarty's confusion. "Erm, never mind. Sorry. And thanks, I'll check these out."

She was *not* another dimension traveler. Or, if she was, she was very deep cover. I rolled my eyes at my stupid train of thought, shoved the list into my pocket, and bolted out of there.

My head down, I trotted down the stairs and out the main corridor. Grateful for an easy and swift exit, I inhaled deeply at the top of the concrete steps. I took in the blue sky, the crisp autumnal air, the quivering V of the birds flying overhead, the brilliant oranges and yellows of leaves still clinging to branches, the guy in the bushes in all black with the camera ... Hang on. The *what*?

"Any thoughts on what they're saying about your podcast?"

Flash-click!

"Did you know about the other kid?"

Flash-click-flash-click!

"When were you last in Germany?"

Cameras and faces emerged from all over and swarmed the steps.

"Wh-what?" I stuttered finally. "I don't—"

A hand grabbed my arm before I could finish and pulled me back inside the school. I toppled back and fell on my bag like a lame turtle.

"They cannot enter inside the school. You are safe in here."

I looked up to see Elke, alert and stoic above me like a mama bird.

"Why are you here? Why'd you do that? I mean, thanks, but, I guess what I'm asking," I stammered as I adjusted the straps on my backpack lamely. "Um, what I'm getting at ... how'd you know they'd be here? I've never seen you around here before."

"You are not very often present through the end of school," Elke giggled, then paled. "*Scheisse*. I do not mean to upset you; I am sorry. I thought—"

"It's cool," I said, smiling as I patted her tensed shoulder awkwardly. "And, really, thanks. But, um, what *is* all that?"

"You do not listen to the podcast?"

"Are you *serious*? All of that is because of that stupid podcast?"

"This is my guess, yes. But also ..." Elke trailed off, glancing quickly around. She pulled me further away from the doors and leaned in close. My pulse quickened. "Remember when I showed you that news article on my phone?"

34

VADE MECUM

I walked for a long time. Nowhere in particular. Not for fitness or for clearing my mind. Not intentionally, anyway. I just walked because it seemed the surest way to pass the time without messing something up, without going mad, without subjecting myself to the nightmares that still awaited me in sleep.

For some reason, my first encounter with Dragon replayed over and over in my mind. Man, I felt on top of the world then! Every stupid little-kid fantasy I ever had came true in that moment.

And now? I don't even recognize myself. Sure, I had gotten a few good nights of rest lately. Sure, I had a few good days at school here and there. But those moments were the exceptions. I was changed. Bitter and jaded and tired, devoid of fantasy, scared to stop moving. As much as I had aged in the past year, I was certain I was too young to feel *that*.

I sat on a bench and looked around. No idea where I was. Sunset drew near. I pulled my phone out of my pocket and looked at the page again Elke showed me.

Under punchy, outlandish headlines, a British news article unfolded the suspicious discoveries of similar-looking adolescent boys who all died from mysterious causes on the same day. This particular story was in a less-reputable tabloid, and it hadn't been picked up by other news outlets as far as Elke or I could tell. Yet.

It was still unnerving, that story, that information.

Elke had asked, *who are these boys?* Her giant, worried eyes as she waited for an answer that didn't come played over and over in my mind.

The other clones, when Jonah died, they must have ... what? Also died? Ceased living? Ceased operating? I like that best – ceased operating. It removed some of the humanity and made the grisly situation more palatable.

I couldn't share this conjecture with Elke, though. So instead, I had shrugged and said, *so weird!* and wandered off without addressing her question at all.

A raindrop hit the top of my head. Then another, and another. A gentle pour ushered me through the streets. I liked it, though. It felt soothing, walking through the rain as the sun set. Like a baby getting a bath at bedtime.

I reached the front door a soggy mess. I jumped back in surprise as my mom swung open the door before I could even turn the handle.

"What the hell is this?" she cried as she shoved an envelope in my face.

I pulled my face away, frowning, and pulled the envelope out of her hands. It was creased, a bit worn, and open. *Abernathy Family Services*, the return address read. My cheeks turned crimson. It was the letter from the clinic.

"When did you do this? And why? And why wouldn't you just ask me?" she cried after me as I pushed past her toward the kitchen.

"Are you kidding?" I sputtered as I twirled around. "How would that have gone, again? Oh, wait, I know how that conversation would have gone because it's gone the same way every freaking time before. I ask about my dad; you shoot me down. Not even, like, an ounce of information. It's something I should know about, you know? So, I took matters into my own hands."

"Your own hands? Going alone to a clinic like that to ask about stuff you know nothing about?"

"Do you hear yourself? If you know nothing about something, then you *ask*. That's what I did," I barked as I swung the refrigerator doors open. "And I didn't go alone. I went with Philippa."

I blindly grabbed food from the fridge and shut the doors dramatically. I stomped off and looked down at my bounty: a can of whipped cream and a container of olives. I sighed. Not my finest haul, but I wasn't about to walk back there.

"You … you went with Philippa?" my mom called from the kitchen. Her voice caught in her throat.

I paused on the stairs and wondered if it was finally a good time to bring up The Phone Call from Chad. I decided against it. But what shot out of my mouth next may have been worse.

"Visiting hours aren't over yet, you can go yell at her, too."

I cringed as soon as I said it.

It wasn't late enough to go to sleep, but I had given up on the day. I tossed the olives and whipped cream on my desk, changed into pajamas, and fell into bed.

I picked up a book, opened it, threw it on the floor. I grabbed my sketch book, opened it, threw it on the floor.

Then, against my better judgement, I grabbed my phone and opened my photo reel to an album called PE.

I swiped through photo after photo of me and Phlee, some dumb, some sweet, most embarrassing. Us at the park with the strangely huge pigeon, us ordering coffee from a fully automated robotic cappuccino machine, us trying to pedal beach trikes when the tide was high, Phlee trying to do a flip off a boat but belly-flopping instead, a series of birds that we swore we'd make into memes later. Hundreds of ridiculous photos shuffled by. I sighed.

Our lives had been pretty good, hers and mine.

Why had I needed to upset the balance by looking for a dad?

Especially now that I knew one was possibly out there for real … and his name was Chad.

Chad.

I was anxious to meet with Gil again.

I knew I needed to. At least, I knew I needed to give it another shot before I shut it down entirely.

I owed Ms. Neally that much. And it's not as though I was without issues needing the time and attention of a therapist or ten.

This meeting was already very unlike my sessions with Malcolm. Instead of sitting across from my cool therapist on a bespoke sofa in an office that I imagined is what one meant by the phrase "effortlessly chic," I was shivering on the twig-laden ground under towering Douglas firs. I usually liked the trees iconic to the Pacific Northwest; today, though, they shot upward with skeptical branches that shook disagreeably in the light autumn breeze.

I just needed someone to talk to, really. I didn't need healing (well, I probably did, but that was a whole thing that likely required a lot of time and effort, which I didn't have), I didn't need psychoanalyzing (again, probably yes ...), I just needed a friend. A non-judgey friend. Who knew about other dimensions and clones and mythical creatures and stuff.

I had emailed Ms. Neally again what was essentially a plea to that end. A swift response arrived in my inbox just minutes after I hit send. *Meeting set*, it had read, with a date, time, and location coordinates listed.

I had followed my phone's direction to those coordinates where I found none other than one Dr. Gil Baudelaire standing next to a sign with "Human Therapy" scrawled in fancy letters.

"You should, uh, probably hide that," I said. "And, um, thanks for seeing me, I guess? How does this work, do I, like, sit on a couch you conjure or something?" I rambled as I spun around, taking in the setting.

"Hmmm, you would like a davenport?" she said and leaned forward. Her eyes bugged out in her convex glasses. "And you are quite welcome."

"The ground's good, I, um ... yeah. Ground's good," I said and dropped down inelegantly.

"Now, hmmmm, we shall unveil the thing that is most troubling you."

Gil, er, should I say Dr. Baudelaire, flitted about with scarves and incense and candles and gems.

"Oh, I, um, don't think you're supposed to light those here. There's usually a burn ban around here. But, alright, you do you. Don't say I didn't warn you," I said as I dodged little sparks that fell from her tools.

The good doctor placed a series of rocks near my crisscrossed legs, stood and regarded them, closed her eyes, and frowned. She looked down, adjusted her glasses, frowned more intensely, then bent and swept up the rocks in a flourish.

She did this three more times before settling on what I guess was the appropriate arrangement of rocks. I knew better than to dismiss any of this. No matter how innocuous, how plain, how old and boring a stone looked, they are not to be trifled with. I knew from experience. Weird, bizarre, unbelievable experience.

I shuddered again in the breeze and tried to be open to this new mode of therapy. Whatever she was doing must hold significance.

"Hmmmm, yes, I see, oh, sweet child. It must be so challenging," Gil Baudelaire said as she paused in front of me and leaned in. Her thick glasses gave her eyes a fishbowl effect. Her giant pupils stared into mine. "It needn't be what you've made it, hmmmm. Burdens grow easily in our minds regardless of their actual heft. Hmmmm. Speak them, and they shrink."

I hmphed. She closed her eyes and brought her palms together. I leaned forward, waiting for whatever fortune cookie phrase she was going to throw at me next. But she said nothing.

"That's it? That's your brilliant fix for my nightmares, and my anxiety, and my anger, and my family being messed up, and my inability to have a friend who's not a mythical creature from another freaking dimension?!"

Her eyes opened slowly, black and huge. She nodded. I was shaking, but not from the cool air. "Hmmmm. You have the strength you need."

I was livid. I had actually gotten my hopes up that I could finally just talk to someone the way I'd opened up to Malcolm. I needed someone to just listen to me. And if we really got on, then maybe they'd be someone to tell me I'm not crazy, to set things in perspective, give me some journaling prompts. I needed someone to normalize stress – once something's not so unique and novel, it loses a lot of its power. Malcolm had shown me that.

Gil straightened her headscarf and extended her hand to me. A small rock sat upon her open palm.

"Strength, hmmmm. Like a rock."

"This is bullshit," I said and stood up.

"Leave fecal matter out of it, if you would, hmmmm?"

"That's all you say? Of course it is," I muttered as I fumbled with my phone to map my way back home. The phone flashed brightly and turned red-hot in my hand. "Ahhh! What the – did you do that?" I spun around and glared at Gil Baudelaire.

"Hmmm? I shan't reward bad behavior," she said as she filed her nails against a pinecone. "Let's begin again, hmmmm?"

I walked back to where she stood, smug and odd with her flowing fabrics and fishbowl eyes. I kicked the rocks that still lay before her on the ground.

"Oh dear, hmmmm. I do wish you hadn't done that."

"Done what? Kicked your stupid rocks? Like this?" I said as I swung my leg over another stone. I missed.

"Hmmmm, please do stop that."

"Why? What are you gonna do? Tell Ms. Neally on me? Give me more dumb fortunes?" I said as I swiped my foot along the ground again and again. "Ooooh, I know. Are you going to read my future in tea leaves? Take out a wand?"

Her countenance darkened. Clouds gathered overhead where there had been none. "Do not mock tea, hmmmm, you have been warned. Do take care, hmmmm?"

"That's it? You tell me nothing and leave me in a forest as a storm is starting? Wow. Where do I leave the yelp review for such an awesome therapy session?"

Her face was suddenly in front of mine, as though she had leapt through the air. Her eyes were as wild as her hair erupting from beneath her purple scarf.

"I cannot help that which does not want to be helped, hmmmm? If, Eve Gwendolyn Genevieve Archer, Dragonlord in Training, you wish to be well, hmmmm, your mind must be open to wellness. It is not so, and so you will not be so."

I suspected that what she was saying might be true. Which infuriated me even more, but for different reasons. I stared hard at the ground, annoyed with myself more than ever. When I finally looked up to apologize, Gil Baudelaire, acronyms et. al., was gone.

"Brilliant," I said as I retrieved my phone once again to set a course for home. The screen was more cracked, but it was working. "What else can I make a mess of?"

As I turned to walk back, a swift gust of wind pushed against me. A faint rattling pulled my attention back to where Gil had been standing. The rocks – the ones she had arranged and I had kicked – were moving. Subtly, almost imperceptibly at first. But as I stared at them, they began to shiver all at once, creating a faint rattle. They subsided, lay still, then gradually began to shiver until each gyrated forcefully. The rocks were moving!

I glanced around. Vacant swings rocked eerily in the distance. A squirrel darted across a park bench. The trees, still not fans of mine, swayed with a little more gusto as the clouds continued to darken and the wind picked up. I walked closer to the rocks.

They had rearranged themselves in a spiral.

I stood for a minute, genuinely puzzled. I looked away and back again. I walked around the perimeter. Yep, that was a bunch of little rocks in a grand spiral, like a nautilus.

Was this menacing? Silly? Foreboding? Hopeful? My brain hurt. My stomach growled. Rain began. A drizzle turned to a downpour. I turned again to go, paused, and spun back to the stones. I snapped a photo of them, then knelt to pick one up. It was cold and smooth like any other small rock you'd find in the woods. I tossed it back on the ground. It skidded and hit another, which rolled just enough to reveal a dark green gleam on its underside.

"Holy crap. Alright, that's something," I said as I swiped the rock and stashed it in my jeans pocket.

I jogged home, a sort of rush propelling me forward. I didn't know what I was holding in my pocket. But it excited me. I ran faster. The rain drowned out my thoughts. It felt nice to just run, wild and ridiculous and wet.

35

VIDERE LICET

I didn't wait for my mom this time. We didn't talk much these days, she and I. It was an odd development. She came from the hospital with this sort of bashful guilt. She avoided eye contact, hid away in her room more than usual, apologized for everything.

I didn't know what to make of it. And, has disgusting as it was, now that she was home and healthy, my bitterness over her keeping information about my father from me had returned tenfold. I didn't know what was worse: the fact that I was harboring such resentment, or the fact that it was potentially over someone named Chad.

Ugh. Why did he have to be named Chad?

So I let the distance sit. And spread.

I liked the quiet and anonymity afforded by these bus rides, anyway. The busses in the afternoons were never quite as full as those in the morning, and I did take disproportionate pride in my new ability to switch busses on the trip from Happy Valley to Clackamas with confidence and accuracy.

Getting on the right bus might be my only win today. I closed my eyes and reviewed the ongoing dumpster fire that had been my school day. I had been late to every class for no good reason, I had forgotten to do every homework assignment, and I was too chicken to wait in line at the cafeteria when I saw the student security guard standing watch at the entrance.

I got off the bus, walked to the hospital, nodded at the reception desk, hopped in the elevator, and appeared in Philippa's room. I didn't even have to think about it. Every movement was depressingly performed on auto-pilot.

Philippa lay as she always did: adorned in her white fuzzy blanket with hedgehog print with hair neatly combed and some variety of ridiculous socks on her feet poking out from taut sheets. I found this reliable scene comforting, which felt really messed up if I thought about it for too long.

I smiled when I saw a copy of Smithsonian open on the chair next to her. Someone was reading the proper material to her. Other more tawdry magazines touting celebrity gossip lay untouched in a pile on the floor. I scooped them up and dropped them in the recycling bin.

"Hey, Phlee! I have something crazy to show you," I said as I rummaged through my bag. I retrieved my phone. I swiped through the camera roll – mostly screenshots of cats doing hilarious things – and found the photo of the rocks I had taken the other day. "Here, look at this. Weird, right?"

I looked over at Philippa. A pleasant hum met the chirps and beeps from her monitors.

"Yeah, I know," I said. "Nuts, right? Anyway, I don't know who to show this to. You always know weird things about ... weird things. Ooh! That's a great idea! Maybe Elke is into nerdy stuff like you?"

I paused and stared at my sister's unmoving face.

"I know, I know ... I'm just as nerdy as you. Maybe nerdier, or at least, a different kind of nerd. You're over there with your calculus and Greek flashcards, and I'm over here, like, 'I can name every known species of dragon.' You tell me who's nerdier."

"Everything alright in her?" a nurse said as she popped around the door. "Oh, it's just you. You guys are so cute. I'd never visit my sister that much."

"Kind of a twisted thing to say, don't ya think?" I said, then reddened. The words shot thoughtlessly out of my mouth.

The nurse frowned, started to say something, then spun around and left.

"Getting me in trouble even when you're in a coma. Kind of a jerk move," I giggled as I looked at my sister. I liked being here more since her breathing tube was removed. I took that as a good sign. And I hadn't realized how upset that had made me, seeing my sister asleep with a breathing apparatus shoved down her throat. I shivered.

"Such a freaking relief," I murmured. "Oh yeah! Like I was saying. Brilliant idea to ask Elke. Foreign people seem to be way smarter." I paused next to Philippa's bed and patted her arm. "You deserve a treat. I shall bring you some of your favorite vanilla pudding. And eat it in your honor. And girl – I know you hate it when I call you girl but I think it's funny – you will not believe what I've been carrying with me."

I took a deep breath, ready to finally divulge the whole Chad conversation to her, when another nurse charged in with a tablet and a clipboard.

"A little behind on my rounds today," she said apologetically. "Don't mind me, just going to get some current vitals."

"It's cool, I was just ducking out for a quick snack," I said as I headed out the door. I desperately wanted to talk about this Chad fellow to someone, and then I desperately wanted to bury it and pretend it never happened.

The only solution: eat pudding.

Fatigue hit me hard as I walked down the halls. I stopped and did my mental checklist: Was anything on my body heavy? Did sounds seem farther away than they were? Had I encountered any giant glowing yellow orbs lately?

I chuckled to myself. I did that a lot lately – found amusement in my messed-up lot of life. Malcolm had said once I could laugh or cry when going through trying moments. But I don't know if he meant it literally.

I found a bench near the cafeteria and laid down on it, not even feeling badly that I took up nearly the entire bench. The place was empty enough; someone needing to sit would have plenty of other options.

I took out my phone and did an image search with the picture I'd taken of the rock spiral. "Labyrinth" was the first hit. I shook my head. Wasn't that like a maze? That couldn't be it. I scrolled and scrolled; phrases like "path of healing," "pilgrimage to enlightenment," "medieval ritual," and "meditative trance" filled the screen.

I thought of Gil, of her grotesque but unassuming coke- bottle glasses magnifying her dark pupils. I wondered what she had seen, how old she was, how much of the universe she surely had experienced. I was so caught up in my own stress, I hadn't considered what she might have to truly offer.

"Huh. How about that," I murmured. "The old weirdo was right – I was closed off. Totally not open to healing."

A warmth radiated from the outside of my thigh. I shot upright and shoved my hand in my pocket. The rock! It was still there! I had sprinted home in that rain and never gave it a second thought. This is why I never do my laundry: for moments like this. I took the small stone out and held it atop my palm, studying it.

The thought that I needed to be more open to healing and change (as trite as that sounded to me then) was taking up a lot of space in my mind. The little rock had a vein of brilliant green on one side, emerald-like and shimmering. Its glow was warm and somehow affirming.

"Why were you in the middle of a spiral? Did Gil leave you there on purpose?" I whispered as I turned it over in my hand.

"Who's Gil? Mind if I have a sit?"

A plump fellow with a cane labored his body down onto the edge of the bench I lay on.

"Nice rock," he said. "What're you here for?"

I scowled and sat up. The rock's glow stopped.

"The pudding," I said as I walked off. I was in no mood for strangers and small talk, however kind. I looked back at the man, small and squatty and alone on a random bench in a hospital hall. I sighed. I knew better. "I'll get you some," I called, feigning some cheeriness.

The rock warmed in my hand again.

What?

36

UTRINQUE PARATUS

That morning, I had only one thing on my mind: Ask Elke.

I liked that phrase. It sounded like an old-timey advice column.

"Nice smile, killer."

Someone knocked into me in the hallway. I didn't look.

"I *said*, nice smile, *killer*."

I spun around.

<SLAP>

A hand hit my cheek with so much force my whole body fell off balance. I dropped my notebook; my backpack slid down my arm. I straightened slowly, my hand already holding my throbbing face.

It was Gillian. The slap from Jonah's girlfriend was suddenly familiar.

"Jonah's mom told me you went over there, trying to butter her up. That's a really shitty thing to do. But I wouldn't expect anything from someone like you, you piece of sh—"

Just as Gillian raised her hand again to strike, Mr. Simmons dove between us.

"Alright, now, Ms., hmmm, I don't seem to remember your name, but no matter. That is enough! Now, you," he turned to me and pointed me toward his room, "to class! And you," he spun Gillian around the opposite way, "to the principal's office! And no funny business; I'm alerting him right now. He will be expecting you."

I shuffled to class, still holding my cheek in my hand. Mr. Simmons walked briskly by.

"Thanks," I called weakly. He didn't turn. He only raised his arm up in a wave and took his place in front of his whiteboard.

I dopped my bag in the back, several rows behind my usual seat, and buried my head in my work. I didn't want to see anyone. And while I would have preferred to just hide out in the bathroom in my present state, ditching the class of the guy who saved me seemed a poor choice.

The bell rang.

I leaned over to gather my things when my desk creaked. I looked up. Elke had perched on my desk. Her blonde hair fell forward as she looked down at me.

"Hey! You are here! I – oh, *schiesse*! Are you alright?"

"Yeah, it's, uh, not as bad as it looks," I said with a shrug. The strap of my backpack barely brushed against my cheek as I heaved the bag up and onto my shoulders. I winced in pain.

"Eh, it looks pretty bad," Elke said.

"Gee, thanks," I said, then looked up. "Hey, you want to get out of here?"

"*Warum nicht*?" she shrugged.

"K. I'm assuming that's a yes. Follow me," I said as I led her out of Mr. Simmons' room.

I gave him another nod on the way out as he began sputtering in protest. I pointed to my cheek; he nodded, defeated. And I think he may have even saluted me, but I was too distracted by Elke's scent. The lovely aroma of jasmine danced around her.

"I can wait, no problem," she said as we approached the third-floor bathroom I had grown so fond of.

"Oh, no, we're, like, here. Come on in, it's always empty. And there's this really big, padded bench with, like, a little rug and stuff. It's really nice," I said quickly as I held the bathroom door open for her.

"I thought when you asked if I wanted to get out of here, we would be physically getting out of the school," she laughed.

"Oh. Yeah, um, I can see how you'd think that. It's cool, you can go. It is kinda weird," I said, wishing I had a bathroom inside this one to hide in. Or die in.

"It's perfect," Elke said and dropped her bag on the bench. She presented a bag of gummies. "Want some?"

"Hell yes," I said and took a handful. "These are the best kind!"

"My Tante Agnes lived about 40 kilometers from the Haribo factory. She is always bringing us Haribo. Even here, she sends me boxes of it."

"You're saying that like it's a problem," I said and took another handful.

She giggled. We were quiet for a long time, just skipping class and eating gummies on a bench in the bathroom, as gals do. I looked up suddenly.

"Hey! You know stuff. Or, at least, you seem like you do. Have you ever seen … anything like this … ah ha. Here, this rock spiral. Does this, like, mean anything to you?" I said as I held up my phone to her.

"You are into ancient runes?" Elke said as she peered at the screen. She looked up with a mischievous smirk. "I do not know the word … I need to look it up. Ah, yes. Pagan. Paganism? That suits you."

'You don't know what suits me," I chuckled. And blushed. Was she flirting with me? *Focus*, I yelled inwardly. I cleared my throat. "How'd you know the word 'runes' in your second language? That's, like, impressive. But what do you mean? The spiral rocks are Pagan runes?"

"No, not exactly. But they look like a … don't tell me the word, I know it … a labyrinth! A labyrinth."

"Labyrinth? Dude. Why did I not see that?" I said, only half-faking my astonishment. I had come across that in my internet search, but I hadn't given it any credence.

"I know a lot about labyrinths. It is a fascinating culture to me," Elke said and paused with a shy smile. "Even John Lennon loved them."

"You know the Beatles?" I squealed, then straightened, trying to be cool. "That was Yoko's influence. Can't be trusted."

"Fair," Elke smiled. "So the labyrinth, it always represents, eh, something … spiritual. A pilgrimage. Do you know this?"

I shook my head. I couldn't wait to tell Philippa. But first, I had a meeting (even though my brain wanted to call it a date, which I know is gross and wrong for many reasons) with Ms. Neally. And before that, I had to make it through the rest of school. And before that, I had to figure out if Elke was just a cool, maybe-friend, or if she was operating as some clone spy.

My phone chimed.

I looked down at the screen at the reminder banner that had popped up.

"What is 'hearing prep'?" Elke asked.

I sighed.

"You really wanna know?"

37

FIDE NEMINI

"I'm sorry to learn you and Gil didn't, eh, mesh," Ms. Neally said quietly as she arranged the cups and a tea kettle on the tray. "No sugar. Shall I ask for some? Gil did wonders for my health when I had to process what happened during … never mind. I'm just sorry it didn't help. But I do understand that one being trained in therapy doesn't necessarily mean everyone is compelled to open up to one."

Rain drummed against the windows of the coffee house that afternoon. Brightly colored umbrellas filled the canister near the door. My wet raincoat squeaked as I shifted in my seat.

"Yeah, I dunno. I think maybe I was partly to blame," I said. Saying that aloud made me feel small. I hated it. "But there was something … at the end. That maybe you can, like, help me with?"

"Oh?"

"Yeah, um, this," I said as I pulled the little grey rock out of my pocket and placed it gently on the table. Ms. Neally frowned. "Oh! Sorry. Yeah, like that it's just a plain old rock. Here," I said and flipped the stone over to reveal its emerald vein.

"Oh! My, Gil must really believe in you. I've not seen one of these since … never mind. You were right to retrieve it."

"You know what it is? Hold up, how'd you know I had to 'retrieve' it?"

233

"If there had been a direct exchange betwixt you and Gil regarding this, you'd know that you have a fiducia stone. Since you don't know this, I'm assuming you found the stone on your own?"

"Um, yeah," I mumbled, my face growing red. "I mean, she kinda gave it to me; she put it in this spiral – a labyrinth, is what I'm told – for me to see but then ... yeah, I grabbed it after she left. I didn't know it had been there."

"You showed this to someone? Whom?"

"No, no ... I, uh, I did, like, a quick image search. And not of this rock, this federal- what you'd call it? I only searched the photo of the spiral rocks. And then maybe asked my friend, er, this German chick, because it seemed like something she'd know about. And she did. She said it looked like a labyrinth."

"German chick?" Ms. Neally repeated. She looked up. "Eve! Not the one who could be—"

"She's not. Trust me."

"How do you know this?'

"I just do."

"You will need to get proof. Concrete evidence that she is completely unrelated to any of it."

"I think I can handle that," I said coyly.

Ms. Neally smiled and poured hot water into a mug for me. She presented a lovely tea caddy with all sorts of herbs and mixtures I'd never heard of. Russian Brick, Panda Dung, Awabancha. I hoped I didn't make a face. I grabbed a satchel labeled Tomato Mint – the least intimidating – and hoped for the best.

"Fiducia. It means confidence. That bit there, yes, that lovely green, is jade. When placed at the apex of a labyrinth, it's meant to draw out a more positive outlook and action," Ms. Neally explained. She smiled. "That was very sweet of Gil to try to take you on that journey. It's a lovely way to heal."

I took a sip of tea and almost spit it out.

"Was it something I said? Oversteep your tea? Oh, my. Did something happen to your cheek?"

"Yes," I grumbled.

We sat quietly, I sipping my disgusting tea, Ms. Neally steeping her third tea bag.

"Your brain is noisy," Ms. Neally said with a smile.

I looked up. I hadn't realized she was watching me, studying me. I reddened.

"Yeah, there's a lot going on up there," I chuckled half-heartedly.

"Anything in particular you want to discuss?"

"I mean, I have Malcolm for the ... human stuff. And Gil for the ... not-so-human stuff," I sighed. "I don't want to add a third victim to the list of people who listen to me whine."

"Don't self-deprecate."

"I don't see the point in these so-called therapists, anyway," I said and took a swig of tea, forgetting its flavor. I grimaced as I swallowed. "I go, I drudge up a buncha crap, and then I leave. Nothing changes. Nothing gets solved."

Ms. Neally cocked her head as she swirled a small spoon around her tea. She stopped, looked out the window, and folded her hands. I swallowed. The posture seemed serious.

"Eve. In my many, many years, I have withstood great strife, just as you. Not the same as you, of course, but significant stresses, nonetheless. So I tell you this with perspective and warning."

I looked around and stared at the door, wishing that someone, anyone, would come in and halt whatever this conversation was.

"The advantage of having a team of people whom you can confide in is monumental. The simple act of talking allows you to break down problems into smaller parts, so gain perspective, to find empathy and support," she said sternly, then paused to drink her tea. "Your thoughts and feelings are very much in a pressure cooker so long as they're kept inside. If you don't release them, an explosion is imminent."

I shrugged and played with some sugar packets. She sighed and adjusted her small, round glasses. I liked it when she wore them, especially with her skirts. It gave her a 1920's flair.

"Think of it spatially, then," Ms. Neally said, clearly losing patience with me. "Within the confines of *you*, thoughts and feelings expand and take up all of the room. Speaking them, why, it allows them to float out into the vastness of air, diminishing their importance and freeing up much-needed space in you."

"Yeah, okay. That makes sense. But I still feel like I'm just whining."

"Do you feel better after? Lighter or less tense, at the very least?"

"I guess so."

"Then lean into that benefit. Keep talking to your therapists. Everyone should have a safe, objective space."

"Yeah, that's true," I said. "Hey, so you've been around for, like ... a long time, right? Where you around when I was born?"

"Even without having ancient age, I, as a human older than you was around when you were born," she said with a little smirk.

I reddened. Geez, I was dumb sometimes.

"Right, right ... duh. But what I mean is—"

"No, I did not know you or know of you at your birth," she said quickly. "Why do you ask?"

"No reason," I mumbled.

My phone buzzed just then. It startled the teacup right out of my hand. The little porcelain cup shattered as brown liquid streamed down the table and onto my pants.

"Crap," I said as I wiped up the mess. A tiny shard of porcelain stuck in my pinkie. "Double crap!" I carried the mess to the trashcan, wiped my hands, and pulled out my phone. "Gah! Triple crap!"

It was Libby. Another podcast episode was out. That was the gist of her misspelled, almost incomprehensible texts. I looked up the podcast only to be greeted with the latest and greatest, entitled, "Happy Valley to Hamburg." I groaned. So, the investigative prowess of Channing and Guy had led them to the reported deaths of the Jonah look-alikes. I couldn't wait to learn how they connected them to me.

At least the alliteration was clever.

"Eve, the fiducia stone," Ms. Neally called after me. I spun around.

"Oh, sorry. Do you want it? Is it for you?"

She smiled and held up a hand.

"Have you noticed it reacts at all to your conclusions, your ideas?"

I frowned and shook my head. She smiled.

"You will. Warm thoughts, Eve. Warm thoughts."

I gave her a wave and shuffled down the steps of the coffeehouse, grumbling the whole way.

"Warm thoughts? About what? About stupid podcasts by stupid people because stupid dead Jonahs keep popping up around the stupid world?"

I tripped on the sidewalk. A car sped by and splashed me with muddy water that had puddled against the curb.

"Thanks a lot!" I screamed after the car. "I'm only trying to save the very world you exist in! Jerk!"

38

NIL DESPERANDUM

I had played with the fiducia stone late into the night. If it meant confidence, as Ms. Neally had suggested, then why did I feel like garbage? Like inept, incapable, weak garbage, to be precise. In my sleepless state, I had emailed Malcolm's office requesting an appointment. When I awoke that morning, just a few hours after sending it, a response with an appointment time later that day was awaiting me.

There was a constant tug-of-war within me lately. One side that wanted to just forget about everything and run away pulled fiercely against another side that was ardently duty-bound to seeing Philippa healthy and awake and Obrenox put away forever.

And the real rub? Neither side had any confidence that I could handle either scenario. My own psyche, trapped in dichotomy, had given up.

I moved through the day with all the speed and color of molasses. When my phone's calendar alert went off, I was relieved and even beat my mom to the car.

"You're never this punctual or eager with your therapy appointments," my mom said as she drove me. I just shrugged.

I found my way to favorite chair and sunk down into it with a sigh of relief. Ms. Neally was right about the safety aspect of therapy – I felt safe here. Unknown to the rest of the world for the next hour. There was no expectation, no to-do list. Just me, in this cozy chair, with a fellow whose job it was to withhold judgement on the ridiculous crap that bubbled out from my brain.

It was nice.

"How are you feeling about your upcoming ... event?" Malcolm said finally, seeing that I was there solely for the chair at that point.

"You can say trial. It's fine," I said as I kicked my toe against the leather ottoman. I preferred this to the trees and strange stone patterns of Gil's therapy.

"Noted. Without displacing any of the magnitude of what it is, I'm happy to see you accepting this part of your life. Very strong of you," Malcolm said slowly as he scribbled in his notebook and crossed his legs,

"I don't know how to feel about it," I said with a shrug. "It's not like I have a frame of reference for any of this; I don't know if things are going well or if they're, like, hopeless ... I know I didn't do it, and I also know I don't have a way to prove that, and, and, and do kids go to jail? I mean, I know I'm not a kid, but –"

"I see this line of thought is upsetting you," Malcolm said quickly. "And while you do have the privilege of doctor-patient confidentiality in here, perhaps it is best to focus on your feelings around the ... trial ... rather than any details salient to the legal procedure."

I glared at him.

"You ask how I feel, so I tell you," I snapped. "But apparently, I told you in the wrong way. Why didn't you tell me what I'm supposed to be feeling?"

"An expected response would be fear, worry; maybe guilt, not from responsibility but from not being able to fix it," Malcolm said calmly. "My concern is that you easily grow detached from things that overwhelm. Stress demands a balance between apathy and emotional consumption. It's a difficult tight rope, but one that proffers the greatest health and stability, ultimately."

"What are you even talking about?" I said as I got up and sat in a different chair. This one spun around. I settled into the tufted leather and gave myself another hard quarter-turn. My foot hit a lamp as I spun. It toppled over; its clear globe and bulb shattered into a million glittering shards on the wood floor. "Crap. Sorry. I'm so sorry!"

"Don't worry about it," Malcolm said. "These floors were due for a cleaning anyway. Shall we take a walk around the building? Seems like you're needing some movement."

My cheeks burned. *Donotcrydonotcrydonotcrydonotcry*. Ah, my old, familiar mantra.

It didn't work.

"Leave the mess. Let's go. After you," he said as he held the door open.

I hadn't cried in what felt like ages, and now, I knock over one lamp in the office of one of the kindest people around and I'm all waterworks. I wiped my sleeve across my face.

"Something hit a nerve. A lot of stress is coming from this nerve," Malcolm murmured. "Why don't we look at what that is?"

I stayed quiet as we rounded the corner to the lobby. I nodded silently as he held out his hand toward a small garden trail that wound its way around the front and side of the building. We walked one lap all the way around, then another, and then another before either of us spoke.

"It's just that—"

"Why don't you—"

We broke the silence at the same time. Malcolm put his hand up.

"Please, go on."

"It's just that," I started again, "what if I don't care anymore? That seems really bad, to not care. Like, really big things are at stake, and I'm all, meh! Either that, or I'm having extreme panic attacks and puking all the time. I don't even remember how to just be – how to just wake up in the morning, and do normal morning things, and then go to school, and do normal school things, and have regular freaking feelings."

I stopped and wiped my face again.

"Eve, you *are* feeling something. You do care. What are you feeling right now, as you tell me this?"

"Like I wanna punch you in the face," I mumbled.

"Hmm?"

"Desolate," I said. "Hopeless."

"If you feel hopelessness, that's reason to know you haven't given up."

"Don't follow," I said and wiped my face again.

"If you'd given up, were completely apathetic, as you say, you wouldn't feel anything, good or bad. You're aware of your lack of hope, and you feel badly about it. You inherently know something is wrong with that," he said and stopped, smiling. "Awareness is good. It means you haven't lost everything."

"Yet," I said quietly.

We stopped before the last turn to the main entrance. The sun shone but there was still frost in the shadows. I shivered and blew into my cupped hands.

"We're out of time – need to warm up anyway, huh? But before you go, I leave you with one last thought to consider," he said and looked at me for approval.

"Yeah? What's that," I said through chattering teeth.

"There's another danger of hopelessness," Malcolm said warily. "Once we deem something hopeless, we're in a sense giving ourselves permission to give up on it, as though it's beyond our control. Something that could be managed, even with difficulty, gets to win, because we dub our influence over it as hopeless and therefore moot, unneeded, ineffectual. If it's hopeless, you don't have to try at all."

I stared at him. My toes were numb in the late autumn breeze. *That* was what I stayed in the freezing cold to hear?

"You done?" I grumbled, finally looking up at him.

"Yeah," he nodded and looked down. "All done. Just … just keep a healthy respect for the power of possibility. Everything had to happen once, once."

My mom pulled up just as Malcolm entered the building. I trudged to the car and took my frustration out on the door I slammed shut, the seatbelt I yanked into place, the volume knob I swatted off.

"Geez, take it on easy! What'd my little car do to you?" my mom said with some nervous laughter.

"Nothing, sorry. Just ... therapy bullshit."

"I liked it better when you worried enough about swearing to do so only in your head," my mom said with another nervous chuckle.

"Yeah," I muttered. "Caring was nice."

But then, I thought, Malcolm's words swirling around my mind, if I'm sad I'm not caring, that means I *am* caring because I'm sad about it, and being sad about not caring *is* caring and ... .

I squeezed my eyes shut and rubbed my temples.

"Still up for visiting your sister?"

"Of course," I said with a sigh.

My mom turned on the radio. Her Bluetooth connection chimed and Ringo Starr singing "Goodnight" filled the car.

I leaned back, humming a little here and there, and stared out the window.

I sat straight up. I swore I saw a white, dappled Australian Shepherd trotting down the sidewalk parallel to us on the road. And I swear the dog looked over at me and winked.

Poppy?

39

ABUNDANS CAUTELA
NON NOCET

"K, Phlee, are you even ready for this?" I said to my sleeping sister as I dabbed some lip balm on her sleeping lips.

"You say something?" a nurse said, suddenly appearing in the doorway.

"Um, no, just, um, talking to my sister," I mumbled.

"Good! That's so good for her! Don't let me keep you. I'll let you be," she said with a smile and pulled the door shut.

"Okay, let's get into the nitty gritty," I said, turning back to Philippa. "First, putting lip balm on you is so gross and you totally owe me. But here is what you won't believe. Remember that chick Channing I told you about? She and her douchebag friend – boyfriend? I don't know, I don't know how to tell – have a podcast. But that's not the insane part. Their podcast is called 'OreGone' – I know, it's upsettingly clever – about murders around Oregon and guess who's featured on it currently? That's right. Yours truly."

I sunk down in the chair next to Philippa's bed. I watched the monitors and screens. It was the same scene day in and day out: Vitals were good, brain waves healthy, I'm told.

But that only confused me more: if everything about my sister was good and healthy, why was she still in a coma? We were going on – week four?! That couldn't be right! I shuddered as I looked at the calendar I had taped next to her bed. Row after row of crossed-out boxes showed a month was indeed quickly approaching.

Week four?! I had done a billion internet searches, cleared the browser history and did a billion more, and all of them produced the same damning fortune: A coma rarely lasts beyond two to four weeks.

And here we were, at the tail end of what was rare in the modern medical community. Fear pricked at my eyes. It was wet and salty.

"Anyhow, I have the trial in two weeks. Yeah, it got moved. It was supposed to be tomorrow – ugh, just saying that makes me want to vomit. I mean, could you imagine? Tomorrow? Not that I know if anything groundbreaking is going to happen between now and two weeks from now, but still. There was a change in judges or something," I said as I stood and smoothed Philippa's blanket for the umpteenth time. "It's just ... I already felt like the whole world was watching, but now with this stupid podcast, everyone's even more into it. God, Phlee. It sucks. This all sucks."

Chirps and beeps sounded in agreement.

Evechild, you are not safe.

I jerked up. Dragon?

Evechild, you are not safe.

It was Dragon's voice, alright, louder, piercing into my brain.

Evechild, remove yourself from that space at once!

I scrambled to find *Fortis Librae*. Just as I was about to port back to my room, I glanced at Philippa. I couldn't leave her in potential danger!

"Psst! Aye, lassie! It yer *mingen' charaid*, reporting for duty!" Baert hissed as he suddenly poked his head out from beneath Philippa's bed. He saluted and bowed. "Neither wound nor wallop shall befall yer bonnie *piuthar*. Now, skedaddle, don' be a balloon. On with ya!"

I nodded and heaved open the mighty book. A glance of gratitude at Baert, a glance of worry at Philippa, a great whirling confusion, and I was back on my bed. I shoved the book off my lap; it slid onto the floor with a great thud.

"What the—" I said as I heard a crunching, crumpling sound under me. I pulled up a small roll of paper, now flattened by my butt, and unrolled it. "Dragon!" I gasped.

Dearest Evechild,

I write because direct contact is far too perilous presently. I have learned that what we feared is true. There are confirmed cases of clones masquerading as students in seven other countries. None seem to have the extent of power yours had while alive, but we cannot risk it. You are almost certainly a known target, as is your family. Find your uncle and flee as swiftly as you can. I shall try one final time to communicate this telepathically to you; my radius has been miscalculated and thus I do not believe you to have received any of these warnings internally.

Ever your mate,

Dragon

p.s. don't let me down

I frowned at the postscript. Why would I let him down?

"Probably not the most pressing tidbit to focus on," I grumbled as I paced around my room. Where did Dragon want me to go? With shaky fingers, I texted Uncle Seb.

No response.

I jogged down the hall to check on my mom. She was on a yoga mat in her room, humming along to whatever was on in her headphones, stretching and eating chocolate cake. She looked up, chocolate on her mouth, and reddened.

"Just doing a little multi-tasking," she giggled.

"Are you safe?" I barked. Her eyes widened. "Are you? Lock these windows, and, geez, keep your bathroom shade drawn," I said impatiently as I darted through her room. "Could you keep your headphones off? I, um, I just need you to be able to hear me."

"Weird request," she said as she slid the black headphones away from her ears. "But we live a weird life," she sighed. "Around and around, without rhyme, but definitely with reason."

She closed her eyes and stretched her arms out, then smiled at me and offered me a bite of cake.

I sniffed the air. Something sweet and earthy lingered.

Ah.

My mom had discovered a new way to manage pain and stress.

"Mom, ma, listen. There's something bad out there. I don't know what, but Dragon left this cryptic note for me and—" I stopped, realizing I rarely spoke of Dragon to her.

Her face darkened.

"This is all his fault. If your uncle hadn't started up those dumb missions, spurred on by our own mother, of all people," my mom groused, then stopped and closed her eyes. "Just breathe. It's fine. Just breathe."

I don't think she was talking to me.

"Mom. Did you hear me? Not safe? Uncle Seb is on his way. Seriously, let's go," I barked.

She finally followed, but not without shoveling another forkful of chocolate cake into her mouth first.

Coats on, shoes on, phones in pocket, doors locked. We were coasting down the highway in a small British car in no time. Driving just to drive. Going just to go.

"Music, anyone?" my mom said as she fidgeted with the radio.

"Stop that, you're ruining it! Ugh, you grimed up the knobs with your grimy paws already," Uncle Seb said as he swatted her hand away.

"You're a grimy paw," my mom mumbled back and giggled.

"Is she—?" my uncle said as he looked at me from the rearview mirror.

"Yeah," I sighed.

He smiled.

"Good for her."

"Is it?"

Before either of us could say anything further, John Lennon's voice filled the little MG.

Don't let me dow-ow-own!

Don't let me dow-own!

"If I could go back in time, I'd go back to Savile Row and watch The Beatles sing their hearts out in that rooftop concert before the London coppers busted in. God, to just perform on the roof in the middle of the day like that," my mom said dreamily.

I was about to scold my mom for being so – detached? unhelpful? delusional? I didn't know what – when something hit me.

The rooftop!

Is that why Dragon had included that phrase? Was he leaving me a clue?

"Uncle Seb!" I cried. "I know where we have to go."

I gulped.

At least … I knew where *I* had to go.

The flashy MG looked out of place at the rest stop among semitrucks and RVs and sedans.

"You sure about this, Egg?" Uncle Seb said, his hands on my shoulders.

"Yeah. Yeah, I think this is what Dragon meant."

"And if you need to get out … You can't go back home, not until we've gotten an all-clear."

I frowned, flipping through different locations in my mind. I wished I had taken in more of that one coffee house. But I didn't have any one spot of it memorized well enough. I looked up,

"The school," I said. "There's a spot at my school I think I can get to."

Uncle Seb frowned.

"You think or you know? I don't know much about this stuff – technology from another timeline I don't dare mess with. But my understanding is you've gotta be dead-certain where you're landing or, or … shit gets scrambled, I don't know," Uncle Seb said, looking more freaked out than I'd seen him before.

And I'd seen him in some pretty dicey situations.

I swallowed hard and nodded.

"I got this. Just … make sure she doesn't see," I said, gesturing toward my mom in the car. She had fallen asleep. "I don't wanna freak her out more. Or again. Or whatever. Anyhow, I guess I'll text you or something?"

"You don't have to be so final," Uncle Seb said with a nervous laugh. "Go around the back of those restrooms, no one's over there. And Egg … be safe."

Clutching the giant book under my arm, I walked briskly in the cold evening air to the other side of the restrooms, as instructed. I was alone. And a bit shaken. I was unused to seeing emotion like that in my uncle.

"Never mind," I muttered as I opened *Fortis Librae* and recited its Latin code. The page illuminated; ancient figures lit up in a brilliant sequence. Spinning, compression, tightness, and then …

Another cold breeze. Sounds of the city.

I choked hard and opened my eyes.

The rooftop of the hospital expanded before me. Something moved in the shadows on the far corner. Something giant, something with wings … Dragon!

He smiled.

"You are clever, Evechild. Well done."

40

AB IGNE IGNEM

"Let me get this straight," I said as I fidgeted with my coat zipper. "You don't know who, or when, or how, just that something bad is going to happen to me?"

"Well, when you say it like that, it has an air of absurdity, I suppose," Dragon said as he crossed his arms.

"And we're 'hiding,' here," I made air quotes with my fingers, "at the place where my sick sister is, defenseless. Where I just was and heard you. But instead, you lead me on this wild goose chase ...."

"That bit is regrettable. I assumed that you would have known my location by virtue of being in telepathic proximity. It's fortuitous that I left you that note after all," Dragon sniffed. "And your sister is not defenseless; the mightiest leftenant to ever walk the Isles is standing guard over her. And finally, we're not hiding. We're strategizing."

"Strategizing," I repeated.

Dragon suddenly straightened, his eyes alert on the dark horizon. He drew his wings in tight against his body and stared hard to the east.

"Dragon? What are you looking at? What is – oh my gosh!"

I gasped.

A blaze burned in the distance. A small flame, tiny from where we saw it, sparked and grew. Smoke billowed. Within minutes, fire trucks sounded, followed by the cry of other first responder vehicles.

I squinted, trying to tell where the fire was coming from, and why Dragon was so interested in it.

I turned to ask him just that. But seeing him made the words pile up in the back of my throat.

His dark eyes, wide with too much knowledge, were wet. A stream of tears silently crept down his scaled cheek.

I softly put my hands around his talon.

"Dragon?"

"Yaël," he whispered.

No sooner had he murmured the name of his childhood beloved when he turned, threw his wings open in their full expanse, and, arcing his back, let out an achingly loud primal roar. A mighty blaze followed the sound. I ducked down against the cool concrete rooftop wall and pressed my hands to my ears, hard. He screamed out fire with blood-curdling wails and rapped his tail against the concrete with such might I thought he might punch through the roof.

I felt his warm breath overhead; in a flash, I was on his back. In three, four, five rapid strides we were in flight, swiftly heading toward the roaring blaze.

Flying, especially this fast at night, was quite a jolt to my system, to say the least. Adrenaline fired, my pulse pounded, and nerves danced to the beat.

"Dragon! I still don't fully understand what has happened!" I cried.

In battle as in life, information is power.

"I don't know what that means!"

They have gone after the keeper of information.

My eyes widened. Ms. Neally!

As we neared the scene of the fire, the roar of the hoses overtook the roar of the flame and the blare of fire truck after fire truck, police car after police car. Powerful streams of water shot out and up, only to be swallowed by orange and red. Only, it wasn't a house that we were approaching …

"Dragon? Why was Ms. Neally here? Are you – are you sure she was here?" I asked as I surveyed the site.

It was a long building; the central section was ablaze inside and out. Through the windows of the wings that shot out on either side, you could see the fire on its warpath. Trees lining the perimeter crackled and smoldered.

It was Beecher.

Smoke pummeled out the windows and falling walls as the epicenter of the blaze raged on and grew. And it grew from … I gasped.

Obrenox and his goons had set a school library on fire.

Dragon suddenly jerked into action. A desperate cry, like a horse snorting and blowing, nearly startled me off his back as he launched into the air again.

"Dragon, you have to slow down! I'm losing my grip!"

"She is close!" he roared. But his roar turned into a piercing yelp, primal and strange.

I looked down, following the angle of the speeding dragon.

And I saw her. Sooty and bloody, crawling along the ground away from the burning building.

"Prepare! I will only swoop to collect her, not stop!"

I understood a little better now how telepathy took way more energy and effort than speaking, but Dragon's roaring speech left my ears ringing painfully. I reached up to rub my ear just as he swooped hard to the left.

I screamed.

I was … falling?

Wind and a thumping pulse. That's all I was aware of.

Then a tree, a bush, *oomph!* My lungs – can't breathe. But soft grass ... ah, the ground!

I stared up at a black splotch. In my periphery, the fire lessened, became smaller. Then the black splotch grew.

My body hurt.

I closed my eyes.

**

"You left her out here alone?"

"Why, I was coming to rescue you!"

"I can take care of myself. You insult me with your insolent chivalry."

"The way I found you suggests otherwise."

I blinked. I was still outside. I was still flat on my back. It was still dark. My body still hurt.

I tried to sit up and groaned.

"Evechild! You're awake!"

"You shouldn't have left her to fall asleep in the first place. She is likely concussed. Eve, Eve, open your eyes. Yes, look at me. I'm going to help you up, ready?"

Ms. Neally gently scooped one arm around my shoulders and, holding her other forearm in front of me like a safety bar on a carnival ride, propped me upright. I toppled forward a bit; her arm was a ready brace. She steadied me long enough for Dragon to move into place as my support.

"I'm going to check you for injuries," she said gently as she crouched lower to me.

"Thanks, but I'm okay. But you – oh my god! The fire!"

Black ash dusted Ms. Neally's dewy skin. My eye traced an injury, fresh and pronounced, from her swollen right eye to the gash oozing blood through her blouse on her right shoulder. Her skirt was tattered, frayed, blackened.

Her escape had been a narrow one.

I was glad Dragon left me.

"Really, I'm fine. Are you, um, you know, alright? You look ...."

"Like I'm cannon fodder, yes," she said as she rubbed her eye. The other one was already swollen shut. "I was able to beat one and hide from the others, but then ...oh my. Oh, this is terrible!"

Ms. Neally had turned, her small frame silhouetted by the charred school. Sunrise slowly revealed the expansive, smoldering damage to Harriet Beecher Junior High.

"Unconscionable!" she whispered as she turned her attention back to me. "No major injuries that I can tell, but some deep contusions, and," she paused and smiled as I blinked one eye and then the other, "likely a nasty concussion."

"There's where you're wrong," I said as I cracked my wrists. "I've had concussions, and the tell-tale signs are dizziness and vomiting."

I worked myself into a standing position, ready to dazzle them with a smug tah-dah. But I felt a wee bit woozy. I promptly yakked and stumbled forward, narrowly missing my own puke puddle.

"The good news, Evechild, is you may return home now, you and your mother. The coast should be clear for another good while, now. Although—"

"Although, they'll discover they didn't get me nor the book," Ms. Neally finished. She clenched her jaw and looked back at the school. "Centuries, eons, of history, lost now."

"Eons? Maybe I, like, didn't hear you right, concussed and all," I said with a chuckle. "Owww, laughing hurts. Anyway, like, eons, though? In a middle school library? Maybe a bit dramatic?"

"It was the perfect place to hide such ancient writings. What is visited and scrutinized less than a public junior high library in the Pacific Northwest?"

She had a point.

As Dragon slowly helped me upright once more, something shiny caught my eye. On the ground, under the Eve-shaped outline of smooshed grass, was my phone. Its screen illuminated as it vibrated again and again.

"Goddammit," I said as I examined its screen, more cracked than ever. "A whole 27 missed calls from my mom, 14 from Uncle Seb. Think we should tell them we're alright?"

I didn't have to get home on Dragon's back, gratefully. Or with *Fortis Librae*. Ms. Neally had parked serendipitously far from the school. One small act of vandalism on her beautiful Maserati on the school grounds was all the reason she needed to walk four blocks from a patrolled lot down the block where she parked instead.

I spread my bruised body out on her backseat. The leather was soft and smelled rich and warm. I guess I dozed off back there. I awoke to my mom and Uncle Seb gingerly easing me out and carrying me up to my bed.

I could hear them talking but didn't care enough to listen in. Under my blankets, I felt like a little kid again, hiding from the grownups.

"So this is the famous Ms. Neally!" I heard my mom say loudly. More chattering, more yammering. "No, really! I'll be fine!" I heard Ms. Neally say. More chitchat, lowered voices, raised voices. "She's stronger than you think!" I heard Uncle Seb cry. Arguing. Swearing. A door slammed. Then another.

Then quiet.

Then my mom crying. Down the hall. Defeated sobs escaping between coughs.

I sighed.

When would this be over?

41

AB INVITO

I went to school the following day.

Pretty bruised, really sore, and very much in need of something semi-normal.

"Hats are not conducive to our academy dress code," Principal Fernhouser chirped as I shuffled down the hall that morning.

I spun around and glared at him. I pushed my hat back to reveal the very bulbous, very purple, very veiny contusion at the side of my hairline. It fit the category of "looks worse than it is," but it was nothing I wanted to flaunt.

The principal gasped and brought his hand to his mouth like a terrified woman in a black and white movie.

"So, okay to keep the hat?" I asked flatly.

He just nodded, wide-eyed. As I turned to continue down the hall, I swear I saw him shudder.

I pushed past a group of sophomores, who were definitely the meanest grade in school. I had observed thusly: freshmen are scared try-hards, seniors are all grown-up and over it, juniors live the stress of their futures hinging on the success of tests and transcripts for upcoming college applications. And sophomores? They're not old enough to be mature or noteworthy, they're aware of the stress awaiting them as they grow up, but they're finally not the young pups anymore. So, they're just mean.

"Hey, nice hat! Don't think you can wear these in the clink, though!"

Someone grabbed my brown bucket hat off my head. A sea of nasty sophomores played keep-away around me as I lamely swiped around in the air. Someone turned to look at me; his taunting melted away as his face went white.

"What the hell is that!?"

"Ugh! Look at her face!"

"That's disgusting!"

And just like that, the pack, now repulsed, grew bored and moved on. One of then tossed my hat behind them. It landed on the floor. I leaned down to retrieve it, but an old friend beat me to it.

"Ah, thanks, Poppy," I said to the wagging dog. "Haven't seen you around in a while."

"Weird hat, but glad to help, Sheila. Where you off to? Had brekkie?"

"I'm not falling for that again. You always promise avocado toast, and I have yet to have any avocado toast. Besides," I said as I shifted my backpack onto my other shoulder to distribute the pain a little better, "I need a normal, non-weird day. So, it's algebra for me."

Poppy licked my hand and trotted off.

And I went to algebra, happy to be there. Happy with the long, boring lecture. Happy with the disproportionate amount of homework. And very happy that Elke gave me a smile and nod.

Uncle Seb and Dragon were both at my house when I got home that afternoon. I heard them laughing in the backyard, which lowered my anxiety a bit, but not much. Why were they both here?

"Egg! Finally. Hey, we helped ourselves to some of that yogurt, the Icelandic stuff. Hope you don't mind."

"It brings back fond memories of those mighty ships alighting the coast...." Dragon wandered off. "Oh my, yes, the reason we are here. I can see that's what you'd like to know, yes."

"We've gotta try going back."

"Sebastian, good god! I thought we were going to break it to her gently. You know, ease her into the idea!"

"That was gentle. You want a softer voice? Eve," Uncle Seb said, looking at me with a cocked head, "it's time we attempt going back. Nothing fancy, we just need to test a new portal. Easy-peasy. Quick in and out."

Dragon was quiet.

My head hurt.

"I just wanted one normal day," I said finally. "I gotta lay down."

"Egg! Is that a yes?" Uncle Seb called after me as I trudged inside.

"Whatever," I grumbled.

As I headed inside, I heard a knock at the door.

"Ma! Mom, someone's at the door!" I called from the kitchen as I gathered some cheese and crackers to eat in bed. It was my secret little luxury, eating in bed at night. On the days I remembered to eat, I looked forward to it more than I should admit.

Another loud knock made me jump. I groaned and shuffled to the door. And I immediately regretted opening it.

"Evelyn Archer, just the delinquent we're looking for!" Detective Jasper said.

"You can't talk to me without my lawyer. And my name's not Evelyn."

"Yeah, yeah, yeah, we're here on different business," Detective Serrano said quickly. "The fire. At your old school. What to do you know about it?"

"The fire?"

Jasper had his skinny notebook out, his pen poised above it, ready to write down the compelling information I was sure to share. They both stared at me.

"So?" Serrano said and shifted her weight.

"So what? I don't know anything about it," I said. "There are a billion kids at that school, past and present. Why are you singling me out? I, uh, don't think you're supposed to do that. But I should just check with my attorney just in case," I said as I pulled my phone from my pocket.

"Don't be a smartass. We're leaving; just doing you the favor of allowing you to volunteer any information you have *first*," Serrano said with a glare. "It's connected to you somehow, I can feel it."

"I can feel it," Jasper repeated as he flipped his notebook shut. "We'll be back."

"I'll have donuts waiting," I grumbled as I shut the door. Outside, I could hear them arguing.

"That's not even an accurate stereotype!" Jasper wailed. "Have you ever seen anyone at the station eating a donut? A croissant, sure. Maybe a coffee cake. But a donut?"

"Shut the hell up, Jasper. Let's see if that principal's around yet."

I heard car doors shut, then an engine whirring away.

"I just wanted a normal day!" I groaned as I shuffled upstairs. "One! One. Go to school, come home, go to bed. That's it. *Normal*."

Outside, the voices of Dragon and Uncle Seb crept through my half-open window. I didn't want to know what they were cooking up, or how much of my yogurt they were eating. I slammed the window shut and pulled the curtains.

One. Normal. Day.

I popped some Tylenol and melatonin and fell into bed.

My dreams were unpleasant.

42

SCIENTIA NON OLET

I knew it was time to go back.

The Stinson awaited us outside the hangar, small and unassuming. Outfitted with new landing gear and snazzy seat cushions, it looked as pristine as ever. These cosmetic changes were a relief; their newness held off the memories of my last escapade in that plane. Or they flowed into my brain more slowly, at any rate.

But yeah, I knew it was time to go back. It had been nagging at me, like a homework assignment I'd procrastinated.

I just hadn't given much thought to what might be waiting there.

I shuddered as scenes of shattered tubes, bleeding Jonahs, and scorched Amythystics in smoldering piles flashed through my mind.

"You good, Egg? It's bit late to turn back," Uncle Seb said. I nodded. It didn't matter how I responded; his words were empty. We were heading back on recon no matter what.

I fastened my seatbelt more tightly and popped another motion-sickness pill. "You got the water?"

I held up the bottle of glittery syrup to Uncle Seb. He gave me a thumbs up and pulled his goggles down over his eyes. I looked back to the small cargo hold. My heart stung; I was half-expecting Baert to peer from behind one of the crates just then. But there would be no Baert today.

I dinnae need the pair of 'em! Cut me down tah two, pure barry and right. Baert's solution to easing his lung trauma made me smile. He hadn't stopped sulking since he learned that a body needs both lungs optimally, and that you couldn't just cut the ailing one out. His condition had since improved, but we weren't going to risk stressing a still-recovering collapsed lung.

No Baert on this trip, and no Dragon.

We must ascertain the viability of a different entrance point and how guarded the lair is. Strictly a fact-finding expedition, Dragon had said as he insisted just my uncle and I go so he and Ms. Neally could work on trial prep with Kip.

I didn't know if that made me feel better or worse.

"Bottoms up, here we go," Uncle Seb called with a little whoop as he raised his own shimmery bottle.

I grimaced with the first sip. *Just do it, you weakling*, I thought. I frowned and chugged it, and I did so just in time. An unwelcome familiarity of compression took over. A flattening sensation rolled me through the smallest loop in this galaxy's dimensional web. Pounding, pulsing; then gasping, heaving. And a hiccup. We were through.

"Not bad, Egg. Very smooth," Uncle Seb said as he rocked his neck side to side. It cracked twice. I winced. He laughed. "Oh, a neck popping disgusts you, but getting your guts squished though a portal is nothing."

"Is that what happens?" I squealed. "Our guts get squished out?!"

"No, relax," he laughed. "It's more of – ufff. Shit, that hurt. I – uuuuuuh-hhh."

"More of a what?"

I looked at uncle and froze.

His head bobbed and his body slumped over the cockpit controls. A high-pitched whistle pierced my ears. I unbuckled and scrambled over. A tiny stream of air shot through the tiniest hole in his left window. The little plane jostled, unhappy and uncontrolled.

"Uncle Seb! Get – oomph – up!" I cried as I heaved my shoulder under his chest to push him upright.

His head dropped back lazily. I felt around his neck for a pulse; something pricked my agitated fingers. I pulled a tiny stone lodged in his neck.

"Gah! Uncle Seb, talk to me!" I cried as I felt around his neck for any signs of injury – blood, welts, anything.

The little gem hadn't pierced the skin very badly, but it landed close enough to his carotid artery to make an intense impact, I surmised.

I flicked it onto the ground and kicked it away. It sparked and skidded into the cargo hold's shaking shadows.

"Uncle Seb, Uncle Seb!" I cried as I shook him desperately. The plane dipped.

His eyes opened. His lips pursed, he blinked and felt along his neck.

"What the – shit, the Amythystics? Did you – Damnit! The plane!" he cried. Uncle Seb's groggy speech quickened as he shoved me out of the way to regain control and purpose of the plane. Within seconds, he righted the small aircraft. The circuits and meters hummed and chirped. If they were calm, I could be calm.

"There more?" he coughed.

"More what? Oh, stones? No, I didn't see any. I didn't even see anyone who could have shot it. Oh, and it, like, cut a teensy little hole in your – oh, yeah, you see it."

Uncle Seb, in a storm of expletives, had one hand on the controls while the other grabbed for a kit bag stuffed behind his seat.

"I can find it! Let me," I shouted as I moved his searching hand next to his other on the controls where it belonged. "Describe it, what am I looking for?"

"Why are you shouting? I'm right here. Christ, that little bugger really did a number on me," he said as he rubbed his neck. "A thick roll. Grayish-silver, round, eternally binding."

My mind raced; what other-worldly instruments that science had yet to explain awaited me? Silver, round, binding? I rummaged through various bags and cases and found nothing but items that didn't fit the description. Then, something.

"Oh my gosh," I groaned. "Duct tape? Don't tell me this is what you were after. You couldn't just ask for duct tape?"

"Yes! Toss it here!," Uncle Seb, ignoring me. "Ah, awesome. We are good now."

"Explain it in a more complicated way next time," I said and rolled my eyes. "I dare you."

I leaned back in my seat and buckled my seatbelt with a sigh meant to engage my uncle. He whistled as he finished a small small crisscross pattern of duct tape affixed to the window. He waggled his eyebrows and pointed at it with his thumb.

"Not bad for a guy just attacked and injured."

"I guess," I said.

"You're a little snarkier than you are usually."

"Hard to be pleasant when we're doing what we're doing."

"You mean defying space and logic and introducing new concepts in quantum physics to the world?"

"I mean flying to Canada to slip into another dimension for some murder recon."

"I didn't know you hated Canada so much," he said. I could feel his grin. I ignored it. I would not admit how funny that was.

"Anyhow. Tiny victories," he said pointing to his duct-taped patched again.

"Tiny victories," I repeated. The phrase gave me a tinge of homesickness for my mom. She said it often.

"Except," Uncle Seb continued.

"Except what?"

"Except that this hole and that stone means someone spotted us. And by that killer aim, I'm assuming it wasn't a friend, and that our presence has been made known."

"You said flying all this way to use that portal instead of the one three minutes from home was a surefire way to evade capture!" I cried as my panic level rose. "I remember because you used that exact dumb phrase: 'Egg, it's a surefire way to evade capture,' remember?" I mimicked his low voice. "So we flew five hours north, first to freaking Mt. Rainier, which I didn't even get to see, and to some portal on the US-Canadian border, and now you're telling me they know we're here for some reason?!"

"Seems a good summary, yes."

I clenched my jaw. The whole point of this trip was to get some insight into alternate routes to Obrenox' lair, to take in the landscape and potential obstacles. It was hard to do that if we had to focus on evasive maneuvers and a quick escape.

"There are always variables, you know that. Do your breathing exercises or whatever," Uncle Seb muttered. "And watch over there, wouldya? Drahk was adamant that we get a specific number for him."

"And he couldn't do that with his dragon-y dragon powers?" I shot back mockingly.

The little plane shot upward. The rapid movement slammed me hard against the back of my seat. Uncle Seb pulled back on the throttle; the plane hovered at the uncomfortable angle. I swallowed hard.

"Let's get one thing clear," Uncle Seb said without turning his hard stare away from the pastel mist swirling about us. "I actually do know what I'm doing, and Drahk deserves a hell of a lot more respect that than. I don't know why dragons are so infantilized, some silly creature in fairy tales and movies and whatever. But Drahk is a badass. And a conqueror. And a survivor. And a millennia worth of things you could never understand. In fact, I think most dragons probably are. But they're mammals. They're not magic. They have skills, abilities, mystical predispositions, and all that. But they're not some kid's toy at a magic show with 'dragon-y powers.'"

He breathed hard. I hadn't heard him rant like that in a long time, if ever. He must have had more than a few encounters with naysayers – small-minded people with no respect for the extraordinary.

"I'm sorry," I said quietly. "I didn't mean anything by it. You're ... you're totally right."

"Of course I'm right. And if he needs us to find something out for him, it's one hundred percent because there is no way in this galaxy that he could get it himself."

"I get it. I said I'm sorry."

"Good," he shot back and cleared his throat. "And another thing, Egg."

"Yeah?"

"Do you have any of the dragon scale water left? Because we need to cloak and blast outta here, like, yesterday."

Uncle Seb swiftly flipped three switches and adjusted two levers. He popped open a small case mounted under the instrument panel I hadn't ever noticed. Without even looking, he turned a dial and pushed a button under it.

"Come on, come on," he said under his breath. "Let's go, calcite. Cue the electromagnetic radiation ... Uh-huh. There it is! Cloaked!"

I looked back, or rather, down. A growing black cloud still billowed toward us. Plumes of charcoal crested and hung in the air, an inky trail.

"The big guy himself came to welcome us, how about that," Uncle Seb grumbled as he maneuvered the tiny Stinson through billowy effervescent toward a familiar gauzy tube forest.

"I didn't bring the spheresaii," I said suddenly.

"We'll be good, so long as you can warn me if anything starts coming outta that black cloud back there, or if any more Amythystic buggers are around."

I swallowed hard and concentrated. I remembered when I last encountered those angry purple elfish guys with the deadly green gems.

"Coast is clear! Why didn't he attack? Are we that fast, or is he that slow?" I said as I watched the trail of black grow faint behind us.

"Obrenox? Both," Uncle Seb said, relaxing a bit. "He may not be quite ready for confrontation, maybe he was hoping just his presence would intimidate us. Or whatever that breathing problem is that he has could be confining him a bit. He's likely stronger in certain types of gravity and oxygen levels. Drahk didn't mention this?"

My head hurt. For so many reasons.

"Um, no, in super villain class we did not cover that."

"With them off our tail, we should manage at least a little info-gathering ... Oh, nice! Yes!" Uncle Seb continued, ignoring me. "There! To your right! See that batch down there? Yeah, that cluster of bluish tubes. How many you think we got?"

I pulled out my phone, focused the camera, and hit record.

"Recording? I've never tried that here. Never trusted the technology to not get scrambled going through portals. Egg, you counting? I gotta feeling time's up," Uncle Seb said as he pointed to a mass of gray moving toward us. "Yep. Let's move. Gotta compress and punch through the other side. It's right above us. Pulling her up now!"

I shoved my phone back in my pocket just in time. Sounds, colors, shapes, detached and pressed down on me with the weight of a hundred moons. Darkness, confusion, and then ... we slipped back into our own dimension.

The plane shot out among the pretty treetops of the North Cascades. We cruised over Mt. Baker and toward Mt. Rainier's foreboding peak.

"Getting any easier?" Uncle Seb asked with a cough. "Keep hydrated."

"Not easier," I choked, "maybe just less terrifying? Why do you keep over the mountains like that?"

My uncle launched into an excited lecture on gravitational force and high altitudes. His voice turned into background noise to me and, as my nerves (and my innards) decompressed, I focused on the vast green whizzing by below.

Dragon's words hung in my mind: *Obrenox means to destroy Earth.*

The whole planet? But wouldn't that mean destroying himself, I had asked him. Not the whole planet, Dragon had corrected, but as much of whatever exists on it as possible. People, animals, plants … Anything that wasn't destroyed would be assimilated. And from there, he'd move on to as many dimensions as he could slip into.

I shuddered, imagining a world in which clones and drones took over all life.

Uncle Seb looked over at me, frowned, and tossed me another water bottle.

"You don't look so good. That last one not take?"

"Do you ever get used to it?" I asked, still lost in my thoughts. "It's pretty insane, what we're just casually doing on a Tuesday."

"Well, Thursday was out because someone has to have her day in court," Uncle Seb chuckled.

"Not quite ready to joke about it, thanks."

"Snarky *and* touchy," he sniffed. "Egg. I – never mind. What's got you so pensive? Besides … that."

I shifted in the small bucket seat, my eyes still affixed on the sprawling verdure below. It was gradually transitioning into farmland and specks of suburbia.

"It's just, I don't know," I said and folded my arms. "One guy taking out the entire planet? Isn't that just a teensy bit … dumb? Ok, maybe not dumb, but at least improbable?"

Uncle Seb's jaw tightened. He said nothing. I said nothing. Hours flew silently by. At last, he grunted and pulled a little more tightly on the yoke. The plane careened toward webbing waterways.

Normally, I loved flying over the Columbia and Willamette Rivers – their convergence at the states of Washington and Oregon always seemed poetic-somehow. Like two friends meeting up to go to the coast.

I shook my head. I was good at replacing one stupid thought with another.

"It's not one guy taking out a planet," Uncle Seb said finally. "It's the cul-mination of careful, practiced tactics and plans. It's, it's … it's mayhem. It's execution that's been in the works for who knows how many millennia," he said, flustered, and pulled his gloves off. "From what I can tell, shit, from what I've *seen*, this is a master plan that's snowballed into something that has little to no hope of being stopped unless we—"

"Unless we what?"

"Annihilate everything in there."

Tall buildings popped through thick clouds below. We were moving, quickly, toward the hangar. Yet time felt stilted.

"Annihilate everything? But ... what happened to just doing a sneaky little takedown of Obrenox? You can't just ... What are you saying?"

"I'm saying, we annihilate everything in there."

"You want us to blow up another dimension?" Hearing myself saying something so ridiculous aloud actually calmed my nerves. "Did we just become the plot of a bad sci-fi flick?"

Uncle Seb didn't say anything. I wasn't used to seeing him so ... so anxious? Discomfited? I was uncertain what adjective to apply, but I knew I didn't like it.

He silently pulled on the yoke again to bring the plane angling toward a familiar runway.

"I know that, uh, I don't understand a *ton* about how dimensions and timelines and – what'd you call it? – quantum ... tangles," I trailed off and fidgeted with my seatbelt.

"Entanglement. Quantum entanglement," Uncle Seb corrected.

"Right. Yeah, that. But I *do* know that no one knows what will happen if we mess with any of it. Especially ... on *that* level."

My uncle was quiet, save for some jibberish about landing that he radioed in. I heard the familiar affirmations of Kip. The plane slowly teemed forward.

"Egg, I know I've not said a lot about my time doing ... what I do," Uncle Seb said finally.

"Hmph," I snorted. "Not 'a lot?' Try hardly anything."

"But I've seen more – too much – and been exposed to more than I'd like to share," he said, ignoring me. "I just need you to take my word for it, that there's been a whole lot of planning in there, and it's not good. And I don't know if it will work the way our pal Obrenox thinks it will work, but I'd rather not find out."

"Yeah, you've alluded to that, to being there more. Why won't you talk about it?"

He was quiet again. The plane's steady hum sang us toward more familiar fields. The hangar grew closer. The runway, small and narrow, came into focus; a swarm of Kips readied it for arrival.

"Your buddy Jonah," Uncle Seb began as he continued our descent, "he was basically a clone lord, yeah?"

I nodded, uncomfortable with the question, uncomfortable with the memory.

"And he was just one, that you knew. But we saw armies of cloned individuals, coming after us, and baking and growing and hanging and Christ knows what else in those godawful tubes."

"Yeah, so?" I said slowly. Dread filled my stomach. Wherever this was headed, I knew I hadn't considered it.

"So, what are the odds that you would know the only guy cloned? Not great. But you knowing one of maybe hundreds? Statistically, the less rare something, the more likely you are to encounter it, right?"

"Right," I said, dread still rising.

"Egg, these guys have been getting planted around the globe for who knows how long."

The Stinson's wheels hit the pavement. Uncle Seb swerved the little plane in an S shape. It obediently slowed. The Kips ran alongside, waving and jumping. Every reunion was a grand reception. I liked that about them.

The plane groaned to a stop. I unbuckled, ready to feel this dimensions' ground, but Uncle Seb stayed, his hands on his lap. The Kips slowed their dance;

some cocked their heads quizzically, others paused with the lack of movement. Another Kip came running out of the hangar with a tray of beverages. He glanced around, read his surroundings, and halted so abruptly a bottle of orange soda tumbled off his tray and hit the ground. Orange foam fizzed in shattered glass at his feet.

Uncle Seb suddenly coughed, rubbed his eyes, and hopped out of the plane.

"C'mon, Egg," he said with a nod toward the hangar. "I think it's time I showed you something."

43

ADAEQUATIO REI ET INTELLECTUS

I sat across from Uncle Seb at his desk. Well, the thing that he called a desk, anyway. A small iron beast that was more Soviet-era than not teetered under piles of books, graphing tablets, notebooks, blueprints, and what had to be an unhealthy amount of gum wrappers. The light, the very one I had clutched under this very desk that dreadful day, sat on the corner, duct-taped but shining.

"Why don't you get a new desk? I mean, the rest of you is so clean," I said, uncomfortable with the silence and the strange request I join him in his postage-stamp-sized office.

"Sentimental reasons. Anyhow, Jesus, I can't believe I'm doing this," Uncle Seb leaned back in his chair, fidgety and sweaty. "Alright, Egg. What I'm going to show you is, well, it's stuff I never intended anyone to see. Sometimes you just write to get stuff off your chest, or to try to work it out, you know?"

"Sure, but that's normal ... and why would I have to see—"

"Maybe a part of me intended for you or your mom to read it one day. I don't know. I can't vouch for my state of mind when I wrote. Christ, I haven't even read any of it since I wrote it. But, alright. Enough with the disclaimers. Enough with the goddamn buildup. It's probably not even that interesting." He paused and rubbed his neatly shaven beard. "No. It is."

He unlocked a safe behind the chair I had never noticed. Why would I? It was draped in old jackets and NASA pamphlets. (Those seemed like something I would have noticed, though.)

"Egg, I need you tell me something first."

I looked at my uncle, who had turned and was holding a thick, worn book in his hands midway between us. His eyes were glistening. I gulped.

"Yeah, anything. What is it?"

"Could you tell me you love me? I don't know what kind of relationship we have, and I don't know what a normal uncle-niece dynamic is, but, uh, hell, it'd sure be great to know you love me too. Because I love the hell outta you, Egg."

His arms were trembling as they stayed partially extended, holding the journal. His eyes were wide, wet, and earnest. I had seen my uncle in a lot of unique situations, but emotional and vulnerable was not one of them.

"Sure, um, yeah, of course I do," I said. "Of course I love you, Uncle Seb." He handed the book to me and sat back down heavily.

"I just needed to know. Before you know ... all of that," he said as he gestured toward the tattered journal now in my arms.

"Do you, um, want to talk about it, er, like, is there a specific thing you want me to read?" I said slowly, still wholly uncomfortable with everything happening.

"Just read it. Know that I love you, that I love your sister and your mom, and that I'm me, and just ... just read it. I love you, Egg."

With that he got up, grabbed his leather jacket, and walked loudly out of the little office. I heard his brisk footsteps on the hangar floor, then the sound of an old British engine firing up. He drove off. I sat back down, thumbing through the pages. It was filled with his writing, a beautiful scrawl, peppered with small drawings and numbers that looked like something you'd see in a physics textbook.

Wild with curiosity, I got up to leave.

"Just locking up, yep!"

"Good lord, Kip! You scared the bajeezus out of me!"

"I shall replace your 'bajeezus,' yep?" he said, cocking his head to the side in confusion.

This must be one of the younger Kips. I smiled, remembering how Uncle Seb described the crew of Kips as "a copy of a copy of a copy that fades a bit more each time."

"No need, Kip. Thanks, though. And for locking up; I wasn't sure how to do that."

He nodded dutifully.

"Will you wait with me until my mom gets here? I, um, was going to get a ride from Uncle Seb."

"Father has driven away, yep! And wait I will, yep!"

"Thanks," I said. I followed him outside. The night breeze was cool but affable. I leaned against the hangar wall with Kip. I felt already like an eternity stood between me and when I'd get to read the journal Uncle Seb had so peculiarly entrusted to me.

I kept the book tight against my torso, hidden under my hoodie from my mom. I don't know why. Just an impulse. I hugged my sides all the way home, scurried up to my room after some hasty good-night pleasantries, and burrowed down into my blankets.

Lamp on, pillows optimally arranged, I opened the journal and read throughout the entire night.

8 July

First entry. Not because I want to keep a journal, but just so I can prove Eamon wrong when he sees I actually wrote something in here. (Suck it, E)

This thus binds my winning, and E doth owe me $40 and a new Oculus headset to replace the one he lied about breaking.

Signed,

Sebastian Ulysses Barras

1 Aug.

Going a little crazy. Got visited by some old friends I never thought I'd see again. Everything I knew about quantum physics is wrong. Again. Scared to write more, but it was this or scream or go insane.

12 Aug

A plane shouldn't be able to do that. I've been flying all my life. Inspired by Drahk, of course. Since junior high, shit has it been that long? But to slip into another pocket of time like that ... time that so closely parallels our own that if it weren't for the weird plants and atmosphere you'd swear you were just having a fever dream. Are there more? I feel like there's something he's not telling me, in showing me all of this. BUT. If you can't trust a dragon, especially after all these years, who can you trust?

18 Oct.

Time's gone missing again. Worried I'm in too deep.

9 Dec.

I'm not supposed to write this shit. I'm not supposed to know any of this shit. I'm not supposed to be alive. But I have to write this and get it out. I have to get it the hell out. Nightly it taunts me, I wake up in a panic and question where I am and when I am. Panicked. Always panicked. I race all day, confirming people know who I am, that I know who they are, that today is still today.

There was a time I didn't know. I didn't know any of that shit. I knew I was me, I knew it was dark, I knew something was in me making me breathe. I don't know if I moved. I don't think I had thoughts. But I don't know? I remember but I don't?

And then I'm back here. Back in my shitty studio apartment off Clickitat. This is where I live, in the basement of one of those fancy old timey Portland foursquares, and I see that couple – the hipster owners who are always growing herbs and shit – daily. And they claim they saw me, brought me soup because I seemed sick, but I don't remember being sick and I sure as hell don't remember soup. I'd of remembered something kind like that.

Something's missing from my brain. I'm scared to ask Drahk; I'm scared to know. Because I think I know. I gotta write this. I gotta get it out.

Eamon's dead.

I didn't, I don't know how, except I think I do and what do I tell my sister. Christ what do I tell her

24 Feb

I had the same dream again. They say if you talk about a dream, you won't have it again. Let's see if writing it has the same effect.

Flashes of light. Yellow, bright, and warm. Something makes me move forward, but I wanted to, I wanted to go, and my heart pounds. And it's like I step through this yellowy heat and then … nothing. Just black. And inside I feel like I'm thrashing but I can't move. It's just black, holding me in place, and I desperately want to move but I can't for some reason. I can't speak, but I'm yelling, and I can't move, but I'm kicking.

And then I wake up in a cold sweat, gasping for breath. What is that? What does it mean? Why do I keep dreaming this? Again and again … infrequently, at first, but now, of the past month, it's been nightly. Nightly. I'm terrified of going to sleep. And I'm so tired.

It's the kid's birthday. I should go. But I'm so tired. I haven't been out much. I blink and I see remnants of that dream, lingering flashes, like I'm being haunted. And what kind of uncle shows up like that? She'll see something's wrong, she'll send Phil off, and try to give me a drink and get me to talk. But I can't. I can't talk to her. Not yet. Three months since the funeral. Is that when I first had the dream? Eamon's funeral was beautiful. My sis handled it like a champ, like she does everything. And I, I crumbled. I left her house, drunk, pathetic, full of self pity, not even offering to help clean up or quiet the crying kid.

I think that is when the dream first happened. I guess writing things out is helpful after all. If you could call this helpful.

1 May

I finally talked to her. I hadn't realized I missed my sister so much. And get this, she called me. With what I guess she thought was great news. She got herself pregnant. I asked by whom, she said no one. Obviously I went to see her. It's a test tube baby. I'm not supposed to call it that; she punched me in the arm when I said that and, shit, my heart flipped. I haven't had human touch of any kind since that last hug at the funeral. Christ, that's been almost eight months ago. Freaking weird to get yourself artificially inseminated when you're newly widowed, but she loves a project, and I know she loves being a mom. She and Eamon always planned on two kids, and damnit if she wasn't going to fulfill his last request. God, she's a saint like that. How are we even related. She suffers this insane loss, and she's moving onward and upward and doing good in the world. And me? I'm drinking and scared to go to bed. I haven't even flown. Not since that day I woke up and somehow knew Eamon was dead.

The dreams haven't stopped.

And I'm going to be an uncle again. Another kiddo without a dad. Why do I feel like that's my fault?

What are these dreams trying to tell me?

2 Oct.

I finally flew today. Not in the way I know how, just little stuff. But god, I hit his air pocket and I was ready, fangs out, conning and dipping. Ridiculous. I'm not reactive; I'm not twitchy. What has me on edge? Was it just that I hadn't flown in so long? It's been 10 months. I feel like something imprinted on me and I can't sort out what or when and I'm so goddamn exhausted.

I tried calling her. To check in on the kid. I do love that little weirdo. She asked if I wanted to FaceTime. I figured that was a good sign? But as soon as I saw Philippa's little face, I lost it. My god she looks like Eamon. I made some lame excuse to get off the phone and puked my guts out. The byproduct of flying? My stomach churns every time I try to remember him, though. I loved him. He was my brother-in-law, but he was more than that. We went to academy together. Survived actual dogfights. Got outta that racket and started flying delivery services with him, safer, more security, more time with the fam, all that shit. Safer, yet ask him that now. He's gone. And I can't remember how or why. Just that it's my fault he was there in the first place, it's my fault part of him still lingers in a different freaking dimension. Dead or alive? I don't even know. Dead here. God, I think I'm gonna be sick again.

I don't know what's wrong with me.

12 Oct.

Drahk came to check on me. Has it been a year? He had met me after the funeral, and I had been such a dick to him. I don't know why, but I remember being certain he had something to do with Eamon's death. It's still weird to write that. I've been holed up here in this stupid room, leaving only to grab bagels downstairs or try to find some thrill in lifting at the gym again, without any contact with the outside world. Like if I stay put long enough I'll wake up and everything will be back to normal and Eamon and I will meet at Nob Hill and eat burgers we shouldn't be eating and talk shit about sports we nothing of.

But that's in the past, I guess. Christ, I'm tearing up writing this. Drahk was weird, quiet, almost hesitant. I wanted to hug him. I saw him and I missed him. God, I miss everyone. I miss flying. I miss flying there – god knows why. The thrill? I was worried that's what he came to talk about, about going back to that messed-up dimension for who knows why. But it didn't come up. Why am I scared to write about that? I should have talked to him more. I invited him for tea, not even beer, goddamn tea. He asked about my dreams. And I lost it. I told him to get the hell out. How does he know? Drahk's got some amazing abilities, but knowing my dreams?? Or does he just suspect? I could have found out more from him. This temper of mine lately. I've never had a temper before.

How did Drahk know about my dreams? What do they mean?

24 Nov.

My sis had the kid. All on her own. I mean, ma was there. She's still no friend of mine, so it's good I didn't show. What do I give a widowed mother who chose to get knocked up or inseminated or whatever (I don't know the deets of the pregnancy, just that she was) just so her kid will have a sibling? I think we know it's more than that though – she and Eamon were already talking about adding another rugrat to their perfect life. Some sort of twisted homage to her dead husband, carrying out their final conversation. I hope she knows what she's doing.

Still having the dreams. This last one was crazy, though, more forceful. I think I was flying. It was noisy, I think I crashed into something. Started with the same lights, ended with the same darkness. But that middle bit, that's new. I got the sweaty bedsheets to prove it.

9 Dec.

Shit I guess one year turned into four, and this stupid book is still stashed in my bedside table. Still don't get out much, but today was awesome. My sis called me. Reunion! God it feels good to write that. I met the new kid, I hugged my sis. Ma wasn't there, but our old crew – Eamon's and mine – showed up with bad gifts and booze that was too expensive, even though they know my sister doesn't drink. I felt normal for a minute. Well, human anyway. I don't know what normal is anymore. But hugging her, hugging Phil, meeting the new one – it all felt so good. She named her Eve Gwendolyn Genevieve (after our ma and Eamon's), which is sweet and all, but how did she miss that the kid's initials are EGG? We had a good laugh.

Feeling good. Better, anyway.

15 May

Years fly. Like me: I'm flying again. But Egg's all caught up in this bullshit now. I don't know what she knows, but all we can do is move forward. I hope Drahk knows what he's doing. That place changes you – how could it not? And if she gets taken, if she gets locked away with the seas of hanging clones, shit I'll never forgive myself. I barely recovered, how could a kid?

25 June

It happened again. I don't know what or how but it did. I came to, desperate and crazed and barely breathing, Drahk staring at me and muttering his Latin shit. He told me we had to go get Egg, that he knew where my bird was. Why was it not at the hangar? And then what happenened after that, shit, there aren't enough pages in the world to describe what happened. I went back there, I went with Eve, we had to get her mom and Phil. God it was nuts. I'm not okay. I don't think Egg's okay. We're alive, but that's about it. And Philippa, she's still in the hospital. And Drahk keeps asking if I want to talk about it when he damn well knows I don't. All I can do is write this insane stuff in here and, I don't know, probably just burn this book one day. But I gotta get it out. I gotta figure out why I'm able to fly places people don't even know exist, why Egg's got this weird power too. What a thing for a kid to carry. It's eating at her. I see it. Her mom has to see it. But, god bless my sis, she operates on a frequency of cheer and optimism that isn't normal.

None of this is normal. Phil hooked up to tubes, police poking around everywhere, Egg getting sued. I hope she pulls through this. I swear if anything happens to her I'll never forgive myself. I already can't.

279

44

MANU PROPRIA

My hands trembled. What did I hold? What had I read? Not just a journal. This was a confessional, a record of my uncle, started almost a decade ago, relaying secrets not meant for this world. And it lay in my hands, tattered, smudged, and so damning.

I heard footsteps outside; I shoved the green leather-bound notebook under my bed.

"Eve, my love, I'm going to get to the hospital a little earlier. Would you – oh! Are you feeling alright?" my mom said with a frown as she stepped into my dimly lit room.

I looked down. My heart pounded in my chest so hard I was certain my mom could see it. She felt my forehead with the back of her hand. I jumped at her cold touch.

"Dear lord, you are on fire!" she exclaimed. "And so ... so pale. Even for you. Oh, Eve. Did you sleep in your clothes?"

I just shrugged. Was I scared to meet her gaze? I was still in my clothes. But I hadn't slept. I had read and re-read my uncle's journal until ... I guess morning? The sun was starting to stretch and shine, but it stayed mostly hidden behind some clouds, like me under my blankets.

I forced a chuckle and pushed her hand away. I slid forward just enough to feel around the edge of my bed; I had to ensure no rogue journals were sticking out. My mom frowned more.

"Just, uh, finding ... this! This sweater," I said as I awkwardly put on a dirty sweater in what I deemed a successful coverup.

"Sit this one out; try to rest. I'll bring you back some spicy Pho around lunchtime. It'll knock those germs right out of you, sound good?"

I smiled and gave her a thumbs up. She blew me a kiss and pulled the door shut. I listened for her footsteps on the stairs, then darted out of bed and grabbed the notebook.

"What do I do with you," I murmured as I flipped through its pages for the millionth time.

For every revelation in there, a dozen new questions popped up in its spot. I let the pages ripple back and forth and back again. I was stumped. Overwhelmed. A little angry. And really, really stumped.

"Hold on, what is that," I whispered as I fingered pages in the back. Something had caught my eye, something I hadn't noticed before. I thumbed through, ready to give up, when I found it. I opened the notebook wide to reveal a scrawled paragraph, barely legible, framed by clusters of mushrooms doodled in green pen just two pages away from the end of the book.

Seb,

I can't believe you keep a diary. Some real asshole must've given this to you. Ha. Anyhow. I promise I won't ready any of the dumb shit you write in here. Haha. Grabbing the opportunity to remind you of a conversation you and I recently, and my thoughts about it. Maybe you'll read this one day, maybe you won't. But I wanted us to remember it. I think we were on to something.

Everything in nature is disposed to defect. The universe shows its vulnerabilities again and again, from collapsing stars to inexplicable and unanticipated genetic mutations in cells – cells of humans, cells of plants, cells of animals .... Nothing is perfect and consistent. Each tree grows a little differently, every snowstorm paints white a little differently, every meteor shower shoots warnings a little differently. If everything in our natural universe can glitch, so to speak, why can't time? Why shouldn't there be little wrinkles and upsets in the fabric of time and space? Why do we demand perfection of science, but not of self?

Fly on, brother.

-E

I sniffed and wiped my cheek. I never had any insight into Eamon. He was a phantom, a handsome fella holding his pregnant wife in a photo, with no further description. I'd never even heard an adjective applied to him. And there, in my hands, was his voice, his feelings. His writing felt earnest. I think he was excited about the possibilities wrapped up in physics. And I think he loved my uncle.

I sniffed again. I bet he would have loved Phlee.

45

AUDI ALTERAM PARTEM

School, hospital, homework, repeat.

Sometimes I threw in a meal or two in there, sometimes a rogue meeting with Dragon et. al., sometimes an hour with Malcolm. But that was the gist of my life lately.

I was okay with the monotony, the predictability of it all. I needed that, when so many bizarre and terrifying question marks taunted me all the time.

There was nothing monotonous or predictable about today, though. Just giant question marks. Mean ones. Marching with spears.

By the time I rolled out of bed, my mom had already had two showers, a workout, and changed her outfit seven times.

"Eve! You didn't lay out your clothes! Do you want to borrow a suit? How about the brown one? No, I think navy is better. Did they tell you what to wear?"

My mom's voice came from down the hall, muffled and frazzled. I knew she'd pull it together in time, but this was not the best energy to greet the day with.

Today.

The Trial.

My mom and I rode with Ms. Neally and Kip in her fancy Maserati. In my smart suit (I went with my mom's navy three-piece) and snazzy loafers (which I'm certain Philippa would have let me borrow), I almost felt cool. In another life, I'd be dressed all dapper and getting out of this beautiful car for a much, much, much different reason ... like, like –

A gloved hand knocked against the back window aggressively. Swarms of cameras and microphones crowded the black sedan as we pulled into the parking lot of the courthouse.

"Eve Archer! What is going through your mind at this moment?"

"Mrs. Archer, what did you notice different about your child growing up?"

"Why doesn't your attorney have any web presence whatsoever?"

That last question made my head shoot up.

"Darn," Ms. Neally murmured. "I thought we covered all of our bases."

"Wait here, yep, and I shall escort you! Your door, yep! Hold on!"

I clutched Kip's arm has he led me through the frenzied media. *Head down, keep walking. Head down, keep walking. Head down* – My head shot up at the sound of a familiar voice.

"Channing?"

"You've just heard the voice of a murderer – *alleged* murderer," she said dramatically into a microphone.

"Alleged, for now," Guy chimed in from behind.

"Make haste, make haste, yep," Kip whispered as he pulled me along. "Count your steps, yep. It helps. Yep, it helps."

We went from shouting and chaos to quiet and order. The courthouse lobby was palatial; only the click-clack of shoes on marble and the security scanner beeps echoed into the wooden doors.

I took a deep breath.

"Good, do your breathing exercises," my mom whispered. The whisper didn't hide the shaking in her voice.

I paused and looked at her with a little bit of astonishment. What a godawful and singularly bizarre experience for a mother.

I hugged her then. For a long time.

She pulled back, finally. Her eyes were wet.

"Are we ready? Eve, how are you feeling?"

I looked at Ms. Neally, at her still slightly swollen eye and her chic ivory suit. I looked at my mom, her eyes still glistening, in her just-pressed black suit. I looked at Kip, chomping on a Ritz cracker, in his modern gray suit.

They all smiled expectantly at me.

"I've, uh, I've gotta go … Just, be right back," I stammered as I bolted for the bathroom.

I hadn't eaten anything that morning. But, I was reminded by the vomit in the toilet, I *had* given in to a little midnight stress-eating and had downed an entire row of oreos and a sleeve of saltines.

The courtroom was empty. I paused, feeling uncertain about going in.

"You can come in," a large man perched on a stool called from the front of the room. "But I have three more minutes left in my nap break, so kindly keep it down," he said with a wink.

"That's the bailiff," Ms. Neally whispered, as if I knew the roles and functions of court officers.

She smiled politely at him and directed me to a bench in the back.

"Don't we sit up there?"

"Would you like to sit up there now?"

I froze. Tears erupted.

"I – I don't know!" I whimpered. "Ms. Neally, I … I think I'm really scared."

My hands were tingly. My chest felt tight.

Evechild, you can do this.

I brightened. Ms. Neally looked at me knowingly.

Of course I am here. Remember just one thing: you are so much stronger than you think. You have strength yet untapped in that heart and brain of yours. This is not where your story ends.

"You don't know that," I whispered as tears fell.

"Eve, my love. They're saying it's time we take our seats," my mom leaned down and whispered to me.

I hadn't trusted my mom much lately. For a lot of reasons. I didn't trust her stability, I didn't trust her to be forthcoming with me. I didn't trust her to be the grownup. But as I watched her stride to the front of the courtroom, composed in her elegant suit and heels, I think I somehow understood her better. And I think I even felt that she would be alright. Whatever the outcome, she would be alright.

I sat down next to Kip on the left side of the courtroom. He tapped me on the arm and pulled a bag of animal crackers from his pocket. I shook my head and attempted a smile.

The din of the courtroom grew louder behind me. How many people did this place seat? I wanted to turn back and look the same way you try to catch another glance of a gory wreck on the side of the road.

Jurors shuffled in.

Twelve people who might as well have been cards in a game of Old Maid stared ahead with my fate in their hands.

"Ms. Rosencrantz, yep, how do you do," Kip said, shaking the opposing counsel's hand.

"I do very well, in here and out there," she quipped.

I stared at the ground, at my shoes, at the holster on the bailiff's belt. A different bailiff had come in. He had a scraggly mustache and a dark scar along his jawline. He caught me staring and glared.

My eyes darted back to my shoes. I didn't know where to look. Mostly because I didn't want to actually see any of it.

"All rise!"

The benches creaked and the floors cracked as the full courtroom stood.

"The Honorable Judge Penelope—"

The judge, an austere, lean woman who was more cheekbones that not turned her pointy, blonde head toward the bailiff with a loud cough.

"It's Pehn-nahl-OHpe, must we go over this again?"

The bailiff shifted uncomfortably. The court stenographer stifled a giggle as she dutifully pecked at her keyboard.

"Apologies, mum," he said, clearing his throat and letting his West London accent escape. "All rise, ehm, that is, remain arisen, for the Honorable Judge Pen-ah-LOPE Roderick-Beauregard, now presiding."

I started to sit, but Kip grabbed my elbow. I rocked side to side, antsy and anxious, as I fought the strange urge to look at the chorus of rustling bodies behind me.

"After I swear in each and every one of you dear jurors," the judge began, "I shall hear opening statements and then presentations of evidence. We shall go from there, yes? Yes?"

"I still didn't find anything out about this judge," Ms. Neally whispered behind Kip and me. "The change in appointment for the case was so last-minute, and, as I understand, quite unusual."

"Yeah, you told us that already," I hissed back.

"Sorry, I am rather nervous, I suppose," she whispered. "Nervous, but optimistic," she added with a gentle pat on my shoulder.

It took forever for all the jurors to get sworn in. An elderly man needed everything repeated. A woman in the front row couldn't stop sobbing. A clean-cut gentleman behind kept shushing her.

"Are you sure you're able to proceed?" the judge asked flatly.

The crying woman looked around, panicked, and pointed to herself and mouthed "me?"

"Yes, you. The one crying in my courtroom. Can you kindly put the histrionics on hold?"

She sniffed and nodded. I looked at Kip, who sat with perfect posture and a pleasant smile, staring forward.

"Yikes," I heard my mom whisper to Ms. Neally.

Finally, Swan Rosencrantz stood.

"Members of this sacred jury," she began with all the theatre of one reciting a Macbeth monologue, "members of this hallowed courtroom, and, of course, most esteemed and honorable Judge Roderick-Beauregard."

"Yes, we're all very grand and important. The court hopes you will use more brevity and less editorializing in your opening statement," the judge interjected. She drummed her fingers on the podium and dropped her cheek onto her palm.

"Who among us are mothers, fathers, parents?" Swan continued without acknowledging the judge's comment. "Who among us love children? Their innocence, their zest, their ... their pure, untapped potential! Imagine such a child. An only child, beloved by his parents, encouraged in astrophysics, aerospace engineering – oh, to have such ambition as a teen! This is the type of person we talk about today."

Swan took a dramatic pause, then pointed to a screen on the opposite wall. A portrait of Jonah appeared.

"This boy was found dead on his doorstep. He had no enemies. He was involved in no dangerous pursuits. But," Swan stopped and gestured toward me, "he had one dangerous friend."

A hushed murmur snaked through the courtroom.

I wanted to throw up.

"It will be proven to the court today that this boy, Jonah Minh Nguyen, found an early end to his promising life by the hand of Eve Archer. For hers was the only name found in his personal effects. As you review evidence today, you will see theirs was a complicated and tumultuous relationship, the stuff of soap-operas and film noir. But, the crime of passion here is no fiction."

I stared at the gobsmacked jurors in disbelief, their eyes affixed to the performative opening statements of Ms. Swan Rosencrantz, esquire.

A crime of passion? Could anyone possibly be buying this? One of the jurors was already writing something down.

I looked frantically at Kip. His expression was unchanged: mouth turned up in a slight smile, eyes fixed forward. Ms. Neally lightly patted my shoulder.

"The facts will cut through the drama and the pandering," she whispered.

Will they?

At last it was Kip's turn to offer his opening statement. He cleared his throat, stamped his foot twice, and straightened his tie.

"I am Kip, yep, Kip Sebastian, for the defendant, yep. Who is kind, and a straight-A student, yep, with strong family bonds and love of animals, yep, and history. With respect to you, to you all, and to you," he said as he bowed to the jury, the audience, and then to the judge, "yep, I will provide facts, not emotionally manipulative narratives, yep, to prove that there is no way this small girl could be capable of what my colleague, yep, has claimed."

"Yes, Kip!" Ms. Neally whispered behind me. I knew she had been practicing his delivery with him for ages. His speaking was less clipped then usual with only a smattering of yep's rather than a flood of them.

As statements continued and led into arguments, I felt someone's eyes on me. I shifted, slowly, but my wooden chair creaked anyway. I shyly looked over my left shoulder.

I froze. No way.

Crimson lips, the same color that taunted me at the funeral, mouthed something indiscernible. I blushed and spun around, suddenly aware of the stupid face I was making as my jaw hung open in confusion at Libby's presence.

Good luck, she mouthed again. Was she being sarcastic? Geez, this girl was a roller coaster of confusion. She had been nicer to me lately, though. I shook my head. *Not the time to think about girls,* I scolded myself. I turned my attention back to the front of the wood-grained courtroom, wholly distracted.

"Could you repeat that for the court, yep?" Kip said.

He stood perfectly erect, perfectly groomed, perfectly coiffed. He gave a quick nod of encouragement at the witness stand and stamped his right foot.

I hadn't noticed anyone going up to the stand. How long had I been staring at Libby, staring at the reporters lined up, staring at the wooden benches. These benches, gnarled and polished with years of anxiety, stretched out like rows of pews ... like the pews I had been in, where Libby had been, mouthing accusations. But now ... my stomach flipped and churned. I choked down vomit.

I hoped I would never be anywhere with rows of wooden benches ever again. Too much judgement.

"So, please sir, if you'll humor me, yep, you claim the accused," Kip's sharp gaze brought me back to the present as he gestured toward me, "Eve Archer, was present in your class that day, the day the deceased was found."

A tidy man with sharp features and a bald head cleared his throat. He slowly leaned forward and paused dramatically in front of the tiny microphone affixed to the witness stand.

"That is what my attendance sheet indicates, yes."

A chorus of whispers erupted around me. Every *s* sound coiled up and over the pews and hung in my ears. I winced. That consonant still made the hairs on my arms stand on end. I looked down at my hands and focused on my breathing. Replaying scenes with Obrenox was really not needed.

"Thank you, Mr. Darlington, yep."

"Darls is fine."

My head shot up. That's why this angled fellow was familiar – Darls had been a substitute teacher at Beecher! And he remembered me from that day? I frowned; I was still unable to reconcile the passage of time during that fatal trip to the seventh dimension.

Kip smiled. Darls nodded.

"No further questions, judge, yep."

"Counsel wishes to approach the bench," a voice from my left startled me.

A heavy woman breathed hard and stood, her bad suit and spiked hair in stark contrast to Kip's neat demeanor. She stomped forward, Kip floated after, and both tended prayerfully to Judge Roderick-Beauregard's stand.

After more vicious whispering, the woman scowled, Kip smirked, and the judge waved them away.

"She is likely trying to dismiss the attendance record as uncorroborated," Ms. Neally whispered, "and Kip likely rebutted that it is not standard practice for classroom attendance to be checked further once turned in to the office."

Yaël is indeed correct, Dragon's voice came into my mind. *Fear not, Evechild.* I smiled. So that's how Kip was doing it! Not that I thought him unequal to the task ... okay, even as one of the "sharper Kip models," I thought him a tiny bit unequal to the task. Dragon sagely guiding his arguments brought me immense comfort, though.

The merry-go-round of witnesses continued. A teacher, then a child psychology professor, another teacher, a medical examiner, a security guard. One by one, they rotated through the carousel of bible-sworn affirmations and questioning.

Not one had tipped the balance of doubt. I started to relax when a familiar voice, wavering and stammering, grabbed my attention.

"Do I think what? That she's a danger to my school? Well, a little churlish, maybe. Disruptive, perhaps. But, but aren't most teens? But a danger ... do I think she's a danger?" Principal Fernhouser said nervously, then stopped and sat back. He rubbed his chest with his hand. "Do I think she's a danger?" he repeated.

"That is the question, Principal. Kindly answer directly," Judge Roderick-Beauregard yawned into her microphone.

"Yes."

It was almost inaudible, his whisper. My pulse raced.

"Please repeat that for the court, louder."

"Yes," Principal Fernhouser practically yelled into the mic.

The sudden volume combined with the damning declaration sent the court in an uproar.

I looked at Kip, at Ms. Neally, at my mom. Their stoic countenances were unchanged, but their silence belied their panic.

His is not the finite testimony, Evechild. Breathe, breathe. There must be more than one cantankerous principal to bring the worst upon you.

The court still hummed with gasps and murmurs. Jurors were viciously writing and gesticulating along wild whispers.

"Order! Order in this courtroom! My, I never get to do that. How thrilling," the judge said as she smoothed her hair and looked over at the clock. "Counselors, have you any further questions for the witness?"

"Do I need any more?" Swan said with a sassy flip of her hair.

"Yep ... that is, yep," Kip stammered. He stared at the ground in intense concentration.

The room was silent as Kip nodded, mumbled to himself, and stamped his foot.

"If counsel does not have an immediate and specious question, I invite the witness to step down," the judge said as she drank a bottle of water. Not just a sip – she drank the entire bottle in one go.

"Yep! Yep, yep," Kip turned and approached Principal Fernhouser. "You are familiar with a group called Anger Management for Educators?"

The principal's face turned six shades of red.

"W-w-why would you ask me that?"

"Relevance!" Swan called from behind.

"It is relevant, yep, if the witness will answer forthwith."

"Yes," Principal Fernhouser said coolly. "Ok? Yes. I'm familiar. As anyone could be."

"And why, specifically, are you familiar, yep?" Kip continued.

"I see your objection, Ms. Rosencrantz, but I am intrigued. Answer the question, please," the judge said quickly.

"I was ordered to attend."

"By whom?" Kip asked.

"By a court," the principal mumbled.

"Could you repeat that, yep?"

"BY A COURT."

Another wave of gasps and shock rumbled through.

"So, you yourself are an angry person, yep – anger that warranted court-ordered group therapy –and therefore possibly not best-suited to weigh in on who is and is not a danger? Yep?" Kip said gently.

"I'm not angry," he muttered into the microphone. "I have my plants now, and my skills, and, oh, dammit all. My life has been in destruction since meeting Ms. Archer. She should be locked up!"

"But, yep, your testimony here," Kip said slowly, "is to determine beyond all doubt that this child, yep, a child, yep, is capable of murder. Not if she has been a nuisance to an educator, yep."

"Agreed," the judge said loudly. "I'll instruct the jury to disregard Mr. Fernhouser's last statement. Anything further?"

Kip shook his head.

Swan, looking lost, shrugged her shoulders and said, "takes one to know one?"

I watched the principal – *my* principal, from junior high and now high school – skulk down the steps from the witness stand and back to his seat. He had always just been a figurehead, a guy who doled out detention slips from behind a desk, who wandered the halls looking for students to scold. He had been kind to me here and there, but ... he was a caricature of an authority figure to me. A cartoon, not a real human. Not someone who thought his life would be better if I were imprisoned.

I shuddered. That's a wrecking ball of a realization.

The judge called for order, but something else had her attention. Her head down, she squirmed side to side and frowned, then beckoned the bailiff over.

She placed her hand over the mic and whispered something to him. He only nodded.

"The court will take a short recess. Counsel will meet in my chambers in ten minutes. Jurors, you must stay sequestered."

Everyone stood as she withdrew through the back door. Cool exit, I thought. There aren't many positions left in the world that demand that type of response. Just as quickly as I wondered how hard it was to become a judge, another thought scolding me for being a delusional idiot slid in.

46

AUCTORITAS

T he courtroom, even the courthouse, was a circus of onlookers. Voyeuristic and ready for gossip, they hung in packs poised with phones, notebooks, full camera equipment.

We waited a minute after the judge departed. The bailiff gave us a nod; my mom had to pull me up to standing. If I could have blended in with that bench and stayed there, I would have. I stayed close to Kip. Ms. Neally and my mom locked arms behind me. The three shuffled me to a small room, meant to be private for us. But the cacophony of onlookers was ever-present.

"How you doing, my Eve? I think it's going well, don't you think it's going well?"

I didn't answer my mom.

"Where's Uncle Seb?" I asked as I twirled a button on my cuff.

Kip offered me a bottle of water. I swatted it away.

"Your uncle hasn't always had the healthiest respect for the laws of aviation," Ms. Neally said carefully, "so we thought it best he keep a low profile throughout all of this."

My mom snorted.

"Just like him, to make it about himself and leave you here," she muttered.

"No one's saying that, Mom."

"Let's focus on recapping the trial thus far, and what we can affect in this next part," Ns. Neally said brightly.

But before she could continue, Kip stamped his foot and held up a pocket watch.

"Time to conference in chambers, yep!"

"You have a pocket watch? Can I see it?"

"Eve, honestly. The weird things that grab your attention, even during …this," my mom half-chuckled, half-groaned behind me as we shuffled out.

We approached a set of mahogany doors, the opulent carved ones I'd see in movies. I started to follow Kip in when Ms. Neally grabbed my arm.

"Counsel only," she whispered.

"No, let the child enter!" a voice barked from within. "It'sssss fine."

That hissing *s* from the judge made me uneasy.

The room was dimly lit and completely paneled in dark wood. Wood floors, wood shelves, wood wainscotting. My eyes traveled the bookcases to the ceiling. Not wood. I wondered if all judges had chambers like this. When did a chamber stop being a chamber and just be an office? Or a study?

"Focus, young Egg, yep," Kip whispered.

"There is new evidence," the judge said, the *s* sound still sticking out like a sore thumb to me. She coughed and pushed some hair out of her face.

"Which is?" Swan said impatiently.

The judge looked up from the mammoth desk. Her face, still angular and austere, was different somehow. Her skin looked … loose. I shook my head. It had to be the low light and seeing her up close.

"Which is," the judge continued, "a recording, yesssss. Here, I've one for both of you."

Her speech was stilted and slow. Her shoulders hunched into little points as she labored to open a drawer and pull out two envelopes, which she slid across the table to us. I hadn't noticed how bony and gnarled her fingers were. They shook as she pulled her hands back to her sides.

"We'll need time to review," Swan said, nonplussed. "I request a continuance."

Kip nodded, though I could see from the way his head was cocked that something wasn't sitting right with him either.

"Good. Fine. We will adjourn. Next sssssession – ahem, sssssorry, I have ssssomething ssssstuck in my throatssssss – will continue, erm, Friday."

My head shot up. Something about the way she said that last phrase sent my heart racing.

It wasn't the judge.

It was her chambers. It was her robes. It was her sharp cheekbones. It was, presumably, her leather chair. But sitting on that chair was someone else in a Penelope Roderick-Beauregard skin suit.

I inched away toward the door. Kip stood quickly, stamped a foot, bowed, and grabbed the envelope.

"Until then, yep," he said quickly.

"I have not disssmissssed you!"

"We haven't settled on a time, darlings!" Swan called after us as the door shut.

Kip and I rounded a corner to an unfamiliar hallway toward a set of doors marked as an exit. Bur a mob of reporters was waiting outside that door. They went alert like a pack of predators and charged toward us. We spun around to go back inside, but there was no exterior door handle. We made a beeline for the back parking lot where another pack of ravenous beasts were camped out.

"Here she comes!" Channing called from within them.

"Hey! Over here!"

Someone grabbed my arm and pulled me behind a hedge, out of sight. I looked up.

"Libby? I don't really have time for whatever this is," I said as my eyes darted around. I had lost Kip.

"I'm parked just over there," she said. "They're all over there and won't see us. Come on."

"This better not be a trap," I barked as I followed her, hunched down, along the hedge to a battered red Civic. I pulled on the doorhandle; it wouldn't give. "I can't open it!"

"You've just gotta, like, really pull on it, yeah, there you go!"

I slid onto the passenger seat, which was torn and taped, and locked the door after me. Libby rummaged through a bag, fussed with some makeup, and then turned to me.

"No trap. Just looked like you needed a hide out. So that trial is bonkers, right? I mean, I totally forgot about Darls. 'Call me Darls,'" she added with a giggle. "But it's, like, *so* much. I don't think I'd be okay at all."

"This ... this is your car? Wait, you drive?" I said as I looked around at the tired, old automobile, decked out in peeling vinyl, broken knobs, and a screwdriver where a stick shift should have been.

"Yeah, it's like, whatever. It gets me around," she retorted. "And, yeah, I drive. I'm, like, a whole year older than you."

"You are? Then why are we in the same grade?" I asked as I turned around to look in the backseat. "You got anything to eat in here? I can't tell if I'm hungry or what—"

I stopped abruptly. A gym bag with clothing spilling out of it took up most of the backseat. It was clothing I recognized from school with Libby. A toiletry bag slumped near it; several pairs of shoes were scattered atop the dirty floormats.

"I travel a lot," Libby snapped when she saw where my eyes had wandered. "And not everyone's parents enroll them in school in, like, a timely fashion, or whatever."

I felt there was more to the story, but I didn't press. Even if I had wanted to, there was no way my brain was going meaningfully process anything. Not after that courtroom, not after that judge ... in those chambers ... I gulped.

Who was that?

What was that?

"You don't look so good, Dragongirl," Libby said with a meager smile. I guess that was a fun little nickname for me now after all. "Hey, isn't that your mom?"

Standing in the parking row across from us was my mom, pacing, her phone pressed to her ear. Ms. Neally and Kip were gesturing wildly to each other. I pulled out my phone.

"Yeah," I chuckled as I showed my phone to Libby. "A grand total of 23 missed calls. And that's not even her record. I should get going. Um, thanks for the hiding spot."

"Anytime," she said.

"Hopefully not!" I called over my shoulder as I darted from the little red car to my motley legal team.

"Fine then!" she shouted after me. I stopped and looked back, flustered.

"No! I meant, like, hopefully it's not needed anytime!" I shouted back.

"There she is!" a guy with a camera yelled.

A group charged after him, toward me. I sprinted to my mom.

"I don't know where they went!" she cried as she spun around and around.

A sleek black Maserati screeched to a stop behind her. My mom and I piled in, and Ms. Neally raced off, leaving black tread marks as she squealed out of the parking lot with insane speed.

Now that was a cool exit.

47

ÆGRI SOMNIA

"**H**e's *here*?!"

"He is."

"Like, *here*. In *this* dimension."

"Yes."

"In this state."

"Yes."

"In this city."

"Yes, at the moment, at least."

Dragon and I stared at each other, uncertain what to do with this information.

"You're sure?" I said after a long pause.

"You were there. You heard him, saw him," he said quietly.

"I heard a creepy judge lady speak similarly to him," I countered.

Dragon smiled, but his eyes were sad. Baert, Uncle Seb, and Ms. Neally stayed silent. Their reserve made the empty coffee house, usually warm and bustling with curiosity, seem cold and even quieter. Not even the orange-haired barista was present. Upon entering, Dragon had shot her a knowing glance, to which she nodded and cleared the place out for us. "Unsafe pipe issue," she had explained nonchalantly to the tourists and regulars, who sulked as she ushered them out.

"Indeed," he said at last, and, before I could interject, he continued. "It is curious. I have never known him to breach a portal into this dimension, nor am I aware of any documented occurrences of such."

Dragon looked searchingly at Ms. Neally, who only shook her head and looked down.

"All we know is that he is here now," she said.

More silence. Mugs of coffee scattered between us had turned cold. Rain battered the windows. The flicker of the fire had gone out. It was bleak.

"For how long?" I asked finally.

Dragon looked around the table. No one made eye contact with him. He sighed and stretched.

"How long as he been here, or how long will he be here?" he responded.

"Both?"

"Dunno," Uncle Seb said, finally speaking up with a cough. "We can't trace a route, Egg. But he can't have been here long."

"Nor will he be able to remain much longer," Ms. Neally murmured as she sipped her cold tea.

"Because of some breathing problem he has, right?" I asked, brightening at Uncle Seb. "You mentioned something about that when we were there last, remember? So, like, can't we just take advantage of that and just, you know, take him out here?"

"Aye, that's thah spirit, lassie!" Baert said suddenly, jumping up. "We creep in on thah beastie, and then – *ah-hah! en garde, a bairnie!* – we take him swiftly, with me bare hands if I have tah! Aye, a good laldy is good for thah soul."

Uncle Seb clapped at the elf's sudden flurry of fighting movements. Baert took a bow and climbed back into his chair, panting.

"Perhaps you're not quite back to fighting shape, Leftenant," Ms. Neally said gently and reached her hand across the table to his. He scowled and pulled his hand away.

"It is true, the atmosphere in his dimension is more methane-rich than this one," Dragon said. "As well as having inconstant pockets of helium. His type have adapted to it, to a point. And certainly prefer that air to this dimension's atmosphere."

"Yeah, yeah, yeah, save me the science lecture for later," I said with a groan. "Just tell me what the issue is with taking him out *here* versus taking him out *there*?"

"We do not know where he is," Dragon said.

"We don't know who he's trained to come pouring through the dimensional portals, or how many," Uncle Seb murmured. "There's no home-turf advantage. Too many unknowns for us."

"Oh," I said and looked down.

More silence.

The scene was indeed bleak.

Suddenly the door burst open. A gust of wind shot through the café, rattling tea cups and disturbing old frames on tired walls. Standing, panting, in a whirling of gauzy scarves and wild hair, was Dr. Gil Baudelaire.

"Hmmmm! There is a disturbance," she wheezed. Kicking the door shut behind her with her heeled boot, she fell dramatically onto a weary couch by the window. "They speak to me. All is not well."

She thrust her hand into the folds of her skirts and produced a fistful of small stones, which she tossed upon the floor in front of her.

"Gil!" Ms. Neally cried as she jumped up to greet her old friend. But Gil thrust her hand out, palm up, to stop Ms. Neally's approach. She stared intently at the scattered stones.

"Gil," Dragon said curtly, suddenly moving in front of us. He crossed his arms and pulled his wings taut against his back.

"Hmmmm, have we met, hmmmm, regard these," Gil said, breathy and dismissive.

"How dare you pretend to not remember me," Dragon snarled.

"Easy, Drahk," Uncle Seb said, and then turned to me in a whisper, "What are we waiting for?" Who the hell is this?"

"They, like, move or arrange themselves into something," I whispered back. "And don't ask. Some kind of therapist. But I don't know why Dragon has beef with her."

"Ssshhh! Ye'll disrupt the barry stones!" Baert hissed.

We waited, watching the little rocks. Ms. Neally slowly lowered herself back into her seat.

One by one, the tiny stones started to shiver. Gyrating more fiercely, they began to move, tittering this way and that, quivering past each other. Gil's eyes were closed, her arms outstretched over the movement.

"Ow! What are you doing?" I hissed as Baert jostled me in the ribs.

"I dinnae see th'action!" he hissed back as he crept onto my chair. "Give me a boost, lassie."

Dragon glared at us both and brought a talon to his lips.

"Look!" gasped Ms. Neally.

The stones had stopped shaking. Their pattern was set. Finally Gil opened her eyes, looked down, and smiled.

"Hmmm, they have spoken," she said, obviously pleased. Then her eyes widened as a grotesque, throaty shriek came from her curled mouth.

I peered at the stones: one long line with a central triangle protruding, like a pointy P, to the right lay on the ground, still and precise. Something glimmered at the triangle's peak, the same glimmer I had spotted in the labyrinth that one day at the park after my "therapy session" with Gil.

"The thurisaz," Dragon murmured.

Baert, Ms. Neally, and Gil all murmured with similar concern. Uncle Seb and I looked at each other. He gestured toward the stones with a furrowed brow; I shrugged.

"Hmmmm, chaos awaits you, hmmmm," Gil said, deep and breathy, as she skipped toward us with her eyes still on the floor. "Can't step there, hmmm, oooh, so sorry! Hmmm, this place quivers with worry, much has been discussed here, much has been seen, hmmmm."

She made her way to us, one slow hopscotch game later, and shimmied her large, gossamer-covered rear onto our table. She leaned back and stretched her neck, shaking her head side to side. Some twigs and a plastic fork fell from her wild, purple hair.

"*This* is who Yaël sent to help you?" Uncle Seb said as he elbowed Baert to keep from sniggering. "No wonder you're still all messed up in the head."

"I know, right? Hey, wait a minute!"

"Oh, I, uh, I mean ... that just came out, Egg, I didn't mean it," he mumbled. I frowned. "But it's not as though you've been yourself, and, and I get it. Who would be?"

"What's a *thuruh*—whatever you said?" I said, looking at Dragon and ignoring my uncle.

"Hmmm, what isn't it?!" Gil cried. "The thurisaz, hmmm! It means many things, hmmmm, but primarily—"

"Chaos," Dragon finished quietly.

Baert leapt onto the table in a swashbuckling fashion.

"Aye, my specialty!" he shouted.

"Not like this, Cuithbaert. Not like this."

The rain pounded even harder against the windows in response. The gem in the middle of the pebble rune shivered.

"Hey, what's with that thing, anyway?" I asked suddenly. "You left one in the labyrinth last time, er, like, one appeared or something. Ms. Neally called it a ... a ... fiduciary... ."

Gil slowly turned her head to me. She blinked heavily as if focusing her eyes for the first time.

"The fiducia stone, hmmmm, appears as needed. Hmmm, you clearly need much, and often."

"There's that awesome therapy again. Thanks," I snapped.

I sunk down in a chair by the big stone fireplace. This all seemed pointless. I went from being in a real trial, to learning that an evil overlord was impersonating the judge, to fleeing reporters, to having a secret meeting at our "hideout" in a well-known coffee house in Southeast Portland. Now, this other-worldly being pops in with her fortune-telling pebbles spouting nonsense.

"This is trying," Dragon said softly as he rested a talon gently on my shoulder. "There are many pieces to this puzzle, Evechild. Pieces I have never encountered for a puzzle I have never fathomed."

"Again, super helpful," I grumbled.

His wings fell limp. Never a good sign.

"Perhaps we ought to write out what we know," Ms. Neally finally spoke up.

"I dinnae think this jabbering is helping thah wee lassie," Baert said, chewing loudly. He had left his fighting stance to swipe some pastries from the kitchen. He licked his fingers and smacked contentedly. "What we barry need," he said between bites, "is right action."

"He does have a point," I said as I turned toward Baert. I gasped. "Baert! Goddammit! What are you eating?" I cried as I swiped the dessert from his hands that were swelling and growing blotchy right before my eyes.

"Thah skan treat said banoffee!" he cried as he vigorously itched his arms, his legs.

"Baert, that's peanut butter. I don't have an epi-pen this time!" I said and looked frantically at Uncle Seb, who shrugged, and then at Ms. Neally.

"Benadryl. I'll fetch some. There's a market just down the street."

"This is as good a time as any to adjourn," Uncle Seb added. "Egg, you come with me. Baert, you dumbass, go with Yaël. And you," he paused and looked at Gil who cocked her head coquettishly and gave a wink, "go back to whatever crystal ball you crawled out of."

She let out a long, throaty laugh and twirled her skirts about. A moth came flapping out of somewhere ... somewhere *on her*.

I turned to find Dragon, but he had already left. I followed my uncle out the door and swiped the fiducia stone along the way.

"Hmmmm, I saw that!" Gil called behind me. "Confidence in chaos, Eve Archer! Confidence in chaos!"

I jogged down the steps with her husky words bouncing around my brain.

My stomach growled and my phone chimed.

I wished the world would stop for just a minute.

Just a minute.

Just a ...

Minute ....

A thick wave of sleep overcame me, and I tumbled down, down, down ...

48

AUDIO HOSTEM

y head hurt. My chest heaved under an enormous weight, but when I finally got my eyes open and looked down, there was nothing there. Just my ratty blue hoodie.

I was warm. Not just warm; I was hot and sweaty. I looked up from where I sat, still on the steps of the coffee house. A long, twisted finger poked my cheek.

"Sssssssooooo, she ssssleepsssss no longer."

I looked up, groggy and exhausted. Judge Penelope Roderick-Beauregard stood over me, skin loose and saggy, eye sockets dark and empty. She thrust a tennis ball-sized yellow orb in my face and cackled. The familiarity of it all, the heaviness, the sleepiness, the burning of Peridiote, the sound of that disgusting being, rippled through my body.

She threw her head back again in sickening glee and, just as another maniacal cackle burst out, a black MG skidded onto the sidewalk and up to the steps. A screech, like an animal who just took an arrow to the chest, pierced my ears. Penelope – Obrenox? – buckled forward and collapsed against me. Uncle Seb threw the car into reverse and was ready for another go. I wiggled beneath the bony load and waved my hands in desperation; the car screeched to a stop just in front of me.

The Peridiote tumbled out of the sinewy grasp and rolled down the steps. The possessed judge, eyes dark but wild, rolled away from me and tried to stand.

The warmth dissipated.

The heaviness lifted.

But the headache, the fatigue, that was still very much with me.

"Egg, let's go! Drahk will take care of this," Uncle Seb hollered from the car. I stumbled away and heaved open the door. Before I could even pull it shut, Uncle Seb hit the gas and lurched the car forward more.

Another piercing screech.

The MG pulled away, leaving a writhing something in a burgundy suit shrieking on the steps. Wings flapped overhead.

My eyes closed. I tried to keep them open, I really did. Uncle Seb jostled me awake as my head knocked against the window. He was talking to me. In between drooping eyelids, I spotted a familiar Australian Shepherd running down the street next to us again.

But stranger than that, I swear I saw ... No way. It couldn't be.

Philippa?

That brush with a peridiote stone must have really rocked my brain. That had to be the only explanation, right?

49

MALA TEMPORA CURRUNT

Uncle Seb didn't walk me inside. He did all but kick me out onto the curb. I had barely turned to wave when he had already sped off.

"Mom?" I called as I pushed the door open. It seemed heavier than usual. The lingering effects of a Peridiote orb. "Mom, are you home?"

My head still pounded. I was still in my mom's navy blue suit. I wondered how hard it was to get pit stains out of a wool-gaberdine blend.

"I wondered when I'd see you!" my mom said as she bounded down the stairs. Her chipper movement made my eye twitch. "I, um, well, I wasn't sure how you were feeling after this morning, but," she paused and fidgeted with the newel post, mumbling how she'd get around to tightening it, "Oh, this banister! But never mind, what I was saying, I figured that you'd perhaps need time with your, eh, your ... you know ... friends?"

I brushed past her on the staircase with two goals in mind: pain relief, get to the hospital.

"Or maybe they're not your friends? Your uncle and a teacher? I guess those are hardly friends. And the others," she trailed off as her brow furrowed with the incredible task of naming a dragon and an elf as "friends" in present-day.

I threw my head back and popped some acetaminophen caplets into my mouth and greedily drank cup after cup of water. I changed from my respectable court attire back into my daily garb. My movements were robotic, mechanical. I was focused.

If I let my mind wander to the day's events ... I shuddered and slapped my cheek. That review would break me, I knew it. I set my jaw and headed downstairs.

"You going to the hospital?" I said as I bounded past my mom, still on the stairs, leaning pensively against the banister.

"What? Oh, sure! That's a great idea," she said and grabbed her keys.

"You need shoes on," I said and pointed to her feet, both in different socks, as we walked out the door.

"Oh! So I do!"

The drive to the hospital was silent, as they tended to be these days. I didn't know what to do with my mom. With her, about her, for her ... It all evaded me. One minute she was sharply dressed, magnetic with her conversation and poise; the next, she was uprooting unripe potatoes in the garden at midnight if she even got out of bed.

We both carried similar lots, she and I. Lots that would remain heavy so long as that silence persisted. For all it really said, if it said anything, was that neither of us trusted the other with those lots.

"You're in more of a hurry than usual!" my mom cried after me as I blasted out of the car and into the hospital. The car alarm beeped behind me. I was already in the elevator, the doors ready to close, when her hand reached through the silver doors. "What's gotten into you? Geez. We're both going to the same place, for the same person, you know."

I charged down the hall. My heart pounded. I swung open the familiar door in the ICU with my breath held.

There, in the dim light surrounded by happily chirping monitors and a jungle of IVs, was my sister.

"Philippa!" I cried and fell upon my sleeping sister. "Thank goodness! You wouldn't believe what I thought I saw."

My mom appeared, panting, followed by Jürgen, frowning.

"Ah, good! You are here," he said as he entered the room and pulled the door shut. That was odd. The door was always open unless I closed it. "Listen, I feel I need to ask you something. There are some strange things happening. Things that I do not know how … ehm, I cannot make sense of it."

I gulped. What did he know? What had he seen?

Do not react, Evechild.

Dragon? My head jerked up. I winced; the post-peridiote headache hadn't completely dissipated yet.

There has been a development.

"What development?" I said aloud. Jürgen frowned.

"I suppose you could call it a development, yes. I believe," he stopped, looked around, and lowered his voice, "I believe I have seen someone going in and out of her room. A friend, perhaps, in a sort of robe. And… and, this is awkward."

"What's awkward? What kind of friend? Describe him?" I spoke rapidly. I think my voice trembled, for I already knew what he was getting at, what Dragon was getting at.

"A shorter guy, I think. He's come in and out at least three times. I saw … *Scheisse*, how do I say this, I think I saw him trying to, you know, make out with her."

"What?!" my mom squealed. "Eve, do you know anything about this? Phlee doesn't have a boyfriend … does she?!"

"Hold on, calm down," I said impatiently. "Jürgen, are you certain that's what was happening? Or was someone just kinda, like, bowing over her, with his back to you?"

Jürgen tilted his head and folded his arms. My mom looked from him to me and back again, her mouth agape.

"You know what? I think you may be right. I think I may have made an incorrect conclusion. That makes more sense," he said, looking relieved. "But, if you know who this is, you need to tell him it is very important he sign in on the ICU guest registry. We cannot have people just coming and going here."

I nodded but said nothing. My brain was spinning out of control. There was only one reason an Amythystic would be sneaking in and out of here.

"And – this is the really strange thing," Jürgen continued, "I think he's leaving some kind of jewelry or something. I have found a gemstone on her head before. I think she has an allergy to it, however, as it leaves a sort of contusion on the skin. Near that same spot that was burnt by the curling iron recently."

"What? Who would do that? You can have allergies to rocks? When did you curl her hair? Eve?"

My mom's barrage of questions fell unanswered down the hall as I charged toward the elevator bay. Top floor to creepy hallway to fire exit. I walked out onto the hospital roof and looked around. Pigeons clustered in a corner stopped to cock their heads at me.

I walked menacingly toward them and flapped my arms until they jumped and scattered.

"I see Baert has advised you well!" Dragon laughed behind me.

I spun around. Sunset was starting; Dragon's frame was formidable against the jewel-toned sky. I didn't hug him. I didn't smile.

"That's why she's still in a coma. The Amythystics are keeping her like that," I said as more of a statement than a question.

Dragon's face fell.

"I did not know, Evechild," he said softly.

I didn't believe him. He looked up. His imploring eyes told me he had heard that last thought of mine. I didn't care.

"They've never attempted something so bold, creating from a human in this dimension. I could not have predicted this. You must believe me."

"What are talking about? Creating what?"

"Obrenox has found a new way to garner power, to augment forces."

"But you – you finished Obrenox, right? Or whoever that was as the judge? So ... so shouldn't it be over?"

"I wish it were that simple, Evechild," Dragon said and extended a talon. "Come with me, we've much to discuss."

I shrugged it away and folded my arms.

"We stay here. Tell me right now. Who was that judge? I – I saw Uncle Seb run over her! She spoke just like him, it ... it had to be him, right?"

I shook all over. Not from any one emotion. Maybe from all of them, shimmying around in my system, in one frenetic wave of exhaustion.

"What we can ascertain, Evechild, is that they've mastered gene-splicing, in essence," Dragon said, then looked at me expectantly. I waved my hand impatiently for him to continue. "The Amythystics are not just using their cloning techniques via tubes, which you and I saw. It seems ... it seems they are taking material from multiple subjects and creating replicas therein."

I was silent. A pigeon cooed behind me. Several more shuffled about and pecked at my laces. I kicked my foot hard and felt contact with a little grey body. Feathers floated in the air as the pigeons alighted once more, with one now limping behind the rest.

I shouldn't have been pleased with that moment of unexpected violence. But I was.

"There are at least six others," Dragon said quietly as he cleared his throat.

"Six other what?"

"Six others ... who ... who look like—"

"Who look like what?"

Dragon looked away. My whole body trembled under the weight of knowledge I didn't want to carry.

"Who look like what, Dragon?" I said again, the aching knowledge already in me. But I knew neither of us wanted it said aloud.

"Philippa," he said at last. "Who look like your sister Philippa."

50

SUNT OMNES UNUM

I had never been much interested in cloning.

Other concepts at the crossroads of medicine and science fascinated me more. Cloning was ... fine.

My mom had recounted the craze that overtook the world when Dolly the Sheep was successfully cloned while she was in high school. I had met this information with a chuckle and a shake of my head, but had made little to no effort to follow up on the science of it all. Until all this tube business in the seventh dimension came about, I can't recall a single time I've considered the process of cloning something or someone.

Now it was all I could think about.

How much and how many of my sister existed beyond that hospital room?

"Ms. Archer, are you going to ask your question, or keep us all in suspense?"

"What?" I said, suddenly aware of Mr. Simmons talking to me. Well, talking *at* me.

"Your hand has been raised for quite some time," he said as he rubbed his brow. "I've paused my lecture to address your query. So?"

I looked up. My hand was indeed raised. I lowered my arm as my cheeks reddened.

"Uh, you answered it. Just ... um ... just stretching."

There was some snickering behind me, and then the class fell silent as it acquiesced to Mr. Simmons' high voice droning on and on about polynomials.

This dumb algebra made my heart sting; I remembered Philippa celebrating a perfect score on her own exam on polynomials and monomials.

Would a clone of her know about that? Do these copies of my sister get her memories?

I shuddered. *Copies of my sister.* Is that even what they are?

I pulled out my laptop, opened an algebra worksheet first to cover up what I was really doing, and typed *how to cloen hymans* and hit the enter key.

My face reddened. Big time. I scrolled down line after line of search results explaining female anatomy in picture and in word. What the hell had I looked up?

I rapidly hit the backspace key as I realized the *u* and the *y* are next to each other on the keyboard.

"Hey, what are you – oh, ehm, sorry," Elke said over my shoulder. "Should you be researching that on a school computer?"

Now my face burned.

"I mistyped," I grumbled.

"What were you meaning to type?" she asked.

I was in a pickle. Do I take the humiliation if accidentally looking up hymens? Or explain to her that I was doing a little research on cloning humans, and then open myself up to the questions that would inevitably follow? What rational reason could I have for researching cloning? What rational reason could I have for researching hymens on a school-issued laptop?

I didn't have time to follow through with either mortifying scenario. I looked up, feeling eyes on me, to Mr. Simmons pointing at me. A small man in a pink striped shirt who looked too young to be balding stuck waved me over.

"Eh, Ms. Archer, is it? If you could just step outside with me for a moment? Perhaps you'd like to bring your belongings, however?"

Everything out of this guy's mouth was a whispered question. Head down, I obediently followed his upturned instructions. Once we were in the hall with the door closed, he gestured for me to follow him once more.

"Let's walk and talk?" he said in a quiet voice. Quiet and apologetic. "You are aware of our technology here at Willamette Preparatory Academy?"

I nodded without looking up. I clomped in my untied sneakers alongside his soft, measured steps.

"Then you understand why your most recent search was immediately flagged and brought to my attention, per our technology protocols?"

My head shot up. I clearly understood very little about their technology, protocols or otherwise. Or technology in general.

"It happens that fast?" I said, totally missing his point. "I mean, I barely hit *enter* before you showed up. That's pretty amazing."

"Regardless of speed," he said, flustered, "you really shouldn't be looking up ... such terms?" He stopped, still flustered, and brushed his hand along the top of his bald head. "Not that I would feign to discourage one from ... learning about one's ... anatomy? But perhaps such searches ought to be left to ... one's private device? Preferably off campus?"

"Of course. You're completely right," I said right away, trying to get the encounter to end as quickly as possible. "I mean, it *was* a typo, for the record."

"I'm sure it was? They usually are?" he said with a smirk. "I'll need to report this to Principal Fernhouser, of course? And I'll be confiscating your device for the remainder of the day?"

"Yeah, sure, whatever," I mumbled. Then I looked up. "Hold on, it *was* a typo! I wasn't looking up ... you *know*. The letters are next to each other!"

This nameless Defender of Chaste Technology walked silently away, nodding his head and waving back at me. Patronizingly. He stopped and motioned for me to come over again. I groaned but followed.

"Are you giving me my laptop back? Because I can't really do my homework without it."

"I thought you might like to hear the bright side? I try to focus on positives in these teachable moments?"

The phrase made my eyes roll. I had no control of them.

"Yeah, hit me. What's the silver lining here or whatever?"

"I had managed to block what I deemed were all possible search terms and phrases of questionable or moral ambiguity? But yours, well yours was one I missed! So, now you've helped bolster the protectors of decency within our little world of technology? A stronger and safer browser experience for all?"

He was so pleased – I think I even heard an exclamation in his voice rather than a question – that all I could do was shrug and attempt a smile. He waved my laptop in the air and gave me a nod, then turned and continued his careful, soundless walk back to whatever nook Principal Fernhouser kept him caged in.

"Ah, good! I found you! I brought the rest of your algebra assignments," Elke said, walking quickly toward me. I liked her walk. "Why were you taken out of the class? Who was that man? Another teacher?"

"Some IT guy, I gathered," I said with a shrug. And then, before Elke could connect the dots, I hastily continued, "my laptop's broken. Super glitchy ... yeah, like, I think it has a virus or something. Yeah, that's right, it just, sort of, had a mind of its own."

She didn't press further. I breathed a sigh of relief and continued to my next class no more informed on the ways of cloning than I was before. If anything, I think I understood less.

"You know anything about cloning?" I said without expecting Elke to have that word down in her second language, let alone have an answer about it.

"Clones?" she asked. "I do not, specifically, but my uncle has studied medicine and science his entire life. He recently showed me a film on a sheep in Scotland—"

"Oh my gosh, what is it with that generation and Dolly the sheep?" I cut her off, laughing.

"You know this film? Oh, it was fascinating," she said. "Why are you laughing? It was so important in science!"

"It's just an obscure reference to have at our age, I think. It's ... it's nothing, don't worry about it. But your uncle is a doctor?"

The bell rang before we could finish our conversation. With a wave, she was off.

That seemed to be the theme of the day: unfinished thoughts.

51

AUT VIAM INVENIAM AUT FACIAM

I couldn't believe what I was hearing.

Uncle Seb, Dragon, Ms. Neally ... they were all speaking nonsense. Jibberish.

I even had the momentary suspicion that it wasn't them at all, but some strange clone-body-snatching situation, like that one encounter with an Uncle Seb clone. I shuddered and felt along the back of my head. I still had a welt there from my tuck-and-roll out of his car.

"Egg, you know we have to act."

"I'm afraid the timing is imperative, Evechild."

"Eve, I believe you are capable of this. You have the strength."

I stared at each of them, unable to speak.

"This is pointless. The kid's been through enough," Uncle Seb said, turning to Dragon.

"Alas, she is our only option presently!" Dragon wailed.

"She is not a last resort but a trained gift," Ms. Neally said gently.

Uncle Seb snorted. Dragon scowled at him. Ms. Neally turned and knelt in front of me.

"Eve? Do you understand what we're asking of you?"

I nodded slowly.

"Can you," Ms. Neally started, then glanced nervously back at Dragon and Uncle Seb, "can you verify what you believe your role is now?" she said carefully.

"You want me," I said finally, slowly, "to go back into the Seventh. Without any of you."

"Yes," Ms. Neally said, nodding her head encouragingly. "And then?"

"And then," I started again, slower still, "and then find Obrenox and ... and," I stopped, and swallowed hard, "and give him ... give him ... a drink? Of something? Because a Kip reported, from an unknown source, that he is, um," I shifted uncomfortably, "sick from injuries he sustained here," I paused and looked at Uncle Seb, who nodded and gave a little salute. "And therefore ... he is ... easier to take down. Especially if the plane isn't there to alert anyone."

"That is the gist of it, yes. Well done," Ms. Neally said softly, her smile looking forced now.

"Yeah, that's the gist of it," I mumbled. "We don't even know if this ... whatever this syrup is ... is going to take him down, but at least we have the gist of something."

"It's an ancient elixir packed with zeolites. They consume methane, which Obrenox needs. It will almost certainly prove fatally toxic for him," Ms. Neally said. "We wouldn't contrive such a plan without the belief of success therein."

"Yeah, I get it. It just seems like a lot of question marks. And ... and," I coughed, "I don't know why, I, um, you know, just thought we had more time. More time before ... before, going back. But ... but, I get it. I get it."

Ms. Neally smiled faintly. Dragon sighed heavily. Uncle Seb turned and threw his hands up in the air.

"Pointless! Are you hearing this, Drahk? The kid can't wrap her head around this. Hell, I can barely wrap my head around this. You know it's," Uncle Seb stopped and glanced at me, then leaned in close to Dragon. "It's basically a suicide mission."

"Enough," Ms. Neally said abruptly and stood up. "You are poisoning her mind. And dismissing her strength and your skill in the process. Shame on you, Sebastian."

Uncle Seb shook his head, fetched a pebble from the gravel at his feet, and flung it hard. The tiny rock puttered down the gravel drive. We all watched it for some reason. The harvest sunset cast a warm glow on the gray rock. The hangar gleamed a bright white, another fresh coat of paint on it compliments of the Kips. It was an otherwise beautiful day. But we four couldn't see beyond a gray pebble flung out of frustration with a futile mission.

Dragon muttered something Latin sounding. This roused Ms. Neally, which incited Uncle Seb, and the three began arguing all over again. Languages I recognized and some I didn't swirled in front of me.

"I'll do it," I said quietly.

They raged on. I felt like the little kid at the dinner table trying to get the grown-ups' attention because the milk had spilled but didn't want to be blamed for it.

"I said, I'll do it," I stammered, my voice shaking as I tried to raise it.

Dragon looked at me first. His brow softened and his shoulders dropped.

"Oh, Evechild. It is still possible," he said, then looked anxiously at Ms. Neally, who folded her arms and looked away, "that is, there's a small possibility we can find an alternative solution."

"Egg, listen, it's a crazy shot, and I don't agree with it, but if you're willing," Uncle Seb paused and looked at me hard, then coughed, "we, well, shit, we probably oughtta try."

"I get it," I said in a whisper. "I can do it."

Ms. Neally put her arm around me. Dragon sat down next to her. Uncle Seb remained standing, unsoftened.

"Then let's get on with it already," he growled.

"Evechild, you still have the spheresaii?"

I nodded.

"Well, I have them in there," I said, gesturing toward the hangar. "You think I'll need them again?"

"Better safe than sorry, you know that," Uncle Seb grumbled.

Ms. Neally glared at him, then turned to me.

"You understand we are not intending you harm. But we have this opportunity, wherein Obrenox' health and virility are compromised, and it is ... prudent – yes, prudent – that we take advantage of this," she said quietly.

I nodded again.

"I'm sure you've many thoughts and questions," Dragon said all-too knowingly. "Is there any one thing you would like addressed presently?"

I looked over at him. His eyes were staring right through me. I dropped my head.

"You know what I'm wondering," I murmured.

Uncle Seb walked over and dropped onto the ground next to me.

"You're worried you won't make it?" he asked. Ms. Neally shot him a look.

"No," I said softly. "I don't care if I make it."

Before Uncle Seb could protest that statement, Dragon rose up.

"Your mother," he said solemnly. "You wonder if you should tell her you're going this time."

"Yeah," I whispered.

"Shit," Uncle Seb muttered.

"Toth help us," Ms. Neally said quietly.

Dear Mum,

Hey, Ma. It's me. Egg. Your favorite child. (That joke is kinda messed up now, you know, considering everything. But I'm writing in pen on my last piece of good paper, so it stands.)

First, I love you. I really do. For a lot of reasons that I should probably run down for you some time. But I'll save that for later. Because there will be a later.

I have to go for a while. I'm still not entirely certain how the time difference works in different dimensions, but, as I understand it, to you I'll only be gone for a few hours. So maybe I don't even need to write this.

But I do have to write this. I just need you to have something to read from me in case –

I stopped writing for a minute to wipe my nose. This was a little harder than I thought it would be. I shook my head, trying to release the image of my mom, alone, one daughter lost to a coma, the other lost to …. I shook my head harder. A giant tear fell and smudged the last two words. I drew my sleeve across my wet eyes and pressed on.

In case I'm not able to tell you in person, for whatever reason. I need you to know that you're a great mom. I know things haven't been easy for you – I understand that better and better as I get older – and I really appreciate all the little things you do for me and Phlee to keep life great. I've never had to launder a shirt a day in my life, and my favorite pop tarts are somehow mysteriously always stocked. You'd leave good-luck treats for us in our backpacks, with little notes on everything. A lot of kids never got anything like that. And I think I've never really said thank you. Because I am thankful for it. For you.

And second, I'm really sorry.

I paused and took a deep breath. Why was I even doing this? I sat back, almost acting on the urge to just crumple up the paper and throw it away. But something tugged and pulled inside of me. I rocked my neck side to side and stared the wall. It was decorated with artsy black-and-white photos of my sister and me, like nearly every other wall in the house. I smiled faintly, a lump rising in my throat again. My mom, the art history major, preferred to look at my and sister's ugly mugs on her walls over the loads of fine art prints she had stashed away somewhere.

So, so sorry. For so many things. I wonder if I had been a more normal kid, who didn't dream of dragons and watch physics videos on YouTube, if I could have avoided all of this. Like maybe someone else would have been "called" to take on this task instead of me. I wish I had told you about the things that were happening around me; maybe I could have at least gotten you to be on your guard more so you and Phlee never ended up hostage in the first place. The irony of you getting taken – you're the strongest person I know, and the only one I know who brags about teaching self-defense at the community center. But it was awful. I wasn't okay when I was without you. I'm sorry that happened to both of us. And I need you to know you are important to me.

Go enjoy a green juice. Listen to some Beatles for me (preferably the White album). Play the piano more. I really like it when you play.

I love you.

egg

p.s. I might secretly like running.

Satisfied, I wiped my nose again and folded the paper into neat thirds. I stretched and ran upstairs to my room. I rummaged around my drawers and shelves until I found another piece of paper I was saving: a sheet of creamy marbled parchment left over from a school project years ago. I smiled.

It was perfect. Philippa would love it.

My breath caught in my throat as the reality of writing a similar letter to my sister crashed upon me. I blinked hard. Tears pricked the corners of my eyes.

I rounded the corner from the stairway to the dining room and stopped.

My heart dropped.

"Eve? What is ... what is this?"

My mom stood trembling; my letter lay balanced atop her shaking hands.

325

52

CANIS CANEM EDIT

"Eve, it is important you know you are in a safe space," Malcolm said quietly. His eyes were unmoving, unblinking. "We are here to keep you safe."

I looked at my mom with annoyance.

"This guy makes house calls?"

"I assure you, in-home therapy is a credible and viable platform, particularly when families are ... in distress," Malcom said quickly. "And was presented in the literature about my private practice."

"Seem awfully defensive, Doctor," I muttered.

"Eve, he's just here to help ... you ... and me ... help you," my mom stammered. She got up from her chair in the corner and began tidying things. Again.

"Look, I'm not ... suicidal," I said, choking out that last word. "And if I were, this wouldn't be helping anyway."

"Eve, you have written what is clearly and intent-to-exit letter to your mother. I'd like to help you examine what drove you to that action, and what your thought process for ... executing your plans might be," Malcolm said. The way he intellectualized the concept, making it sound more like a plan of action for assembling a shed, was oddly disarming. Maybe he was good at his job after all.

"Eve, please, my lovely child, I didn't know what to do so I called him! I think he can help, though! If you'll let him!"

I looked away, thoroughly at a loss. Do I tell her what the letter actually meant? Do I tell *them*? Like, hey, Malcolm, I'm not trying to off myself, but the end-result of my slipping into another dimension to poison an evil clone lord while he has the sniffles might be the same. So I wrote my mom a nice letter to read so she doesn't think I ran away or was kidnapped or something.

I snorted.

"You can say anything here, Eve. Anything. It's okay. You are safe," Malcolm said, leaning forward earnestly.

"I know I can. This is my freaking house. And I *was* safe," I said with a nasty look at my mom, "until I was made to sit in this ... this ... whatever the hell this is, an intervention or whatever," I said as I stood up. "I'm leaving."

I paused and looked back at them, Malcolm and my mom, their heads both cocked sympathetically to the side like prairie dogs watching their friend get slaughtered.

"To be clear, I'm going to bed. Alive. With plans to wake up that way. Goodnight," I barked as I marched up the stairs.

I didn't brush my teeth. I didn't even change into pajamas. I just dove under my covers and stared at the ceiling, a thousand thoughts swirling around me. I heard their voices downstairs, low and serious, then an out-of-place guffaw from my mom. The front door creaked open, then closed. A click of the lock, then footsteps on the stairs.

"Great," I muttered. "Super pumped for this conversation."

"Eve?" my mom said gently as she lightly tapped on the door.

"Yeah, come in."

"Eve, I know you must have so much on your mind, and I'm so sorry I haven't really asked you how you're doing or what's going on in your world, but I – but I – oh, my Egg, I'm so sorry you feel like this!"

My mom collapsed on me, heaving and sobbing.

Christ, I felt awful.

"Mom, Ma, hey, no, it's not like that," I said gently, pushing lightly on her shoulders. A jolt of something – guilt? rage? – pulsed quickly within me. For everything she had just said was true. She never asked me about anything. She never asked how I was doing.

"It's not? Then why –" my mom said as she sat up, sniffing.

"The letter," I said, pausing to breathe deeply, "well, it was just a little something to have because I have to go ... to, um, that place ...." I trailed off looking at her huge, earnest eyes, so full of worry. "Jesus, Mom, I have to go back to the Seventh. If you had actually read what I wrote, you can totally see I was talking about going to another dimension. Not freaking offing myself," I barked. "They think they figured out a way to get rid of Obrenox. For good. So, I'm going. And I wrote you that stupid letter in case ... in case ...."

I couldn't finish. I was numb.

My mom stood up, brushed her fingers against her cheeks, and straightened her sweater. She stood in front of my bed for what seemed like an eternity. I resumed my ceiling stare.

"I don't know what to do with this," she said finally. "But I love you."

She turned to leave my room and paused at the door. Her eyes stayed on the floor.

"And I'm proud of you."

The door shut quietly. I heard her sniffling as she padded down the hall. I heard her bedroom door squeak open. I heard the stream of water, then the dull thud of a shower door shutting.

The shower was her favorite place to cry. She once referred to it as poetic and metaphorically cleansing. I've taken a billion showers and I've never found any poetry in there. I finish them barely cleaner than when I began, let alone metaphorically cleaner.

She said she was proud of me. A year ago that statement would have sent me over the moon. But now? I shrugged off the statement like an old coat – I wore it because I needed it, but I definitely wasn't parading around any fashion shows in it.

I pulled on my covers and tucked the blankets all around me. I liked that feeling. I snuggled into them and closed my eyes, fully expecting the exhaustion of the overwhelming day to pull me right into sleep.

No such luck.

"Ugh, forget this," I said as I thrashed around to release my body was tightly tucked blankets. I slid out of bed and grabbed my backpack.

"To Philippa I goooo," I sang softly as I heaved *Fortis Librae* onto my lap and opened it to an increasingly well-worn page. I closed my eyes and quietly chanted the Latin recitation. Baert had told me I could only use the book's travel function if I had one of them with me. An accidental appearance at my favorite doughnut counter that I used to frequent with Phlee proved that statement wrong.

I coughed and opened my eyes. *Yes, I did it!* I grinned and waited, listening, behind the sterile curtain tucked in the corner of Philippa's hospital room. A close call with an unsuspecting nurse last time had me plot logistics a bit better. So, I had memorized every seam of this curtain, its skinny stainless-steel poles, and the mint-green and beige checkerboard tiles it stood upon.

All I heard were the familiar beeps and chirps of the equipment lording over my sister in her bed. I poked my head out. Coast clear.

Walking around the perimeter of the room as quietly as I could, I made my way to the door, and, taking care not to draw attention, gingerly pulled it closed. Through the thin window in the door, I caught the concerned glance of a woman seated at the counter facing Philippa's room. She got up with a frown.

"Crap!" I hissed and looked around. Panicked, I tucked myself behind the closest lounge chair and pulled a recycle bin against it to shield my backside.

"Is someone in here? Visiting hours are long gone," the woman said as she shuffled around Philippa in bed and knocked on the wall next to the bathroom.

"You in there?" The door to the small en-suite restroom clicked open. "Hmm. Strange," she said and lumbered back to her station.

She left the door to the room open. *Open.*

"Gah!" I groaned. I slumped down in my spot and pouted. "Thwarted," I mumbled.

Across from me, shieled from outside view by Philippa's bed, a small cabinet door creaked open. A tiny hand appeared. It pressed against the inside of the door, then withdrew. One leg slowly slid out, then another, then a purple tunic-clad torso, then a mass of red hair.

"Baert!" I hissed, then recoiled.

That same woman's head shot upright and stared hard in my direction. Baert, however, was oblivious. He crawled, silently, up the side of Philippa's bed. He peered over the rails, then hoisted himself up and over next to her. I started to object, then shut my mouth.

I watched the little elf reach inside a small satchel and take out a miniature hairbrush and a tiny glass bottle. Tenderly, he selected a length of hair, his tiny fingers working through tangles, and brushed it. He hummed a bit as he did so, softly, until Philippa's whole mop of dark brown hair was smooth and placed elegantly around her face. He dabbed a bit of the contents of the glass vial along the side of her neck, just under a scrawled scabby wound.

Still humming, he shimmied to the end of her bed and, placing her feet in his lap, opened his satchel once more.

My vision blurred. Baert held my sister's bare foot in his hand, and with all the tenderness in the world, ran a pumice stone gently against it. One foot, then the other. Some lotion, an emery board along her toenails, then a pair of knitted socks I hadn't seen before.

My throat caught. Baert silently replaced his tiny tools in his satchel, tidied the blankets around my sister's sleeping body, and withdrew back into the cabinet with as little disturbance as when he arrived.

I sat, unmoving, with my hand against my mouth as my body heaved great sobs behind that blue vinyl chair on the floor of my sister's hospital room.

My dear friend, that sweet elf!

I wrapped my arms around me and clutched my sides.

"Oh, Phlee," I whispered into the still air. "I don't want this to be the last time I see you. I don't want to remember you this way, I don't want you to remember me as … as … Oh, Phlee!"

I gave up and sobbed. Loudly and openly.

I must have fallen asleep there, in the shadows between that chair and the wall. A toe pushed into my side.

"You supposed to be here?"

A different woman's voice jolted me awake. I looked up, wild-eyed and groggy. "Oh. It's you. Didn't see you sign in. Make sure you get that name on the register, I ain't covering for your skinny butt again when they do the security audits, no ma'am."

The nurse wandered out of the room, still grumbling about her thankless work. I stretched and tried to stand. My leg buckled and I fell.

"Ooooh! Yikes! Crap," I said and massaged my foot. It was dead asleep. Pins and needles. "Ugh, you have no idea how terrible this is."

I looked up at my sister with a chuckle. Her monitors beeped back, not entertained. But I think she would have laughed.

"I don't know why, I thought you'd magically be awake," I murmured as a limped over to her bedside. "I have to tell you the sweetest thing, Phlee. It's Baert. You can't even imagine – oh my god, but first, you remember Elke? That German foreign exchange student I told you about? Well, she actually lives here, well, kinda, but anyhow, that's not the point."

I babbled relentlessly to my sister's unmoving face, laughing here, shrugging there, accepting her solemn silence as agreement on some points. I stroked her hair, so soft and smooth from the love of an elf.

That lump rose in my throat again.

"Phlee, there's another reason I came here. I mean, like, I wanted to tell you that stuff, for sure, and you totally need to know it, but, um, ok, here goes," I said as I pulled a chair over next to her bed.

"You should put on some music when you talk to her."

I startled, then glowered. Who was interrupting me?

"Oh. Hi Dr. Daas. Um, long time no see," I mumbled as I wiped my sleeve across my face and moved away from the bed. "I, er, I'm just leaving."

He didn't look up from his clipboard and continued to write as he spoke. I didn't know that was even humanly possible.

"Remember to bring music. Remarkable research around the brain and music," he murmured, still scrawling away on his pad. "Your mother in later?"

"Dunno. Probably," I said. But then my blood suddenly froze. "Why? Should she be? Did something happen? Is there any update?"

"No, no, nothing like that," he said and finally looked up. His brow softened. "I just hadn't checked in with your mom in a while, that's all." He smiled and gave me a wave. "Toodle-oo."

My jaw clenched. I shoved my hands in my pockets and trudged down the hall.

"Toodle-oo," I grumbled to myself. "He floats in, all casual, like it wasn't his fault she's lying in there in the first place." I kicked a paper cup lying on the floor, then turned, picked it up, and walked it to a recycling bin. I caught a glimpse of my reflection in the colorful mirrored walls as I walked. I jumped. "Yikes," I said aloud. "Forgot I slept here."

I spun around, looking for the exit, then groaned. The book! That's how I had come here. And I left it in Philippa's room.

As I stomped back, my mind turned back to Baert. My mood softened; so did my steps. Eyes blurry, I kept my head down as I shuffled past Dr. Daas and team. My book safely back in my hands, I headed down the hall with their voices trailing behind me.

"Yes, isn't it wild? One sister in a coma, the other on trial for *murder*."

"Those poor parents."

"Just a mom, as far as I know. And she was admitted herself not too long ago with cardiac arrest or something."

"Christ, I'd just off myself."

Laughter. Then the beep of the elevator door arriving. Those were the last sounds I heard.

53

OBTORTO COLLO

My head hurt.

My wrists hurt.

They were bound behind me.

But not well, it turned out, as I jostled about and freed my hands.

I was in the backseat of a car. There was a strip of tape over my mouth. It was dark out. Two guys in dark hats I didn't recognize were up front. The one driving was breathing hard and beating his hands against the steering wheel.

"Man, that was such a rush!" the driver said between whoops and hollers. "I can't believe we did it. Man, are you feeling this?!"

"Yeah, yeah," the guy in the passenger seat said. "We've seen enough movies, and it's not rocket science. And anyway, I'm not a huge fan of this. So, let's – shit. She's up. Yo, shut up back there!"

I stopped thrashing and looked up. Something about that voice was familiar.

"Man, I actually wish we were being followed right now, you know? I'd love to see how I'd handle being chased. Man, I would ace that shit!"

"Let's just get her back, yeah?"

"Yeah. And get paaaaaid!"

I paused trying to peel the tape from my mouth. Someone was paid to kidnap me? A human? Strange as it was, an abduction by some mythical creature seemed more likely, given my life lately.

The car slowed as it approached an iron gate at the base of a long drive. The driver leaned out the window to punch in a security code. My heart pounded. He was distracted. They both were. The car was stopped. I had to act.

I scanned the backseat for anything weapon-like: scissors, a pencil, a bag, anything! But it was immaculate. Slowly, slowly, I inched to the left toward the door.

"Dude, how many times are you here? How do you not know the code?"

"Relax. Shut up. They must've changed it. Here, she's texting me right now. I'll get it."

Now! I heaved my body against the door as I pulled hard on the handle.

It didn't budge.

I braced myself and pushed again.

"What the—? What are you doing back there?"

The guy in the passenger seat spun around and reached back. I kicked at his hand while I lunged to the other side and tried that door.

"Hey, idiot, the child locks are on. C'mon, the gates are open. She's already all pissy that we're late."

I slumped down in the backseat as the car slowly drove up the winding driveway. I wiggled my lips under their sticky prison; I felt the bottom corner loosen. A palatial home loomed in the distance. I knew there were pretty nice houses in Happy Valley, but this one took the cake. Why on earth were we at that house? Whose was it?

The car pulled around the circular drive and stopped in front of the main entrance like we were in the valet zone of a hotel.

"Shit, that's her. That means she's been waiting. C'mon, let's get this over with," the driver sighed as he turned off the ignition. The other guy had already gotten out and was waiting outside my door.

"Got her right here for ya!" he called to someone in a coat and hat walking quickly toward us. Blonde hair spilled out from under a fur cap. The coat flapped in the cold wind and revealed a woman dressed in pajamas that were fancier than my nicest concert dress.

"No way," I breathed through my tape.

The driver walked up to her and attempted a hug. No such luck.

"Well?" she squealed. "Where is she?"

"Gotter right back here," the guy in front of my door said. He pulled on the handle. The door remained locked. "Bro, can you be a pal? The locks?"

The driver rolled his eyes and hit his key fob twice.

"Why is she locked in your car? What is that?! What did you do?"

"Channing, babe, you said to pick her up and bring her to you. So, uh, obviously that's what we did."

"Like this?! This isn't a goddamn heist movie! I meant, to just get her like a normal person. As in, 'hey, would you like to come by for a coffee or something,' and then go? What the hell is wrong with you two?"

Channing Reagan Barrenton swatted at both the bandits – the driver I now recognized as Guy. She opened the door and offered a hand. Her smile turned to a scowl as she straightened and yelled at her lackies once more.

"You put a goddamn gag on her?"

"Babe, it's just tape."

"You two are sociopaths."

"You're the one who asked we get her."

"I can't ... I just cannot with you two. Cannot handle. C'mon. Come inside," she said as she leaned into the car again and offered her hand.

I tore the remaining tape from my mouth. Gosh, how it stung! I already held duct tape in pretty high regard, but that gave me new, hateful respect for it.

"I'm not going anywhere. I'm calling the police. You all are psychos," I stammered as I checked my pockets for my phone.

"We got rid of her phone," Guy said nonchalantly from behind Channing as he scrolled his own phone.

My eyes narrowed and my blood turned hot.

"You did *what*? That phone had my only photos – *all* of my photos – of my sister on it," I growled.

"Give her her phone," Channing clipped.

"Can't," Guy shrugged.

"And why is that?"

"Threw it out the window."

My eyes filled with tears. Rage took every other nook and cranny in me.

"Oh my god, then go *get it*," Channing screamed at them. "Look at her, she's losing it. God, it's like watching a badger or something rabid."

With that, she jerked me out the car, shooed the boys back into the car with instructions to find my phone *or else*, and forced me up the giant steps to her giant house.

"Hey, sweetie, what you said earlier," Channing said gently as she steered me down an opulent hallway toward her kitchen, "about calling the police? You're not really going to do that, right? Let's think this through. That's such an overreaction. And, my dear, kind of a bad one. Because, honestly, who are they going to believe? *Moi*, helpless and home alone with, *ahem*, no record. Or you, who, well, you know what you've been accused of and are on trial for."

White hot rage. It hadn't stopped.

Neither had the tears.

I looked down. A tear splattered on marble tile by my foot. She was right.

"Alright, so let's skip the pleasantries and get to the skinny," Channing said as she set up a small microphone aside her iPad.

"What are you calling pleasantries," I grumbled then reddened.

She said nothing but continued with whatever strange preparations she was focused on. A pen, a legal pad, a phone – all perfectly parallel with the iPad – and a cup of tea placed *just so*.

"Tea? Water? I've prepared a list of questions you're welcome to peruse before we dive in," she said as she adjusted her seat.

"Dive into what?" I asked. "Questions about what?" I eyed the microphone again, the questions, and my pulse quickened. "Hold on, I'm not, like, being interviewed for your stupid show or whatever. That's why you brought me here? That's why you ... why your friends *abducted* me?"

My hands shook. Channing stared at me and sighed.

"Wouldn't you rather control the narrative yourself? As it is, I'm just going to relay information as it has come to me. And, like, I make no guarantees of the verity of the suppositions in these cases and strictly underscore before every episode that any conclusions are my own."

She paused to sip her tea. I gulped. This chick was good. Smart and entitled – that's a dangerous combination, you know. Intelligence and ego generally pave the way for some entitlement; add wealth and status to that and there's no way in hell this girl wouldn't get her way. She was conditioned to precisely that. She yawned and stretched. Smart, entitled, and very, very beautiful.

And also a kidnapper! I scolded myself. Man, was I out of sorts. My stomach grumbled. Which for some reason made me realize how badly I needed a bathroom. I mumbled as much to Channing. She rolled her eyes and gestured toward a hall.

I shuffled in that general direction. Boy, was I light-headed. The white of the marble rose all about me; I put my hand out to brace myself. A dull sound of something cylindrical spinning pulled me from my dizziness; I had knocked against a giant vase. It's tapered base rocked around its narrow stand. I steadied it with a shaky hand and scooched it against the wall just a bit. I breathed. It had stopped.

I glanced back at Channing, who was focused on her sound check and lighting and who knows what over there. Something plinked on the floor; I looked down and retrieved a tiny shard of porcelain. What the ... the vase! Slowly a crack formed from a chink in the rim. It must have hit the wall and dislodged that piece. The crack stretched down the entire length of the vase. I gulped. That ghastly tube that had held Philippa cracking and exploding replayed in my mind. Oh dear. The dizziness was back.

I stumbled down the hall, found the bathroom, pulled the door shut and leaned against the counter.

Deep breaths. I splashed water on my face. *This is not related to Obrenox. You are okay.* I repeated that over and over until I felt my breathing deepen and my heartbeat slow down.

I was abducted by two of the most popular people in school. So they could ... use me to make their dumb podcast better? I shook my head. I needed to get this over with. I didn't have time or energy for this bullshit.

"Hey, um, so why go to such dramatic lengths to get me here?" I asked as I came out of the bathroom, feeling a little better. "Why not just find me at school? This is, uh, pretty messed up."

Channing stopped writing and looked up. She sighed loudly and rubbed her temples.

"Look, I know this isn't ideal. I truly intended for those idiots to ask you over for coffee or something. I'd rather not dwell on that point. You're here now – not at school surrounded by schedules and distractions – so let's make the most of it, yes?"

"Umm, no?" I said with a snort. "I was drugged and brought here against my will. Those idiots abducted me, bound me, put tape over my mouth! I don't care if I have a freaking rap sheet or whatever, those are the facts and this is so not cool. You're a psychopath if you don't see that. And ... and what's really messed up? Your stupid goons grabbed me at the hospital where I was visiting my sister. *A hospital.* What the hell is wrong with you guys?!"

My voice quivered. My hands still shook. I had to get out of there.

"Let's all take a breath and re-focus. I don't know anything about a hospital. What I do know is that they asked your weird friend. The blonde one. Who is, like, pretty mean. She told them where you'd be after school."

"Libby?" I started. Made sense; she'd sell her soul to be welcomed by the popular upperclassmen.

The front doors crashed open. The two partners in crime walked through waving their arms.

"Your princes have returned victorious! Here, check it out. Barely even scratched."

"My phone!" I cried and lunged toward the guy. Not Guy, but his stupid lackey. He pulled it back just as I reached for it.

"Uh-uh! What do we say?" he said with a sickening smirk as he waved my phone back and forth.

I stared at him. Then I kicked him between the legs, swiped my phone, and ran the hell out of there.

I could hear Channing screaming in the distance. I ran all the way down the absurdly long driveway, catching myself before tumbling forward several times as the grade steepened. Panting, I reached the bottom. The gate was closed. A tall stone fence stretched from either side of it.

I sunk down on the ground, fully ready to capitulate. This day had officially kicked my ass. Or maybe this day was the straw that broke the camel's back. Either way, I sat, cold and shivering in the dark, fully exhausted.

"Guess I'm stuck here," I muttered as I leaned my head back. It slid off the metal post and fell backward through two of the gate posts. "Hold on," I said as I spun around. "Can I – can I fit? Ah-ha! I can! Ha! What a stupid gate. What's the point of that?" I said as I stumbled through the foreboding gate spires. I took off toward the road, chucking at my good fortune.

"Ayo, Sheila! What are the odds I'd meet you out here? You trying to track down your dragon friend?" Poppy said, appearing suddenly on the sidewalk next to me.

"Poppy? Why on earth are you here? At night? I – Poppy! Oh my gosh, Dragon! That's a great idea!" I said as I picked up my pace. "I can see if Dragon's within telepathic range!"

I focused all my brain's energy on syncing up with him. All the while I jogged, half-certain I was moving in the right direction. The city lights were brighter up ahead, at any rate, and I could make the hills dotted with the lights of my neighborhood. Just as I was about to stop to rest, a gust of wind from broad wings flapping overhead greeted me. \

"Hell yes, Poppy. Great idea," I said as I slowed. "Dragon! I can't believe that worked! God, this day, though. Can you just get me home? Hey, Poppy ... Poppy?"

Dragon cocked his head and studied me as he lowered himself for boarding.

"As luck would have it, indeed, I was on an evening constitutional over the lake and got just within distance of your thoughts calling to me. But Evechild," he said with a frown as he hoisted me upon his back, "who is Poppy?"

"You know, Poppy, the dog? Australian Shepherd you sent me? White with brown and black spots, Australian accent?" I called as we launched into the night sky.

"I do not know of anyone by that description," Dragon answered.

"Well, maybe it was Ms. Neally's doing," I called back.

"Unlikely. Yaël has a terrible canine allergy and would balk at befriending a species she deemed 'speciously loyal.' No, no, this Poppy must have come from elsewhere."

"Hmm," I said, fully confounded.

"Hmm indeed," Dragon echoed.

His wings stayed outstretched as we glided through the dark, cold night. Our silence was the loudest part of the conversation.

Before we touched down in my backyard, Dragon hovered for a moment. My feet dangled precariously; I had already began sliding down the side to dismount.

"Evechild," he said firmly, "this dog is of unknown origins. Unless—"

"Unless it's from the seventh?!" I blurted suddenly, alarmed and still clutching his scales to keep from sliding all the way off.

"No; that dimension generally eschews non-humanoid Mammalia. Evechild. I – oh, gracious, you are nearly falling; here, I will descend fully. There you are, safe on the ground. Anyhoo, Evechild, what I was going to say," Dragon said and paused, coughed, and looked at me with the most doleful eyes, "it is possible this Poppy is a, ehm, that is, a psychosomatic manifestation, a stress response... Do you see?"

"See what?" I said and stared at him. Not indignant, not sarcastic, just confused. Thoroughly confused. "What are you even talking about? Poppy is a dog."

"Yes, to you," he said quietly. "I shall mention this to Gil, if you'll allow me. If I can stomach speaking to her, that is."

"Gil? Yeah, why would I care? She was there one time, with Poppy and me. Man, I am starving. Dragon, thank you for the ride. I – geez, this is another of those days that I can't even begin to process."

I was rambling, stumbling toward the backdoor. The kitchen light still on inside.

"Yes, yes, I understand. You must get your rest. But, Evechild, may I ask you one thing? Did Gil and Poppy interact?"

"Of course they did," I said with a shrug. Then I thought harder about it, seeing the look on Dragon's face. "I mean, I thought they did ... I guess ... maybe Poppy, like, ran that way while Gil went there ... or maybe ... Oh, I don't know! What does it matter? I'm going to bed. Night, Dragon."

"Rest well, Evechild," he said somberly and sprang up into the cloudy, dark sky.

54

SEDET, AETERNUMQUE SEDEBIT

It took several glares from people sitting around me on the bus before I realized the terrible chiming of a phone was coming from me.

"New ringtone, sorry," I mumbled as I rummaged through my bag for my phone. It was a number I hated that I recognized.

The hospital.

I refused to save it in my contacts list; that felt like I was giving in. No, I had told myself, I would not need to save this number, for Philippa will be there such a short time it's certainly not needed.

"Ah, hallo! Good, you answered. This is Jürgen, just calling to see if you heard the news."

"News?" I said, my heart beating quicker. "I'm, like, on my way there now. What has happened?"

"Ah, good. There is good news. Your sister, Philippa, she is awake."

"What?!" I squealed into the phone. Several bus riders looked back with annoyance. I didn't care. "She's awake?! Holy crap! On my god! Ok, I'm almost there. There are – uh, like four more stops. She's awake!"

"There is more, but yes, her waking up is wonderful news. Alright, I will see you soon." Jürgen hung up. I beamed. Everything would be okay. I could feel it. Finally, I could feel it.

I exploded out of that bus with hope and happiness and – cue record scratch. My mom greeted me at the hospital entrance, her eyes swollen and black with smudged eye makeup.

It didn't look like happy tears. She hugged me. Hard.

"Let's go see her, yeah? Just, brave, happy faces only, okay? Ugh. Okay. Here we go," my mom prattled as she held me against her down the hall to the elevators.

I couldn't process what was happening. I just stared and followed.

A group of white coats and blue scrubs were gathered around Philippa's bed. Academic tones and head nods pinballed around them. Jürgen spotted me and walked over.

"She is asleep again, very common for anyone coming out of a coma," he explained. "But you can come in, come talk to her. Your voice may rouse her again."

I nodded, confused, bewildered, uncertain what I was supposed to be feeling, and followed him in. The doctors and nurses stepped aside to make room for me. I still didn't understand what was happening. Her monitors chirped happily, the beeps and lines hummed optimistically, her breathing tubes were removed. I looked up at the faces gathered, still in deep conversation.

"...I believe it was T4 that gradually compacted ..."

"...I concur, it's a shame the coma prevented further testing ..."

"...x-rays during a coma? Not typical, not when the surgery had appeared successful..."

"...paraplegia can have recovery aspects ..."

Their erudite, cold phrases hung in the air around me. I felt suffocated by their words. Paraplegia? Did I know what that was? Was my survival instinct preventing me from defining it? I spun around and stared at my mom. Her arms were folded at her chest, one hand holding a makeup-stained Kleenex. She sniffed loudly. She caught my gaze and began crying again.

"Mom, what the hell is this?" I whispered, going over to her. "I thought she woke up?"

"Yes, but, there's more now. Um, gosh. She, um, after the surgery," my mom spit out words between sobs, "God, the surgery only repaired part of the spinal damage. Philippa is … she's … she's paralyzed."

The words hit me in the gut, hit me in the throat, hit me in the nose, hit me everywhere that would knock the wind out of you and render you a useless mess.

But I didn't cry.

The room spun a bit. I felt like I couldn't breathe in. I hugged my mom, more to steady myself than to comfort her. I looked over at my sister. Her head was turned to the side. Holy cow – I hadn't seen her in any other position than perfectly supine in weeks! That small movement, it sent a wave of victory rippling through my bones. I stepped back and held my mom by the shoulders.

"Mom. Mom! Christ, are you overlooking the most important part? Phlee's awake! She's awake!"

My mom looked up, pathetic and tear-stained, and forced a small smile. "But she doesn't know she can't walk."

I dropped my hands. My heart broke.

"Oh."

The doctors filed out of the room, Jürgen behind them.

I looked over at the hospital bed once more. Sterile white sheets adorned with my sister's favorite fuzzy blanket dotted with hedgehogs, little tubes spiraling from her arm, and a clipboard left carelessly atop her feet. I marched over there and grabbed it, suddenly furious.

"Whose is this," I demanded, stomping out of the room. "Who's leaving their shit on my sister? What ambivalent, cold, unfeeling, medical professional," I said those last two words with a snide voice and air quotes, "thinks it's okay to leave their shit on. top. of. my sister?!"

The nurses had stopped and looked up from their stations. A wheelchair being pushed came to rest. A doctor drinking coffee stopped mid-sip and looked up.

"Apologies," he said as he walked over.

I held up the clipboard in front of him, then whipped it away and tossed it to my side. It fell with a clatter on the sterile tile floor a few feet away.

"Eve Gwendolyn Genevieve!" my mom hissed behind me.

The doctor made no response. He walked slowly, his coffee mug in one hand, and retrieved the clipboard. The entire reception area remained silent.

Jürgen reentered from the opposite hall just then, whistling and holding a jump rope. He slowed, read the room, and stopped, confused.

"On my break I will be, uh, jumping rope. Healthy body, healthy mind, you know?" he stuttered nervously, looking around.

A lab tech stood on tiptoe and whispered something to him. He looked up, surprised, stared right at me, and then began laughing. "She did? Really? Oh wow."

The hum of the hospital slowly resumed as he strode over with a smile.

"You really threw his clipboard? Good, that guy is an asshole," he said.

"You're telling me," I said gruffly. I turned and pulled the door to Philippa's room shut, just as Jürgen was coming over. "Shit," I muttered and swung the door open again. "Jürgen, oh, good, you're still there. Totally did not mean to slam that door in your face. Um, I didn't mean to be rude to you. It's … it's just a lot. I don't know."

"No apology necessary. Take your time. Be with your family. I'm here until 7 p.m.," he said gently. "Like I said, I am on a short break now anyway," he said and held up the jump rope. I smiled. At least, I tried to smile.

"Hey, butthole … is that you?"

Philippa's voice reached me, soft and meager and good-natured. My heart swelled inside my chest.

"Yeah, it's me," I said, my voice cracking. "It's the butthole."

347

55

TUUM EST

"What's a coma like? Draw four, new color's green," I said, yawning, and laid down an UNO card.

"Weird. Like stretches of nothing and then a dream that's way too real, but not like a dream you know in sleep, a different kind. I don't know, does that make sense? Ha, reverse. Back to me," Philippa said as she slapped a yellow card down on the stack. The little bedside table shook.

"Easy, you'll spill! Don't know your own strength yet, huh? Uno," I said with a smirk. Philippa held up a particular finger as she drew card after card. "Could you hear us in there? Reading to you and talking or whatever?"

"Aw, you read to me?"

"Well, Mom did. I mostly ranted and complained."

Philippa grinned and shrugged.

"I win!" I cried as I threw my final card down. I pumped my arms in the air.

"Wow, you beat a coma patient. Big moment for you," Philippa laughed as she gathered the cards and started to shuffle them.

"Um, ex-coma patient; give yourself some credit. And trust me, I need the win."

"Trial tomorrow?"

"Trial tomorrow."

"You gonna win?"

"You're awake. That's, like, a win enough," I mumbled, a lump suddenly rising in my throat.

"Sure," Philippa laughed and tossed her pillow at me.

I shrugged and wiped some moisture from my cheeks.

56

HABEUS CORPUS

"**O**rder! Order in my courtroom!"

My head jerked up. How long had I been asleep?! Of all the inconvenient places to nod off. I brushed my hair from my face and adjusted my body on the mahogany bench. Kip looked down at me and smiled. There was a wet spot on his upper arm. Ah. My drool. I must have dozed off with my head against my fearless attorney's fetching gray suit.

"It just looked like you were overcome with emotion," Ms. Neally whispered suddenly from behind me. "No one could tell you were sleeping. And it was only a handful of minutes."

I relaxed. Sleep and I weren't so well acquainted these days. My nights were spent talking with Philippa; making my time in bed scare. Which was fine since bed only meant the gateway to nightmares and horrible replays was opened. I yawned, stretched, and looked around.

Swan Rosencrantz was leaning dramatically against the table in front of the plaintiff bench. She stretched an arm out to reveal a gold watch under her red suit sleeve and very theatrically checked the time. I followed her gaze, along with the turned heads of every other person in that courtroom, to a great commotion in the back.

"I have a right to be here!" a familiar voice yelled.

"You are obstructing justice by intentionally manipulating allegations in an active case and trial!" an older male voice yelled. Each word was louder than the last.

I sat up more and peered over Ms. Neally and my mom, who were also turned in rapt attention at the hullabaloo.

Two police officers, with several news outlet folks greedily filming, were attempting to force someone out of the courtroom. Someone who was putting up quite a fight in a pink chevron-striped suit while spouting non-sequitur amendments ... I gasped.

"Young lady, what is your name," the judge barked into the tiny microphone atop his podium.

"Channing Reagan Barrenton, Your Honor," she cried as she wrestled against an officer who was doing little more than holding his arm outstretched as a barrier, "this is unconsented and unlawful contact! You are denying me my right to observe judicial process!"

"Barrenton, hmm? Why is that name always a pain in my *tuchus*? Ms. Barrenton, you have given me reason in excess to request your removal from my courtroom at this time. Would you like me to read off such reasons so they may be entered into court record, or would you like to depart willingly before I have the chance to do just that?"

"This is unjust. You are unjust! Geez, I'm leaving. But you were all witnesses! I was intimidated by legal personnel!"

"Shall we add contempt to the list, Ms. Barrenton? You can join others by that name on that very least, in fact," the judge added dryly.

I smiled. The door shut heavily. A collective jostling as everyone turned forward once more was met by a long sigh from the Right Honorable Judge Singh.

"I knew I should not have accepted this case," he muttered. The mic still picked it up. "Now, where were we? Ah, yes, Ms. Rosencrantz. Please continue."

My smile fell. What had I missed? I caught Ms. Nguyen staring at me from the other side of Swan Rosencrantz. She looked away quickly. She held something in her hands on her lap. Something red, and fuzzy ... it was one of Jonah's beanies. I'd recognize it anywhere. The recollection stabbed my heart and stole my breath.

When you're in survival mode, you blast from one activity, one need, to the next, like cannon fire. No time to think, just strike the match and go. And then you have a moment like seeing a stocking cap of a dead friend and you're jerked back into the reality of humanity – feelings and emotions and questions and memories.

I couldn't swallow. When had I started crying? Oh, this was a fine time to have an emotional reckoning!

"Pardon me, Ms. Rosencrantz. Mr. Sebastian is your client quite well?" the judge said with a frown.

Kip elbowed me in the rib. I waved him away and rubbed my wet cheek against my left shoulder. Makeup I was unused to wearing left a creamy patch on the lapel of my blazer. I couldn't stop sobbing, wheezing. The harder I tried to control it, the worse it got! Kip opened his briefcase and pulled out a sleeve of Ritz crackers, which he placed on my lap with a little pat on my arm.

"This is too much. Jurors, counsel, we will recess for – what time do you have, Ms. Martinez? – for 12 minutes. I will see you all promptly at half past the hour."

The judge struck his gavel loudly and commotion through the courtroom resumed. Everyone had a question – who was this Barrenton girl? Why was Eve Archer crying so hard? What happened to the other judge? Does the coffee shop serve sandwiches?

"Eve, let's get you to the restroom," my mom whispered. "Get some air and some water."

"Everyone's leaving. I'll just stay here," I said as I shook my head. "I – I don't know what happened. I saw Jonah's stupid beanie and I – I – crap, I can't stop!" I wailed as the tears poured even harder.

Ms. Neally placed her hand atop mine. Kip gave me a thumbs-up. My mom checked her phone. I glowered at her, but before she realized my glare was for her, she smiled and showed me the screen.

"Seb's with Philippa, see? Ah, doesn't she look great?"

I sniffed and wiped my cheek against my other shoulder. That picture slowed the cannon fire, stopped the tears.

"I wondered when the dam would break," Ms. Neally said gently. She smiled at my confused look. "You've been holding a lot in for a long time; holding it together for a long time. All of it was bound to come out eventually."

I smiled. A funny thought came to me just then – could seventh-grade me, the Eve who had just met Ms. Neally in the library at Beecher Junior High – ever fathom that pretty librarian would be giving her a pep talk in a courtroom one day? I thought back to that moment; I had been so self-important and without any idea Ms. Neally the Librarian and my uncle Seb had a mutual acquaintance. Not me, but a dragon.

Geez, life is weird.

I took the tissue and bottle of water my mom had found for me. I breathed in, I breathed out. I brushed my hair out of my face and tried to wipe the makeup smudges from my suit collar.

"Okay, so – hold on, can you all, like, wipe those stupid sympathetic looks off your faces? That's definitely not helpful – can you catch me up on what's happening so far? I really, really dozed off hard for a minute."

"Of course," Ms. Neally said at the same time my mom started to speak. Both were too deferential to continue talking over the other. I rolled my eyes and stared at Ms. Neally. She looked a little embarrassed, but continued. "Judge Singh usually presides over corporate cases. I'm uncertain how he'll weigh a juvenile case of this caliber. After the last judge –"

"Pen-ah-lope," I giggled.

"Yes, that judge, was, *ahem*, out sick," Ms. Neally stopped and looked at each of us, "he was really the only judge available within a reasonable time frame."

"Wait, so we could have just waited for a different judge instead of getting back here so soon?" I cried.

"Eve," my mom hissed, "do you really want this freaking trial sitting over your head indefinitely? We've got to get out from under this thing."

I kept my mouth shut. My mom didn't sound decisive, she sounded desperate. You mean *you've* got to get out from under this thing, I thought.

"Your mother is right," Ms. Neally said carefully. "Ms. Rosencrantz has been laying out … concerns … yes, I think that's the right word. That's all you missed."

"That and Channing losing her shit in the back!" a voice giggled behind me. I spun around.

"Libby! What are – how long have you been standing there?"

"Relax, Dragongirl," she smiled. I guess she really did think that was, like, a cute nickname between us now. "I only just walked up. Here, I brought you something. You're, like, so always hungry all the time."

She held out a granola bar and string cheese.

I didn't take either.

"You here with Channing? Let me guess, you're reporting this little meeting to her after you leave, right?"

"What? No – I … I just remembered how cavernous you were last time, and I thought –"

"You thought you'd help your bestie Channing. Thanks, but no thanks," I said and started to turn around. I stopped and look over at her again, still standing there, impeccably dressed, mouth agape. "And it's *ravenous*, Libster. I was *ravenous*, not cavernous."

"All rise for the Honorable Judge Cartwright Singh!"

I hadn't clocked that first name. I wished I could cannon ball back in time to an Eve who would have giggled at those two names together. For no logical reason other than they sounded silly. Because when you're not enmeshed in rage and fear and despondency all the time, things like that *are* silly. And you have the energy for levity, for giggling.

"Ms. Rosencrantz, you may continue," Judge Singh said, he eyeline fixed firmly on the clock on the back wall.

"Ah, thank you, Your Honor. Now, if we don't have any more up-and-coming Coppolas trying to turn my case into fan fiction," Swan paused and flashed the courtroom a winning smile. A few jurors smiled; members in the audience chuckled. "I will continue with what I can only describe as a shocking turn of events that, as a sworn upholder of justice I will obviously deliver with impartiality, but," Swan paused again and took a dramatic step forward, and then another, her red heels perfectly matched to her red suit pants, "as a fellow human, I cannot condone, let the record show."

"The court will remind counsel to avoid, with prejudice, editorializing or inserting personal bias as that does, of course, undermine counsel's integrity as a representative of justice for the plaintiff as well as this fine state."

"Geez, it's getting intense in here," I whispered to Kip.

"Very serious stuff, yep," he whispered back.

"So redacted, Your Honor," Swan said with a sigh. "And so it goes, and so it goes ....," she hummed.

"The court will also remind counsel to avoid singing," Judge Singh growled into the microphone.

"Even Billy Joel? I had you pegged for a BJ fan. But I digress," Swan said with a little smile as the courtroom hummed. "Back to serious matters. Yes, I am afraid that I need to announce, on behalf of my client, Ms. Nguyen, that the family – goodness, you really want me to do this?"

Swan stopped and stared at Ms. Nguyen. Not with any theatrics, but with real, earnest concern and struggle. Ms. Nguyen still held the beanie. She pursed her lips, looked over at me, back at the beanie, back at Swan, and nodded.

"Counsel, kindly get to the point," the judge said louder than he needed to.

"The Nguyen family would like to withdraw their suit against Eve Gwendolyn Genevieve Archer. There, I said it. Ugh," Swan Rosencrantz said rapidly and then sank dramatically back onto the bench. She rubbed her temples with her fingers and sighed.

The courtroom buzzed.

"Am I to understand," Judge Singh said slowly, "that the Nguyen family, specifically you, Ms. Nguyen, to whom I express my deepest condolences, no longer wishes to press charges against the defendant?"

Ms. Nguyen nodded solemnly. Swan threw her head back and waved her hands in the air.

"That's right, You Honor! Do with that what you will."

"Alright, alright, everyone quiet down, please. I need a moment to consider this situation," the judge said, his brow furrowed and his chin atop his palm.

The courtroom silenced.

The whole place seemed to hold its breath with me. My equilibrium felt off, like I couldn't process things as they were happening. Like I had to consciously tell myself what was going on. This is a courtroom. That is Jonah's mom. That is Jonah's mom's lawyer. They just told the judge they're not pressing charges against you.

I still couldn't process it.

57

DUBITANTE

The silence felt like it was going to break the courtroom. Too much pressure, all that silence. It would surely burst.

"This is your prerogative, Ms. Nguyen," Judge Singh said finally. "However, in the matter of the State versus Archer, we still have some loose ends. A boy was murdered, an accusation was made, and the burden of proof had been on the plaintiff. With the latter facet removed, we are left with the fact that a boy was murdered, and such things cannot dwindle without closure and justice. Thus, I must inquire of the State its intentions."

The silence held.

"Sir?" a meager voice asked. A frumpy woman, made even frumpier by her proximity to Swan Rosencrantz, had her hand raised.

"Yes? And you are?" the judge said as he frowned at the woman.

"Ms. York? You've – we've already spoken, Your Honor. I've been here every time? Representing the State of Oregon?"

The judge frowned even harder, then sighed and waved his hand.

"Right, so, I'm Ms. York, representing the state. The state of Oregon. And, and, yes, as Your Honor has stated, a boy was murdered."

"The court implores the state to be succinct, if you don't mind, Ms. – eh, Ms. –" the judge trailed off.

357

"York, sir. The state will not rest without justice in this crime," she said quickly, "and will thus keep the investigation open, as it is already undergoing ... investigation ... that is, um, it is already being investigated, so it will continue. Yes. Yes, it will continue."

"The State does not wish to redirect or cross-examine with either the existing defendant or another suspect in mind?" the judge asked as he rubbed his eyes.

"Um, no. But the state *will* find the guilty party," Ms. York said quickly and sat down.

"So present."

My heart stopped. That voice behind me – she wouldn't. She couldn't.

"Pardon? Who spoke?" the judge asked he scanned the courtroom.

"I did, You Honor."

I turned to see Ms. Neally, beautiful and poised in her herringbone skirt suit, cheekbones as sharp as her intellect, standing and speaking.

"And you are?" Judge Singh said incredulously.

"Yaël Neally."

"And you are ... confessing?"

"I am, sir. Yes."

Gasps pinged about the paneled room. The judge pounded his gavel.

"You are only just now feeling compelled to offer an admission of guilt? Yaël Neally, I must ask," he stopped, looked at his bailiff and muttered under his breath, "Good lord, what a shitshow," not far enough away from the mic. He cleared his throat and leaned in. "Counsel and the confessed, please approach."

Three attorneys and a librarian approached the bench. Well, two attorneys and a ... a Kip. The judge held his palm against the mic as he leaned forward. It made an awful thumping sound. The five held an intense conference of whispering, hissing, gesticulating. Finally, the judge sat back, shook his head and sighed. He shooed the four back to their places. He started to speak several times before grabbing the mic and speaking forcefully into it, as if against his will.

"Pending an investigation to verify the confession and confirm soundness of mind, the court accepts a plea of guilty in the murder of Jonah Minh Nguyen from one Yaël Neally. The court furthers finds that the matter of State versus Archer shall be dismissed, with the caveat that Ms. Archer may be the subject of further investigation as deemed appropriate by law enforcement especially as Ms. Neally is questioned and found culpable. Court," the judge paused his rapid run-on sentence to take a deep breath and bang his gavel, "dismissed!"

The courtroom exploded.

People yelled. People cheered. People screamed threats. People cried my name. Reporters in the back, allowed in on the condition they remained silent, were chattering away into their cameras.

I felt my mom's arms wrap around my shoulders from behind me. The bailiff and several other armed guards strode toward me, past me, and to Ms. Neally, who stared stoically ahead as they put handcuffs around her delicate wrists and led her from the courtroom. She looked back at me, smiled faintly, and winked.

"Come, young Egg, yep! Let us be on our way, yep," Kip said and pulled me upright.

"What just happened? Why ... why did she do that?" I said, feeling unable to turn words to sentences.

I looked across the room. Ms. Nguyen was already gone. The room seemed more packed than before with everyone standing. My mom wrapped her trench coat around my shoulders and pushed me forward. Normally the action would have irritated me, but now I was relieved to someone acting for me.

My executive function was failing. Had failed. Will fail.

We three ploughed through the masses and out the back. The halls were lined with the same question: *How'd you get your teacher to take the fall for you?*

"That's what they think?" I said to Kip. "What's going on? Why'd she do that? Kip?"

"Hmmm, yep. That's what they think. Yep, but it'll work out. She's smart, yep," he said as he fumbled in his coat pocket, produced a key fob and held it up with a smile. "Now I understand, yep! She told me to hold on to her automobile key, yep!"

"How about that," my mom murmured. "What a saint."

I frowned. This was beyond saintly. It didn't make any sense, moral or otherwise. We serpentine around the back parking lot to Ms. Neally's Maserati, clean and chic as ever. Kip got in the passenger seat, my mom and I both piled into the backseat.

"Oh," my mom chuckled. "Ok, I guess I can … um, where to?" she asked as she buckled into the driver's seat.

"Philippa," I said. "I'm not going to believe any of this until I say it aloud. Plus, it should be quiet at the hospital, right?"

Wrong.

As we drove along the roundabout in front of the hospital, several news crews were already setting up camera equipment. Seated in a lawn chair across from them, sipping from a thermos and taking selfies, was none other than famous local podcaster, Channing Reagon Barrenton.

"Oh lord," my mom said with a sigh. "How do we get in? It's a hospital, not a hotel! There's just the one way in!"

"We park over there, at the E.R. There's a skybridge connecting the buildings," I said.

"How on earth do you know that?" my mom cried as she swung the car around. It revved eagerly. "Ooh, a bit more power than I'm used to."

"You were in that emergency room, remember?" I said flatly, not trying to hide my annoyance. But annoyance at what? That she didn't remember or that she was there in the first place?

I swallowed hard. Both. I was annoyed at both.

"You have been through so much, Egg," my mom said barely loud enough to hear.

We parked and ducked into the E.R. lobby. We were almost in the clear when I heard a man behind me start yelling.

"Hey! That's her! The girl on the TV right now, she just walked through here! Yeah, right over there!"

I didn't wait long enough to find out how the rest of that conversation went, or if there was a pursuit involved. I just ran.

I ran until I was next to Philippa.

Honestly, I cannot recall the mode of transporation that got me to her. Or the time that elapsed. It was like I had been suspended in slow motion, one long blink happening, while the world raced on the other side of my eyelids.

I didn't care.

Panting, sweating, I fell atop my sister and hugged her.

"Bro, you're squishing me and all my vital tubes," she squeaked.

My mom and Kip appeared. Not panting, not sweating.

They both fell on top of me, on top of Phlee.

"Guys? This group hug is, like, super special and all, but I can't breathe," she squeaked again.

A monitor started chirping. Another beeped, faster, faster, faster.

Jurgen came charging through the door, stopped, and laughed.

"Oh, my! This is lovely, but, eh, you are squishing her just a little bit. Can you breathe okay?"

"See, I told you," Philippa said, giggling through her wheezing.

"You're fine," I said and smiled at her.

"You're acting weird. Even for you," she said as she gingerly propped herself against her pillows. "What's up?"

That phrase – it was something Jonah had said to me more than once. That was all it took. The dam, brittle though it was, broke again and the tears flooded out.

I sat down next to my sister and relayed the entire, bizarre day to her.

Every detail ... except the bit about Libby. I couldn't go into *that* with an audience. I looked over at my mom in the recliner by the window. She had nodded off. I wasn't angry with her. I understood. I had fallen asleep in my own trial, for heaven's sake. Kip stood near her, his yo-yo in hand, honing his craft.

Once the words stopped and the tears abated, I sat back and breathed heavily.

"Shit, that's a lot," Philippa said quietly. I nodded. "And that's just *today*?" I nodded again.

She reached her hand out toward me. I smiled and put my hand in hers.

"Ew, don't be gross," she said as she swatted it away, "I was asking for a pudding."

I laughed.

Actual laughter!

"Pudding. Vanilla. On it," I said as I got up.

"Thanks for being less of a butthole and getting me a pudding," she said.

"Thanks for being alive."

"Kinda heavy, don't ya think? Let's keep it lighter in these rooms of healing!"

I turned back and hugged her again.

"I mean it. I'm so happy you're ... you're...you know."

My voice caught. She sniffed.

"Smarter than you?" she said at last, with a little hiccup that let me know she had been crying too.

"Also a butthole," I whispered.

We giggled through our sobs and just leaned into each other for a while.

58

CLARERE AUDERE GAUDERE

I should have felt lighter.

Happier?

More optimistic?

Optimistic at all?

I paused, as if listening to my soul deny or confirm optimism. Memories of last night with Philippa flashed in my mind. I relaxed. That was reason to be more optimistic.

So I felt mildly lighter.

Based on my mom's revelry last night, I should be the lightest, more carefree person in the world. *Philippa's awake! Eve's trial is over!* she sang and paraded around the house after we got home from the hospital. They had let us stay a full hour past visiting hours. Extenuating circumstances, the nurse had said with a smile. Someone else had popped in with a bottle of champagne. It had been sitting forever in the staff fridge; what better reason to bust it out, they had said.

My mom wasted no time popping it open and guzzling it down as soon as we got in the door at home. She offered me a small pour. I brushed it away; not for any moral or legal reason, but because I found champagne genuinely disgusting.

She fell asleep on the sofa in her clothes, smiling and hiccupping. I covered her with a blanket. I was glad she felt happy, hopeful.

I pulled my blankets around me, ignoring the sun, and sunk back down in my bed. The same questions, the ones that hung like heavy chains around my neck, kept yelling at me.

Why did Ms. Neally take the blame?

Did Philippa remember anything about how she ended up in the hospital?

What were the other Jonah clones around the globe up to?

My heart stopped at the next question.

What about the Philippa clones?

I flipped and flopped around under my covers, frustrated and fearful. Then I moaned loudly; one more question hit me:

Who the hell was Chad?

Something moist hit me in the face and roused me from my nap.

"Ugh! What is that!?" I squealed and squirmed in the blue pleather lounge chair I must have dozed off in. "Did you ... throw something?"

Philippa remained silent in her bed, her eyes closed. I settled back into my chair and folded my arms.

I had taken to going straight to the hospital from school. It made for long days of long bus rides or long car rides driven in somber silence. Strangely, though, I found I was the most relaxed at the hospital. Philippa was there, it was clean, the cafeteria grilled cheese was not bad, and, of great meaning to me, it was a haven from news and gossip and reminders of the complicated life I'd stumbled into this past year.

But if I thought too long about it, I'd scold myself for that last bit. The fact that I was in a hospital with my crippled sister was glaring evidence of that complicated life; it felt a little icky to enjoy my time there. But I did.

Today, though, I had forgone school altogether (unbeknownst to my mom). I had a lot of feelings to hold let alone unpack, and their weight was no place for a school laden with entitled opinions. So, off the to the hospital I went. And napped.

A moist washcloth landed in my lap. I jerked upright.

Philippa giggled. She was awake, sitting upright in her hospital bed. She dipped another washcloth in a cup of water on her tray table and tossed it at me. I squealed again.

"Dude! Why?" I laughed, fetching not one but five moist washcloths scattered on and around me. "How can your aim be this bad?"

"My aim is impeccable. You were really out."

"You couldn't let me sleep?"

"It's dark out; you've been asleep since you got here, basically," she said with a shrug. "And you were snoring."

"There it is," I said with a smile as I stretched. The homework I hadn't even started slid off my lap and fell to the ground in a flurry of papers. "Sorry, Phlee. I, uh, don't really sleep at home or whatever. And this chair is super comfortable. Gah! Your stupid washcloths landed on my essay!"

Philippa rolled her eyes and offered me a can of soda from the collection of snacks accumulating on the table opposite her. It had been four days since she found out. Since she found out that … Christ, I still can't admit it.

"How is our star patient today? Your vitals are looking excellent," Jürgen announced as he strode in. "Ah, you are awake. Good. I brought you a Coca Cola. Would either of you care to watch a movie? I've noticed your television is never on."

I started to answer but Philippa shook her head. Jürgen smiled, studied her monitors and tubes, and turned back toward the door.

"I'll leave you to it," he said. "When you'd like to discuss what we were, eh, discussing earlier, just press your call button and I'll be right back in."

He and Philippa nodded knowingly at each other. Jürgen eyed me suspiciously, gave Philippa a thumbs up, and departed.

"Discuss what? What the hell was that about?"

"Just … don't worry about it. But look. I've gotta ask you something and I need you to answer honestly. And, also, not think I'm crazy. But if you think I'm, like, I don't know, a dazzling genius or whatever for figuring it out, you can tell me that."

I giggled, but her disclaimers made me uneasy. I didn't know where Philippa was headed. What did she remember about her injury? Did she remember how it happened? The accusations? The ongoing trial?

"Fire away," I said, a little too upbeat.

"Ok. So, it's like, I have had about a million dreams," she started.

"No. Nope. No, absolutely not. I am not listening to another one of your crazy dreams," I said laughing. "I love you or whatever, and, yeah, there was a time when I missed you so much that I would have given anything to hear about your dumbass insane dreams. But I've gotta put a hard stop to your dream interpretations."

Philippa threw a pillow at me. I fluffed it and stuck it behind my neck with a smile.

"Hey, give that back. And that's not what I'm saying! No, it's like, a really specific, super-weird dream – even for me – that I keep having all of the time," she said as she adjusted the remaining pillows around her.

"Yeah, that's still pretty on-brand for you," I said as I took a swig of coke. The soda seemed to be the go-to offering of my only favorite nurse, Jürgen, whom I discovered was basically the Godfather of nurses.

"Bro, listen," Philippa said. Her wide eyes grew even wider, making her resemble one of her favorite Anime characters. "For real. Ok. Did you … ever … um, like, you know, know someone, or, I mean, something … ugh." She stopped, laughed awkwardly, and nervously looked around. She leaned closer and lowered her voice. "Dammit, Egg. Is there a dragon?"

"Like, in general?" I asked, choking on a giggle.

"No! Like, in your life!" Philippa wailed. One of the monitors chirped faster.

"Take it easy, relax," I said, giggling. "And, yes. Yes there is."

"Ohhhh," she said as she fell back against her pillows, relieved. "Thank the sweet baby Jesus. I'll probably have more questions as I piece together some weirdass memories."

"You were worried there wasn't a dragon? That's really the pressing thing on your mind?" I said, still chuckling.

"It's just that I had such vivid memories of you and a dragon, but no one else, and I genuinely feared my broken brain was creating a *Fight Club* situation."

She stared at me so earnestly, so fretful and innocent. I burst out laughing. Right in her earnest, fretful face.

"Figures that'd be your rationale!" I chortled. "You are a woman of science, so I must be your Tyler Durden! And dude," I wiped away a cheerful tear as I caught my breath, "your brain's not broken. Don't say that."

"I think the dragon would be Tyler Durden," she said, clearly deep in thought over the plot of Fight Club. She laughed, then winced in pain. "Oof. Not ready to laugh that hard yet. And I think that'd make you Marla."

"Durden's love interest?!" I squeaked. "Ew!"

"Why don't we just ask Chuck who would be whom," Philippa giggled between choking and more wincing.

"Chuck who?"

"Oh my gosh. The guy who wrote the book. He lives in Portland," she said, once again throwing a pillow at me. "I can't ever remember how to pronounce his name."

"Maybe he's my dad."

"Stop making me laugh, it hurts!" she cackled.

"That wasn't a joke!" I laughed and threw the pillow back at her. For a moment, life felt normal. And I liked it.

A scuffle outside drew our attention toward the door. It swung open dramatically as my mom pushed her way in holding several brown bags whose enticing aromas made me cast aside any annoyance I had for her just then.

"Thai food for my girls!" she sang, ignoring scolding voices behind her. She hit the door closed with her hip. "I couldn't remember if you like Tara Thai or Thai Chili Jam better, so I got you both," she added proudly.

Philippa stretched and smiled. She pulled a tray table closer to her, then put her hands on either side of her on the bed.

"Here, let me move over and make some space. We can see what movies are on – I, oh. Right," she said, her face instantly falling and her voice dropping. "I can't ... do that," she whispered, looking down.

My mom and I were silent. I looked at the pile of wet, cold washcloths on my lap. My mom adjusted the brown bags, now showing discoloration on the bottoms from the steam and moisture of the fresh Thai dishes stowed inside.

"Well, I'll serve these up, then! You'd like some of both?" she said quickly and jumped awkwardly into action. "I love these trays, so handy. Oh, I forgot drinks – oh, wonderful! So many sodas! Do you want some water, though? Tea seems appropriate. I wonder if they're still serving—"

"This looks great, Ma," I said abruptly, cutting off her nervous rambling. "Here, take my seat. I'll check out the tea action."

My mom nodded sheepishly. I glanced at Philippa. Her head was still down, her shoulders drawn in. She looked so small, just then. Awareness of a missing motor skill must do that to a person. Make you feel small. I swallowed hard and left.

"You know visiting hours are over," a gruff woman at the intake desk outside Phlee's room said.

"You don't have to visit, then," I said as I marched down the hall toward the coffee station. I smiled, quite proud of that quick retort.

I poured hot water into paper cups. "One cup, two cups, three – ah!" My counting aloud was interrupted by someone's hand on my shoulder. I held the knuckle of my forefinger against my lips, soothing the burn.

"Sorry to surprise you," Jürgen said. "Let me help you. You're getting green tea when it is night? Maybe I should try that. I have four more hours to go. Anyhow, how is your sister?"

I let him take the two cups from me while I carried one in one hand and kept nursing my other hand.

"She's … she's her old self. Like, joking and happy and all, and then something happens and she, well, God it sucks. I see the minute she realizes all over that she's … um … she's … you know."

"Paralyzed," Jürgen finished.

"Right. That," I murmured.

"Paralysis takes many forms, and is often temporary," Jürgen said. He stopped and looked me squarely in the eyes. "I do not mean to get your hopes up. But it is not a death sentence. You cannot think that way."

"I wasn't, geez," I said with a nervous laugh. "It's a lot, though. You know?"

"I do not know, no. Not about this. But I am truly so sad this has happened to your sister and to you and your mom. But I am here for you."

I smiled. I believed him.

"Hey, what were you and Phlee talking about? When you left just earlier?"

We had reached Philippa's room. I could hear television and forced laughter inside. Good. Jürgen paused, and then walked a few steps back, motioning for me to follow.

"We have yet to discuss her discharge planning," he said quietly. "She knows she needs to meet with different specialists and do wheelchair training."

"There's training?!" I blurted too loudly. The gruff nurse – the one who was anti-visitor and anti- joy – looked up with a scowl. Jürgen nodded.

"There is. These are important next steps to be discussed, especially now that she has been awake and strong consistently these past few days. I am worried she may be in some denial."

"Well, yeah," I snorted. "Wouldn't you be? But why would you two keep that a secret? You seemed like you didn't want me to know about it."

"Ah, yes," Jürgen said, his eyes softening. "Your sister didn't want to discuss it in front of you. She was worried it would upset you."

Of course she did.

My heart.

59

FAC FORTIA ET PATERE

My mom insisted on having a party.

I understood to a point; Philippa coming out of a coma was a big deal, and certainly worthy of celebration. But the rest of that bit, the paralysis, that was a hard thing to celebrate around.

"Do you think she'd want Lauren and Lindsay there?" my mom asked as she scribbled away in her notebook. "They're such beautiful people. They'd just be happy we're all okay, right? Not be all nosey. She'd want them there?"

"Of course she would! But Ma," I scowled at her, "we don't even have her home yet. We don't know how long she'll be on paid meds, what her mood will be, anything. Maybe, uh, hold off on the grand plans?"

"I was just looking forward to celebrating and, you know, putting the worst behind us," she said quietly.

"I know," I said. "I get it."

"Ugh, now *she* would be nosey," my mom said as pressed her pen hard and struck out a name on her list. "And him, no way. He posts *everything* immediately. Oh, shoot! I forgot to make us dinner!"

"Didn't even notice, all good," I said with a forced smile. Honestly, I couldn't remember the last time my mom made dinner. Pre-Obrenox, the three of us would dine together pretty regularly. With the trial stress turned down and Philippa's return home getting closer, my mom had taken to picking right back up in life as though she hadn't been a checked-out ghost of a person for the last several months.

Not that I was bitter or anything.

But I was painfully aware of what can happen when your blood pressure gets too high; every day since my mom's "cardiac episode" (her term, not mine) had been a balancing act to not stress her out.

I swallowed hard and kept my head down in my homework.

So, yeah. The worst wasn't behind us. Some exquisitely bad things were back there, for sure. Hopefully over. But The Worst? I didn't even know what that was at this point. The bad that had happened so far was in a league of its own, a category of bad no one could even imagine.

It was so bizarrely bad, I didn't even have a book to compare it to. No plucky protagonist to draw inspiration from, no zany plotline to draw parallels from.

Just new, original, crappy BAD that turned worse and could get worse yet.

So was the worst behind us? No. I had no reason to believe that.

Something rattled against the window; I jumped, immediately on alert.

"What the ..." I trailed off as I watched a piece of paper slowly appear in the corner.

"You say something?" my mom said.

"No, just, um, locking the windows," I said as I darted across the dining room.

My mom nodded without looking up from her notebooks. I crept toward the window, all the hairs on my body standing on end. Closer, I peered into the window; some grubby fingers held up a paper with something scrawled on it.

Sister room 2310h, bring scan biadh

I recoiled. Baert's eyes twinkled under the paper, which he promptly crumpled up and popped in his mouth. With a wag of his fingers, he dove through the hedge and was gone.

I smiled. Even bad news was made better by Baert. I didn't know if what awaited me was bad, but secrecy wasn't usually employed for good things.

"Going to bed," I said as I strode back to my spot at the table. I closed my laptop and stretched. "That's enough homework for me."

"Hmm? Proud of you, Eggie. Sweet dreams," my mom said and blew a kiss.

I ignored her. On all counts. I didn't want her pride; it increasingly meant very little. I was tired of the intermittent nickname usage; it popped up disingenuously. I hadn't had a dream that smacked of anything sweet since I was, like, seven and dreamt of marrying a dragon and becoming queen of a dragon land I made up. My face scrunched up; that last bit probably wasn't so sweet as seven-year-old me thought it was.

And that blowing-a-kiss thing?

Gross.

In my room, I pushed some pillows and dirty clothes under a blanket in an Eve-shaped lump on my bed. I unplugged the lamps, knowing lack of light would deter my mom from lingering should she enter.

Satisfied, I grabbed *Fortis Librae* and jumped through whatever little wrinkles in the fabric of time the universe afforded me through this book.

I felt the familiar punch in the gut this particular method of travel brought as I tumbled forward into my sister's hospital room.

"Aye, lassie! Ye deciphered my code," Baert cried as he pulled back the curtain I was crouching behind.

"Is that my loser sister?"

"Yeah, it's me," I said between coughs.

"Your relationship communication is perplexing," Dragon said.

"Gang's all here. Hey guys," I said as I stood and stretched. "And Baert, it wasn't so much a code as a very simple instruction," I said with a laugh. "Oh, before I forget, here you are!"

Baert smiled and grabbed the plastic bag I held out for him. He opened it, took a whiff, and smiled even bigger.

"Hey, uh, wanna be a pal? Share whatever that is in there?" Philippa asked.

"Lassie gave them tah me," Baert snorted between bites, his beard and mustache speckled with crumbs. "And besides," he said as he choked down a final bite and turned the bag upside down, "aaallll gone!"

"Baert! There were, like, 11 snickerdoodles in there!" I said.

"What is a snickering doodle?" Dragon asked, his head cocked.

"Only my favorite cookie; thanks a lot, little elf-man," Philippa said with a chuckle. "So what's this big meeting about?"

Baert's eyes flashed red and his nostrils flared. His little fists balled up as he turned and squared up toward Philippa.

"Oh geez, I know what that means," I said, stepping between Baert and my sister's bed. "She didn't mean it, buddy. She doesn't know. To her, 'elf man' is a compliment ... like, a mighty elf combined with, um, you know, a super-strong man," I rattled quickly.

"Quite right, Cuithbaert. No need for machismo defenses," Dragon said, giving me a nod.

"Yeah," I continued nervously, "Phlee here, uh, totally knows what a mighty general you are and to never mistake you for like, a house elf or something."

"There are different types of elves?" Philippa asked.

There go the nostrils, flaring again.

"Phlee, what a weird sense of humor!" I said and shot her a look. "Anyway, yeah, why are we here, Dragon?"

"Quite right, Evechild. Let us tend to the business at hand. Cuithbaert, if you would, sir."

Baert looked up from licking the bag. Dragon sighed and rolled his eyes.

"Eye rolls are my thing, Dragon!" I cried, delighted. I hopped up next to Philippa. "Sorry about the snickerdoodles, Phlee. I, uh, probably should have brought separate bags so Baert wouldn't devour them all immediately."

"Dinnae mean tah."

"Night is swiftly passing, and we need to maximize our time, if we could," Dragon said, a twinge of impatience in his voice. "Ms. Neally is not here for, eh, obvious reasons," he said, his voice softer then. He looked away and coughed. "As for your uncle, we thought this particular conversation might be better left to the present company."

I had no idea what that meant. What could I know that Uncle Seb couldn't?

"You're aware of the stories, the reports, of," Dragon paused, lowered his voice and leaned in, "of certain someones with similar visages?"

"Of what?" Philippa blurted.

"Shhh! Yeah, go on, Dragon."

"There has been another report."

"Oh no," I groaned. "Where now? Let me guess, you heard it on that stupid podcast."

"In Colombia," Dragon continued, ignoring me. "Cuithbaert, could you – good heavens, Leftenant, are you quite done with that bag?"

Baert jumped, dropped the bag, and looked up sheepishly.

"Colombia?" I asked.

"Santa Marta, specifically," Dragon said.

"Highest point in the Sierra Nevadas," Philippa said as she lurped the last of her apple juice loudly through a straw. She looked up at all of us staring at her. "What? It is."

"Indeed," Dragon said. "Indeed."

"Ah-ha! I knew ol' Baert had the wee bit. Git off yer aft and have a look, lassie," Baert said as he pulled a crumpled paper from within his tunic.

I took it from him, shook it free of crumbs, and smoothed it out.

"Another news clipping? This is in Spanish though ... I, uh, kinda failed my seventh-grade Spanish elective and never really attempted it again. You got anything else I can read in those crumb-filled pockets?"

"Haud yer wheesht," Baert said, not entertained. "Look, lassie."

He drummed his finger against a grainy photo on the wrinkled paper. Dragon paced, muttering something in Latin. Philippa sipped loudly.

"Phlee! I think your drink is gone," I said and grabbed another bottle of apple juice from the counter near her bed. I had stocked them earlier; I smiled, pleased my sister was drinking all of them.

"Lassie!"

"Geez, what? Ok, I'm looking. See? Happy? ... Oh my ... holy shit."

I felt all the blood drain from my face.

I dropped the bottle.

"Is that—"

"Your uncle, yes," Dragon finished.

"Uncle Seb's in Colombia? Hey, my juice! It's leaking!" Philippa said.

I looked at Dragon and knew immediately that no, it wasn't my actual uncle in that photo.

"How many of him are there," I whispered.

"Dinnae ken," Baert said. "But I'll give every clipe a right skelping."

"What do we do? Why Colombia?"

"The trees, the mountains, these are natural, ancient guardians of realms within the folds of the universe," Dragon said quietly.

"Yeah, I remember Uncle Seb yammering on about that when we were coming back last time. I, uh, geez ... I probably should have listened better," I said.

"Coming back from where? How many of who?"

"Phlee, I'll fill you in a bit more later," I said as she yawned. "You need to get to sleep. And I should get back home too, anyway."

"You're lucky I'm still all weak and too out of it to fight you on that," she said, yawning again. "Because this sounds like some pretty messed up stuff."

"Evechild, this is much for you to process."

"Yeah, it just gets piled in with the rest of the weird shit at this point," I mumbled. "I'm guessing you have a plan, though."

Dragon was quiet.

Baert shoved his hands in his pockets and rocked back and forth.

"C'mon guys, you can't show me this crap and, like, not have a plan."

"We have examined many options, many angles. And given the project time-frame, other variables and such, and so forth," Dragon stammered and coughed.

"Spit it out, Dragon."

"We either eradicate the clones, or we eliminate Obrenox."

Baert nodded his head solemnly. Behind me, Philippa let out a loud snore.

"Either, or?" I whispered, stepping in closer to them.

Dragon nodded, then looked beyond me at Philippa, concerned. My heart pounded. I had nearly forgotten about that part … the part about there also being clones of my sister out there …

"Vanquishing Obrenox means the life force of these clones is snuffed out," he said carefully, quietly. "Exterminating the clones does not seem to affect him, however. He loses the ability to control them into an attack, true. This is a boon. However, they can continue to propagate – or be propagated? I am unclear on the scientific specificity – until … until …"

"Until the host is killed. Like Jonah," I said hoarsely.

"This is also my understanding."

We stood there, the three of us, silent under the heaviness of truth, for what seemed like hours. When I looked down, I realized Baert's hand was in mine.

Another snore from Philippa jolted us all back to the present.

"Well then. There you have it," Dragon said abruptly.

I just nodded. What was there to say?

I *did* dream that night.

Still wasn't sweet.

Unless getting attacked by clone armies of everyone you know is sweet.

60

FALSUS IN UNO

I wasn't very kind that day.

Sometimes when you wake up, you can feel that tingle, anger with nowhere to go. And you decide you deserve to indulge in that anger. So you walk around all day with a scowl on your face and an insult in your heart.

This wasn't that.

I woke up, neutral but placid, and headed to school. The walk was pleasant, quiet. Quiet until I entered the side of the school.

"Ew, here she comes now. You have your lucky stuffed dragon with you?

Libby stood, posing, in a group of upperclassmen. A few snickers and laughs bounced around the group. She beamed.

I shot her a look. But her face fell when she saw me. Crap, I hoped she didn't see that was actually hurt.

I kept my head down until I was seated, my bag stowed under my chair. I scanned the classroom for Elke, then kept my eyes glued on the door like a puppy waiting for its master.

No such luck.

That's when I became irreversibly cranky.

So cranky that I couldn't think of a single thing that would turn my mood around.

Every situation, thing, whatever, I could fathom had only bad angles. I was incapable of seeing good.

I collected my things and bolted out the door before the bell even finished ringing.

"God, watch it," I snapped as my books toppled out of my arms. I looked up to see who ran into me. I groaned. "Just leave me alone."

"No, no, no! It's not like that, what you saw earlier, I was just, like, making them laugh," Libby said, starting strong but trailing off.

"That's exactly what I saw earlier," I growled. "You are using me as a way to get upperclassmen to pay attention to you."

"It's not like that," she whimpered.

"You're delusional. And I was delusional for thinking there was a decent human being in there," I said, snubbing my nose at her and turning the other direction.

I walked angrily down the hall. Down a hall. Down a hall I'd never been in before. I spun around. Had I been here before? I turned back; the hall seemed to extend in front of me for a billion miles.

My head hurt.

Someone tapped me on the back. Before I could turn around, a girl ran by, laughing and waving her arms. Her short brown hair bobbed as she ran in her croc-leather loafers. She turned head back, a crazed smile plastered under vacant eyes. I gasped.

"Philippa?"

The girl laughed; it was then I realized there was no sound of laughter coming from her. Her mouth hung open, her body shook in nothing more than a grand pantomime of laughter. Shivers shot down my spine.

I caught up with her. Before I could say anything, she had one of my hands in hers. She pressed something into my palm and closed my fingers over it. It immediately burned. Hotter and hotter. I yelped and tried to pull my hand back but she held it tight. A crazy smile, not Philippa's smile but still somehow

Philippa's smile, stayed unnervingly still under her dead eyes, unflinching. I squealed and twisted away until I broke free.

Then I ran.

I ran past my third-period class, down the stairs, out the door, and through the parking lot. I darted through rows of cars, uncertain if that ... that thing was following me. I cut down the center to a row at my left. As I popped between cars on the other side, I heard the screech of brakes and smell of burnt rubber.

A red coupe, beaten up and smoking, was stopped inches from my right leg. I pounded on the top of the hood and threw my arms out, indignant and fevered. Libby's terrified face stared back at me, her knuckles white atop the steering wheel.

"What the hell, man?" I screamed.

"Oh my gosh, I'm, like, so sorry!" she cried out the window.

"Why were you going so fast?"

"Why are you running through the parking lot?"

I was quiet. She was quiet. Finally she threw her arms up and motioned for me to get in. I shook my head vigorously. She stared at me. I don't know why that worked, but it did. Plus, I really needed to sit down.

"Why are you cutting school?" I asked as I brusquely slammed the door shut and buckled my seat belt.

"Why are *you* cutting school?" she shot back.

I was quiet again.

"Not a great day for me," I mumbled.

We looped around the neighborhood streets aimlessly. I was okay with it. It gave me time to close my eyes and review what I had just seen.

Philippa? A burnt palm?

I froze. It was a clone. With one of the those stones from the Amythystics.

"Are you, like, okay?"

Libby's voice startled me.

"Yeah, I was just, um, sleeping."

"Your eyes were open."

"They were?"

Libby didn't say anything. More aimless driving. I didn't recognize anything. Rows of houses climbing up a steep neighborhood road.

"Look, I, like, really am sorry," Libby said at last. "Back at school … it was … pathetic. But they were actually talking to me! Like, if I could just get in with two or three of them…"

"Libby, why do you care so much? You have your own crew to fawn over you."

"Yeah? Where?" she shot back, her voice catching.

I thought about that for a minute. This whole school year, early yet though it was, I hadn't seen her usual band of lemmings. It hadn't hit me before that Libby was generally alone.

"They're at a different school. All my friends. Or, whatever you want to call them. Haven't had a text, call, nothing, from any of them. Not a single one," Libby sniffed.

"That, um, that stinks. Sorry," I muttered. "But that doesn't mean you get to be an asshole, just because you're lonely."

She didn't say anything. Rain fell softly. I shivered. She turned up the heat in the car; something buzzed for a minute and then a smoking smell came pouring through the car.

"Ooooh, that's not good," she grumbled. "You know anything about cars?"

"No, but I know someone who does. Hang on; I'll map it," I said as I pulled out my phone and opened the map.

Twenty-two minutes later, we were driving up to Uncle Seb's hangar.

The hangar door was open; the plane looked bigger than usual tucked into that space. The lights were off; I frowned.

"Uncle Seb?" I called as I got out and walked around the hangar. Libby turned off her car and followed me inside. "He must be back there," I said as I motioned toward his office. I could see a thin line of light from below the door.

We stopped, alert. A thud, subtle but real, came from within the office. And then another, louder, and another, even louder.

"What is, like, going on in there?" Libby asked.

"Ssshhh! I don't know, but it's not normal," I whispered.

"How do you know?" she hissed.

"Does that sound normal to you?"

The thuds were met by several thumps, then a girl's whimper.

"Stay here," I whispered to Libby as I held my hand against her arm.

"Ew, why is your hand so sweaty? And no way am I staying here. What weird shit is your uncle doing in there?" she whispered back.

I took a deep breath and wiped my hands on my pants. They were amazingly sweaty. I turned to Libby and stared at her, hard. Her eyes softened; so did my resolve. I had to look away and remind myself quickly what a raging jerk she's always been to me.

"Look, you might see something that ... what I mean is ... my uncle's not a bad guy, there's just some stuff going on with, like ... uuuuuggggh. Just don't say anything, ok?" I said, flustered.

She nodded and motioned for me to take the lead. We crept past the pristine plane, past the impeccably organized shelves and bins, to the metal office door. The sounds grew louder, louder, and then – nothing. Silence.

I held my finger to my lips, then gestured toward the door. Libby nodded, shoved her hands in her pockets, and pulled out a tube of lip gloss.

I shook my head wildly. And threw my arms out.

She shrugged and produced another tube of a different flavor/color combination.

"How do you not know the international sign for 'be quiet'!?" I hissed.

"Your lips are, like, so chapped, naturally I thought that's what you were asking," she hissed back.

"Never mind. Let's go."

I opened the door, slowly, carefully, peering through the crack. I saw my uncle; he was alone. I sighed; my shoulders relaxed and I threw the door open the rest of the way.

"Uncle Seb, what the – oh my god!" I cried as I stepped inside.

Uncle Seb turned; at his feet lay a girl, face down, in a familiar cardigan and corduroy pants with croc-leather loafers.

"That was the most messed-up thing I've ever had to do in my life, Egg," he said. He was breathing hard.

I motioned for Libby to stay away; she understood that one and backed away. I was scared to come any closer to my closer, any closer to ... to the thing on the floor.

"Was it – was it just the one?" I asked, suddenly feeling queasy. "No, please don't turn her over!" I cried as my uncle leaned down to examine the body.

"Yeah, just this one, but they typically travel in pairs, or packs," he said grimly.

I jumped; a hand was on my shoulder, a familiar warmth creeping through my body. I spun around just in time to see the face of my sister collapse before me. In her place stood Libby, panting, holding a giant wrench.

I looked down at the fallen clone, at Libby, at the clone, at my uncle, at the other clone, at Libby.

"Yep, travel in pairs. Nice one," my uncle said simply. "Who's this?"

"This is, um, uh," I stuttered, unable to comprehend my present situation.

"I'm Libby," she said, dropping the wrench and offering her hand. "Dragongirl's BFF since, like, fourth grade."

"Dragongirl? Well, as Egg's BFF, I'll go easy on you and ask nicely that you, one, pick up that wrench and put it back where you found it, and two, never mention anything you saw here to anyone, ever," my uncle said as he stepped over one clone, then the other. "Got it?"

"Egg?" Libby asked.

"Got it?" my uncle repeated gruffly.

"For sure. But like, who are you, and who are they? And, oh my god, I totally forgot! We're here because my car was doing this funky screechy thing with maybe just a tiny bit of smoke coming out, and she said you're, like, this amazing mechanic and –"

"The shop's closed. You need to leave," he said as he pushed past her and toward his car. He paused and looked around. "Strange, they were all here earlier."

"Who was?" I asked.

"The Kips. I wonder," Uncle Seb said as he jogged around the back of the hangar. "Dear god, Kip! Are you alright? Egg, Egg! You have that fiducia stone on you?"

I ran after him and stopped in my tracks. Sitting, leaning, pathetic and bound in glowing Peridiote cuffs were three Kips. Two were asleep; the other looked up with the saddest, most woeful eyes and burst into tears.

I didn't know Kips could cry.

I raced back to Libby's car and rummaged through my backpack. I didn't dare leave something so bizarre and potentially important in my room; my mom, with her energy returning, was prone to a lot of cleaning and organizing these days. It took one close call with the spheresaii bag for me to wise up and stash things better.

"Here! I have it!" I cried as I ran back. "But don't you need the other one?"

"This one should do the trick," Uncle Seb said as he yawned and placed the stone inside the central Kip's fist. "It's strange, though; usually once the host wielding these things is done, they lose their power. But we should see – ah! Yes, Kip, old pal! Can you bust free of those?"

The Kip in the middle looked around, eyes wide and frightened, then nodded at my uncle, clenched his fists tightly, and pulled his wrists free. The yellow glow dissipated and fell to the ground and fizzled and steamed in a snake-like show. Kip held the stone near his ankle and pulled his feet apart, freeing his legs as well. He hopped up.

"Good as new, yep! Now to save brothers, yep! Oh, oh, nope! Duck, yep!"

Uncle Seb ducked just in time; a Philippa clone stumbled forward, swiping at the air, a dagger in her fist. Kip laid her out with a swift punch.

"Kip! Kip! I can't breathe!" I wheezed as someone squeezed tightly around my neck. I pulled hard at the fingers. I recognized the bluish-green nail polish on them. I had bought it for Philippa as a good-luck charm; the colors were those of a college she was hoping to get into.

I wrestled out her grip and turned to face my sister. Not Philippa, but Philippa. She held a Peridiote up to my neck. I couldn't swallow. She threw her head back and opened her mouth wide in laughter, but no sound came out.

I fought through the heaviness, the sleepiness, and lunged toward the stone. I grabbed and threw it as hard as I could. It sparked and flashed angrily on the ground, not all that far away.

I turned to run. Libby was leaning against one of the Kips, fast asleep with him, propped up against the hangar. I shook her, hard. It was no use. The other Kip had a clone in a headlock, while the third sprinted from around the hangar. He held something in his hand, which he tossed expertly to my uncle.

"Egg, look away!" Uncle Seb screamed as he charged after the clone following me.

A gunshot sounded. I screamed.

One, and then two clones were again on the ground.

The yellow cuffs sizzled, sparked, and vanished, leaving just remnants of slithering ash on the ground. Kip opened his eyes, then Libby.

"Get her out of here," Uncle Seb barked.

But the Kips were already on it.

"Right this way, miss, yep!" they echoed as they led a very shaky Libby the opposite direction around the hangar.

"They don't shut down unless you kill them," he said quietly between heavy breaths. "You gotta spill their blood, or whatever it is. Or ..."

"Dragon told me," I said quickly, not wanting him to complete the sentence. I knew what the other option was for shutting down the clones while Obrenox was still alive.

I shouldn't have looked, but I did.

61

FIAT PANIS

"Sooooo are you going to tell me what the hell all of that was, or just sit there?" Libby said after about eight minutes of driving. "You've been silent forever."

"We've barely been driving. And no, I'm not; and yes, I will just sit here," I said flatly. Then I added quickly, "but thank you, um, for driving me home, at any rate ... yeah."

Libby's hands gripped the steering wheel. Her jalopy drove better than it ever had; better than I had ever experienced, anyway, limited though my time was in that car. Within minutes of popping the hood, Uncle Seb was closing it and yelling that it was "good to go, just a coolant leak from a janky gasket."

"You can't just not tell me," she said with a flip of her hair. "Where do I turn again?"

"At that next intersection. Yeah, that one, take a right."

"Eve," she snapped, "there were two dead girls getting carried off by some twin guys – or triplets? I don't even know – and I, like, passed out for a minute or something. What the actual hell is going on?"

In our years of classes together, elementary school until now, I had never heard her call me by my actual name. Not once. I had no reason to be certain she knew what it was.

"Yeah," I muttered. "Pretty messed up."

Honestly, I was playing it cool but underneath I had no idea what to do. I couldn't trust Libby with any of this; who's to say the first look from Channing wouldn't have her spilling her guts? And every time someone in my life knew anything about the other dimension, something bad happened. Take Philippa. Totally innocent in all of this, not even a role to play. And she has suffered the most.

"You're seriously not going to explain anything? Like, at all?"

I shook my head. Libby slammed on the brakes. I quickly checked behind us; our abrupt stop in the middle of the road wasn't ideal. Luckily, we were the only ones on the road that night for the moment.

"That's so, extremely, totally messed up. Even for you, Dragongirl."

So, we were back to that name being an insult. I felt her staring at me, glaring at me, but I didn't budge. I kept my eyes fixed ahead, moving them only to check the side mirror for traffic approaching.

"Fine. Be that way. See if I help you again," she grumbled as she hit the gas with a little too much gusto. We shot through the intersection as the light turned yellow.

"That was where you were supposed to turn," I said evenly. "And you don't get it. It's like, the less you know, the better. Just trust me. And whatever you do, do *not* talk to anyone about this."

"Like they'd believe me anyway," she muttered as she flipped the car around, a precarious maneuver in the middle of a four-lane road.

We drove the rest of the way in silence. I was sure her silence was born of frustration, fear; mine was too, but any emotion was blanketed by extreme exhaustion. Even if I had wanted to talk to Libby more, I don't think my brain could have even formed coherent sentences at that point.

"Thanks, and, um, sorry. I know this is all pretty freaking messed up," I mumbled as I got out of her car. The passenger door creaked and squeaked, and I worried for a minute it wouldn't close.

"It's ... whatever. Tell your uncle thanks for helping with my car," she said simply and drove off before I could say anything further, let alone check that the door had latched.

A gust of warm air and the smell of cinnamon greeted me as I walked inside. Two unfamiliar things. My mom rarely had the heat on, and I could count on one hand the times she had baked in recent memory. Yet there, on the kitchen counter, were piles of freshly baked snickerdoodles. I grabbed one and took a bite; it was better than any of my attempts at baking Philippa's favorite cookie.

I headed upstairs. Music came drifting down the hallway; I followed it to my mom's room. She and Philippa had records fanned out on her bed. On the record player on my mom's dresser, an old Otis Redding album played.

"Phlee! You're home!" I cried as I hugged my sister. My knee hit something hard. "Oh, sorry; did I hurt you?"

"Nah. Just the edge of my MotoThrone5000," she said as she lifted her blanket to reveal the wheelchair underneath.

"Wait, that can't be what it's called," I said, laughing. My mom danced in from the bathroom and shot me a look.

"Obviously your sister wasn't going to cruise around in a regular old wheel-chair," she said. "So we renamed it."

"Oooh, can we hit a bottle of champagne against it? Like how they christen boats?" Philippa asked.

"I think I have a seltzer water; will that work?" my mom said.

"Nah, it's gotta be the real deal," I said, throwing my bag down and picking up a record. "I forgot you even had a record player in here."

"Honestly, so did I!" my mom said as she danced while folding laundry.

"This should be in the queue," I said, picking up a Wes Montgomery album and handing it to Philippa.

"Oh, agreed! But it will be, like, number nine in line. I've gotta pretty intense playlist set up," Philippa said as she tossed an album to my mom, who caught it between her palms. "Nice catch. Next one, if you will, please."

My mom beamed. Still rocking her hips side to side, she carefully removed one record and replaced it with the next. The record player hummed with that soft static – I loved the sound of a new record starting – and then Barbra Streisand's inimitable voice came on.

"People ... people who need people," Philippa sang along to the iconic song.

My mom started to cry. Unabashedly. I coughed down the lump in my throat.

It was a beautiful moment. But I had no interest in leaning into emotion.

"I'm gonna go to bed," I said as I kissed Philippa on the top of the head.

"Ew, did you just put your lips on me?" she said.

"You know it. And there's plenty more where that came from," I said, giggling. I grabbed my bag and headed out of the master bedroom, giving a wave to my mom. "Goodnight, ma."

She looked up, her cheeks wet, and blew me a kiss.

"What is with all of these public displays of affection?" Philippa said, laughing. "Why did PDA become acceptable while I was away?"

I mindlessly did my nightly routine. My heart felt lighter with Philippa home. But my thoughts were heavier than ever.

I fell asleep almost immediately. But not for long; my eyes shot open to the sound of voices. I sat straight up on high alert. But it was only my mom and sister calling goodnight to one another.

"We continue with your record selections tomorrow!" my mom sang down the hallway. Phlee sang back, and I heard the thump-thump of her wheelchair hitting her bed.

That sound stabbed at my heart. I ought to be grateful, my mom reminded me a few days ago, that Phlee is able to be home from the hospital and mobile. *Mobile.* As if that should have ever not been a certainty.

I floundered around under my covers. The sweet moments of the evening had given way to bitterness, frustration. And this time when I closed my eyes, all I saw was my uncle choking a clone, a clone of my sister, who had toppled forward with blood oozing from somewhere under her dark brown hair.

I craved sleep.

I craved restful, healing sleep.

It was so strange that entire generations relegated sleep to nothing more an a byproduct of weakness. *Sleep when you're dead*, they'd say. I suspect they did, though perhaps much sooner than they thought.

Bodies and brains need sleep.

My stomach growled.

...And they probably need food.

62

LUPUS EST HOMO HOMINI

D id I want to go to school?

No.

Did I want to stay at home alone with my own thoughts?

No times infinity.

My mom and sister had already left for Philippa's physical therapy. It was the first of many upcoming marathon sessions with a team of people all tasked with various components of my sister's functioning: walking, talking, memory recall, cardiac health, and even appetite.

Turns out not a lot of people stay in a coma that long. Even fewer make a full recovery. And fewer still are as young and disarming as my sister.

She was a medical anomaly, and a sweetheart of one at that.

Reporters, researchers, grad students, medical residents, everyone was clamoring to get a moment with her.

I checked my phone for the millionth time as I trudged to school. No new updates from my mom since the last text informing me they had made it, that Jurgen came down to help stave off the crowds, and that Philippa was eager to be a star student as usual. I don't know why I was so nervous; I couldn't pinpoint the exact emotion, but it was something akin to nerves.

"Ah! Hallo! *Wie gehts*?" Elke greeted me at the rear stairwell as I ducked through crowds of students shuffling in.

"I don't remember that one – are you asking me if I'm hungry?" I giggled as I nodded hello. I think Elke was the one person who could illicit a giggle out of me, especially given my state lately.

"*Bist du hungrig*; see? That word sounds like 'hungry' in English," she said. "I just asked 'what's up.' Sorry; I should not be so casual."

"That's a strange thing to apologize for," I said, still giggling, "and I'm always hungry."

"I have not brought any extra food with me," Elke said, her smile dropping. "Here comes another apology."

"Not what I meant. Man, lost in translation is a very real struggle today. On to algebra?" I said as I nudged her in the arm good-naturedly.

"On to algebra," she said with a faint smile.

I sensed something was wrong. I sensed I should ask. I sensed this is what normal human friends do.

Instead I said nothing and slumped down in my usual chair. Elke paused in front of my desk briefly; I didn't look up from rummaging through my binder for my homework, which I never found. Probably because, as it turned out, I didn't do that homework.

I groaned and looked across the room at Elke. Sometimes she sat at the desk behind me, but usually she sat in the same place I did just on the other side of the room: fourth desk back, last row against the wall.

I frowned. She typically had perfect posture; today she was bowled over, head propped up on her hand, absentmindedly sketching something. I shrugged and went back to staring at the blank page in my notebook. Who am I to judge someone having an off day?

"Your assignment, please, Ms. Archer," Ms. Simmons' whiny voice startled me as his long fingers wiggled in front of me.

"Oh, um, I did this one," I said as I pulled out a different homework sheet, "but I guess I never got the new one."

"You've had more than enough time to complete it," he said impatiently, his hand on his hip. "I gave it out last week. You were – oh, oh my, that's right – occupied with … never mind. See me after class and I'll give you your make-up work."

My cheeks burned.

I was at a trial. Just say it. I was in a courtroom with a bunch of grownups trying to convince a bunch of other grownups that I could commit murder. That's why I missed that math assignment.

Good luck finding that reason on your attendance report.

I glanced back over at Elke again. Her head was down in her folded arms on top of her desk. Very unlike her. The period dragged on and on. When the bell finally sounded, I jumped up and charged to her desk.

"Hey, let's get out of here," I said, gently shaking her arm. She looked up. Her cheeks were pink and showed the pattern of her sweater. Her eyes were red and glossy.

"Yeah, okay," she said as she gathered her things.

"Ms. Archer, your work? You have quite a bit of catch-up to do, I'm afraid," Ms. Simmons called from his desk.

"I'll, um, be back at lunch," I called over my shoulder to him. "Got an emergency."

I ushered Elke out the door and swiftly upstairs to my favorite bathroom. I directed her to the little sofa and sat her down.

"Spill it. *Wie … wie … kates?*" I said, lamely attempting her German greeting. She smiled.

"Close enough," she said. "My papa is requesting I return sooner than we had planned."

"What? Why? Is everything okay?"

"There? Yes, all is okay. But here … well, he has safety worries. He is concerned … about my friends here."

She looked around uncomfortably. I stared at her, confused, before it dawned on me what she was getting at.

"Oh," I said quietly.

"Yeah. Oh," Elke said, looking so very defeated.

"Are you ... concerned?" I asked finally.

She grabbed my hand and pulled me down to the sofa next to her. We sat side by side, silently, for a minute. She kept my hand in hers.

"Only because I am growing feelings for you," she said quietly. "My papa and I, we were in a fight yesterday over this during our phone call. I thought it was okay, though. He is my parent; I do miss him. And I understand his worries. But then today I see you, and ... and ... *schiesse, Ich hasse das. Es ist nicht Gerecht.*"

"For real," I said solemnly. I didn't know what she had said, but context clues can get you a long way with empathy.

Elke giggled. My heart pounded. She, with her perfectly smooth blonde hair and warm eyes, stared at me, with my tangled blonde hair and tired, puffy eyes. Our fingers were intertwined, though I don't even know when that fully happened.

She leaned in. I gulped. Her lips were suddenly the only thing that existed in the world.

"Holy crap, are you kidding me? This is too adorable for words!"

A familiar voice tore through the moment and ripped it to shreds. I looked up, suddenly aware of how flushed and sweaty I was. Channing held her phone toward us, obviously recording.

"So, you've found love in the midst of murder!" she chortled. "Love really does conquer all. Ugh. What a story this continues to be!"

"Um, who is this?" Elke whispered.

"Oh, you don't know? Allow me the pleasure of your introduction to me," Channing said as she held a limp hand in front of Elke. "Channing Reagan Barrenton. I'm sure now you're realizing, dear. It's fine; we all have our forgetful moments."

Elke stared at her, unimpressed. She didn't take Channing's hand, or even further acknowledge her in any way.

"Never heard of you," Elke said as she stood up, gathered her bag and looked at me. "Let's go?"

I quickly grabbed my stuff and scrambled out of the bathroom after her.

"Oh my gosh," I gushed as I jogged up to Elke. "I can't believe you just said that. Her face, and your reaction, and her reaction, and I think that was just one of my most favorite moments ever! Hey, slow down! Man, you walk fast."

Elke bolted down the rear stairwell – the very one we had greeted each other on barely two hours ago – and out the back doors. As I charged after her, a rustling in the bushes that lined the parking lot caught my attention. I slowed down and looked at Elke, gaining distance, and at the bush, shaking vigorously despite a complete lack of wind.

"Ugh," I groaned. "Please just be an animal. A squirrel. Please be a squirrel," I muttered as I approached, phone in hand.

"Ne'er a wee squirrel, boot yer favorite bonny lad!"

Baert's eyes twinkled from within the arbor vitae. He thrust his head through, his red hair showing brilliantly against the dull green.

"Aye, tis itchy!" he cried as she barreled all the way through and landed at my feet.

"Yeah, next time pick a rhododendron or something with smooth leaves. Any kid who's ever played outside can tell you exactly which ones are murder bushes," I said with a chuckle. "Why are you here? What's going on?"

"Murder bush?!" he said with wide eyes. And then, mimicking me with a whiny voice, "why are you heeeere, why would Baert feign to visit meeee?"

"That's not what I said," I giggled.

"Lassie! Back!" Baert said as he pushed me away from the hedge. "I dinnae ken a murder bush tah be yer final captor."

"I was exaggerating, Baert. That bush just sucks to retrieve a lost ball from or, like, fall into. You'll be itching forever and finding those tiny needly bunches in your hair forever. It sucks. Royally sucks."

He eyed the tall hedge suspiciously.

"Um, you were just hiding in that one. So, clearly not murder-y," I said and tugged on his arm to pull him away from sizing up the nefarious evergreen. "Just you? Dropping by to say hi or what?"

"Aye, Lassie, if only the presence of yer *mo charaid* were just that!" Baert wailed. "Boot I'm a balloon!"

I glanced around, suddenly very aware I was truant in the school's parking lot with a crying elf. I had no idea where Elke had disappeared to. She had her own stuff to deal with; I'd text her later to check on her. That's what normal human friends do, right?

I frowned. The fact that I was lately trying to ascertain what was "normal" and "human" in friendly behavior wasn't great … I made a mental note to discuss with Malcolm what the hell friends do.

"Baert, this is not the best place in the world to be … doing this," I hissed as I pulled him around the hedge to the other side of the school grounds. "What's going on? What's happened? And," I paused, eyeing him and remembering a few key traits of braunies, "I really am so happy to see you. Always. Um, I'm glad you're here with me."

Baert's whole demeanor softened. He took a deep breath and bowed. He motioned for me to follow him, then sat down under a cluster of branches out of general eyesight. I crouched down and joined him. A twig jabbed my ear. My butt felt the growing cold of wet ground.

"Ya see, Lassie – could ye be still? – ever since the great judgement, this Leftenant's been right lost! Alone! How d'we free her?"

My heart dropped. Ms. Neally.

"You mean … you didn't have a plan?" I asked slowly. Baert looked up and shook his head mournfully. "You guys didn't know she … that she was going to confess?" His big eyes grew bigger, sadder. "She just stood up and took the blame all by herself, without … without any plan?!"

"Aye!" Baert cried. He hit his head against the thickest branch closest to him, again and again. "Ye peely wally radge, Baert! Yer heid's full o'mince! I'd of told thah fair lass, Yaël, yer aff yer heid! Boot here I am, and there she be!"

I let him cry. It seemed like he needed it. And I guessed his other company – Dragon and my machismo-packed uncle, specifically – didn't offer a space for storied war generals' tears. I rubbed his little back, small but muscled. His tunic was soft and smelled of lavender. I smiled.

"Baert, your tunic smells lovely," I said, thinking I might take his mind off his sadness.

But that backfired. Big time.

"'Twas her!" he wailed even louder. "She cleaned, and a *gie it laldy*, that!"

"Yeah, she was … the best," I said, still uncertain how to respond when Baert's conversation was peppered with Scottish sayings, Gaelic sayings, and Scottish Gaelic sayings. Blindly agreeing with him seemed to work just fine thus far.

Baert sniffed and leaned back.

"So, Dragon and Uncle Seb," I started.

"Dinnae nary a plan," he finished.

"But we at least know where she is? Uncle Seb has visited her?"

Baert nodded.

Slowly, an idea started to take shape. My heart beat a little faster. I patiently waited for the thoughts to form like someone waiting with outstretched palm for a timid animal to approach. A little whirl of excitement grew with the idea.

"Baert," I said with a smile, "if Uncle Seb has been there, and if we can get you there, then we have a way to break her out."

Baert looked at me, his eyes now wide with mischief instead of sorrow. He grinned.

"Thah book," he said resolutely.

63

HORRESCO REFERENS

I walked home in the middle of a school day. Normally such an audacious quest would have had me sprinting, serpentining, skulking about side streets and small shops lest someone be able to track me. But now I walked carelessly, gallantly, along a straight sidewalk toward my house.

It wasn't the energy from realizing we might have a way to save Ms. Neally from the clink, although that was elating. It wasn't knowing Philippa and I would be eating Thai food together tonight at home in front of the tv, although that was equally blissful.

It was realizing I almost had my first kiss. With a singularly beautiful and intriguing German girl.

Almost. My. First. Kiss.

It was exhilarating! So much so that I couldn't even fathom what the actual kiss itself might feel like!

As I floated down the sidewalk, my thoughts happily consumed with all things Elke, I didn't notice a shadow gaining on me, a shadow so close that it comingled with my own. I didn't notice another shadow scurry across the street in front of me.

I didn't notice much of anything until a dark throaty voice pierced my reverie and reset my reality.

"Eve, hmmmm."

I looked up, but saw nothing. My foot hit something uneven on the pavement. I looked down; a group of pebbles was just under my shoe. Then, one by one, tiny stones rolled toward me. A few at first, then more and more until they had settled into a pattern. My blood froze.

"I've seen that," I whispered to myself. "Why is that familiar?"

Something caught my eye. Something dark, moving, then something flowy and brilliantly colored.

"Hmmm, she doesn't pay attention, and now she must run! Run, hmmm! RUN!"

Gil appeared suddenly before me. Her hand reached out over the pebbled pattern – a thurisaz! That was it! – as something leapt from the shadows behind her. A girl – a young woman with wavy brown hair and a plaid cardigan – jumped on Gil's back and pulled fiercely on the old gypsy's scarves. Gil wheezed and rocked. The girl looked straight at me. Philippa's stolen eyes flashed dark.

I darted around Gil and pulled on the clone. Its body looked identical to Philippa's, but it was cold to the touch. I grasped ahold of its waistband with one hand and grabbed a fistful of hair with the other and yanked hard. The clone's mouth shot open and it toppled back, noiselessly, atop the cement.

"Go, hmmm! I shall tend to this, hmmm, creature!" Gil cried as she pulled something shiny from the folds of her skirts.

I didn't hesitate. I didn't want to see what Gil would do. I ran, but not fast enough to escape the sound of Gil's throaty war cry as she thrust a blade through fake flesh. Then, farther away, screams, sirens.

I didn't stop running until I was inside my house, doors locked. I collapsed, panting, on the stairs. Within minutes, the door rattled open. Philippa's head appeared around the corner. I lunged down the stairs toward her, my adrenaline still streaming through my veins. She shrieked and backed through the door. I launched through the air from the fourth step, ready to fight, and fell, hard, on the wood parquet floor at the landing.

I laid there huffing, the wind knocked out of me. Philippa's voice sent my pulse racing again.

"Dude, what the hell? I know you're excited to see me, but the flying banshee is maybe a bit excessive," Philippa said as she peered down at me. "Now, if you could move your body so I can get to the kitchen, that'd be swell."

The tinny hum of her wheelchair snapped me out of rage mode. That, and it was her real voice! Those clones, the Philippa ones, they couldn't emit vocal sound for some reason.

"Oh, Phlee, thank god!" I cried as I scurried upright. I hugged her tightly around the neck.

"Ah, I love it! You girls are so sweet to each other," my mom cried as she came into the house. "I'm a witness!"

"Hey, uh, lock the door, would you?" I called to my mom. I was still panting.

"You're home already?" my mom said with a frown.

"Yeah, uh, school let out early ... um, some stranger danger alert or something," I said lamely.

"Oh, gosh! Everything okay? Philippa had a banner day, acing her tests as usual," my mom sang as she casually locked the door. I hit the deadbolt after her. "Wow, you must really be spooked, huh? I don't think I've ever seen you lock a door in your life. Anyhow, your sister. What a rockstar. Tell her all about it, Phlee!"

"Yep. A rockstar," Philippa said between bites of cookie. She grabbed a handful of snickerdoodles from the counter and rolled into the family room. "I'll give the debriefing after some downtime."

My mom frowned. She started to say something, but I quickly cut her off.

"Ma, it was probably a lot for her," I whispered out of earshot of Philippa. "Even good can be a lot. Just, um, let her be, yeah? Maybe we just all, like, take a beat and breathe for a bit?"

She nodded and headed upstairs to change, but I could tell she was pouting. The adult was pouting. While I, the child, had to keep order.

I grabbed some crackers and plopped onto the couch next to Philippa. I had pushed all the furniture *just so* to accommodate the wheelchair without it being too obvious. The last thing I wanted was for Phlee to feel like an imposition in her own home.

"Saltine?" I asked as I offered her the sleeve of crackers.

She shook her head. Her eyes watered as she clicked through shows and movies.

"Oof. I can get you Ritz instead, my bad," I said in a lame attempt to lighten things up.

"No, I'll take it," she sniffed as she grabbed the package. "It's just so … strange. All of this. I can't … I don't even know where to start."

"You don't have to start," I said quietly. "I can't imagine. It's, like, so much, Phlee. You don't have to say anything. We can do whatever. Watch whatever. Even if you steal all the crackers."

She smiled then.

"Everyone knows the proper serving of saltines is one sleeve. You want to watch this with me?"

My giggling turned to groaning as I looked at the screen.

"Yes. I've been saving this exact, weird, likely suggestive and cringey anime to watch with you," I said.

"Really?" she said, brightening.

"Hell no!" I laughed. "But nothing would make me happier in this moment than watching it with you. For real. You start it. I'll get more snacks."

"But you'll miss the exposition!" she called behind me as I leapt to the kitchen.

"Exactly."

Rummaging through the pantry for snacks while Phlee yelled her television narrative at me, lest I miss any crucial details, had me smiling, relaxed, existing in a reality that felt normal.

Normal.

Ah, what a word!

My favorite books never addressed that bit. Teen protagonists heroically leapt from one impossible task to the next, fueled by altruism and duty. Never did they burrow as far as possible under their covers in an overwhelming spiral of despair and anxiety. Not that I was critical of my unrealistic novels – I loved them! There are all these human emotions that connect you to characters in books: fear, loss, protecting friends and family, love conquers all, blah, blah, blah. And they keep going. But that stuff impacts you, good and bad. You don't come through a hero's journey without a little damage.

I paused and chuckled at my own thoughts. If I were presented with a book like that, would I even read it? Like, hero has problem, hero tackles problem but scary things happen in the process, hero can't get out of bed because everything freaks hero out now.

But then something more concerning landed in my mind: Did my favorite books and stories simply not include the non-sexy parts of Herculean tasks intentionally, or was there something really, really wrong with me?

What would the headline of my story be? Will my story even be known? "Villain vanquished, world saved." That hardly tells my story. A more realistic headline would be, "World saved, hero naps."

"Yo! You're missing everything! What's the cheese situation in there?" Philippa called from the sofa.

I shook my head, shouldered my self-loathing, and grabbed the tray of snacks. I tripped over my backpack, slumped against the counter where I had thrown it down earlier, and dropped everything. Crackers and cheese slices swam in fizzing puddles of seltzer water on the floor.

"It's like I didn't even miss a beat," Philippa said, peering over the back of the sofa. "Oh, hey! It's not that bad! Let me help you!"

"No, no, stay there," I said as I dropped, defeated and crying, onto the kitchen floor. "I'm the idiot who dropped it, I can clean it up."

"Pretty harsh commentary on a simple accident," she said, frowning. "Ah, you must be devastated at the thought of letting me down. Is that it?" she added with forced laughter. It worked. I caught myself smiling at my sister as I mopped up the soggy mess. "There, see? You're basically done already. And I'm not upset in the least."

"Thanks for the pep talk," I chuckled. "Popcorn?"

She gave me a thumbs-up and turned back to the television.

I stared at the microwave as the bag enlarged and little kernels popped and bounced inside. The sound was deafening. Had microwaving popcorn always sounded like gunfire?

I finally returned to the sofa, victorious with snacks and beverages. One look at Philippa, though, and I jumped and dropped the bowl of popcorn all over her.

Blood dripped from a bullet hole in her forehead and oozed from a gash in her neck.

"Geez, you are so shaky today!" she said. "You don't look so good. Don't get me sick! Here, I think I got most of the popcorn."

I blinked and looked at her again: brown eyes wide with worry, wavy hair clean and dry. No blood.

"It's just been a weird day," I said as I exhaled and sat down next to my sister. "Maybe I am sick."

64

GRAVIORA MANENT

I didn't really understand time anymore. Events shuffled back and forth on either side of my present moment like a deck of cards. Some were more significant than others, like drawing a face card on Tuesday versus a lowly two of clubs on Thursday. Planning how to save the world from Obrenox or trying to finish my lit arts homework; it was all so random and conflated by stress.

Have'nt heard from u. Hope u R ok. (This is ubcle Sad)

**Seb not sad*

I cringed. Uncle Seb texted like an old person, complete with typos and outdated abbreviations. His texts should have made me smile, should have softened my heart. But I awoke grumpy and was determined to stay that way.

I had made up my mind to talk to Ms. Nguyen after school. It was the type of thing I would have loved to consult Ms. Neally about. But she was currently being held without bail in a state prison. The same detectives – Serrano and Jasper – had visited my house again late last night.

"What was she hiding in that library?" Serrano had demanded.

"Nothing! At least, nothing that I would know about. I don't even go to that school," I had told them several times.

"But you did. And we have multiple eye-witness accounts of you skipping class to hang out in that library," Serrano had countered.

"Yep. From different sources," Jasper had added smugly.

"That's what multiple eyewitnesses means," Serrano had barked at him. "Now, what were the two of you up to? Why this boy? Why this family? What had he discovered that prompted you to keep him quiet?"

"By killing him?" Jasper said as he folded his arms.

At that point, my mom had stood up, collected their beverages, and invited them to leave.

"We're not done here," Serrano had snarled. "We can only give you so many opportunities to tell us what you know. The bigger this gets, the worse it gets for you."

I had said nothing. My mom opened the front door and told them their time was up.

"Mind if I take my seltzer water to go?" Jasper had said. Serrano smacked it out of his hand. "Great. Now I must stay and clean that up. And I'm so parched!"

"I'll clean. Please leave. I shouldn't have let you in without our lawyer, anyway," my mom had said with a scowl.

Later that night, Uncle Seb had shown up. I was upstairs, tossing and turning per my usual midnight ritual, when I heard him and my mom arguing.

"Don't wake them! Either of them! She's still way too stressed; she has to sleep!"

"But this is important, dammit!"

"Then you can tell *me*. You don't get to be absent forever, hop back into our lives when you need something, and repeat."

"You're always so ready to throw that shit at me. Did it ever occur to you I lay low for your own safety?"

"For my own sanity, you mean."

"Just tell Egg that they've taken Yaël to state jail. They raided her place, found enough that they think she set the fire to library to destroy evidence ... that ... combined with her insane, fake confession in court ...they've taken her, sis. They've taken her and I can't do shit about it."

I heard my uncle's voice break. It was quiet for a minute. Then some indistinct mumbling, whispering. I strained to hear, but no luck.

"Look, I'll tell her. You need some rest, too. You can stay here, I guess; I can make up the sofa for you."

More silence, then the door opening, shutting, locking.

I had fallen asleep replaying that day in court and wondering if Baert and Dragon knew. Of course they knew. They had to know … right? The plan Baert and I had come up with, to use Fortis Librae to bust her out, it could still work … right?

These same thoughts danced around in my mind as I wove in and out the day's duties. I don't know why I thought talking Ms. Nguyen might help. But when an idea nagged like that, I gave in.

"Oh! Hallo! I need to apologize for last time," Elke said, her bright face suddenly appearing before mine. "Maybe we go for coffee after school?'

"I can't, sorry," I grumbled, still absorbed in grumpy thoughts. She nodded and looked down. "Ugh, that's not what I meant – I really have plans after school. But, um, maybe tomorrow?"

"It's a date," she said as she pulled out her phone. "It is in my calendar now. So it is official."

I was instantly warm all over. I guess I couldn't be so snide and dismissive of the "love conquers all" trope in books now. If a smile and a date from this lovely creature could melt the ice of current stresses, imagine what full-blown love could do.

As I trudged from one class to the next, the series of insane events seemed farther and farther away. Dragon and Ms. Neally and school fires and clones and Gil, it was all just a bizarre dream, right?

I chuckled to myself as I walked down the hall, running my fingers along the wall. There was a time I had wished for a dragon, certain that the presence of one would make all my problems go away.

It did the opposite.

I had more problems than ever. I sighed. I guess that's what Shakespeare meant by "ignorance is bliss." I got why that saying stuck around.

My dear bard also noted that 'ignorance is the root of misfortune,' but you do not hear the laity throwing that one around.

I spun around. Nothing but empty halls. Had I daydreamed right through the fourth period bell? Was I daydreaming Dragon talking to me?

Indeed you have. And no, you are not. Also, this roof is not structurally sound. Someone ought to inform the headmaster that this skylight is one pigeon dropping away from crashing in.

I glanced around, tightened my backpack straps, and headed out the back door. On the way, I patted the stair rail affectionately. It reminded me of Elke now.

"Dragon?" I called as I jogged a few paces away from the building and looked up. I squinted in the low winter sun. A flutter of a wing confirmed he was up there. "Uh, what's going on?"

"Your classmates, Evechild, are a rather curious bunch. They take to truancy with such ease; trying to get to you has been quite a nuisance," he said as he glided down to the pavement beside me.

"Yeah, these rich kids kinda do whatever they want," I said dryly as I recalled my unsavory encounter with Channing and Guy and their hostage-happy lackey. "Hey, what's your stance on revenge, by the way?"

Dragon snorted in disgust; a plume of smoke burst from his nostrils.

"Ok, ok, unfavorable on revenge. Got it, geez," I said, backing up.

"Gil has informed me of your encounter, Evechild," he said hastily. "As has Sebastian. All is not well, here. We cannot ascertain how many clones were fabricated of your sister, only that they were done so in haste and are thus ... lacking somewhat."

I nodded, listening, not realizing we were walking toward the back of the school stadium.

"There have been many, but they lack in muscle composition and communication abilities," he continued.

"Quantity not quality," I murmured. "And they're silent. Which is way creepier."

"Indeed. Your sister shan't be denigrated by such paltry things much longer."

"How's that?"

Dragon paused, sat back on his haunches, and stretched his wings. Their pearly undersides were gnarled by fresh scars. Some sort of stitching was still visible along his torso. He caught my gaze and immediately folded his wings to his sides.

"You shall destroy Obrenox."

"Uuuuggghhh, this again?!" I wailed. It was cold in the shadow of the stadium. I shivered and leaned against its brick exterior. "I know that that's this endgame or whatever, but can you and my uncle stop speaking in such dramatic, sweeping statements like that? I mean, do you hear how impossible that sounds?"

Dragon cocked his head and frowned. A pigeon descended on the ground near us; at least a dozen more followed and pecked at the frosty ground.

"Away, ya wee beasties!" I cried in my best Baert impression. I stomped at them and waved my arms until they flew off.

Dragon looked up suspiciously, then quietly hovered above the ground. He rose higher and higher until he was eye-level with the top of the stadium.

"*Dégage! Ficher le camp*!" he yelled. The pigeons squawked and took off en masse, settling on some nearby powerlines. They cocked their little heads in time with each other, staring down at Drgon. He broadened his chest and flexed his wings toward them. "*J'ai dit dégage!*"

The flock squawked and took off. Dragon snorted at the few stragglers; bursts of smoke sent them on a frenzied flight after the others.

"Was that ... were you speaking French?" I asked as he floated down.

"*Bien sûr*. Everyone knows pigeons are French."

"They do? They are?" I eyed the birds, now just dots on a building several blocks away. "There is so much in this world I don't get."

"That is the most intelligent thing any human could ever admit," Dragon said. "Admitting lack of knowledge opens up infinitesimal possibilities."

I scrunched up my face. I really didn't have a long, philosophical lecture in me, as much as I typically enjoyed Dragon's wisdom and perspective.

"Anyhoo, Evechild, we are running out of time," he continued, eyeing my face. "Every day we wait, a new crop of clones grows readier, and Obrenox' health improves."

"How do you know?"

"I – pardon? – why, it is an obvious conclusion, a sound supposition," he stammered. I wasn't used to hearing Dragon flustered.

"What if," I started slowly, "he's just running out of clones *and* getting sicker. Or, like, at least staying sick. What about that? Do we know for sure there are more clones and that he's still sick?"

Dragon was quiet. I paced in front of him, growing more excited in my thought process.

"We know his last few attacks haven't worked – we've bested him every time. And, that's right! Oh my gosh, Uncle Seb even managed to hit him with his car! And if those Amythystics hadn't arrived in time to carry him off, who knows what would have happened. And, I mean, he came *here* in the first place? Isn't that kinda desperate?"

"You raise compelling points," Dragon said quietly as he drummed his talons against the stadium wall. He left a tiny groove in the brick as he did so. I smiled; I didn't point it out.

"Even Gil was able to stave off one of those things," I added. "*Gil*. Who is, like, basically made of silk and hair."

"I am uncertain of her composition, actually," Dragon said with a furrowed brow.

"I gotta ask, how do you even know her? Doesn't really seem like, uh, your type."

"We are fellow collectors. Her accumulation of Beatles recordings as well as Byzantine chants surpasses even my own, if you can believe it. It really is titillating, her collection. Why, I get a thrill just thinking of it!" he said as his wings fluttered. Then his face darkened and his demeanor changed. "On paper, one would think Gil and I would be the most famous of mates. Her storied friendships, her famed tutelage of several of my favorite Johns, including Lennon and Tolkien and, of course, her water polo accolades," he trailed off wistfully.

"You should be besties, but she's a giant weirdo. I get it."

"Not quite. Well, yes, but, I'm afraid our tale takes an untoward turn. You see, I had Dr. Baudelaire built up in my mind as a fellow superfan. But upon finally meeting, I discovered she ... oh my, it's so difficult to say as the pain is still quite fresh," Dragon said, looking down.

"Geez, what is it?" I asked, figuring an errant fortune had been cast or something of that ilk.

"She ... she ... collects as an investment. She's in it for the money!" Dragon wailed.

"Oof. What a let down," I said, trying not to giggle at Dragon's dramatic tail thumping.

"Indeed. One gets one's hopes up, believing one is to meet one whose interests intersect with one's own at an unparalleled level, and then one learns .... Oh, it is so disappointing, Evechild. And, to make matters worse, Yaël took a liking to her," Dragon said with a sigh.

"Yeah, about that," I said, a little nervous. "What do we do now that she's being held in Salem?"

"Why, we get her out, of course."

"Well duh, but how?"

Dragon sighed again and dropped to the ground.

"I honestly do not know."

"What about how to get rid of Obrenox – 'destroy him,' as you say?"

"I honestly do not know."

"Cool, cool, cool … So, um, not to sound rude, but why'd you come here today?"

Dragon was quiet again. For a long time.

"Your uncle," he said at last.

"What about him?"

"He's dying."

65

MALA TEMPORA CURRUNT

I threw a garbage can.

One of the big metal ones outside of the bathrooms.

It made a terrific clamor on the tiled floor. Which felt really nice.

Dragon had offered to take me home, take me anywhere. I didn't want to be home. I didn't want to be anywhere.

So I returned to school. Which was a mistake.

The first person I ran into was Libby. She smiled big, her eyes wide and expectant. But her face fell as I glared and pushed past her.

"I know a lot about you, you know!" she yelled after me. "All your stupid secrets, Dragongirl!"

I charged ahead, then stopped dead in my tracks when I heard another voice join Libby's behind me.

"You know a lot about her? Her, Eve? Allow yourself to be introduced to me. I'm Channing Reagan—"

"I know who you are," Libby said. "And yeah. I think I do."

I ducked into the bathroom, seething, raging, and waited until the bell rang and the voices cleared.

I wanted to scream. I wanted to punch something.

"Ouch!" I snarled at the garbage can as I banged my elbow against it on my way out.

That was all it took. I kicked the metal contraption. It moved easily. So naturally I picked it up and chucked it as hard as I could down the hall.

God, it was satisfying. The lid came off and clattered down the stairwell. Metal on tile echoed down, down, down each step. The drum continued to roll down the hall, spilling its contents as it went.

"What is the meaning of this?! I should hope this was an accident! Oh. It's you," Principal Fernhouser said as he appeared at the top of stairwell, bin lid in tow. "I think I see who is responsible for this boorish, churlish disruption. Clean this up, immediately, Ms. Archer."

"It was an accident," I said evenly as I stared back at him.

"I do not believe it was."

"Prove it," I said and stomped off in the opposite direction.

Such an encounter would have typically set me off in a sweaty, palpitating mess. But I was cool as a cucumber as I stomped out of school that day. I swung open the front doors, unabashedly shameless. I took one step down the grand stone entrance, stepped on my shoelace, and somersaulted down the rest of the steps.

"Owwwww," I groaned as I lay at the bottom. "Is that – am I bleeding? Gah! I hate today!"

"Y'alright, Sheila? Got a bit o'comeuppance, didya?"

"Poppy, not now," I said as I pulled myself upright and examined my bloody elbow. "Wait, don't go. I got some questions for you, man."

"Don't spit the dummy, then. Let's have it," she said as I stood up and dusted off my backside. "You look like a dog's breakfast."

"I don't know what that means, Poppy," I muttered. "C'mon, walk me home. But first," I paused and blushed, "could I ... like, what I mean is, um, you're a dog, and I'm having a really crappy day ... well, day/life ... and could I maybe, you know ...?"

"You wanna have a pet, then?" Poppy said and wagged her tail. "G'on. Git it done, then."

I pet her head. I rubbed her ears. Then I dropped to my knees and hugged the little dog. Oh, she was soft and warm and wagged her tail and licked my cheek and did all the things I needed a dog to do in that moment.

"Crikey, you must really be having a dunny of a day. Usually such a whinge. This is a different side of you, Sheila."

I wiped my eyes as I got up. Had I been crying? Never mind that; I straightened my bag again and started home.

"Can I talk to you about some stuff?"

Poppy nodded.

I took a deep breath. For the next eighteen minutes, I spoke in one long, rapid-fire run-on sentence, listing every woe, foe, and worry in my life. Things I couldn't Malcolm. Things I wouldn't tell Gil.

When we got to my house, Poppy ran into the yard and ate grass. Aggressively. She choked down great big masses of grass, barely taking time to chew it first.

"Oh, I'm so sorry; I – I didn't realize you were hungry," I said. "I'll run inside and grab you something."

"It's not hunger, mate," she said between desperate chomps, "your problems, they're too much! I gotta bit o' dunny distress, if you catch my drift. Your life ... crikey, I wasn't ready for all that. Gonna yak all over!"

My mom opened the door and started to say something, then stopped and stared at the Australian Shepherd in her yard ripping up chunks of grass. Poppy chewed hastily, swallowed, burped, spit some out. She muzzled a different spot in the yard and repeated the same actions.

"Did a dog follow you home? Geez, it must be sick. Poor thing. Did you feed it something to make it that sick? But never mind that," she said. "Here, I'll take your bag. Philippa's been waiting for you. Her PT session wasn't super great today."

"Does everyone know dogs eat grass when their stomachs are upset? My problems are so bad they make a dog vomitous? How's that supposed to make me feel about myself?" I mumbled to myself as I walked past my mom and into the house. "Bye, Poppy. And, uh, thanks."

"The dog is named Poppy?" my mom asked incredulously.

"Just what I decided to call her. Since she followed me home or whatever. Where's Phlee?"

I headed upstairs and found my sister on the floor surrounded by art supplies. A blanket covered her legs. She looked up and smiled.

"Art project for the ages," she said as she presented a long, bejeweled rod.

"Is that ...?"

"My pimpstick? Why yes, it is!" she said proudly.

"Don't call it that!" my mom yelled from down the hall.

"You, uh, you have a cane?"

"Hell yes, I do. The doctor said I needed a visual goal, something attainable. So, I thought to myself, self, what is attainable and tangible? A CANE."

I hugged my sister and ran out of the room. I called behind me that I really needed a bathroom.

I didn't, exactly. I just needed somewhere to go cry.

Phlee isn't walking for all the spinal damage she endured. And yet she's here, decorating a cane with gaudy gemstones. She aspired to walk, but being realistic, settled for *walking with a cane* as her goal.

What do I even do with that?

My heart hurt as my chest heaved with each sob. Unloading everything to Poppy had breached the seal. Now feelings were just flowing out every which way. I leaned over the sink and splashed cold water on my face.

I rejoined my sister in her room. She had moved aside art supplies to make room for a much more daunting task: college applications. Her determination to keep her life moving forward was admirable.

"Where do you think you'll apply?" Philippa asked as she typed away on her laptop. My head shot up. I had leaned against her bed, a pile of prospective college brochures and catalogues on my lap, and apparently drifted to sleep for a minute.

"Me?" I asked, dazed.

"Yeah, you, silly," she said, still looking down. The sun had started to set; the glow of her screen illuminated her lovely face. The scars along her neck looked darker and more severe in the low light. Same with the spot on her forehead. I shuddered.

"Wherever, I don't know, really. I guess whichever place accepts me," I said. She frowned at this answer. Should I have answered truthfully? Should I have told her why college was the farthest thing from my mind and that there might not even be a world left for me to go to college in?

"High school's gonna fly by. You really should have at least a short list. Something you can, like, adjust and edit, so you're ready by year eleven," she said.

"Year eleven?" I snorted. "Because I'll have transferred to some posh UK school where they call it 'year eleven' instead of 'junior year,' is that it?"

"It just makes more sense to call it that," she sniffed, ever the Anglophile. "And anyway, I have my list. And it is awesome. I may even let you come visit me."

"Oh, is that right? Shall I venture forth in my lorry to visit you hither?" I said in a very bad English accent.

"Offer rescinded! And a lorry is a giant truck. Don't be daft," she shot back. But she giggled.

As long as I could make my sister laugh, the darkness didn't get the best of me. The darkness that was always *right there* – a shapeless fiend of fear, exhaustion, overwhelm, anger, nihilism. I felt it getting closer, heavier, every day.

And I hated it.

66

GRATIA ET SCIENTIA

I took a deep breath as I trudged up the three neatly painted steps to the front porch of the Nguyen home. The smiling Buddha sculpture was no longer next to the welcome mat. As I raised my hand to knock on the door, it flew open.

"I wondered when I would see you again," Ms. Nguyen said. "Come, come. Hurry in. There are always onlookers. I do not like them."

I wiped my feet and entered. A blast of warm air scented with lemon hit me in the face. My stomach growled immediately.

"You are hungry?" she asked and motioned for me to follow her.

"No, no, sorry. It's just, um, my dumb stomach," I stammered as we came into the kitchen. Delicious smells and spirals of steam made more rumblings happen. Louder, more embarrassing ones.

"Here, you eat. I made too many. I do that, you know. Make food enough for … an old habit," she said and looked away.

"I can't imagine," I said softly as I sat at the counter where she laid out a plate and chopsticks for me. "But really, I don't want to, um, impose and, like, eat all of your food."

She didn't respond but instead heaped spoonful after spoonful of delectable pork and vermicelli noodles in front of me. I stared at the food. I looked at her.

I don't know why I needed to come here. Maybe some nourishment would jog my memory?

"So, you are wondering why I let go of charges in the trial," she said, eyeing me as I fumbled with the chopsticks. I clumsily brought a single bean sprout to my mouth.

"I guess so," I said as I chased a piece of pork around my plate with the chopsticks. I gave up trying to hold the slippery morsel and stabbed it with one chopstick instead. I popped it in my mouth and immediately moaned in contentment. "Holy cow, that is one of the most delicious things I've ever eaten."

Ms. Nguyen smiled and scooped another generous helping onto my plate. I didn't even mind the chopsticks – the challenge was worth it. I happily smacked down bite after bite, realizing I couldn't think of the last time I sat down and ate a proper meal. Life lately had been handfuls of crackers gobbled down between harrowing moments, with the occasional hunk of cheese thrown in.

"This was Jonah's favorite," she said quietly. "I'm so glad you remembered his birthday. I knew you two were real friends."

I looked up mid-bite. It was his birthday? I felt my cheeks redden. I swallowed hard; a wad of semi-masticated pork lodged itself in the back of my throat. I tried swallowing it down; no luck. I reached for the glass of water she had poured me. Water dribbled down the sides of my mouth, unable to breach the pork dam in my gullet.

I couldn't breathe. I felt tingly. My vision turned a greyish-white as I felt arms tighten around my torso and a fist push into my belly.

"Thwuuumph! Guh!"

A hunk of pork sailed through the air in a trail of spittle and landed atop something on the opposite counter. I staggered back; Ms. Nguyen braced herself behind me and guided me to a chair.

"Here, drink some water."

My hand shook as I brought the glass to my mouth. The small woman, unphased, grabbed a paper towel and swiped the regurgitated pork. With no reaction. Like she was picking up a bottle cap, not a semi-masticated hunk of pork covered in throat juice. She tossed it in a compost bin under the sink with one hand while the other grabbed a small spatula.

I marveled at her.

After a few minutes, she turned around, holding a cake.

"See? No problem. You can hardly tell you vomited on this. Not like the laundry. You could definitely tell then. But this cake, I think he would like it."

I wanted to die.

My face burned, my hands still shook. I stared at the floor and wished as hard I have ever wished that I could teleport straight out of there and never relive this moment ever again.

"I didn't vomit. I was choking," I muttered.

"And I saved you," she said matter-of-factly. She set the cake down in front of me. A freshly smeared dollop sat beside the carefully piped words atop the white confection. "I'd offer you some, but who knows what you'd do with it."

When I finally looked up, I saw that she was smiling. I relaxed a bit and forced a smile.

"I will show you something," she said as she got up. "It's why I know you didn't do it."

She disappeared down the hall. I looked at the cake. *#1 Son,* it said in blue frosting. My stomach gurgled, churning with upset.

"Geez, can I make it here one time without destroying this poor woman's house with my stupid stomach?" I groaned to myself.

"I held on to these," Ms. Nguyen said, reappearing a moment later with a small stack of notebooks. "I never let the police see them. Maybe I should have, I do not know. His other things, I haven't gotten them back yet. So I'm glad I kept these. I don't have to worry if I will see them again or not."

I flipped through the notebooks, most filled with anime sketches and graphic novel outlines. A page here and there had school notes scribbled on them, but generally, they were sketch books, collections of Jonah's drawings.

"I knew he liked to draw, but I don't think I realized how talented he was," I said quietly. I turned a page and my heart stopped. "Is that – did he draw--??"

"You. And him. Yes," Ms. Nguyen said warmly. "See? You were friends. He drew you into his stories, look. In this one, you are superheroes together. And if you go forward a few pages, yes, see this one? This is my favorite. You and he have a pet dragon."

Indeed we did. Page after page showed sketches, cartoons, plot summaries of two friends off on wild adventures, saving the world from bad guys. My heart pounded. I didn't know what this meant. But his mom did.

"You never truly know the impact you have on people. You never truly know how someone views you," she murmured quietly, smiling fondly at the drawings.

I said nothing. I just turned the page. My warm heart, though, froze when I opened another notebook.

"You, uh, think I could get some more water?"

Ms. Nguyen nodded. While she was at the sink, I slid the notebook quickly inside my hoodie, tucking it partway into my waistband to secure it. I zipped up my sweatshirt all the way and grabbed the glass of water. I drank it greedily, my hands shaking again.

"You see your hands? You do not have the makeup of someone who could do something so terrible. You cry and you throw up and you shake," she said. Her voice was gentle, but her words confused me. Where was she going with this? She opened another notebook, full of more art. "This is not a drawing of an enemy. He knew you were a friend."

I got up abruptly. My chair hit against the table and rocked it slightly. The cake, already besmirched by me, wiggled faintly.

"Thank you for showing me this," I said as I started toward the door. I paused, realizing suddenly how much of my fate sat in this grieving woman's hands. "And, um, thank you for ... for ... seeing that I couldn't ...," my voice trailed off.

Her eyes swelled with tears. Silent, she opened the door for me. I headed outside, then hesitated on the steps.

"Ms. Nguyen?" I called to her. She stood inside the doorway. "Tell Jonah happy birthday for me."

I raced home, screaming to Dragon inside my mind. He heard me somewhere along the way, for I saw his mighty silhouette descending to my backyard just as I arrived.

"Dragon," I said, panting as I pulled the notebook out. "Look!"

67

ARTE ET LABORE

"Very interesting, indeed," Dragon murmured as he scanned the pages. "It is fascinating ... the level of detail. Yes, very interesting."

We held the notebook between us, Dragon and I, scrutinizing Jonah's drawings. This particular set of pages held a series of images, comic book-style, each featuring a character that was unmistakably Jonah.

"What do you think is going on in this one?" I asked as I pointed to a square showing a bunch of tiny elf-looking things gathered around a sort of bed.

"Excellent use of chiaroscuro," Dragon murmured approvingly.

"Of what? No, like, what do you think it's portraying?"

"Amythystics performing a cloning experiment. And how do you not know the term for artistic use of shadow? But yes, a cloning experiment."

"Seriously? You got that from this?"

"Certainly. Something stood out to you that made you bring this book to me, Evechild. If not that, then what?"

"This!" I cried as I pointed to a square in the bottom corner. In it, a boy – presumably Jonah, based on the similarities to other sketches – laid flat on the ground as a giant gemstone hovered above him. The stone had sharp angles and a series of dashed lines emanating from it. It so clearly was a drawing of a Peridiote stone.

Dragon stared at it for a long time. Too long. So long that I studied it even closer, wondering if I missed something.

"We've several clues, here, Evechild," he said at last. "I think we can begin to better surmise how Jonah came to be under Obrenox' influence."

I nodded solemnly. Of course, my heart was heavy for Jonah. But deep inside, a little thought grew. What if I had come across that giant yellow orb on my own, without Dragon? Would I also be at its bidding now? Is that why I ran into Jonah that one day? Was he returning to ... to rendezvous with Peridiote? Gain access to the other dimension somehow?

Dragon frowned.

"Do not put such responsibility upon yourself," he said, gentle but concerned.

"Stop reading my thoughts," I grumbled. "Dragon, I think this tells us about a biggr problem we need to take care of."

"True, we do need to ascertain the science and engineering of their cloning process," he began.

"Nooo!" I cut him off. "The stones! If there's so much power in some of these rocks, why can't we start by destroying them? It's not like they can fight back."

I stopped myself, realizing what I just said and recalling the many times now Peridiote and its nasty geologic relatives had stood in my way.

"You know what I mean," I muttered.

"Alas, humans are the weaker of the foes, and cloned humans are the weakest of all," Dragon said. "Besides, a stone as powerful as Peridiote cannot be fully destroyed. There is no known element that will obliterate it completely."

"Like a diamond," I murmured.

"Similar, I suppose, yes."

"I can't believe he drew this stuff," I said as I flipped through the notebook again. Page after page showed different vignettes of the same three themes: powerful rocks, stretcher in a science lab, tube gardens. I shuddered. "It's spooky, thinking about him doing this."

"Drawing is a sort of therapy, no? It is not so strange that he illustrated these events to make sense of them, or give them a space to live in outside his mind."

I thought about that for a while. I liked it. If talk therapy was a thing, then surely drawing was, too.

"Eve! We're making tacos! Any requests?" my mom called from the kitchen.

"How is she, anyway?" Dragon asked.

"Who?"

"Your mother. She seems ... nonplussed."

"Oh yeah, she has these crazy mood swings before ultimately settling into, like, total denial," I said with a forced laugh.

"Seems an odd thing to be jocular about," Dragon said, studying me.

"Eh, it's just one of those things I gotta laugh about so it doesn't eat me alive," I said, my voice catching. I hadn't ever said that aloud.

"You are stronger than you think."

"I've heard that before," I said dryly.

"Indeed. And how you have proof that it is true."

I smiled, but turned so Dragon couldn't see.

"I don't really know what to do with this stuff about Jonah," I said as I got up and stretched.

"Nor do I. Yaël would undoubtedly have keen insight," he responded quietly.

"Dragon, snap out of it. She's not gone, she's just south a bit. Go see her."

Dragon looked up and smiled.

"See? There you are again. Wisdom and strength beyond your own realization."

I waved as Dragon lifted off. I turned inside and followed the smell of carne asada to my mom and sister.

I awoke later that night to my phone buzzing. I hated that I had it on all the time now. I hated that I even knew where it was. I floundered around under my many blankets until I found it.

"Uuuuggghhh, what," I snarled at the little device. I blinked and blinked, trying to adjust my tired eyes to the bright screen.

Uncle Seb's name came into focus. I immediately sat up.

Busting her out. More l8r

I didn't know what irritated me more: the fact that they were breaking Ms. Neally out of jail without me, or the fact that my uncle used horrible text jargon.

"Just type 'later,' it's so simple!" I hissed. I slid out of bed and began getting dressed, then stopped. I grabbed my phone and typed a response.

What should I be doing?

I frowned, not wanting to sound too abrupt or upset.

Also, yay! Rescue!

I added in an emoji of a rainbow and a flexing bicep and hit send. I smiled, satisfied, and climbed back in bed, determined to wait for a response. That didn't take long. Another buzz.

Stay put. All door.

**Good not door*

I pulled my blankets back up around my neck.

I must have fallen asleep, for I dreamt that night. But they weren't pleasant dreams. I can't remember all the details, but Ms. Neally wasn't safe and Dragon couldn't get to her. I awoke very unsettled, very unrested, and very anxious.

I yawned and looked out my window that morning. Mine was the only window that faced East, which I used to love. A young me relished in the sunrise being all my own in that house. I'd set an alarm to watch it every morning, then fall back asleep feeling like I had a leg-up on the day having seen its birth. Nowadays, I met the sunrise with ambivalence if not irritation; I really couldn't afford to be awake at that time.

But the first strains of light trickling over the Earth were beautiful. I looked down at the yard and gasped. There, in the grass, lay stones, pebbles, carefully arranged in an intentional pattern, a symbol....

I breathed in.

Another thurisaz.

Behind me, my door creaked open. I breathed out. It was just my mom in her robe and sweats.

"Oh, Egg! You're awake? Do you see that? Those rocks? I was just noticing them when I went to pull the recycling bins out to the curb. Was is that?" she said.

"Chaos," I coughed.

"What?"

"That pattern. It means chaos."

68

LUPUS IN FABULA

Our episode today has more twists than a gymnastics meet, not that our lead suspect would ever take part in a sport. From a shocking court-room development to possible global implications, this story just keeps getting better and better.

When we last dazzled you with deadly details on "OreGone," your true crime podcast dedicated exclusively to murders around the beaver state, our suspect Elle was awaiting trial for murder with charges brought against her by both the decedent's family and the state...

"Do you really have to listen to that when you know I'm right here?" I snarled at Libby.

"Actually, yes. I totally do. Because current events are, like, way important," she said and flipped her hair without looking up at me.

I shouldn't have engaged. I shouldn't have said anything in the first place. But when one has a rage diamond forming inside of them, one doesn't always behave rationally.

"Tell me how," I said evenly.

"What?"

"Tell me how current events are, like, way important," I said mockingly. "And tell me why. Please. Edify us," I said as I leaned back in my and folded my arms.

"Oh, yes, actually I am interested in this also," Elke said, pulling her chair up beside mine.

"What is the meaning of this?" Mr. Simmons demanded. "I was left strict instructions to not let this class, and I quote, 'drift off,' and I vowed to Mr. Poon that, as his chosen substitute, I would not let that happen."

"We're discussing current events," I said. "Totally appropriate for the, um, curriculum Mr. Poon's been following. Yeah, that's it. Libby was just about to educate us."

"Oh, okay then. Wonderful. Shall we hear your thoughts?" Mr. Simmons said as he turned to Libby.

Libby's face reddened. She opened her mouth, closed it, balled up her fists, and finally stomped off in a huff. Amongst giggles and jeers, Mr. Simmons cleared his throat and tapped his foot.

"Back to work, if you please, then," he said. As he turned, I noticed a trail of tissue stuck to his shoe.

"Way to be prepared," I scoffed and pointed at his foot. A few other students noticed and snickered; one snapped a picture on their phone.

Mr. Simmons twirled around and stared. More giggles. I started to wind up with another zinger when Elke's hand landed on my arm. She hushed the students and cleared her throat.

"He does not know it is there, why are you laughing? Excuse me, Mr. Simmons, there is something attached to your shoe," she said nonchalantly.

We all quieted. Elke's reasonable approach made me cranky. She leaned in to say something and I brushed her off. One by one, students turned back to their work. I had made it through most of the school day, but internal pressure was mounting. The rage diamond grew ever potent, and I needed to get outta there.

Alright, "rage diamond" might be a bit dramatic. But I felt the distinct urge to punch something, to run fast, to scream. I didn't know what, just something physical. What does that even entail? How does one go about being physical? *Dear god*, I thought, *the podcast is right – I am no athlete.*

I exited the school, aware that neither Principal Fernhouser nor his obedient office staff would attempt to stop me anymore. It took a bit of thrill out of skipping class, but I suppose I shouldn't have found that thrilling in the first place.

I spit on the sidewalk and adjusted my bag. I looked around, taking out my phone as I fixed my coat. It was cold. Sunny, clear, and cold. Winters in the Pacific Northwest went from nonstop rain to these types of days, where the inside of your noses freezes and burns every time you take a chilled breath in.

I loved it.

The frost on the ground and the quiet streets – not many cyclists and walkers out in these frigid temps – made things feel frozen in time. Like the world turned a bit more slowly and judgment was slow to open its eyes.

I attempted to whistle (still couldn't), and spit again. Red splattered on the ground. I licked my lip. I quickly wiped my nose and mouth with my sleeve and then examined it. I had a bloody nose.

"Oy, Sheila! Crikey, this isn't the first time I've see your face bloodier than an arm fulla mozzie bites," Poppy cried, suddenly in front of me.

"Ugh, so glad I have an audience for this," I groaned. "Got any tissue?"

Poppy turned in a little circle, showing me how dumb a question that was. Where would she keep it?

"Gotta a sec for a quick convo 'fore arvo's out? I hate being out at night, y'know," Poppy said and wagged her tail.

"Sorry, Poppy, I really don't," I said in a nasally voice as I pinched my nose shut. "I gotta get home to get this cleaned up before Malcolm time."

"Before what time?" she said, trotting next to me.

"Malcolm. He's my therapist."

"Good on ya, Sheila."

I knew the comment was innocent if not genuine, but I chose to take it as sarcastic and demeaning. That's just how I was carrying the day.

When I was finally seated in my favorite leather chair across Malcolm, my rage diamond had morphed into a murderous headache. I folded and unfolded my arms. I rubbed my temples and sighed loudly.

"Not feeling so hot? What's on your mind," Malcolm said as he wrote something in his notebook.

"What's in that thing, anyway? What are you writing about me?"

Malcolm closed his notebook, folded his hands atop it, and smiled at me.

"You know what's in it. Bullet points of our conversations, my own impressions in the moment, and so on. So I may keep our time efficient and on topic."

"And so on?" I repeated and winced. "Gah, my head hurts so bad."

"Would you like some water?"

I shook my head. I sniffed. Something warm dripped on my lip. Ugh, gross!

"Is your nose bleeding?" Malcolm said, standing suddenly.

"Is it? Oh, look at that. Something else to add to my list of gifts the universe has doled out lately," I said dryly. I grabbed a tissue from the desk and held it against my pinched nose.

"You believe the universe has treated you unfairly," he said, then leaned forward with another tissue. "You wouldn't feel more comfortable cleaning up in the restroom down the hall?"

I shook my head and wadded up my bloodied tissues as I applied a fresh one. In hindsight, I ought to have cleaned up in the restroom down the hall ... Sorry, Malcolm.

"You were saying? Dig into that, if you'd like, that feeling of unfairness," Malcolm said, eyeing my ball of soiled tissues. "The, uh, trash bin is by the door."

"I was? I think what I was saying is that these nosebleeds don't even cause a blip on the radar. Sure, if things were, like, quiet and normal, would I be alarmed? I mean, probably. But now?" I said, feeling heavy words tumbling out like blocks. I couldn't control it. "When my sister's trying to learn how to walk again, and some evil chick is parading me around on her podcast, and Ms. Neally's in jail for no reason whatsoever, and my mom's lost all touch with reality," I paused to take a breath, "Nothing's fair. What of it? What're you gonna do? Cry over spilled blood?" I said as I spit into a tissue.

"I'd like to take a minute to process what you've just shared while you clean up on the restroom. This has become a safety issue now. For my sake at least, if you would," Malcolm said evenly, gently, and held his hand toward the door.

"Down the hall?" I said as I stood. I was shaky and my face was red. My mouth tasted metallic.

"Down the hall," he repeated with a nod.

I spit into the sink in the restroom and looked up. Oof. I was a sight. I attempted to run my fingers through my hair to smooth it a bit; they got stuck. I splashed cold water on my face and rinsed out my mouth one more time. As I swished blood-tinged water inside my cheeks, my eyes rested on a colorful poster to the side of the mirror. KNOW THE SIGNS! a large mouth shouted. Below, lesser-known warning signs of anorexia were listed.

"Hmm," I hummed as I scanned the list. I gargled and spit. "Shakiness, dizziness, moodiness, metallic taste in mouth, bloody noses … hmm."

I frowned and looked my reflection up and down. Man, had I gotten scrawny. My body, my brain, they never told me to eat. I shrugged. I had *just* eaten at Ms. Nguyen's house … a day ago? Three days ago?

"Hmm," I said again and gave my nose another wipe.

I opened the door to Malcolm's office to find him standing, waiting for me, holding open a book I hadn't seen before.

"Eve, when is the last time you ate a meal?"

"Funny you should ask, I was just thinking about this amazing vermicelli with lemongrass chicken I just ate the other day," I started.

"Eve, I'm serious. Stress and anxiety can manifest in many ways – make us behave in ways we wouldn't typically. Does not eating give you sense of control?"

I faltered at the door. Should I stay standing? Sit down? The dizziness was returning, so I had better sit down … I grabbed ahold of the corner of the desk to steady myself. I made my way to the chair and sunk down.

"What were you saying? This chair is so, so soft. Nice job with the pillow action. And your restrooms are nice. Hadn't been in there before," I said as I yawned and folded my arms. I leaned my head back. "She came in through the bathroom window," I sang, a Beatles song always on the ready on my head.

"Eve, you're not making sense. I am concerned. Let's focus on one thing. Let's focus energy and thought on the chair. Tell me about the chair," Malcolm said as she shuffled about his desk.

As I rambled on about the chair, occasionally sniffing just to check for blood, I was aware of Malcolm covertly picking up his phone and texting. I rambled and rambled, dozed off for a moment, jerked awake and resumed rambling. Just as I was getting to the injustice of Ms. Neally's imprisonment, a knock sounded at the office door.

My mom poked her head in.

"What? No. No, you said this is *our* time, you and me," I said.

"I felt, given the circumstances, that your mother ought to be present for a quick word of counsel at the end of our session today."

"Given what circumstances? So I had a bloody nose, big freaking deal," I said and turned away from them both.

"You did? Oh, Eve, I'm so sorry. Those are miserable," my mom said.

"I'd like to leave you with some recommended reading on disordered eating," Malcolm said as he coolly offered a handwritten list to my mom. "Be advised, no official diagnoses have been given. Based on what I've observed, however, I advise you to call one of those clinics there for a check-up to that end immediately."

I said nothing. I hated that feeling: that ego-crushing realization that the grownups are talking about you right in front of you as though you can't hear them. I grabbed my backpack and stormed out. My mom was still standing in the doorway, so I didn't have to worry about remembering if the door was a push or a pull.

I stomped down the hall and into the building lobby. Its high ceiling and tile floor gave my stomping an especially impactful echo.

It was a very satisfying storm off.

As my mom and I pulled up to our driveway later that evening, she groaned and flashed her lights. A tiny car was parked, but running, in our driveway.

Uncle Seb got out and waved.

69

VERITAS ODIT MORAS

The living room was colder than usual. I watched my mom clench her jaw, purse her lips. Her fingers tightened around her mug. She wanted to say a lot. Likely not all of it good. But she surprised us, and herself, I think.

"I'm sure that was difficult to say," she said slowly. "But I'm proud of you. And I'm here for you."

Uncle Seb smiled and nodded, but never looked up. I shifted uncomfortably on the sofa across from him and beside my mom.

"What kind of cancer did you say? I'm sorry, you just said it all so quickly," she said.

"Colon," Uncle Seb said.

We three were silent. The ceiling creaked overhead. Philippa was moving about in her wheelchair.

"I'm gonna check on Phlee," I said, grateful for the excuse to leave.

I headed toward the stairs, then paused. This all sucked. Every single day presented a new, sucky thing. What it felt like, anyway. I spun around, walked to my uncle, and gave him an awkward hug. He grabbed my hand in his and squeezed.

"Yep. It's fine," he said gruffly and sniffed hard.

I raced upstairs as if I were trying to outrun emotions. I barely made it before they caught me. Tucked inside the bathroom, I cried. And cried. All different types of tears that had lined up, awaiting release.

"Eve? That you? Are you ok?" Philippa said quietly over a gentle knock.

I swung the door open. Philippa instinctively grimaced and looked away, her hands over her face.

"What is that reaction?"

"You're in the bathroom!" she cried.

"And you thought I'd just, like, parade around in here in the nude?" I said, some giggling replacing my glower.

"I don't know! But really," Philippa said, her voice softening. "You good?"

"Allergies," I said and brushed past her.

"What's going on down there? They never hang out that long, or that quietly."

"Uncle Seb," I started, then faltered. It wasn't really my information to share. I frowned. But, he and I were way closer than he and Philippa. I shrugged and motioned for her to follow me into my room. Once inside with the door shut, I leaned down next to her, "he's sick. Really sick. Mom's upset, and I'm sure is finding some weird way to be sanctimonious about it or whatever."

"Solid vocab word," Philippa said. "You seem awfully cool with all of this. I mean, despite your allergies acting up."

I threw a pillow at her but didn't respond. I felt if I moved my face, my stoicism would crumble. So, I stayed quiet.

"Did you like this?" Philippa changed the subject, picking up my dogeared copy of the Kafka compendium I'd been using in lit arts. "I dig the dystopian, existential stuff. But I didn't know you liked it."

I shrugged. In another life, I would have been busting with pride if my brainy, sophisticated older sister engaged in academic conversation with me.

Now? I don't think I had a single cell firing with enough gusto to respond.

"I don't, really. I'm going to bed."

Philippa frowned. I hated disappointing her. Any minute that I felt I squandered with her now was wrapped in leaden guilt. Like, having been without her for so long, how dare I take time with her now for granted?

But God, how I was tired!

"Any music requests to fall asleep to?" Philippa said, ever gracious, ever accommodating of my bouncing temperament.

"Surprise me," I said as I drew the curtains closed. "But just not –"

"The Everly Brothers," we both said at the same time.

I chuckled and buried my head under my pillow. Philippa was already singing down the hallway. Downstairs, the serious tones of my mom and Uncle Seb kept floating up. I didn't have the energy to wonder what they were talking about, let alone care.

It didn't matter, anyway.

Everything was terrible.

With this amount of terrible, there's really nothing to dilute it.

My eyes shot open. My phone buzzed loudly next to me. I swatted around for it, my limbs lame in the sleepy night. I found it and quickly swiped to stop the buzzing.

"Eve? Egg? Can you hear me?"

"What? I answered a call?" I groaned and pulled the phone closer to my face.

"Egg, you were with me tonight. I was at your house," Uncle Seb said into the phone frantically. "Remember that."

"What? Yeah, no duh," I said, wondering why that last phrase from him was more commandment than question."

"All night. My car's still there, in face."

"It is? Where are you? Why are you calling?"

"I had one too many, passed out on your sofa, and accidentally hit your number when I woke up because your contact info was up," he said rapidly, now in a whisper.

"Hold on, you're downstairs?" I said as I slid out of bed, my confusion and curiosity rousing me. I peered down the stairway at an empty living room. "No you're not," I hissed into the phone. "What's going on with you?"

"Just say I was there. I was *there*!"

The phone clicked.

"Uncle Seb? Hello?" I frowned and looked at my phone. The screen only showed the time, 3:18 a.m., against a backdrop of a Beatles collage I'd made years earlier.

I trudged back to bed, my adrenaline letting up and making way for sleepiness. Before I climbed back into bed, I checked out my window. Uncle Seb's little black MG shimmered under the streetlamps on either side of the driveway. Remnants of the thurisaz outline laid still in the grass.

I fell immediately and deeply asleep. I dreamt of buildings crashing as I drove a tiny car through rainbow-painted streets.

That one was new.

So was Philippa sitting in her wheelchair across from my bed, patiently waiting for me to awaken.

"Gah! How long have you been there?" I said as I yawned and stretched.

She said nothing. She just held her phone out and hit play. A news reel started.

A female's voice in stereotypical reporter cadence was mid-story:

...the same woman who read her way into students' hearts through her years as a librarian at Happy Valley's Harriet Beecher-Stowe Junior High. That very library, though, met an unexpected ending when it was engulfed in flames not long ago. Now Neally is officially declared 'on the lam,' as a 'person of interest' in what police are calling a 'an unprecedented and shocking' turn of events.

I looked up, still groggy, at my sister. She sighed.

"What's going on?" I said. "Why are they talking about Ms. Neally? What is that?"

"It's from this morning," Philippa said with another sigh. "It's all over. Ms. Neally is gone – like, escaped – but there is apparently zero trace of any breakout."

I smiled. I ignored the pit in my stomach that told me there was trouble shrouding this good news.

"That's what Uncle Seb meant," I murmured. I looked up at my sister, still smiling. "He got her out."

70

DULCE EST DESIPERE IN LOCO

I resisted the urge to ditch everything and go to my uncle's hangar. First, because I couldn't. Not using *Fortis Librae*, anyway. Uncle Seb must have swiped it when he was over. And second, because I didn't know if my uncle would even be there.

As I helped my mom with laundry and Philippa with her stretches, I caught myself trying to signal Dragon through my thoughts. The morning came and went. Things stayed quiet.

Not that a quiet day wasn't welcomed – I had been longing for one such day, after all. And today, a Saturday, with mundanity all around me at home, had a cozy familiarity.

Except for Philippa's physical therapy. I was conscious of not letting her current condition become too commonplace, too status quo. It needed to stay novel, fleeting.

"You seem especially thoughtful today," my mom said, watching me do algebra homework from the other side of the kitchen.

"Just pensive," I said. She smiled.

"Your uncle?" she asked.

"Algebra," I responded.

"Good answer," she said as she got up to fill the tea kettle.

It was nice, this little morsel of normal. I had almost forgotten about my mom's many near-mental breakdowns and her heart "episode." She sat down next to me and pulled a little orange bottle from her pocket. She popped two little white tablets in her mouth and chased them with hot tea.

"To the old ticker," she said as she clinked her teacup lightly against mine.

"Too soon," I said with half a smile, which was all I could force out on the topic. I poured some hot water into my cup and watched the jasmine tea satchel float to the top.

"The doctor said everything's better and better every day," she said, ignoring me.

"That's so great. Really. But please can we, just today, not talk about all that stuff?"

"Like our lives?" she snorted.

"Exactly. Um, maybe something just slightly more uplifting? Anything. Dictators. A conversation about dictators would be more uplifting," I said as I got up, annoyed.

"Oooh, we talking favorite dictators? Which era? Anyone said Tojo?" Philippa said eagerly as she rolled into the kitchen. A length of toilet paper was wrapped around one of her wheelchair spokes. I giggled. She frowned and continued, "Don't laugh. Hitler, Mussolini, and Stalin get all the top billing for starting World War II, but my boy Hideki Tojo was quite the instrumental mastermind."

My mom noticed the toilet paper; she clapped her hand against her mouth. Her shoulders shook as she held in laughter. A giggle escaped me. Then another. And another. Philipppa looked from me to my mom and back, befuddled. Finally, my mom and I lost it.

"I'm sorry, Phlee!" I gasped and gulped through laughing. "You have ... you have ...!" I pointed and fell back, trying to compose myself. "And maybe don't refer to a dictator as 'your boy.'"

I walked past my sister and have her shoulders a squeeze.

"Ew. What is that touch," she demanded. "And why were you – oh my gosh. Is that what you infants were laughing at?" she said, her voice squealing in disgust as she looked down and saw the white toilet paper on her wheel.

"Yes! But it's all wrapped around, and you came in so hot," my mom started to explain before erupting in laughter again.

I left the two of them in the kitchen and headed upstairs. Something was gnawing at me.

I jumped on my bed and took out my phone. "Neally escapes prison," I typed into the search bar. Myriad results populated the screen; from local news to gossip-mongering social media accounts, her name was everywhere. Photos of Detectives Jasper and Serrano popped up, as did pictures of Beecher, Principal Fernhouser, even Uncle Seb.

"Ah," I murmured. "They've already connected him with her. He needed an alibi."

I continued to scroll, frowning, then stopped. A headline, slightly different from the others, caught my eye: *Ancient chest found in school's charred remains.*

My heart raced as I read. Which, if you can believe it, was the exact moment Dragon's voice arrived in my head, clear and strong: *I will take you to see them tonight at 2200.*

I lunged to the window and looked up. A shadow whooshed overhead and was gone. Downstairs, my mom and sister were cackling about something. I liked their happy voices.

I hoped they would stay happy.

Things were getting weird. Weirder by the day. So weird, in fact, that I had trouble keeping up.

The publicity didn't help.

But their healing – my mom's and my sister's – was a fixed point from which I could navigate. So long as I didn't stray too far from them, I was tethered to some truth. Regardless of what news and dumb podcasts said.

More laughter wafted up the stairs. I shuddered as a flashback to their bodies hanging limp in those tubes shot through my mind. I shook my head, hard.

"Focus. They're ok. They're ok. You're ok. It's under control," I murmured to myself. My phone buzzed. I looked down to see a message from Libby.

Yay! She's out! That's a good thing, right? Hope you're ok. Sorry things went sideways.

There was more, but I wasn't interested in reading it.

I returned to staring out at the window. I looked down and jumped back. A wild-haired Gil, in purple and black gauzy layers floating about her, waved as she stood above an outline of rocks on the grass.

When I looked again, she was gone. But the rocks remained. Always in the same outline, the same sign.

Thurisaz.

Chaos.

I couldn't get away from it.

71

VOLO NON FUGIA

All night I waited. Nervous, anxious, pacing if not physically then mentally. Nothing I did could consume time fast enough.

In a stroke of genius, I gathered all the little gemstones I had – fiducia stones and heliotropes and other little guys whose weird names I forgot. Everything I had gathered from Gil, Ms. Neally, from the Seventh I carried to the bathroom. With the faucet running for ultimate privacy, I felt like a real warlock as I dropped them into a cloth satchel I found under the sink. It smelled of perfume. No matter. I pulled the silky bag shut and regarded it with pride.

Bad idea.

Within seconds, the bag was drenched and warm on the bottom, as if it peed itself. Then it caught fire. I screamed and dropped it in the sink. I turned off the water and watched it smolder, then retrieved the collection of stones from the simmering, steaming clutch.

"Guess they don't like to be all mixed together like that," I said to myself, frowning. "What do I do with them? Hmmm. You know what? Don't over-think it."

I placed each stone in a different pocket of my clothing, recalling I had transported them that way before.

"Eve? You good? I thought I heard a scream," my mom said from the other side of the door with a light knock.

"Oh, uh, thought I saw a spider," I said quickly. "Yep, all good. Just, uh, pooping!"

I heard my mom swear under her breath and walk down the hall. I listened for the familiar click of her bedroom door, which came just seconds later. She had turned in for the night. Any minute I'd hear either the record player or the television ... And there it was. The laugh track to whatever old sitcom was muffled but signaled that the coast was clear.

I patted my jeans pockets. I didn't have a plan for the stones. But, at the very least, maybe Dragon could give me some insight to their origins, powers, anything.

She came in through the bathroom window... a familiar voice sang into my mind.

Dragon!

I peered out the little window over the toilet and saw the mighty wave of a black wing. It gleamed opalescent in the moonlight.

I hummed along as I quietly put on my hoodie and checked that the stones were secure. I crept downstairs, knowing the exact creak of every step. The landing was trickier; its tired wooden planks were unpredictable. At the bottom, I expertly reached a foot out as far as I could, balancing against the banister, until I stepped down, carefully, judiciously.

No creak! Home free.

"What're you doing?"

"Gah!"

I spun around, slipped, and fell against Philippa's knees. Her wheelchair went rolling backward, knocked into the lamp, which crashed into a glass vase on the console table beside it.

"Oooh, I don't know if Secretariat can handle wheeling over glass. Don't wanna pop a tire," Philippa said as she braked her chair and folded her arms. "I'll wait while you clean that up."

"Ugh. Hold on, I've got it," I said. "Wait, are you referring to your wheelchair as Secretariat now?"

She nodded and stretched her arms. "Greatest, most winning racehorse of all time. Seemed fitting."

"Who was shot when he couldn't run anymore. You sure that's the best name?"

She started to laugh. I shot her a look and gestured upstairs, as I brought my index finger to my lips.

Philippa just shrugged. She waited quietly as I cleaned up the glass shards around her and set the lamp upright.

"Where are you going, anyway?" she whispered loudly.

"Just, out. On a walk. Clears my head," I said lamely. I knew she didn't buy it.

"Give that dragon of yours my regards," she said. She paused and looked up, feebly, meekly. "I, um, was going upstairs ... Mom usually helps, but ..."

"Oh, oh my gosh, of course," I said quickly as I turned and leaned down close to her. "Like this?"

"Yeah. Cool, thanks. Oh, sorry; I didn't brake. Ran over your foot a little, sorry. There, yeah," she said as she wrapped her arms around my neck and leaned against me. I pulled her upright and kind of swung her toward the stairs. "If you could let me lean, yeah. Okay, that works, too."

Philippa giggled good-naturedly as I labored to heave our two bodies up one step at a time.

"You and mom do this every night? How strong is she?"

"Shockingly strong," Philippa said, panting a little. "And she helps me up, like, eight times as fast as this. Like, this is the pace of a baby. It's as though as a baby is helping me upstairs."

"Dude, I will drop you," I laughed.

"Probably. Because of your tiny baby muscles."

"Ssshhhh!" I hissed between giggles.

We lumbered all the way to her room, to her bed, somehow without waking our mom.

"Please do not tuck me in. As the baby, that's just not right," Philippa said as she yawned as stretched out atop her perfectly made bed. "But could you hand me that blanket?"

I tossed a giant, striped blanket at her. It landed on her head.

"Your chance to smother me in bed came and went. You missed it," she said.

"That's messed up!" I chuckled. "Goodnight, or whatever."

"Thanks for the lift," she called as I left her room. "Really."

I gave her a thumbs up in response. The feelings around Philippa's who situation were too raw for me to trust my voice.

As I pulled her bedroom door shut, whatever lightness I had been feeling was snuffed out.

I jogged back downstairs, letting the stairs creak and moan, and slipped outside. I was meeting a dragon to talk about a jail-breaking librarian and a clone lord in another dimension. A couple of creaky boards alerting my mom that I was out of bed really wasn't all that worrisome after all.

Dragon's warm smile poked at my frostiness. He cocked his head, then opened his wing and gestured for me to sit.

I stayed standing.

Best to keep my guard up.

Best to keep feelings locked in.

Best to assume the worst will happen.

"Evechild, there is no shame in navigating difficult things with vulnerability," Dragon said softly.

I looked down. My fists clenched tighter and tighter, as if squeezing my fingers like that would somehow prevent tears from forming.

It didn't.

"So, I grabbed all those little stones, the ones left by the amythystics and the ones from Gil and Ms. Neally," I started, pausing to sniff loudly and wipe my face.

"You humans believe that withdrawing emotion is a form of protection, that emotions skew your operability and logic," Dragon continued gently.

"...I mixed the stones together, and, man, they did not like that," I rambled on, ignoring Dragon entirely. "Which got me thinking, they must not be pieces of spheresaii orbs, which is what I was wondering about. But in the bag, the spheresaii, they seem to *like* being together. These tiny guys though," I stopped and patted my pockets, "definitely need to stay separate."

"Nothing is accomplished unless someone cares about it first. Regardless of motivation, care is a provision steeped in emotion that gets things done. Let yourself care about this. Be feeling, be vulnerable. Intentional ambivalence is not strength; it is cowardice, stopping yourself short of feeling something fully. Without feeling—"

"Geez, I *do* care!" I barked suddenly. "I care so much it crushes me! Don't you get that? I'm not cowardly, I'm exhausted. Feeling all this, this crap, it's exhausting. And soon as I start to feel like I'm a little bit on top, like I have a teensy bit of hope or whatever, *boom*, something reminds me how freaking awful things are. I care, Dragon. I care that every time I try to reason that things can't get worse, they somehow get even worse!"

"There is a balance to all of this," Dragon started again. But I kept going, kept raging.

"I'm feeling ok, but then I've gotta carry my paralyzed sister up the stairs. Still feeling ok after that? Hell no. So, what, do I just stare at the reminder of my failures every day in the form of my busted sister? Do I *feel* my way through this incredibly messed up situation? Hell no."

"Evechild, your candor is heard and supported. But I do think—"

"I can't *feel*. I can only *do*. If I *feel*, I can't get out of bed. So, I've gotta task, right? I've gotta get back and take out Obrenox, right? Well, after that's done, then I'll make myself a cute little cup of tea and curl up in a cute little blanket and take out a cute little journal and write about all my cute little feelings."

I was out of breath. And sweating. Dragon was quiet. Wintry wind rustled the rhododendrons, their bushes dry and bony. My body shook in little waves; I was uncertain if it was anger, hunger, or cold that kept me shivering. Probably all three. Up above, a voice startled me.

"I'm not busted," Philippa called from inside her bedroom upstairs. Her window must have been open.

My heart dropped. Tears welled.

I wanted to scream.

"Hop on. Let us go for a walk in the stars," he said tenderly.

My vision blurry, I nodded and stumbled forward. He scooped me up onto his back and silently sprang into the air, higher and higher.

The wind was chilly against my tear-stained cheeks, but the jolt of fresh air gave me new life. I breathed in deeply and exhaled as slowly as I could. Every breath cycle mended a frayed nerve. I could feel it.

"It is nice to talk things through aloud. I've always found it helpful," Dragon said, breaking the silence. "I value being your confidant."

I winced a little. His words were kind, but they had a shrinking effect on my ego.

"I kinda just unloaded a lot of garbage on you. I, uh, talked *at* you more than with you," I said sheepishly. He shouldn't applaud my bad behavior.

"Unloading what burdens you to a trusted source is not bad behavior," he said quickly. "You feel better, a bit, do you not?"

I smiled and nodded.

"Why does talking help? Seems dumb, or selfish. Like I'm just throwing my problems at someone else, so now I've brought someone else down with my crap."

Dragon's wings whooshed slowly, majestically, and reminded me of the long paddles of rowing teams cutting rhythmically through the water. My mom had paddled on a dragon boat team a few summers ago. Smooth and powerful, the long, ornate boats soared down the Willamette River, sometimes with a drummer. It was a soothing memory. Dragon boat to actual dragon. I smiled.

"That is a lovely memory," Dragon said. "Perhaps you'll join your mother in this endeavor in the summer."

"Perhaps," I said.

"Think about the items in your mind, the heavy ones and the lighter ones, all crammed in the space of your brain. Imagine, for a moment, that your mind's capacity is limited. And you have suddenly the equivalent of a closet so jam-packed it cannot properly shut let alone store things properly. Oh, the disarray! The stress of mess!"

I giggled despite being a tad annoyed that he wouldn't drop it already.

"When you talk with someone – without fear of judgement or punishment – you are removing those items from the precious closet of the mind and piling them in the middle of a vast expanse of sand. There, they may simply *be*, or they may get swept away by the sands of time, or the sands of growth, or the sands of change."

"The sands of castles," I added, still giggling.

"Indeed. But whatever the case, in that expanse, those items, those problems and troubles, they lessen. So, talk. Take things from the precious, cramped space of the brain and cast them into the infinite sands of conversation. Close your eyes, can you picture it? A large wooden crate, labeled with a particular stress. As soon as you talk about it, you've wedged it out of your mind. You've just dumped it there, on that sandy expanse. You'll still know where to find it. But it is no longer overcrowding your mind's closet."

I thought about this for a while. The explanation was perhaps a bit grandiose. But I *could* see it: a dozen or so crates, all labeled with different crappy things, strewn about a vast desertscape. The sun shone and cast long shadows. Gentle wind left little divots in the sand.

"Talking is good," I murmured, feeling lighter and lighter in the night sky.

"Talking is good," Dragon echoed.

We soared about for a good hour. We went nowhere in particular, and it felt nice. We swooped here, looped there, dipped and then shot up. The night was clear and the lights twinkled below just as much as above. We headed toward a cluster of hills where the really big houses looked out over the valley.

"Hey, what is that?" I asked.

"What is what?"

I squinted, leaned, and tried to focus on something moving just below. Something small, pointy, with a tiny light, making a faint whirring sound ...

"Holy shit, it's a drone. Dragon, turn around! Go!"

"It cannot be; they only travel in packs," Dragon said. But he obliged and rapidly launched us in the other direction.

"No, a drone, a human thing, like a tiny remote-controlled plane with a camera!" I explained frantically.

"Camera?!"

Dragon shot straight up. I squeezed my eyes shut and pressed my body against his scales and clung about his neck. Not long ago, he had fashioned a sort of harness for me to use while riding. A leather strap looped around his neck, across his belly and diagonally over his shoulder. I had mocked it when I first saw it. Now I wished I had ten more wrapped around him and me.

"How high are we going?" I squealed.

"How high can drones fly?"

I peeled my eyes open and turned my head just enough to peek below.

"I think it's gone!"

Dragon shot forward, then flapped in two, three, four long, powerful strokes.

"Do you spot that contraption anywhere?" he said, panting, as we hovered far higher than I'd ever flown with him.

"Really don't want to open my eyes and look down again," I squeaked.

"I do believe we've evaded it," Dragon said.

We coasted a bit before we began our descent. And we both had the same, horrid question that neither wanted to ask.

As we swooped down into my backyard once more, Dragon's worry was palpable.

"You, uh, need to off-load some clutter? I gotta big sandy desert ready for you," I said, smiling a little.

"We didn't get a chance to discuss the gems. Nor did we discuss Yael's whereabouts. Nor did we acknowledge that someone may now have a recording of you flying atop a dragon."

I stretched and yawned. I didn't have the energy to delve into any of those crates with him. I looked up to the side of the house; Philippa's bedroom window was now closed.

"Alright, then. What are the gems?"

"The short answer is, the Earth is a billion-year-old powerhouse of energetic carbon, much of which, if realized, is cast aside as anomalies. You, Evechild, are very in tune with this energy. So rocks and things, they respond to you differently, and you to them. Naturally, witches and wizards and scientists have studied and researched and –"

"This is the short answer?" I said, cutting him short. I smiled and his face softened. "And Ms. Neally?"

"Naturally, you've already reached a correct conclusion: Sebastian and Baert provided safe passage. They are within the folds of a different dimension – not the Seventh, mind you. But one that is perhaps a bit hostile toward humans and human-like creatures."

"Hostile? But they're safe?"

"As safe as one can be whilst evading the notice of dinosaurs."

"Dinosaurs?" I squealed. Dragon frowned.

"Surely your uncle explained to you where dinosaurs actually went to avoid meteors and ice ages? Well, not all of them; those from the Cretaceous period sadly did not heed the counsel of their Jurassic predecessors. And, indeed, there are the sad remains of the stubborn or intoxicated, too foolhardy to know what was good for them. The Mesozoic era was wild. Simply wild."

"Um, yeah, I don't really know what to do with that information … so, uh, moving on," I said, my brain reeling. "But at some point, when things are, like, calm and normal, maybe we circle back to these other dimensions … and … the dinosaurs?"

Dragon chuckled and nodded.

"You want to meet one, don't you," he said, mischief sparkling in his eyes.

"I can meet one?!" I squealed. But before I could indulge that insane question, my phone buzzed. I pulled it out; an unknown number had messaged me. Three times. Frowning, I swiped and read. Dragon leaned in.

My favorite little rockstar, you've done it again. Just when I think I'm running low on material, Guy's drone returns with the most fascinating footage! Let me know what you think.

<image>

Feel free to schedule a time to discuss!

I clicked on the image to enlarge it, but I didn't have to. A civilian drone's low-light aperture was just sophisticated enough to capture the head and silhouette of a dark, winged flying creature, and, atop it, a blonde-haired teenage girl … .

"Oh heavens, I look ghastly," Dragon murmured over my shoulder.

"Are you serious? *That* is your concern?"

"Well, it is *a* concern, as it would be for anyone," he sniffed and pouted.

"Good lord, Dragon. What do I do with this?! And don't you dare say to toss it into a crate on a sandy beach."

Dragon was quiet.

I was quiet.

Though still dark, somewhere in the distance a bird chirped. Then another, urging the sun to rise.

"I'm gonna try to sleep."

"I think that best. Pleasant slumber, Evechild," Dragon said quietly.

I turned to go inside, but spun around, expecting Dragon's usual one-last-gem-of-wisdom before he left. But he was already soaring through the sky. I was unused to seeing him stumped.

If a millennia-old creature of myth and mysticism was stumped, what hope did I have?

I cursed Channing a million times as I tossed around in bed. And then, just to stick it to me, she snuck into my dreams in a wonderful but infuriating way.

72

ESSE QUAM VIDERI

As I trudged from one class to the next with all the gusto and panache of a zombie, a single thought clung to me.

The longer I put off taking care of Obrenox, the more out of control things were getting.

This morning as I left for school, another pile of pebbles awaited me in the front yard. But their pattern was different. Not a labyrinth or a thurisaz; these were arranged in a line with two smaller lines coming down diagonally from the upper part of one side, like a scrawled letter F.

Pebble patterns spontaneously appearing seemed pretty out of control. With or without clones and whatnot.

I looked across the classroom and frowned; the spot Elke usually sat in lit arts was empty. I was too sleepy in algebra earlier in the day to consider her absence. I would have loved to show her the photo and get her take on what this swoopy F meant.

But then she'd ask *why* I had a picture of a swoopy F in rocks on my front lawn.

I sighed.

My mind was made up.

I had to go back.

But I knew that already.

I had to *do it.*

I drifted down the stairs after the final bell, uncertain what I was feeling. Angst? Anguish? The crushing existential dread that comes with realizing the fate of the world rests on your ability to get out of bed and do a thing no one will ever know about?

"Um, excuse me. I said, excuse me. I'm trying to speak to you."

I looked up. Crowds of students shuffled past. Laughing, heckling, wrestling, flirting. A few pushed by and knocked me against the rail. What did I care? I was going to maybe die trying to take out this crazy evil guy they had no idea about. So they could continue living their vapid lives in this petri dish called a school ...

"I *said,* excuse me. God!"

I whirled around and saw Channing standing on the step above me, one hand on her hip, the other holding her phone out.

"No. No way. I've gotta go," I said and pushed my way through a group filming a dance on the lower landing.

"You may go," Channing snapped, catching up to me, "*after* I have my quote. You never responded to my text, which is absurd. But I'll let it slide. This is you, is it not?"

She thrust her phone in front of my face. She had a photo open of me – plainly me – atop what looked like a dragon. It was a bit grainy, sure. But that was my ugly mug. And that was Dragon.

"What am I supposed to be looking at?" I said coolly.

"You tell me," she glowered.

"I'm not very good with photo editors, so I, uh, don't know what you were trying to get at," I said, suddenly aware of groups of onlookers gathering.

"This is not edited," Channing hissed.

"How'd you get that picture of me, anyway? Why do you have a picture of me in your phone?" I said loudly with disgust, raising my voice for the sake of the crowd. "Channing, I barely know you, and here you are, photoshopping pictures of me from … is that me at my horse-riding practice? You followed me there? That is so messed up!"

I was yelling now, not out of anger, but purely for the benefit of an audience. It worked. People snickered and jeered. Channing's face reddened, as red as her corduroy blazer. She glared at me, hard, and walked slowly toward me, closer and closer. Her face came within inches of mine. I gulped.

"You, um, are you trying to kiss me or something?" I said, stuttering and sweating but not losing volume. "Guy's not enough for you, huh? You gotta go after underclassmen?"

The crowed went wild.

"Big. Mistake," she hissed, overenunciating each word. I hated it when people did that.

But it was effective. Scared the crap outta me. Almost literally.

I bolted to the bathroom and left the crowds to start spreading the tale of my conquest. I hung out in the stall until things quieted. As I scurried out of the school and jogged through the rain on my way home, a comforting realization energized me: I was right. Channing could show that "footage" as much as she wanted; who was going to believe that she recorded a real dragon flying over her house in Happy Valley, much less that I was flying atop one?

One stressful thing crossed off the list.

I didn't know another was awaiting me at home.

My mom's car was idling in the driveway when I arrived. She hurried out of it and helped me out of my wet coat and backpack.

"There was a cancellation, and they can see you today. Now, actually, if you don't mind changing into dry clothes super-fast," she said with a shaky voice.

"What? Who can?"

"The clinic. For … for, what was the phrase you're supposed to use now? Disordered eating. Yes, the – oh, I can't remember the name of the place. But they're booked, like, months out! Scoot, let's go. Please?"

I groaned. I groaned one long groan as I stomped upstairs, as I changed into sweats (which were really, really loose on me now), as I stomped back downstairs, as I got into her car and fastened my seatbelt.

"Are you done? This is important. *You* are important," my mom said nervously as she backed up the car.

"Uuuuugggghhhhh! No, I am not done. Ma, this is absurd. I don't have an eating disorder."

"Disordered eating," she corrected.

"Whatever. Look," I grabbed her purse and rummaged around and pulled out a protein bar. I tore off the wrapper and took a giant bite. "See? I'm eating. Willingly. I'm – ugh! Gross!" I spit out the wad of half-masticated protein bar, which was more cement than cookies-n-cream as the wrapper proclaimed.

"I knew it!" my mom wailed.

"It's disgusting! That was a bad example! Look, I'll force it down. Here, I'm – I'm eating it."

"I'm getting you help!"

"Ma, there are people in real trouble who need help; I'm not one of them, I can't take someone's spot. I – God, this is really so disgusting. How do you eat this?"

I shoved the bar into my mouth, minus the spit-up lump which I had tossed out the window. I chewed. And chewed. And chewed. No amount of saliva could break down that food-product masquerading as nutrition. I tried to swallow. My stomach lurched and flipped. When had I eaten last? Stress and insomnia ... that duo just didn't cultivate much of an appetite in me. More chewing. Another gulp.

My stomach heaved. I clamped my hand over my mouth.

"Oh my gosh, Eve, look at yourself! You can't even eat one measly bar without inducing your expelling reflex! Oh, this is awful! It's all my fault!"

My mom cried, wailed, as she drove quickly – let's call it what it was, *recklessly* – to the clinic, an assuming foursquare downtown with a suspicious number of flowers growing around it.

And I, well, I threw up chunks of protein bar. Mostly on my pants. A little on the door panel.

After we parked and got out, my mom handed me a small towel she had used to wipe the smeared mascara from her face.

"Ugh! This smells worse than the puke!"

"All I had," she sniffed. "I grabbed it out of my gym bag."

I cleaned myself as best I could and tossed the grotesque towel back to her.

"Sorry about that non-induced vomit I expelled," I said dryly.

I followed her in. There was no use fighting her on this, not in the parking lot, anyway.

I sat at a child-size table in the corner and colored while my mom spoke weepily to a sympathetic man at the registration counter. He gently patted her hand and handed her a clipboard with some papers to fill out.

By the time we were called back, I had colored a very fetching scene of a family of a rabbits around a dinner table.

But I had given each of the rabbits little devil horns and had carefully drawn in tiny, intricately detailed humans floating in their soup bowls.

It was some of my finest work.

73

SALTUS IN DEMONSTRANDO

"It's normal to have a difficult relationship with food."

"I'm sure it is," I said.

The woman assigned to "introduce me to healing and treatment" was named Paige. She wore a beautifully colored headscarf, had striking dark eyes, and did not find me amusing in the least.

"Many of our relationships are complicated, if you think about. With anything."

"For sure. But I love food. No complication there."

Paige pursed her lips.

"I don't know if it loves me back, though. Does it think about me when I'm gone? I don't know the last time we had a night together, just the two of us, me and food. Maybe you're right. Maybe it is complicated."

"Eve, I'm your friend in this. I'm your advocate and your confidant. It's important we break down these walls for meaningful work."

"Tell her how you threw up in the car," my mom said behind me.

"You threw up in the car?" Paige said, alarmed.

"No! Well, yeah. But not because I *wanted* to or whatever. It was the world's most disgusting protein bar, and I haven't been feeling that great, and eating that brick on an empty stomach, with her crazy driving –"

"It's common to make excuses. It's ok," Paige said gently.

"It was the protein bar!" I wailed. "It was disgusting!"

Paige got up and gestured for my mom to follow. The two of them gave me knowing smiles, knowing nods, and ducked outside into the hallway.

I groaned.

How was I going to get out of this? I could feel a keen sense of losing time. I was trapped in here while Obrenox was doing who knows what, while Uncle Seb grew sicker, while Philippa was alone ... Who was I to stop the world and get help for a problem I didn't have?

I walked around the little room, decorated in soft colors and warm textures. I scanned the art, the posters, all promoting awareness and healing and acceptance.

I groaned again.

Something gnawed at me, at my conscience. Something like guilt, something that softened my heart. I took a deep breath and opened the door.

"Can you guys come back in? So we can talk for a minute? For real?"

Paige and my mom looked at each other, nodded, then nodded at me and came back in. I didn't care for this little nonverbal alliance they had formed.

"Look, I think it's important you know that I understand the value and the need of this place and places like it," I began slowly, trying to keep my voice cool and level. "I also understand how you came to the conclusions that you did based on my, well, my, *this*," I said and did a sweeping gesture across my body. "But I truly do not have a mental ...um, hang up, or whatever the appropriate word is to use around disordered eating. Truly. But thank you for caring enough to try to help me. What I'd really like is a cheeseburger. And fries. And some pie."

Paige and my mom frowned, looked at each other, nodded, and frowned at me even more.

"I'm so happy you're open to this dialogue," Paige said.

"Happy to end this dialogue, you mean, as your services won't be needed," I said cheerfully.

"This is what I'm talking about," my mom said quietly to Paige.

If ever there were a time for me to snap, that was it. I wanted to punch the walls, throw the chairs, kick the trashcans, run screaming up and down the halls.

But I did none of that.

"Fine," I said. "Check me in. When's dinner?"

I flipped through a magazine on the table closest to me. It was a Popular Mechanics issue filled with articles about the Mars rover, which I loved. No stupid celebrity gossip rags here; those didn't exactly promote the healthy body image mentality this place touted. But space? Hell yeah.

"I noticed you had several servings of the roast chicken," a man said gently as he sat down in a chair beside me. He wore pale yellow scrubs, which didn't match the penny loafers on his feet that had actual pennies in them. They reminded me of my sister. I immediately missed her. "I'm Lars, a clinician here. May I ask when your last lavatory visit was?"

"Oh yeah, it was so good. Is there more? Like, are we allowed snacks?"

"We endeavor to not utilize words like 'allow' when referring to nutrition intake. But yes, if you feel true hunger and need another little bit for satiation to encourage fuller sleep, we are happy to oblige. I must press you on my latter question, however; may I see your bathroom log?"

He spoke so gently, so lightly, that you barely noticed how convoluted his sentences were. One word glided into the next to create the most serene conversation ever.

That is, until he said the phrase "bathroom log." That one made me giggle. Lars' face fell with such disappointment. It was as though I had laughed at a puppy. An elegant, gentle puppy.

"Um, no," I said, shifting uncomfortably in my chair. It shifted under my body weight and made a farting sound. "That was the chair!" I said quickly. Lars nodded. "It was. And no, no bathroom logs for me," I grumbled.

"Let's you and I talk further, if you're amenable. Are you free in, say, thirty minutes?"

"Am I free?" I said, looking around at the mostly empty room of pastel-colored lounge chairs and large floor pillows. "Yeah. Yeah, I think I'll be free in thirty."

"Wonderful. We'll convene in the Meadow Room."

"Meadow room?" I said, looking up, but he was already gone. I saw him gliding down the opposite hall, one long, smooth stride at a time, and wondered if he were an ice skater in another life.

Those were the thoughts in my head. Not Obrenox, not clones, not rock runes. All of that seemed worlds and lifetimes away while I whittled away the hours in this soft-colored sanctuary of roast chicken and body-positive mantras.

I was ok with it.

I felt like a pause button had been hit on all of that. The world and its stresses were suspended, mid-action, while I pigged out on nutritious snacks and took naps on a giant pink bean bag after reading about the Mars rover to my heart's content.

I may never hit play again.

Thirty minutes passed quicker than I wanted. I wandered around the hall I had seen Lars skate down and peered through windows into other rooms.

"This place has an art room? Awesome," I said with genuine excitement. "Ooh, and a library! Nice!"

I found the meadow room – a conference room appropriately named with its sprawling mural of wildflowers and rolling hills painted all the way around it. Lars looked up, a look of pleasant surprise on his face. He closed the book he had been writing in and stood, his arms outstretched.

"Welcome!" he said congenially.

"You, uh, you said to come," I said, suddenly feeling very uncomfortable. "Did I mishear?"

"Newcomers are rarely so amenable," he said. "Please, sit or stand or lay as suits you."

"Lay as suits me?"

"Yes, the chaise against the window creates quite an idyllic milieu," he said and gestured toward the wall of windows where, indeed, a sloping chaise sat.

"I'll, um, just sit here. Thanks," I mumbled and plopped into the chair nearest me.

"You do not believe you belong here."

"Wow, you, uh, just get right into it, huh? That's cool, I kinda hate small talk anyway. It's, like, so superficial, talking about the weather or whatever."

"Would you prefer to talk about the weather?"

I stopped and scowled.

"Share what you're feeling?"

I sighed.

"Lars, here's the thing. I, um, have met with a few therapists. You guys are great. Super needed. Super helpful. But you all do this really obnoxious thing where you make an assertion and then just expect me to expound on it for you."

"Go with that."

"You just did it again."

Lars was quiet. I cracked my knuckles. I'm not usually a knuckle-cracker. I don't even know why I did it, then. Sheer discomfort? It really hurt, at any rate.

I hated the silence, and I almost cracked my knuckles again. I decided this guy was alright. So, I talked to him.

I told him how stressed I was. Not all the reasons why, but the bits he could handle. I told him how worried I was. Not all the things that worried me, but the parts he might be able to weigh in on. I told him how sleep-deprived I was. I told him about Elke, about Libby, about Channing.

And after hearing about my sister in the hospital, my mom's heart "episode," my isolation at school, my burgeoning love of other girls, my lack of sleep, my unanswered paternity questions, he sat back and closed his book.

He stared up for a long time, the tips of his fingers drawn together. Finally he cleared his throat and looked at me.

"Eve, you do not belong here."

"I know, I know," I muttered. "I belong in some special center, doped up on anti-depressants. Right?"

"Is that what you've been told?"

I nodded, feeling a lump form in my throat.

"I am not in a position to offer a full diagnosis, but I do not think you are depressed. I think you have a tremendous amount of stress, the likes of which would do in even the most supported, self-aware human of any age. And you are managing it largely alone, at an age when clothing choices are stressful let alone reconciling the compromised health of a sister."

I don't know when tears had started falling, but they fell fast and heavy. I wiped my nose with my sleeve.

"May I speak candidly?"

"Were you not?" I said with a forced chuckle.

"I believe too many young people are prematurely medicated. I am a proponent of medication – any disorder, regardless of causation or type, ought to be appropriately treated. Physical health and mental and behavioral health are all *health* and need parity and equity in treatment."

I nodded. I liked this guy. His gentle voice had gained some fervor. Maybe he just needed to get some things off his chest, too, but what he was saying made me feel good.

"Should medication be appropriate, after thorough examinations and data collection, for lack of a better phrase, then that is what we shall seek. But you, my dear, young friend," he paused he stretched his arm across the table, tapping his fingers lightly toward me, "bear a tremendous weight that must seem insurmountably heavy. I am deeply sorry for that. I do not know how all this came to be born by you, nor why, nor shall I ask, nor shall I endeavor to guess. It just *is*. And it ... it stinks."

I looked up. The tears stopped. I think I smiled. At least, my heart did.

"I am writing the following prescription for you," he said as he pulled out another pad of paper. "One nap, daily, and meals three to five times daily or as needed." He looked at me and smiled. "Too cheesy? Perhaps. But I see you are smiling a little. Are you comfortable with my recommending your return to home?"

I nodded.

"Let's go. I'll show you where you can wait for your mom, if you'd like. But Eve," he stopped me at the door, "your mental and behavioral health can change, just as your physical health can. While it is my opinion that your stressors are unusually extreme currently but your disposition otherwise healthy, be vigilant on their after-effects. Trauma and sustained stress can twist the healthiest of people, wreak havoc on their synapses. Take care of your brain. Watch after it."

"That's kind of a funny thought," I said. "Watching my brain."

"This is very serious. Imagine a small cut on your finger. It hurts, it's bothersome. But you forge ahead. Maybe something else hits the same spot, and the cut becomes bigger. Maybe a foreign body, a bacterium, gets inside. An infection begins, it travels through the bloodstream—"

"Yeah, I got it. Good analogy," I cut him off with a little chuckle.

Talking again had me feeling lighter.

Talking again and having a person of authority validating me had me feeling WAY lighter.

"Would you like me to fetch you a snack while you wait?" he said as we walked back to the room simply labeled "gathering space." I nodded eagerly.

It was late, very late, by the time I was home and in my own bed. I didn't say much to my mom on the drive home. She seemed deflated. Defeated. Sheepish. I know she thought she was doing the right thing.

But if there's anything I've learned through all of this, from my first therapist Brittney until now, it's that grownups seem too hurried to diagnose and medicate as soon as something seems askance.

What's that thing Uncle Seb said once? You can put out the fire, but that doesn't mean you've fixed the broken wire that sparked it in the first place.

Between unloading mental crates with Dragon and finding healing in roast chicken and compassion with Lars, I was pretty maxed out on self-reflection and introspection.

But I slept.

Oh, how I slept!

74

SI VIS PACEM, PARA BELLUM

I ditched school.

I sat in my room, quietly, with a certain book balanced on my lap, weighing pros and cons in my head.

Fortis Librae was exceptional. It defied all logic. Even more than life existing in other dimensions tucked inside the folds of space-time.

The thing about this weird book travel is that it takes a lot outta you. So far, a lot of my exploits and adventures have had a bit of science behind them – stuff that nods toward physics, quantum mechanics ... theories you can really delve into and let your mind go wild with possibilities about the universe's workings.

But *Fortis Librae* ... that stood in a category all its own. The fantasy of any type of travel that transfers you on a molecular level and returns you with intact cells still seems just that: *fantasy*. Yet here I was, utilizing this strange, fantastical element of travel that held no mechanical prejudice.

I had gotten used to bopping about via these mystical pages. Back and forth from the hospital while Philippa was there, ducking out of school covertly and ending up in my bed. I had once even tried transporting from my house to a local burger joint with a stress-induced milkshake and French fries craving I couldn't shake. But my memory must have been a bit off, because I ended up at a Wendy's on the other side of town instead. It was one I had frequented as a kid with my mom, a sort of reward spot that must have burrowed its way into my subconscious recall. At any rate, I shot back home with a frosty, which I enjoyed even though I was too disoriented to remember to order fries.

I opened the book again. Some of the pages had a sort of watermark on them now, a sort of compass with scrolling arrows adorning it. Each one was slightly different, though – inlaid with a floral stamping or little chemistry-like symbols, for example – and, I came to realize, represented a location I frequented.

For a while, the page I'd turn to for Uncle Seb's hangar had the most pronounced motif. And, interestingly, it wasn't a plane, like you might expect, but an intricate ship with sails that gleamed opalescent if you tilted the page in the light. As my visits there dropped off, the watermark faded and faded. Now, if you thumbed through the book and landed on a certain page, you might try to wipe away a smudge that resembled a wave.

Some of the pages were new, crisp, light. Others were rough and heavy. I made a mental note to inquire of this book's origins more committedly with Ms. Neally. My stomach flipped thinking of her. Was she okay? Whatever had been hidden away in the library at Beecher, was it gone forever? I picked up *Fortis Librae* and hugged it to my chest.

"Please don't let me down," I murmured, my eyes closed. "Please. Please let this work." Tears welled again. I threw the book down in frustration. "Goddammit."

"Hey, you still have time to – are you okay?" Philippa said suddenly. I hadn't even heard my bedroom door open. "Oooh, new book? Wait, I've seen that one before. Why are you always carrying it around? Hold on, is that Latin? Can I look?"

Before she could angle her wheelchair through the maze of discarded clothing, homework, books, blankets, and half-empty mugs, I kicked the mighty tome under my bed. She looked up, disappointed.

"It's a surprise," I said quickly before she could object. My stomach somersaulted again. It was a surprise, alright. But not the kind she was smiling about. "Anyway, Mom sent me in to see if you had any song requests," she said. "We've made it through every single Bob Dylan album we have. Can you believe that? Man, that guy's voice, though. What a trip!"

I smiled faintly. Going through our collective records had become almost a nightly ritual. Sometimes the music would start earlier in the evening, soundtracking dinner and homework and bedtime routines. Other nights, just before I'd drift off, I'd suddenly hear Otis Redding serenading the house. This would be joined by Philippa yelling her approval rating down the hall, met by my mom's laughter. Her room had become a healing DJ booth for her and my sister.

Would tonight be the last night I'd take part?

A lump formed in my throat. I swallowed hard and trudged to my mom's room. She was leaning against the dresser, record player open and ready, flipping through a stack of records.

"No, no, done it, done it, shouldn't even own it," she said to herself softly, her brow furrowed with the level of deep thought required to split the atom. Her task, to her, was equally significant.

"Here. I have one," I said as I offered her my selection without looking up.

"Ooooh, a new offering! What do we have – oh. Oh, Eve," she said, her voice hushed as her face crumpled. "Yes. This is a good one."

She pulled a record from a worn album sleeve and delicately placed it on the turntable. That familiar, favorite sound of crackling fired up. I turned and silently walked back down the hall to my room as the music started.

Once there was a way
To get back homeward
Once there was a way
To get back home
Sleep, pretty darling, do not cry

And I will sing a lullaby

Paul McCartney's perfect voice carried me away in a wave of pain, bittersweet and noble, as I pulled *Fortis Librae* from under my bed and opened it again. I leaned against my bed and breathed in, out, all the while humming along with Sir Paul.

I surveyed my room, disheveled but loved. My heart softened as I considered my mom and my sister trying to clean it up. I sighed and got up to tidy things a bit. I arranged my books by color, a project Philippa had started. I set up some frames with photos of the three of us that my mom was always giving me. I straightened my maps and dragon posters on my wall. I kind of made my bed.

"Boy, you've got to carry that weight, carry that weight," I sang along softly. I always liked that next song, how they had the one flow into the next. Now it hit a little harder, as if The Beatles somehow knew the exact words and melodies to narrate this moment. I took another deep breath as the original refrain sounded. I sang along, *"sleep, pretty darling, do not cry...."*

But I did cry.

I cried as I listened to my family sing, as I looked over my beloved bedroom sanctuary. I started to open *Fortis Librae* yet again, when I suddenly remembered one last thing. Philippa's letter. I had finally written it. I opened my sock drawer and retrieved a thick, vellum envelope – the fanciest I could find at the stationary store – with "Phlee" scrawled on it in my best attempt at calligraphy. I placed my stuffed dragon Bartholomew in the middle of my bed and balanced the envelope atop his little wings.

Dear Phlee,

Ha. I called you "dear." Already you're rolling your eyes and coming to make fun of me. But here's the thing, my DEAR sister. I'm not here. I think I'm coming back – that's the intent, anyway. But I had to do something. Something big, important, vital, all that jazz.

But I couldn't go without telling you a few things. First, I'm sorry. God, I'm sorry! If it weren't for me, none of your current predicament would exist. All your pain, your injuries, they're my freaking fault. I was the one who agreed to go along with a dragon, not you, and you somehow got caught up in all of this and I hate it. Phlee, I hate it so much! You must know that. Please know that. Please know that if I could take it all back, I would. I'd tell Dragon to scram, to find some other sucker to save the world lol. But really, I would.

I've been forced to experience life without you. And I can say, unequivocally (using this word from your SAT vocab prep! you proud??), that it's no life for me. Life without you isn't life at all. All I could think about is that I should have told you how you're the first person I want to share good news with, how you're the person I want to go to when I'm upset, how you're the only one who understands the proper way to prepare mac n'cheese and that one box does indeed equal one serving. I should have told you how much I look up to you, how much I actually love your singing, how no one makes me laugh as hard as you do.

I should have told you all of that and so much more. And I should have told you more that I love you. Without any dumb joke or facetious disclaimer attached. Just I love you. So I'm telling you now. You're the best sister, friend, human.

Wish me luck. See you soon, loser.

p.s. don't worry, we'll never speak of this letter again

I stared at the envelope perched atop my childhood friend for a very long time. The music had stopped. The lights were off in the hall. Another deep breath in and out. I stretched. I wondered if I should change my outfit.

"C'mon, Eve, stop procrastinating," I muttered to myself as I plopped down, legs crisscrossed, with the book on my lap once more.

I had gone over my plan a billion times. I played out each step with such detail it was though it had already happened; I had conjured a reality where I had already gone and come back and everything was fine. But now, the realness and immediacy punched me in the face and left me reeling for balance and vision.

"Okay. You can do this. You've thought out every part. Step one," I said slowly, "you use this book to transport back to the seventh, right back to Obrenox' lair." I closed my eyes and recalled that ghastly place with its arching stone ceilings, gem-splattered ante-room, and cotton-candy outer atmosphere with perfect clarity. It was easy. Nightmares never let me forget it.

"Eve, little Egg – oh! You're up! I was just saying goodnight is all," my mom said suddenly as she pushed my door open a few inches.

Without thinking, I got up and hugged her. Hard.

"Goodnight, mom," I said, then added, "love you."

"I ... I love you, too, my sweet child," she said, genuine but surprised. *She* said that emotive stuff all the time. I definitely did not. "Okay, off you go. Sweet dreams. Ride tomorrow?"

"Uh, yeah, sure. Tomorrow, thanks. Goodnight."

I pulled the door shut behind her and locked it. Then, thinking better of it, unlocked it and returned to my spot with the book.

"Where was I," I mumbled as I ran my fingers over the soft leather and traced along the worn, embossed words. "Okay. I get there. I find him. I make him drink ... this," I said as I reached farther under my bed to retrieve a plastic bag. In it was a bottle of fruit juice blended with water hemlock, a very poisonous plant that was conveniently native to my own, dear marshy state.

I was pretty proud of this concoction. I couldn't take full credit for the idea. One of the books Ms. Moriarty had recommended to me a while back was a story about a woman who poisons her abusive husband with something from her own garden.

That had planted a seed (heh) that grew into an approved hypothesis with Dragon. There had been many a conversation betwixt my curious crew about the best way to poison Obrenox, whose mammalian characteristics seemed similar enough to humans until you considered the methane-heavy atmosphere of the Seventh Dimension.

And there we stayed, hung up on that point, at odds with each other's ideas.

Until one day, in my algebra class of all places, it occurred to me that if I wanted to take him down, I had to focus on the similar parts, not the different ones. If he had human traits, how could I best attack them?

Poison, yes. But with what?

A few cleared search histories later, I was on a nature walk with Elke on a fine wintry afternoon. I strategically steered toward a trail system whose forested walkways ran parallel to freshwater marshes. Armed with a plant identification app on my phone and some latex gloves I swiped from the lab at school, I pinched a few stalks. I had to be quick, so I brought scissors, and cleverly got Elke to turn the other way to photograph the sunset.

I smiled a sad smile. I hadn't written anything for Elke. Whatever was budding between us was too new. Our friendship even was too new. Plus, I suspected her German sensibilities wouldn't care for a syrupy farewell letter proclaiming my unspoken love.

But I had to tell her *something*. Should the worst happen … I shook my head. "Don't be melodramatic," I scolded myself. I grabbed my phone, quickly typed a message to her, and hit send.

Hey, you're really incredible. Thought you should know I'm grateful to know you.

I frowned. Uncharacteristically heartfelt. I stared at the little blue text bubble, then, in a panic, tried to unsend the message. But the magic window in which that's allowed had passed. I sighed. Maybe it wasn't so bad.

My phone pinged. I looked down. Elke had responded.

Are you high?

I smiled for real that time.

No, listened to too much good music and got all sentimental or whatever. Disregard lol.

My heart pitter-pattered, light but quick with excitement, as I awaited her response. No message came, but a little heart appeared atop my last text. That was pretty good. A heart. I could live with that.

"Geez, enough of this already!" I yelled aloud and stuffed my phone in my pocket. I zipped up my backpack and checked that the bottle was secure beside one other secret weapon of choice: the white orb from the spheresaii. "Okay. It's okay. Let's just freaking get this done or I'll never do it."

I opened *Fortis Librae* resolutely. I turned to the blank page and began reciting the activation chant. Who knew that *this* is why Latin would turn out handy? If I make it back – *ahem*, rather, *when* I make it back – I'd have to tell Philippa. She'd get a kick out of –

Colors compressed. Air was thin. My ears rang. A thousand rolling pins flattened my insides and then ... *Oof!* I toppled onto cold stone. I opened my eyes. Everything was dark, dank, and familiar. Jagged stones shot upward, seemingly unending. But if you squinted just so, your eyes could fix upon a final point, shimmering ever so slightly. At the peak of this grand hall was that dizzying mosaic and just below that, a black cloud gyrated and swirled.

"Holy shit, it worked," I gasped. I clamped my hand over my mouth and scurried into the shadows of a mammoth stone balustrade.

I leaned back and looked up again. If he was way up there, and I'm way down here, does it make more sense for me to go up or for him to come down? I pulled my pack off and opened it. I hastily put on the latex gloves, then carefully transferred the juice bottle to the pouch of my hoodie and zipped it. The orb tittered and shivered within the pack.

"Not yet, little buddy," I whispered as I pushed it further into my pack to fit the giant book in with it. "Not until –"

"Until whatsssssss? I am sssssso curioussssssss, yesssssssss."

75

BIBAMUS, MORIENDUM EST

Before I could even turn, a long, black, snake-like something swirled around my ankle. I yanked, hard. It hissed in disappointment as I darted away.

I don't know why I thought I could outrun it. Everything in my body screamed RUN. So I did. But that hiss. The hiss hung behind me, like it was drafting me, as I sprinted along the outer wall and unwittingly pulled it along. I finally slowed and spun around. There he was.

Obrenox. Adorned atop his inky plume by slithering appendages, he clapped and giggled. His black robes shuddered in a ripple that started at his bony shoulders and moved down to the grotesque twisting serpents at his hem. It was sickening.

I gulped and looked around. It was just him and me. So far. No amythystics, no clones, no dronettes.

Could it be that easy?

The hall grew quiet. Like the kind of dead quiet that brings that high buzz to your ears. Obrenox stared at me. I stared back.

"It'sssssss jusssssst you?" he said finally.

I nodded. He tapped his foot impatiently. A baby blue silk slipper peaked through the dark robes. Obrenox sighed and stretched. His red kerchief had been swapped out for a blue, woolly scarf that he wore thickly wrapped about his head and neck.

"When are otherssssssss sssssset to arrive sssssso we may sssssssssstartsssssss the funsssssss?" he asked, then broke into a coughing fit.

It hadn't occurred to me that this other-dimensional overlord might maintain strict battle etiquette. I stifled a giggle.

He held up a bony, gnarled finger as he turned his head to cough – hack, really – into his sleeve. The cuff of the sleeve shuddered and hissed as he wheezed into the fabric over and over.

"Oh!" I said suddenly and unzipped my pouch. "I have something, for, um, you ... for that ... that cough." I started strong, eager, but looking at him drained all of that out of me as I spoke.

"Yessssssss?" he said and leaned forward. His scarf opened just enough for me to catch a glimpse of his face.

Yellow eyes, sagging skin that was both pockmarked and creased, is all I saw. And yet, something in that glance tugged at me, something familiar.

"YESSSSSS?" he hissed loudly, raising higher and swooping forward over me.

"Oh, um, right," I stammered and gulped as I held the poisoned fruit juice forward. "H-h-here."

His skeletal hand wrapped around the bottle, one bony finger at a time. I shuddered. He raised the juice up and stuck out his hip, dropping his other hand onto it with a *hmph*.

"And whatsssssss thisssssss?" he said peevishly. His robes rippled and hissed in response.

I took a breath in and tightened my grip on my backpack straps.

"It's juice. To drink. With, um, you know, plants and vitamins and stuff ... to heal, for, um, healing you."

"You helpsssssssss Friar Obrenox?"

"Friar?" I said without thinking. "Like, like the Benedictine guy with, um, monks or whatever?"

"Like Friar Lord Jesssssusssssss, to whom even your precioussssss pope prayssssssssssss," Obrenox roared, growing larger and emitting more smoke and snarling snake folds.

"The pope? He's, um, not really important, like, even to Catholics," I mumbled, feeling my face redden and palms sweat. What was I doing? Having casual conversation with the thing that wants to destroy everything I know? I looked up. "Wait, did you mean *fair* lord Jesus? Like the song? Or scripture or whatever? It's ... nevermind...."

"Your speciesssssss reveresssssssss the popesssssssss," Obrenox wailed.

"Maybe, like, four hundred years ago. Now, uh, world leaders ... don't do anything with, um, the pope, really ... I think," I sputtered. What was I doing? Now I was rambling about the global involvement of the pope?

"Itssssss a trick! To hurt Obrenox, yessssssssss!" he wailed louder.

"I don't want to get sick!" I blurted quickly. "Yeah, I don't want, um, your germs ... Gross!"

Obrenox cocked his head and folded his arms. His hem hissed. He tossed the bottle up in the air.

I've never been what you would call an athlete. I haven't been on one of those fancy sports teams, I don't know any mascots, I don't own a jockstrap (whatever those are).

But in that moment, I forgot this. I dove through the air, arms outstretched. I sailed through the edge of Obrenox' cloud. It hissed and billowed. I landed hard on the cold, unyielding stone.

I looked down. Clutched in left hand against my stomach was the bottle of fruit juice. *In my left hand*. (I'm a right-handed non-athlete.)

"Juice?" I blurted as I thrust the bottle toward him from the ground.

He grabbed it with a loud sigh, uncapped it, and drank the entire thing instantly. He smacked his lips loudly and turned toward me, hands on hips.

"Sssssso? I am not sssssssssick now?"

"I mean, maybe give it a minute, but, um, yeah?" I stammered as I stood up and backed away a few steps. I reached a hand behind to pull the zipper on my backpack a bit. I wanted to be ready to get out of here through *Fortis Librae* as swiftly as possible.

Suddenly, Obrenox stood erect, burped, then lurched forward. His skinny, gaunt hand clutched at his belly while his other clasped over his mouth. Another burp, then he thrust his neck out as a berry-colored stream of hemlock-spotted sputum shot out of his mouth.

He stopped just as rapidly as he had begun. He cleared his throat and straightened his shoulders. I said nothing. He raised his hands out, ready to speak, when another little burp popped out from within the blue wool scarf, now fringed with vomit.

Obrenox lurched forward and yakked again.

And again.

And again.

Each time more horrifically theatrical and odorous than the last.

Vomit spewed around me, over me, every which way. And the sound, the cacophony of it all. If he wasn't yakking, he was wailing, screaming in anguish like an ill-tempered child.

I tilted my backpack over my head as a cover and felt the orb roll forward. The white orb!

As quickly as I could, I snatched it, held it out, and screamed every Latin phrase I could remember at it. One of them worked, for it gleamed, shone, then shot straight up.

76

TU STULTUS ES

White swirls of frost climbed up the walls. A silence so pure it pierced your inner ear hung in the frigid hall.

"Sssssoooo ch-ch-chilly!" Obrenox stammered as he withdrew into his shivering robes. His hems slithered and hissed in discontent.

Icy trails etched upward on the stone, higher and higher. And then, suddenly, the white orb shook and shuddered, flashed a blinding white, and shot a blanket of ice out that fell in a dome atop us.

That wasn't good.

Being trapped in an igloo in Obrenox' lair wasn't something I had planned for. But at least he wasn't puking everywhere anymore.

"Ohhhh, it hurtssssssa and ssssssstabsssss," he whimpered. His bony hands again clutched at his stomach. "Sssssyrup was a trickssssss!" he wailed. Then he stopped, burped, and held a wiry hand out as if to halt something. Another burp, another heave. Oh no, I thought, backing up.

A stream of vomit shot out from his cloaked face. In the extreme cold, it froze, almost instantly, in a long arc of pink and sickly yellow. Obrenox screeched with disgust or delight – I honestly couldn't tell – and the frozen puke ribbon fell to the ground and shattered.

It was enough to make my own gag reflex act up.

The black cloud he rested on began dropping charcoal-colored snow. Gradually, it shrunk. And shrunk. The snakes slithered and hissed a stuttered, shivered hiss. Obrenox yowled and heaved all the while, not noticing this. But I noticed it. I kept backing farther and farther away, sliding my back along the ice dome's wall. A plan was stirring.

Inside my pocket, my hand clasped the green stone Gil had left me in the labyrinth, the same kind that appeared in the thurisaz pattern. It singed my palm, but its heat only fueled me. If chaos was what it wanted, what it signaled, then chaos is what it would get.

Finally, the inky snow cloud gave out and Obrenox hit the ground with not a thud but a clatter of frail bones and frozen serpents. He laid on his side and dry-heaved and shivered in a pile of black snow and pink puke chunks.

He was weak. He was sick. And getting sicker.

In a flash, I pulled *Fortis Librae* out of my pack and held it tightly against my side while I flung the tiny gem has hard as I could at the apex of the dome. It impaled the ice like a miniscule dart. Within seconds, cracks shot out every direction along the dome. My eyes traced a long crack, creaking all the way down the side closest to me. I kicked at it as hard as I could and busted through the ice.

But I hadn't just kicked the icy dome layer. I had struck one of the outer stones in the mighty keep. Frigid and brittle, the stone cracked. A whirr of hot air streamed through, high and piercing like a kettle.

What happened next, I'm not entirely sure of. I thrust open the book and called the little spheresaii back to me as the entire palatial stone hall filled with green light. That one stone broke more; steaming air poured through. Hot mixed with cold and a violent column of air began to rotate. Its rope-like swirl formed a funnel and whirled about the perimeter, bigger and bigger, faster and faster, until a tornado of sorts overtook the whole lair.

The last thing I heard was Obrenox shrieking the same word over and over: "Chaosssssss! Chaossssss!"

I had to look.

In the eye of that strange storm, writhing with his hood dislodged, was Obrenox. And though his eyes were sunken in and his face gaunt under his veiny, balding head, there was no mistaking the resemblance.

All that was missing was a pair of dark sunglasses.

It was Kip.

77

VIDEO SED NON CREDO

My landing was less than elegant.

I blasted into my kitchen, soaked and shivering but generally intact. I laid on the floor for a minute and just listened. I could barely hear anything over my own panting, over my pounding heartbeat.

"Aye? Lassie? *Ciamar a tha thu?*"

I rolled over and pushed myself upright. I blinked and blinked – my vision was exceptionally blurry – until Baert came into focus. He crouched down in front of me, his red eyebrows knitted with worry.

"Baert! I did it? I did it! I – I made it! Holy crap, it's him, he's him, I mean *they're* him," I rattled, my teeth still chattering as my whole body convulsed in shivers. "He's sick, but I think still alive; he drank the poison, and, like, puked *all* over. But he's ... you'll never guess."

"I dinnae what yer sayin', my bonnie lass, but it's a braw thing tah see ya, Lassie."

"Help me up, I've gotta tell – wait, did you come back with Uncle Seb?"

Baert was quiet. He heaved his little body under my arm and pushed me upright.

"Oh, *schiesse*! Oh, wow, that hurts!" I cried as I collapsed back to the floor. I gingerly pulled my right shoe off. My sock was drenched with blood. I tried to wriggle my toes and yelped in pain. "I think I broke my toe when I kicked that stupid ice," I muttered. "Can you, uh, get me a wet washcloth and some gauze or something? God, this sucks. Baert? Baert?"

He popped his head out from within the pantry. Crumbs dotted his beard. He held out a half-eaten graham cracker.

"Aye? Right scran, this one. And look! No rashies," he said happily with a full mouth as he displayed his little arms.

"Yeah, cool. Glad you've learned. Baert, listen. Did Uncle Seb come back with you?"

He shook his head, releasing more crumbs from his beard, and shoved another graham cracker in his mouth.

"Baert, I saw him," I said as I pulled myself up against the counter and leaned into it.

"Saw who?" he said, chomping away.

"Obrenox."

"Aye, we've all see that radge bampot."

"No, you don't get it. Baert," I said with such force that he stopped chewing and looked up at me. "I know who Obrenox is."

"Yer erse is oot thah windae!" he said with a snort and put two more crackers in his mouth. He chomped down hard, satisfied with the crunch. "Of course y'know – he's that radge Obrenox."

"Ugh! Where's Uncle Seb, he'll know!"

Baert looked up again, his cheeks bulging and his eyes wide. He started to speak; it was muffled with crumbs. He held a finger up as he chewed. And chewed. And finally swallowed.

"Tis sick," he said simply and went for another package.

"Not so fast," I said as I swiped the wrapped crackers from him. "Uncle Seb is sick? I mean, I already knew that, about the diagnosis or whatever. Where is he? Why are you not hearing me? Obrenox was—"

"Bandage that up; tis a blootered, boke sight," he cut me off, disinterested. "Aye," he sighed, took the graham cracker package from me and stashed it inside his tunic. "Let's be on with it, then."

We waited at the coffee house, Baert and I. Groups and patrons came and went. The orange-haired barista served the best coffee drinks and desserts in the world with her usual listless ambivalence. From Dragon to gaggles of tourists clamoring for photos at the piano, I sensed there was little that would fluster or amaze her.

"Lassie," Baert whispered to me, "relax."

I jumped. I had been guzzling cup after cup of delicious concoctions – most of them caffeinated. Not intentionally, you see; I had a very rudimentary working knowledge of coffee drinks, which was not typical for a native North-westerner. I was suddenly aware of my non-busted foot tapping incessantly.

"Sorry," I muttered and took another bite of a pastry. "What are we waiting for, anyway?"

"Hmmmm, you're so glad to see me! Ah, you've made it, hmmmm!"

Gil appeared in the doorway, a blustery arrival of scarves and shimmering organza skirts. She strode to our table in the corner, not caring that she knocked over two chairs and stepped on a purse on her way.

She sat down with undue pomp and held her arm out as she regarded the café while looking at nothing in particular.

"Hmmmm, to be among friends, hmmmm, tis a welcome thing. And you, young heroine," she turned to me and gasped loudly, "by Toth, what havoc was wreaked on you, young thing, hmmmm? You're, hmmmm, positively bedeviled with strife!"

"Good to see you, too," I grumbled. "I used your stupid rock and took down Obrenox. In case anyone was wondering."

Baert looked up from his cocoa. Frothy chocolate clung to the tips of his mustache. Gil stared at me, hard, then waved her hand dismissively.

"Hmmmm, he has not been taken down, hmmm. No, no, not yet, hmmmm, not fully."

I started to object, but she held a bauble-covered hand up and continued in her deep, breathy musings.

"It is not over yet, hmmmmm. I do feel, hmmm, yes, I do feel there are terrible forces yet, hmmmm. They linger."

"What the hell do I do with that?" I griped quietly, mostly to myself.

"Hmmmm. You take your battle victory."

I glared at her. Baert, whose small body barely let him see across the table, reached over and patted my hand. I withdrew it and scowled.

"Come, hmmmm, let's see him," Gil said and stood up with a stretch. A moth came flapping out of somewhere on her. Then another.

I was too tired to question her. I winced in pain as I stood; I already forgot about my broken toe. I had wrapped it as best I could with Baert's help. And by help, I mean he held my phone as I watched a video on how to bandage a broken toe. I hobbled after them as they headed up the staircase and down a dark hall.

A sliver of light came from the bottom of a door in the back. Gil turned to us, put a finger to her lips, and made a shushing sound. We were already silent, and her shushing was louder than anything going on in that building at that moment.

With just a single light knock, the door fell open.

"Hmmmm, this ought to be more secure, hmmm, kindly lock it, yes, hmmmmm, in you go."

I shuffled in after her and gasped.

Propped up in a rocking chair, wrapped in blankets and horribly jaundiced, was my uncle.

"Egg!" he sputtered weakly. "Hey! You're back!"

He turned off the television he had been watching on mute and tossed the remote onto a little bed against the wall. The dim lamplight cast shadows that made him look even more gaunt and sickly than I wanted to believe he was.

"Tell me all about it," he breathed.

This was not my uncle. This was some sad Victorian-era bloke who subscribed to leeches and bloodletting as medicine. No way was this my machismo-brimming, womanizing pilot uncle. No way.

"Aye, I've just thah thing!" Baert said. He opened an armoire and pulled down a leather jacket. Standing on tiptoes, he gently draped it about Uncle Seb's shoulders. My uncle beamed and my heart dropped.

Alright, it was him.

I just didn't want it to be.

"Tell him, Lassie," Baert whispered and nodded toward the frail man shrouded in leather from another lifetime.

I swallowed and took a step forward. I looked at Gil, who had tweezers out and was pulling hairs from her knuckles. I looked at Baert, who stood steadfastly by Uncle Seb, his eyes fixed on his dear friend.

"This, uh, whole situation," I said nervously, "is a little new to me."

Uncle Seb smiled weakly.

"A lot of radiation, you know?"

I frowned and shook my head slowly.

"Flying in and out of different dimensions," he said, then stopped to cough. He coughed and sputtered so laboriously I wanted to tell him to stop, to just go to sleep, that everything is fine and he needn't worry. Baert brought him a glass of water, which he choked down. "Think about what that does to a body. A lot of unknowns, but you'd have to assume there's some radioactive energy in that kind of space travel."

"I guess so," I said and looked down. How many times had my uncle flown in and out of different dimensions? Had he known the risks? Was this because of that?

"That last trip damn near killed me," he coughed.

"Last trip?" I asked.

"To hide her," Uncle Seb finally after his coughing abated. "Couldn't risk keeping her here."

"Ah," I said, a thousand questions about Ms. Neally bubbling up in my brain. A look from Baert told me to keep them to myself.

"Radiation poison, they call it. Causes cancer. Colon cancer, in my case."

"I keep tellin' him, take my colon," Baert grumbled. "I dinnae need it."

My uncle and I smiled.

"Anyhoo, enough of my bullshit. You've got news for me, I suspect, Egg."

I nodded. He pointed to a chair across from him.

I sat down.

I didn't know where to start.

"Your mom's been keeping me updated on Philippa. God, that's good news, her progress," he said, as if reading my mind. "You can fill me in on the other stuff," he said and coughed more. For a really long time.

By other stuff, I assumed he meant anything related to my latest trip to a big stone lair in the Seventh dimension.

So, I took a deep breath, and I told him every detail I could remember. He nodded continually, a sort of open-mouth smile plastered on his yellow face. But after I detailed what I saw last before ending up on my kitchen floor, his mouth clamped shut and his eyes met mine.

"Holy shit," he breathed.

"Yeah," I said. "Holy shit."

"You got him to drink the poison."

"Yeah, but he was still ... mostly alive, I think, when I left."

"And you saw his face?"

I nodded, still dumbfounded over this point.

"And you're sure you saw—"

"Yes," I said resolutely.

"I knew it."

"Wait, what?" I said, jerking upright.

78

VEXATA QUAESTIO

It was nice to awaken in my own bed. It felt like an eternity since I had been there, snuggled in my blankets listening to the sounds of the morning. My mom's familiar gait padded up and down the stairs, up and down the hall. Philippa sang in the shower, sang over the racket of getting in and out of her wheelchair. They called back and forth to the other with breakfast requests, schedule reminders, questions about PT and homework assignments.

"I'm using my crutches!" Philippa screamed with glee. My mom clapped and whooped somewhere in response. I smiled as I heard the delight in her voice. "I'm just gonna slide down the stairs though, no judgement!"

I had a weird sensation then that they would be perfectly alright without me. They were already perfectly alright without me. I had gotten myself all worked up for some deathly showdown with Obrenox, and here I was, there and back again, with just a story about evading some vomit and a peculiar weather event.

It seemed too easy.

I couldn't shake the feeling that it wasn't over.

Probably because I knew that it wasn't.

But for the moment, I could assume Obrenox' ability to destroy this dimension was crippled. The trial had come and gone. I was still a source of notoriety in the community. I was still dodging those obdurate investigators. I still missed Ms. Neally and worried tremendously about her. And now I had to process

Uncle Seb's … situation. I wasn't good at using the word *cancer*. Mostly because I didn't believe it would take him.

Nothing could take that guy.

For today, I would focus on the good things. I stretched and smiled. There *were* good things.

"Hey, loser, you awake?" Philippa said with a gentle knock.

"Yes, loser, come in," I said with a giggle. "Shall we smoothie it up for breakfast? I'll even make you an omelette. All proper."

Philippa pushed the door open. Her expression didn't look like one who was there for a lovely breakfast date. She was out of breath, but lumbering around on crutches has that effect. Still … my pulse quickened.

"Those detectives, they're here again."

"I don't know anything about that fire, or the library, or Ms. Neally's weird confession," I groaned as I stomped across my room and grabbed a sweatshirt.

"It's … it's not that," Philippa said, shifting her weight against her crutches. "I think you had better talk to them."

Somewhere my phone buzzed. Over and over. Frowning, I fished it out of my blankets and opened my messages. A bunch from Channing, which I ignored. And one from Elke.

I just learned about your friend. I am so sorry. I hope you are ok.

I pushed past my sister – gently – and raced downstairs. Who was she talking about? What friend? Did I have a friend?

"Ah, Ms. Archer. Sorry for the early hour. Couldn't wait," Detective Serrano said abruptly without removing her sunglasses.

"What have you done this time," Detective Jasper said with a whistle.

"*Ay dios mío*! Cool it, Jasper," she snapped at her partner. He just shook his head and popped a toothpick in his mouth. "You know her?"

I looked down at the photo she held out to me.

"Libby? Sure, we've been in the same class, since, like, third grade or something," I said, my heart still pounding. "Why?"

"Missing persons report filed on her. And this," she pulled out a plastic bag with a smartphone in it and held it up, "was found in a pile of dirt at the site of that burned-down library."

I didn't have to ask whose phone it was.

"So ... so what's happened to her?" I asked shakily.

"That's what we're here to find out. You're the last one contacted in her phone. In fact, you're one of the only people contacted with any regularity. Anything you want to tell us? You know how this goes."

I shook my head. At least, I think I shook my head. It was spinning. Everything was spinning.

"You're the common link in all of this you know – ouch! Gah, splinter in my tongue," Jasper said, spitting the tooth pick out. A trail of spittle followed it.

"I suppose you're conveniently lacking info on the Beecher theft, too, huh?" Serrano said sharply. I gulped. My mind raced. *What was going on?*

"Theft?"

"Don't play dumb, missy. It's all over the news — buncha little shadows snuck into the burn site, took a box or something right from it. Disgusting. Flagrant disrespect," Jasper said, shaking his head.

"Why don't you just feed her her lines while you're at it? Christ, Jasper. You ever heard of getting the perps to tell *us* the story, not the other way around?" Serrano scowled. Jasper spit on the sidewalk.

"Could you, like, not spit on my porch? I'll, um, let you know if I, uh, hear anything," I said and backed up. Behind them, someone else was coming up the walk.

"What's going on down there? Everything good?" my mom yelled from upstairs.

"Nope! Not good!" Philippa called back.

"Really," I said to the detectives, "I, I mean it. I'll tell you if I learn anything. Honest."

Serrano and Jasper looked me up and down, then turned to each other and nodded.

"Be sure that you do," Serrano said.

"Yeah. Be sure that you do," Jasper echoed.

They walked self-importantly back to their patrol car, pushing past a man in a turquoise windbreaker, cargo shorts, and sandals. It was still winter; who was this clown?

"Easy, watch it, broseph!" the man said as he skirted by the puffed-up detective duo. "No reason for the gnar! Good vibes, only, am I right?"

He reached the front step before I could shut the door.

"Wait! I think I'm here for you, little sister."

I lingered in the doorway and looked at him skeptically.

"No thanks. We don't like Jesus or buying things," I said. Behind me I heard Philippa snort. I held in my grin; it was so satisfying making her laugh.

"No worries on both accounts," he said with a West Coast drawl I only heard in movies set in 80s-era California.

"Ok, bye then," I said and started to close the front door.

"No, no, no, no, wait!"

I froze. That voice was familiar. I inched the door open slowly.

"I think you know my dog, Poppy. She's, like, totally righteous and is killer at looking after you. And have you ever met a sweeter animal? I think not," he said with a loud laugh.

"Who ... who are you?"

My mom came up behind me and pushed the door open.

"Who is –" she stopped and turned white. "Chad?!"

"That's right, Daddy's home, and all that jazz, as they say!"

My mom pulled me inside and slammed the door. Then locked it.

"Mom?" Philippa said. "Who is that?"

"It's me, Chad! I'm your dad!" he called from outside.

"Chad?" Philippa repeated.

"Chad," my mom said.

"Chad?" I repeated.

"Chad!" he yelled from outside again.

What was worse: learning that my enemy-turned friend-turned neutral, complicated acquaintance Libby was missing, or learning that I had a father my mom knew about and kept from me named Chad?

79

EPILOGUE

*W*hile we end our tale with more questions than when we started, one thing has become clear: the justice system looms laissez-faire as a stressed-out proletariat does the heavy lifting. A boy was murdered. This is not a sentence that should be followed by "court dismissed." Sure, we've had a confession, but where is the mysterious librarian now? How is she connected to the burning of the middle school library? Who was poking around the charred ground, unearthing some strange trunk?

Something foul is afoot in our quiet town. And we'll keep digging. Metaphorically, and, as recent events might demand, literally. Join us in the mud to find the dirt. Until next time, fellow investigators and champions of justice, on "OreGone," your favorite true-crime podcast.

<unsubscribe>

ACKNOWLEDGEMENTS

Middle-school teachers never get the gratitude they deserve. I had a remarkable teacher in seventh and eighth grades for English and drama, one inimitable Ms. Smith. She introduced me to Langston Hughes and Maya Angelou and told me to find my voice like they had. I still have every piece of writing from her classes; she validated and encouraged something in me that would take me years to pull back out and take seriously.

This book and these words aren't for the many, many voices who told me to get A Real Job, to pursue different paths (I did and I have and it suuuuucked). They're for the few who quietly cheered on an introverted, scared, whimsical-to-a-fault, mentally disordered teen-turned-adult trying to sort out who they are and what they're about.

To the Ms. Smiths of the world, to Randy et Christine (my first customers and favorite editors), to my children, to supportive friends, and to David, thank you for being you. Getting these books into your hands is the culmination of conquering obstacles and clinging to victories and finding mastery in discipline and value in craft.

And finally, Candice Broersma, the most brilliant artist and designer, whom I happened to stumble upon: thank you for sharing your talent and bringing Eve and Dragon to life. (She won awards for the first book's cover i this series, btdubs. And rightfully so. It is awesome.)

About the Author

A.P. Coiteux, a native of the Pacific Northwest, makes her foray into fiction writing with the twisty Eve Archer series. A journalist displaced by career trajectories as pro athlete and concert pianist, she found her way back to writing at the behest of her children. Their brilliant minds and hilarious outlooks – coupled with Coiteux's own experiences coping with and recovering from trauma, grief, and mental health disorders – formed the outline of Eve Archer's zany world.

Coiteux still finds time to coach soccer, teach and make music, and advocate for health reform. After living around the globe, Coiteux happily resides in Washington with her partner, David, in a haunted (by kind ghosts) 1920s farmhouse that has stone lions at its entrance, thus fulfilling several childhood dreams.

Learn more at apcoiteux.com.